Elsebeth Egholm is a Danish autho... Jutland, Denmark. She has written ten books and in 2011 published *Three Dog Night* which was the start of a new series introducing ex-convict Peter Boutrup and was an instant bestseller.

Praise for *Three Dog Night*:

'A rich mix of damaged but endearing characters . . . the narrative has multiple layers without becoming overcomplicated . . . at times brutal but the gruesomeness is balanced with evocative descriptions' *Big Issue*

'A highly recommended, bleak and captivating crime novel' *Information*

'Both plot and characters go full throttle . . . How it all connects is both surprising and imaginative' *Politiken*

'The story is captivating and well told. The book has some cleverly turned twists in a focused narrative where the expected truths emerge during the dramatic final stand-off' *Metroxpress*

THREE DOG NIGHT

ELSEBETH EGHOLM

TRANSLATED BY
CHARLOTTE BARSLUND AND DON BARTLETT

headline

First published in Great Britain 2013 by
HEADLINE PUBLISHING GROUP

First published in paperback in 2013 by
HEADLINE PUBLISHING GROUP

1

Cataloguing in Publication Data is available from the British Library

ISBN 978 0 7553 9783 9

Typeset in Granjon by Palimpsest Book Production Limited
Falkirk, Stirlingshire

Printed and bound in Great Britain by Clays Ltd, St Ives plc

Headline's policy is to use papers that are natural, renewable
and recyclable products and made from wood grown in sustainable forests.
The logging and manufacturing processes are expected to conform to the
environmental regulations of the country of origin.

HEADLINE PUBLISHING GROUP
An Hachette UK Company
338 Euston Road
London NW1 3BH

www.headline.co.uk
www.hachette.co.uk

For Pia

1

ALL HE COULD think about was getting home.

As he walked he put distance between himself and the noise of the party. Behind him, New Year's Eve fireworks soared into the sky, scattering colourful parachutes into the night. Elsewhere, the landscape was lit by snow and the moon.

A few fireworks reached his half of the sky. Ahead of him, towards the sea, there was only silence and a world in black and white. The New Year had been born in an explosion of frost and threats of impending snow; ill-tempered and foul, like a portent of evil, if you believed in that kind of thing.

He liked walking. It made him conscious of his body. He strode as quickly as he could to keep the cold at bay. The freezing temperature tightened his face into a mask. He could easily have taken his van because he'd only had a couple of beers. That was how it was ever since the surgery. He had no desire to abuse his body any more than he already had. Smoking was a thing of the past, too. He was like Lucky Luke now: he preferred milk to whisky. Only occasionally, when he was with friends, would he let go and drink himself senseless.

The closer he got, the more difficult it was to make headway. He could already see the houses. It wasn't far from the party to the cliff, where two of the three fishermen's cottages were illuminated. The lights were on in his cottage, of course – he had left them on – but also in the neighbouring cottage, where a woman had recently moved in. Her lights were on day and night, as though she never slept. He had only seen her a few times. Once he had nodded to her, but she hadn't nodded back. There was something about her that intrigued him, though.

The wind whipped up the snow, forming it into drifts, and over the last fifty metres to the cottage it was up to his ankles. His nameplate was hidden under snow and ice. He brushed off the crystals with a glove: Peter A. Boutrup. He had screwed the sign to the door on the day he had returned, more than a year ago. It signified more than just his name. It was a decision: this was where his life and his future lay, and the past would have to take care of itself.

Perhaps the beers had had an effect after all, or maybe the cold had frozen his brain, because it was only now that he noticed a column of smoke rising from the chimney. The thought was just forming that he had a visitor when he heard his dog barking.

He went to unlock the door and found it open. A second later, he could smell cigarette smoke. The dog stopped barking and came to meet him, grovelling with a guilty expression on its face. And not without reason. The fire was roaring in the fireplace. Stinger lay snoring, stretched out the length of the sofa. There was an empty bottle of vodka on the coffee table and a saucer had been used as an ashtray. Peter counted nineteen cigarette butts and calculated that his guest had only just arrived. His clothes were crumpled, he reeked of booze, smoke and stale sweat, and there were holes in his socks. The tattoos on his hands and arms were blurred and had been scratched until they bled because he had developed an allergy to the cheap ink injected into his skin – probably the same type that Stinger injected into his customers; hence the nickname.

'Wakey wakey, Stinger!'

He tried unsuccessfully to shake some life into the man on the sofa while Kaj growled with hypocritical ferocity. Yes, the dog could be fierce, but it could easily tell friends and enemies apart, and Stinger was a friend, even though Peter was not exactly looking for company right now.

He gave up trying to wake Stinger, put a screen around the fireplace and, as was his wont, dragged a mattress on to the balcony and went to sleep with the dog snuggled up against the Arctic sleeping bag, burying its nose in a lambskin fleece. He could have done with a couple of extra dogs tonight, he thought, his teeth chattering from the cold. Aboriginal Australians used tame dingoes to keep warm on cold nights: a dog on each side and – if it was really cold, like tonight – a third on top. The first night of the New Year was one of those: a three-dog night. The weather forecast had warned that temperatures might fall to minus thirteen.

He wriggled down into the sleeping bag and felt the dog's body close to his. An ocean of stars glittered in the sky and he watched the remainder of the night's fireworks making a feeble attempt to impress. The frost nipped at his face and he closed the top of the sleeping bag until his breathing defrosted his skin. A three-dog night. The words evoked frostbite and fateful events. New Year's Eve partygoers were out in the cold, many in flimsy clothes and a novelty hat, alcohol pumping through their bloodstreams. On a night like this, winter was more than a match for humanity.

Before falling asleep, he suddenly realised why he was so intrigued by the dark-eyed woman in the cottage next door. He had only seen her from afar, but he had seen those same eyes before. Eyes whose questions he could not answer.

He looked up, found the brightest star and longed for his late girlfriend My.

2

EARLY ON NEW Year's Day the light fell sharply across the cliff, painting the sea in violet and drawing the horizon out in a silver line. The snow reflected the low rays of sun in every direction, glistening like precious stones you could pick up and put in your pocket.

Stinger was still snoring as Peter got dressed. Leaving Kaj in the house, he drove down to see his boss, Manfred, who lived with his wife and two children in Rimsø. On the roads and verges he saw New Year's Eve debris: empty bottles and scorched rockets and spent firework cakes. Confetti, paper streamers and a novelty hat or two had been thrown over snow-covered hedges.

'Happy New Year, Peter!'

Manfred appeared, looking well rested, with his dachshund, King. He had a rifle and hunting bag slung over his shoulders, and wore a cartridge belt around his waist. They left the village in his four-wheel drive and went up to the woods and fields surrounding Gjerrild, where Manfred and his uncle had game rights. There were eight hunters in total and after some discussion they spread out across the area. Peter followed Manfred, but he didn't carry a gun. Soon they were walking through the stillness of the forest, scarcely exchanging a word, looking for hoof prints and any other signs of red deer.

'Good time last night?'

Manfred spoke in a low voice as they followed the path through the pine trees. Peter knew that Manfred and his wife had been at home with the little ones. Early to bed and early to rise, that was the rhythm in Manfred and Jutta's house. Peter liked to follow the same monotonous routine himself, as if his temperament was attuned to the rising and the setting of the sun. He and Manfred had a lot in common.

'Not bad,' Peter said as they trudged through the snow in their sturdy rubber boots. 'Villy had a party.'

Manfred's oilskin jacket snagged on branches and twigs as they went. It was ten o'clock in the morning and the temperature was minus eleven. Manfred was a small man, but he could climb along the ridge of a roof like a circus artist and was as familiar with the tools of his trade as he was with books, which Peter greatly appreciated. Manfred was forcing his way through the trees as surefootedly as if he were tiling the vicar's roof.

'It's dangerous on cold New Year's Eves,' he said, still keeping his voice low so as not to frighten the inhabitants of the forest. 'Some of Jutta's friends in Grenå are still waiting for their daughter. She'd promised to come home after a party.'

The snow creaked under Peter's wellies. He, too, was walking and speaking carefully.

'Early days yet. She probably just found a bed for the night.'

Manfred shivered as a branch brushed against him and snow drizzled down under his rollneck.

'I'm sure you're right. But try telling her mum that.'

'Better than the alternative, though?'

Manfred nodded.

'I'm with you there.'

They reached the clearing and walked side by side for a while. Then the dog caught the scent. It sprang around nervously, whirling up snow, its muscles tense with sheer excitement.

'Here.'

Peter bent down and pointed. Deer tracks criss-crossed, gouging up the snow. At first glance it looked as if someone had run a matchstick through the cream on top of a layer cake. But if you looked closely, individual tracks stood out. Manfred, too, bent down and the dog poked its long snout deep into the holes.

'And look here.'

Fresh, steaming faeces lay scattered around. The smell of wild animal seasoned the air and they could see where antlers had swept the snow searching for food. In some places the bark had been peeled off the trees. Peter lowered his voice to a whisper and pointed to the stag's hoof print, which was the size of his boot heel.

'Deer,' Manfred concluded. 'Could be up to eight of them.'

They followed the trail and moved carefully, with the dog on the leash now. Normally they would have been chatting about all sorts of things, combining knowledge and enthusiasm with physical effort, which was what hunting was. Once more Peter walked behind Manfred and the dog as they plodded their way through the snow. Peter and Manfred got on well. Manfred had been taking a philosophy degree at university when life and a bout of depression took its toll, and he had chosen to devote himself to manual labour and trained as a carpenter. He was born and bred in Rimsø. After he had finished his apprenticeship he had set up Rimsø Builders, and after three years of working on his own hired Peter. The business now employed four people, but there wasn't much work in winter. At the moment they had only one job, a new roof on a barn belonging to a pig farmer, and Manfred had been forced to lay off the two newest employees temporarily.

The snow grew deeper and their boots sank into it. Manfred suddenly stopped in front of him. The dog was completely rigid. Peter stared. The stag was standing in the clearing sniffing the air, but the light breeze was in their favour, blowing their scents away from it. And yet the animal had an inkling of their presence, that much was clear. Its winter coat was grey and brown;

muscles rippled nervously under the fur. Its nostrils flared in reaction to an as yet unidentifiable threat and its breath hung in the air like a cloud.

Manfred turned slowly to Peter. In one gliding motion he handed him the rifle. Peter shook his head, but Manfred refused to lower his arm and in the end Peter took it, pressed it to his shoulder and rested his cheek so that he was watching the animal through the crosshairs.

It was a fourteen-pointer, a trophy buck, and he had never seen a more beautiful sight. Its antlers were free of any late summer velvet. It stood there captured in the sunlight, its profile turned towards them as if wanting to show them its best side.

Peter's finger tightened around the trigger. Then the animal turned its head while its body remained in the same position. For a couple of long seconds it stared straight into the rifle's sights and Peter could hear his blood rushing under the gaze of the stag. Then it seemed, finally, to spot him and the rifle. It tossed its head back, stamped on the ground and set off through the snow with the white hairs on its bottom raised like a flag as a danger signal.

The silence that followed was as heavy as melting snow. Then Manfred said: 'You should have shot it.'

Peter handed the rifle back to him.

'It was too old. I thought we were going for the young ones?'

Manfred shuffled his feet in the snow. King stuck his nose into a hoof print and whined quietly.

'It wouldn't have mattered. It would have been all right.'

They looked at each other and Peter was reminded of the long seconds watching the stag. The silence was no longer the same. It contained the warmth, the friendship and the risk Manfred had shown himself willing to take: trusting a hunter who was no longer permitted to carry a weapon.

'I don't want you getting into trouble because of me,' Peter said emphatically. No more needed to be said, and they walked on through the forest.

When he arrived back home, tired and content as always after hours spent in the fresh air, his guest was still asleep.

It was one-thirty before Stinger's snoring finally started to lighten. Fifteen minutes later he woke up, hawking and spluttering and reaching for his cigarette packet, which was empty.

'Here.'

Peter handed him a mug of coffee. Stinger slurped and spilled it.

'Happy New Year.'

Stinger muttered a reply into the mug. Peter left him and went to the kitchen. He fried up some bacon and eggs, made toast and heated a tin of baked beans. When he took everything to the coffee table, Stinger had roused enough to sit upright and rub his face with his scabbed hands.

'So what's up? To what do we owe the pleasure?' Peter asked.

Stinger regarded him with a wounded expression.

'Christ, Peter. I thought friends were welcome at any time? At least that's what you used to say.'

It was true, he still kept the key under the white stone. He was perfectly aware of that. He had only himself to blame. But sometimes it was like living in a railway station when old friends from the past dropped in for the night.

'Got any tomato sauce?'

Stinger looked down at the plate Peter passed him.

'In the fridge. And help yourself to Beluga caviar while you're out there.'

'Bewhat?'

'Nothing.'

Kaj followed Stinger all the way to the kitchen and back – not because he was being vigilant, but because he hoped

Stinger would drop some food. Experience had taught him that he would.

'I was supposed to meet Ramses. That was the deal.'

Stinger squeezed the sauce bottle so hard it spattered everywhere and the plate looked like a traffic accident. Then he went to work with his knife and fork, sending crispy bacon flying in all directions.

'I don't suppose you've seen him, have you?'

Peter shook his head. Kaj spotted the bacon on the floor and took his chance.

'I didn't know he was out.'

'You're not keeping up. He's been out for a while,' Stinger said, chewing. 'We were meant to meet here on New Year's Eve and make plans.'

'But you forgot to invite me?'

'We assumed you would be at home.'

Peter sliced through the yolk of his fried egg. The yellow liquid poured out and mixed with the red tomato sauce from the beans.

'And what's your plan?'

Stinger put down his knife and fork and scratched his hand. A scab came off and started to bleed.

'It's the frost,' he said looking at the blood. 'My skin goes all dry.'

'What plan?'

'We were going to recover Brian's stash. The stuff he hid before he went inside.'

'And you both believe it really exists?'

Stinger nodded with conviction.

''Course it does. He told us how to go about finding it. Separately, I mean.'

'Separately?'

He wolfed down a forkful of beans followed by toast dipped in tomato sauce.

'Well, you see, Ramses knows a bit. And I know the rest.'

He chewed and swallowed. 'Between us we know enough to find the shit. Good one, eh? It's worth at least three million, you know. We can live like kings for the rest of our lives.'

Peter was unable to suppress his laughter.

'Then you'll need one hell of a financial adviser or you'll be dead before your time. Given your consumption of fags and vodka, the money won't last long.'

Once again Stinger looked hurt.

'It's a fortune, you know.'

There were lots of rumours about the stash.

'So what is it you know? And why you two? Why would a dying man entrust his deepest secret to a couple of bums like you?'

Stinger mopped up the sauce, egg remnants and bacon grease with a piece of toast.

'We were like family back then. Don't you remember? Me and Ramses were like the old boy's sons. Behind bars and outside.'

Peter watched as Stinger opened his mouth wide for the toast. Stinger was both right and wrong. All three of them, Brian, Ramses and Stinger, had struck up a kind of friendship, but Stinger was naive. Ramses could be bought for next to nothing, and Brian had always loved playing people off against one other, then standing back and watching the result. Peter wouldn't trust either of the other two. But perhaps Brian had become sentimental during the last few months of his life with the cancer eating him up. Perhaps the dying man had felt the urge to confess to someone, and there were worse people than Ramses and Stinger. They were half-wits, that went without saying, but deep down they were OK. There were lots of rumours going around and some suggested that Brian had once been a big-time drugs smuggler, and if that was the case it was way beyond the combined abilities of Stinger and Ramses.

'So what do you know?'

Stinger swallowed and washed everything down with coffee. He wiped his mouth on his sleeve.

'Brian was crazy about boats, do you remember? An old sea dog was how he liked to describe himself. He had a motorboat called *Molly*.'

Peter nodded. Stinger had learned the art of tattooing from Brian – the old salt had an anchor tattooed on his forearm, a busty girl on his biceps and a clove hitch on his chest. It was no secret that Brian's career had encompassed a range of smuggling activities – especially in the Baltic.

'Anyway, when it got too hot for him, he scuttled *Molly* somewhere in the Kattegat,' Stinger said, scratching the bleeding scab. 'Sealed the stash in a box. That's the bit I know. Where the stash is, I mean. Sort of.'

'Sort of?' Peter had to smile. 'And Ramses? What does he know? Something sort of as well?'

Stinger carried on scratching. Another scab came off, revealing pink skin the size of a one-krone coin.

'Ramses has the other half of the coordinates. Brian told me.'

'And you have the first half, I suppose?'

Stinger nodded and suppressed a belch.

'Great grub, thank you,' he said politely and added, as if he had just finished eating at a three-star restaurant: 'I really enjoyed that.'

3

FELIX SAW THE man leaving the house again just after two o'clock.

She had seen him arrive on New Year's Eve. She had heard the dog barking, and the PIR light next door had been triggered and revealed his presence: tall and skinny and – she imagined – freezing in a very short jacket without anything on his head or hands. At first he had knocked, and then when there was no answer, he had pushed down the door handle. Then, after hanging about for a little examining the snowdrifts, he had come over to hers and rung the doorbell.

'Have you got a shovel I could borrow?'

'There's one in the car port.'

She had pointed it out to him. He sniffed, not that that made much difference. Snot hung from his nose. He wiped it with one hand and she saw it was covered with scars and scabs mixed with some amateurish tattoos. He didn't say thank you, or anything else, just turned around and headed for the car port. Shortly afterwards she had seen him shovelling snow near the lane. He worked away for ten minutes until he came to a stone. He bent down and took something out from underneath it. Then he came back to return the shovel and she watched him open the door to the house and greet the dog. That was what convinced her that he was all right. Plus, of course, the fact that he knew where the key was kept.

And now he was leaving again, with mittens on his hands and wearing a thicker jacket than before and the knitted beanie on his head. She recognised the jacket. Her neighbour – *Peter A. Boutrup* she'd read on his door one day when he was out – usually wore it when he took the dog out for walks. Which he did every day. And it was a fine dog, an Alsatian.

She moved away from the window but didn't know where else to go. The cold and her tiredness were a bad combination. She was always cold in this house. She was sneezing, shivering and coughing so much she permanently had chest pains. There appeared to be draughts everywhere, and she felt like she was walking on cotton wool, she was so exhausted. She knew she ought to eat something, but whenever she tried, the food would stick in her throat and she wouldn't feel hungry any more. If only she could sleep a little. But everything inside her resisted the thought of bed. Only when she was finally worn down by insomnia was she able to ignore her resistance and let go. She wasn't exhausted enough yet, though, so she turned on the television. They were showing the New Year's Concert from Vienna.

She liked the music. The waltzes swayed to and fro inside her. At one time, before the accident, she used dance to find a space for herself. She wasn't trained; she made up her own steps. But her body was made for dancing, she knew that. It wasn't her job and never had been. It was just part of her, like breathing or putting one foot in front of the other.

She rose to her feet, drawn by the waltz. Tentatively, she began to dance to the rhythm of the music. Humming and swaying, she spun around, up on her toes, down again until she was almost in a trance. But she was too weak, and when the music suddenly stopped and the applause erupted, she stood breathless on the floor in her stockinged feet, everything spinning around in front of her. Suddenly it wasn't the dancing on the television she saw. It was glimpses of the accident, everything spinning her around and around and around, until she no longer knew who she was or why.

She switched off the television. Her heart was pounding and she was dripping with sweat. Fresh air was what she needed, even though her exhaustion was now almost insurmountable.

She went into the hallway and put on several layers of clothing. To be on the safe side, she stuffed her mobile in her pocket, thinking about her neighbour, Peter A. Boutrup. He had said hello to her one day, but she had not returned his greeting. She didn't know why, but perhaps she hadn't had the strength.

She was about to venture out into the cold when she noticed he had just closed his front door and was on his way out with the dog. She hated situations like this and felt angry inside. Now what? Her indecision halted her; she was incapable of moving. From the window she saw him embarking on his usual walk up to the cliff in snow up to his ankles, with the dog running alongside him, a bundle of energy after being confined to the house. He tossed treats into the air, which it caught, or threw them into the snow so it would have to dig down to find them.

She didn't open her front door until he had been gone for quite some time.

The air was freezing cold and stung her lungs. She had no option but to follow him and the dog. The snow was too deep in every other direction. She walked at a brisk pace while keeping her distance at the same time. Soon she spotted them. They were oblivious to anything but themselves, it seemed, but one day she supposed she would have to say hello to him, exchange a few words and perhaps make it clear she wasn't interested in being close neighbours.

Suddenly the dog started to bark. She saw Peter stop and she did the same. He stood still for a while, looking down from what appeared to her to be the highest point of the cliff. She tried to follow his gaze. She couldn't see what he had spotted, but the mood had changed and the man and the dog were no longer playful.

* * *

Peter leaned over the cliff edge. He needed to get closer to see what the dog had seen, but walking beyond where the snow had been cleared was dangerous. The drop to the beach was dizzying. He decided to send Kaj down first. The dog would love it.

'Off you go.'

He pointed downwards.

'Find.'

The dog took up the challenge. It ran to and fro along the cliff before deciding where to begin its descent. Then things moved fast. It careered down, skidding on stiff legs all the way to where the waves rolled into the crust of ice along the beach. It soon reached the dark spot on the stones. It sniffed all the way around, nudged it with its nose and barked loudly.

'Bloody hell.'

The dog's instinct had been spot on. He had to get down there. But he already knew what awaited him. Like Kaj, he stumbled, slipped, and almost rolled, to the foot of the cliff.

'What is it, boy? What have you found?'

He approached with caution. He had never seen the dog so agitated. The figure was half concealed by snow, lying on its stomach with one cheek distorted and the mouth open. Dark stubble covered part of the face; one black bushy eyebrow – the eyebrows which had been his pride and joy – was caked with ice. As was his hair. It looked as if someone had scattered artificial Yuletide snow across him, and it had settled like white crystals against the black background. He was dressed inappropriately for the weather: a short, black leather jacket, jeans and a pair of trainers.

Peter knelt down and felt for a pulse, but he knew it was too late. Ramses – who in life had been a handsome idiot, always a sucker for a girl in a short skirt or easy money – was as dead as a doornail. There was what looked like an exit wound in his back, where the blood had stained the snow a rusty red. He surmised that the Egyptian had been shot from the front at close range, straight through the heart.

He heard a noise and turned around just in time to see the woman from the neighbouring house – he recognised her black Puffa jacket – standing and waving her arms at the top of the cliff. She cupped her gloved hands to her mouth: 'Hi. Is that what I think it is?'

He waved and nodded. She started her descent.

'Stay where you are,' he shouted. 'There's no need for you to see this.'

But she was already halfway down. She lost her footing and tumbled, but she didn't seem to care, even though she could easily have broken her neck. She landed at his feet and he automatically stuck out a hand to support her. It was the first time he had seen her close up and he found it hard to take his eyes off her. She was both beautiful and ugly. The beauty lay in her eyes, which shone like a pool of turquoise contained inside a clear, black circle; it was also in the oval form of her face and the colour of her hair, various shades of dark against skin as white as chalk, although only a few strands protruded from under her cap. The ugliness lay in the fact that she looked as if she might faint on the spot and occupy a position next to the corpse. She was painfully thin, her skin waxen, and the beauty of her eyes was framed by sunken, charcoal-grey sockets which made them seem dark despite their colour.

'I suppose you think I've never seen a dead body before.'

'Have you?'

He guessed she was around thirty, the same age as him. How many bodies could she have seen?

She made no reply, just stared at Ramses and ran her hand nervously up to her throat and around her neck, under her scarf and hair, as if something was too tight. There was a wide variety of birds on the cliff all year round, and Peter thought he had seen most of them, but she was the most exotic of the lot.

'Poor guy. Who is he?' she asked.

He hesitated.

'No idea. You wouldn't have a mobile on you, would you?'

She put her hand into her pocket, found her mobile and passed it to him.

He took it, brushing her hand, and felt a sudden urge to touch her, to stroke her cheek. Instead, however, he did the last thing in the world he wanted to do: he called the police.

4

'AND SHE HASN'T been seen since?'

Mark Bille Hansen, the new head of the East Jutland police force in the town of Grenå, had a headache. Not because he had overdone it on New Year's Eve, but for a completely different reason he didn't want to think about right now. He shook some pills into the palm of his hand as noiselessly as he could, letting the person on the line carry on talking.

'We had a party, which finished around two o'clock. She wanted to go home but there was no one to give her a lift, so she said she would walk.'

Mark swallowed the pills dry. Wedging the telephone between his chin and his shoulder, he lined up a few items on his desk: blotting pad, pen, notepad, mobile. He placed his coffee cup in the corner, with a packet of V6 chewing gum next to it. An old newspaper flew into the waste-paper basket.

'How far did she have to walk? Where does she live and where was the party?'

He made a note of the addresses while looking across his office. The furnishings were sparse, not to say austere. Nothing surplus to requirements. No ornaments. It suited him just fine.

'The others said she wasn't wearing much. We're afraid she might have frozen to death in this weather.'

He could see why. A nineteen-year-old with champagne in her blood, dressed in scanty clothing, outside in minus thirteen, was close to a deliberate suicide mission in his mind.

'And you've spoken to her family?'

'I've just this minute spoken to Nina's parents, yes. They're too upset to call,' said the man who had hosted the party. 'Her father's been driving around town for hours. Now they're at home crossing their fingers that she'll turn up.'

Mark coughed discreetly as the pills slowly made their way down. Thank God he didn't have children to worry about on top of everything else.

'Can someone bring us a photo? Or better still, e-mail us a photo that's a good likeness and we'll treat her as a missing person.'

'Is that all you do?'

The man sounded disappointed, but also as if he hadn't been expecting anything else from the police, who had been getting a bad press recently.

'We'll get reinforcements and start a search.'

Mark ended the conversation. What the hell did the idiot imagine? That the police would just let a young girl disappear in the snow without even trying to find her? He started organising the operation, called Århus and explained the situation. After that, he took his jacket and braced himself to visit the girl's parents in Nørrevang.

A cushy number, that was how it had been sold to him when the posting became a reality. In Grenå he could recover in peace instead of rushing off in pursuit of dead bodies with the Copenhagen Homicide Squad. And he did have family in Grenå, as they had pointed out. They would undoubtedly be a great source of support to him, they said. Screw his bosses. They had failed to mention that it took half a day to travel to the hospital – to the kind of hospital he needed, anyway.

He was leaning on the door handle when the telephone rang again.

'Grenå Police. Bille Hansen speaking.'

It was going to be a New Year's Day he would never forget, he thought, as a man who introduced himself as Peter Boutrup informed him, calmly and concisely, that his dog had found the body of a man at the foot of Gjerrild Cliff. The man appeared to have a bullet hole in his back.

Mark quickly ended the call, made a second call to Århus, then got hold of Jepsen and briefed him.

'Go to Nørrevang and talk to Nina's parents. Hopefully the officers from Århus will soon be there with the dogs. They know where, and what it's about, so they can just get started. Otherwise I'm on my mobile, OK?'

Jepsen blinked like a frightened animal. After six weeks he still seemed surprised every time Mark asked him to do something. What were they used to out here in Djursland? A glass of port and a friendly word? A matey pat on the shoulder? He could do neither.

Jepsen nodded, red-eyed but composed. Mark hoped this was because he had let the New Year in with a bigger bang than his boss's own damp squib.

'I'm going to the cliff to have a look. But it won't be long before the others get there: the ambulance crew, the forensics team, the SOC people. Anyone who can do the things we can't,' he said.

Jepsen nodded once more, with panic in his eyes now, possibly in response to the guest list Mark had just reeled off. He wasn't wild about it, either. He put on his coat and gave a last glance round his office. He should have opted for a career in the army.

'See you later.'

Mark closed the door behind him slightly too hard. Århus. He bounded down the stairs, suppressing his irritation that officers from Denmark's second largest city would now be hurrying here to solve a case he could have solved himself if he'd had the staff. He doubted there was a single detective in Århus with more experience than he had after eight years in Copenhagen. But it made no difference. He would just have to get used to the role of rural police officer and having no say in murder cases.

5

PETER WATCHED THE black Puffa jacket as it moved up and down along the shore. She refused to go home. He had offered to stay behind and deal with the police. It was obvious she was unwell. But no. She refused to let anything go, and that included Ramses who was lying there looking as if he was frozen senseless, which of course he was.

Peter looked at the remains of Ramses and cursed him to hell and back. He had been a nice enough bloke, but he had never been blessed with much intelligence. Now the lack of brain cells had probably brought his life to an end and, well, so be it. It was worse that it had happened right here, by the cliff – right in the middle of the life Peter had hoped to rebuild without being dragged back by his past. That had been the plan: a nice, easy life, just him and the dog; seeing good friends when the opportunity arose; the job which he enjoyed; the outdoors; and possibly at some time in the future a dream of the normal family life he'd never had himself. Now that Ramses was lying there, he'd been forced to contact the authorities, people he would have preferred to give a wide berth, and who had never done him any good in the past.

'The police are here.'

It was as if noises were amplified in the clear frost. A car fought its way through the snow, the engine sounding as if it was about to explode with anger. They'd only had time to exchange a few words and she had politely patted Kaj on the head. She stopped doing that now.

'You go back up and I'll stay here,' she suggested.

He nodded and lumbered up the cliff to meet them. The policeman – so far there was only one – introduced himself as Mark Bille Hansen from Grenå Police. He had shoulder-length black hair, like an Indian's, and a lined face that looked anything but Danish. He didn't come across as especially friendly and Peter concluded that he was either stressed or hung-over. The latter was only to be expected on New Year's Day.

They talked for a little while before clambering down to the beach, where the woman in the Puffa jacket was standing guard. The policeman squatted down and studied Ramses carefully.

'When did you find him?'

Peter had checked his watch. It was now a quarter past three and starting to get dark.

'At half past two. I went for a walk with the dog.'

'And you've never seen him before?'

Before Peter had made up his mind, he was shaking his head. The man with the black hair put his ear close to Ramses's mouth to detect any possible signs of life. Then his fingers found the gold chain with the Star of David and held it up.

'A religious symbol?'

The question was aimed at Peter, but it was his neighbour who answered. He didn't even know her name yet.

'It looks Jewish.'

Mark Bille Hansen had another quick look at the body.

'Hm. That might fit.'

Peter let them talk. He could have told them that Ramses was not very familiar with religious symbols. He only wore the star because he liked the look of it and because a girlfriend from the distant past had given it to him and told him it would bring him luck. Peter looked at the star and wondered what luck it had brought Ramses. If this was good luck, he would like to see what bad luck was.

'And you were just passing?'

The question was addressed to the hitherto nameless woman.

'I was out enjoying a New Year's Day walk. I live up there . . . as well.'

She pointed up the cliff.

'As well?'

'We both live there,' she said, with obvious irritation in her voice.

'Together?' Mark asked.

She shook her head vehemently. It looked as if it might come off. She glanced at Peter.

'We don't actually know each other.'

She took off her mitten and held out her hand.

'My name is Felix. Perhaps we should introduce ourselves.'

'Peter.'

Her hand was tiny. It was also ice-cold and her handshake was devoid of any strength. Her eyes directed the strength she had at him while everything else seemed as if it might crumble and turn into dust.

Mark Bille looked at his notepad.

'Peter Andreas Boutrup. What else?'

'What do you mean?'

'Who are you?'

'I live up there. In number fifteen,' Peter said. 'I'm a carpenter.'

Mark Bille nodded. Peter could see he was about to ask another question when they heard the emergency sirens.

More than anything, Mark felt like covering his ears with his hands. His headache hadn't gone away, despite the pills, and the sound of the sirens cut through his brain with scalpel-like precision and found the centre of the pain. Matters did not improve when he saw the two detectives quickly approaching from the car: a man and a woman. The man was tall and sturdy with a young face and short, steel-grey hair, and Mark had never seen him before. The woman he would have recognised anywhere in the world and he could have kicked himself for not knowing where she was now. Anna Bagger had risen through the ranks and she had obviously ended up in the East Jutland Crime Division. Of course he would have known if he'd bothered to keep up in the last twelve months, and now he was standing there like a moron as she moved towards him with her characteristic glide. He went to meet her. When they were close he realised she was just as surprised to see him. But she hid it well; she stuck out her hand and looked him in the eye.

'Mark. I hear you got married.'

Half her smile was professional, probably for the benefit of her colleague. The other half hit him somewhere he didn't like.

'And I hear you got divorced.'

He said it in a low voice. She exhaled and her breath misted in the icy air.

'A lot can happen in two years. I see you've returned to the scene of the crime?'

There were layers of meaning in every single word and in every little movement, from the way she blinked to the way she gasped as she breathed.

'You could say that. I grew up around here,' he said.

She looked around. No one could take in the bigger picture and the small details in a split second like she could: the grey sea, the snow and ice on the cliff, the body on the sea-smoothed dark stones, and a little further away the dog and the two neighbours who had discovered the body. For a moment, her gaze zoomed in on the bullet hole in the man's back before returning to Mark and homing in somewhere between his eyes. Perhaps she was a little rattled after all.

'I didn't know that you were such a country bumpkin,' she

said. 'I want you to meet my colleague from the Crime Division, Martin Nielsen.'

Mark shook hands with the man as relief washed over him. She didn't know. She had been busy with her own life and oblivious to his, something which at this precise moment suited him just fine. She would find out, of course, but he would have that conversation when the time came.

'It's all happening on Djursland, I must say,' Anna Bagger said, blowing a strand of blonde hair from her face.

Again icy breath emerged from her lips and he remembered how she would exhale cigarette smoke by sticking out her lower lip. Once it had touched something inside him, he didn't really know why; perhaps it was the combination of feminine – her finely plucked eyebrows which knitted in concentration, while her eyes were half-closed in pleasure – and masculine, with the sailor-like movement of her lips. It no longer touched him, but then again few things did.

'A missing girl and a dead man, you mean? Yes, never a dull moment here,' he agreed.

She nodded and started walking quickly over to the body and introducing herself to the two people who had found it. She asked her questions in a calm, friendly tone, but Mark knew she was committing to memory the images of the man and woman with photographic accuracy and that her brain had already started combining motive, opportunity and alibi. She was clever. This was her life's ambition. Meanwhile more vehicles had arrived at the top of the cliff and technicians in white overalls were swarming around with more police officers and a pathologist. Anna Bagger finished her round of questions.

'So neither of you has ever seen him before?'

Both the man with the dog and the woman who looked thin to the point of transparency denied having seen him before. At length Anna Bagger seemed to realise they had been standing for an hour and a half in extremely cold conditions.

'Go home and make yourselves comfortable. Someone will be along to take your detailed statements.'

Mark watched them as they and the dog struggled back up the cliff. Every time the man offered to help, the woman pretended not to notice.

6

PETER HELD OUT his hand. She didn't take it, but he could clearly see her exertion and her obstinate determination as she mobilised all her strength and forced herself up the last stretch. She was in need of some sort of help, he could see, possibly medical, but there was also something deeper. It seemed as if her very soul had fragmented, a state he knew only too well.

Before they parted she stood scrutinising him while patting Kaj, who soaked up the attention, a typical dog.

'Why did you lie?' she asked. 'Why did you say you didn't know him?'

'Why do you think I lied?'

She angled her head upwards to see him. She was so tiny.

'I recognise a lie when I hear one.'

'Recognise?'

He couldn't help smiling. He was reminded of Manfred's King, a small dog which thought it was a Great Dane.

'From personal experience?'

'I recognise the sound of a lie,' she insisted. 'And you lied.'

'So what if I did?'

'Who is he?'

There was more than usual curiosity in the voice and eyes that branded him a liar.

'Nobody.'

'And what is Mr Nobody's name? Where's he from?'

She was getting too close. He searched for a way to divert the conversation.

'Felix,' he said. 'That's a funny name for a girl. It must be foreign.'

'Felicia.'

She pressed her tongue against her front teeth on the c. 'My mother's Spanish. It's a nickname. Peter . . .'

She tasted his name. 'You have a namesake in the Bible. He, too, denied a friend. Three times.'

She stared at him as if she could nail him to the cross with her eyes, and he knew exactly what kind of person she was. She was the type that would not be shaken off. She was probably ill or just terribly run-down, but she didn't let go, and again he was reminded of King in a comparison which was not entirely fair.

'Listen,' he said. 'I think we've got off on the wrong foot.'

He scratched his neck.

'Would you like to come in?' he offered. 'I could make some coffee.'

She shook her head in an exaggerated protest before setting off back to her house.

'He wasn't my friend,' he called as she left, but she simply waved a gloved hand in the air without turning around.

Stinger was a friend, he thought. Ramses was merely an acquaintance. It was important to make a distinction or your life would quickly fill up with dubious associates for whom you felt some responsibility.

At first it was a relief when he was able to close the door behind him, but his thoughts soon started to trouble him. She was right. Why had he lied?

For a while he walked around in circles in the house which was no longer the safe haven of which he had dreamed. Everything within him had resisted the moment she had asked whether he recognised the body at the foot of the cliff. The denial had been automatic, but from that moment on he was trapped. In her presence, in the spotlight of her gaze, the denial had been uttered again in front of the police. Bang. Just like that! In no time at all he had wrecked his future, so as to be able to buy himself a little more peace and the illusion of being an ordinary citizen doing his civic duty.

It was already a murder case. Of course they would find the link between him and Ramses. Of course they would dig up everything.

There was only one thing for it: he would have to go back immediately and admit that he had lied.

He had already put on his coat and his boots when the realisation dawned on him.

Ramses had known half the coordinates of the spot in the Kattegat where Brian's boat had supposedly been scuttled with its valuable cargo. Someone might have forced the information out of him and then killed him. Stinger knew the other half of the secret. Whoever had killed Ramses must be looking for Stinger now. Stinger was no angel, but there wasn't an evil bone in him. He didn't deserve to die.

He rang the mobile number Stinger had given him, but there was no reply. He left a message: 'This is Peter. Call me. Quickly. The shit's hit the fan.' But he knew Stinger and his relationship with technology only too well. There was no guarantee he would know how to listen to a message.

He looked at his watch. It was four o'clock and it had grown dark outside. The police had told him to stay at home.

Stinger had mentioned he was staying with his sister in Århus. Peter knew her vaguely. Elisabeth, her name was. What else could he remember about Elisabeth? From time to time she had visited Stinger in Horsens Prison. She had been a biker chick back then, a couple of years ago. Leather, studs and biceps as big as thighs, but kindness itself behind the facade.

He would have to make a couple of calls before he could get her full name and address. He weighed up the pros and cons and ended up concluding it was more important to save a life than clean the slate. The latter could wait. He whistled for the dog and drove off in the old VW van he had recently bought at an auction for 18,000 kroner he didn't have.

7

'AND YOU DIDN'T see him drive off?'

The police officer, Anna Bagger, seemed annoyed, and she had cause to be. There was also something friendly and trustworthy about her, but that was possibly down to pure professionalism. Felix shook her head.

'I was cold when I got back so I took a hot bath. I expect he left while I was in the bathroom.'

'You don't know where he was going?'

It sounded idiotic, but she probably had to phrase the question like that. Perhaps they were taught to do it this way at the police academy. Mark Bille Hansen, who was accompanying her, tried to look neutral.

'No. As I told you earlier, I don't know him.'

'How long have you lived here?'

'One month.'

'Is it really possible for two people living this close to each other for one month not to speak?'

It wasn't an accusation; on the contrary, it was spoken with mild wonder and a suppressed smile as Anna Bagger allowed her gaze to glide over the décor, which was maritime kitsch: a model of the frigate *Jylland* in the window, a porthole in the wall, rope edging round the ceiling and conches on the window sill. Nothing Felix would have chosen for herself.

'We keep ourselves to ourselves.'

'Why?'

'Why what?'

Anna Bagger made a gesture to encompass both the house and the cliff.

'Why do you live here? So far away. What are you doing here?'

Felix had never liked several questions being fired at once. In fact, she didn't like being interrogated like this, and she certainly didn't like having strangers in her house.

'I'm on sick leave. I need peace and quiet.'

'What's your job?'

'I manage a spa in Århus. We offer skincare treatment and sell beauty products,' she explained and added: 'We also do massages.'

She felt herself being scrutinised, but wasn't surprised. Right now she didn't look like a beautician. She hadn't done so for months.

'And you're able to live on your sick pay? I can't imagine it's much,' Anna Bagger said.

'I don't need much.'

She didn't think her private finances or lack of them was anyone's business but her own. Anna Bagger looked at her as if she couldn't make up her mind whether to believe her or not. Felix wished Peter Boutrup had stayed put.

'He found the body. Well, him and the dog. I was just trying to help and I happened to have my mobile with me. That's all.'

Anna Bagger's face took on an inscrutable expression.

'Thank you. That'll be all. For now.'

The police officer sounded a little distant, as if her thoughts had already jumped to the next link in the investigation. They shook hands and she left the house, followed by the rural police officer who looked anything but rural. A car started outside. An ambulance pulled away. Anna Bagger and her entourage also found their cars and soon they were tiny dots rumbling through the snow down the lane back home to Århus.

* * *

Felix unlocked the door to the secret room. Nausea rose in her throat and she started to shake as though she had a fever. She should have stayed at home. What on earth had made her walk to the cliff?

Suddenly her legs felt unsteady beneath her, so she sat down on the swivel chair. When the room had stopped spinning, she looked at the walls, which were plastered with cuttings, photos, business cards and scribbled-on Post-its.

There were survivors. And then there were the dead. She was a survivor. Why this was so, she had no idea, nor did she want to know. Her neighbour was another survivor. She had seen it in his eyes. There were only the dead and survivors. Everything in between – the living – was another country to her. As indeed was life at this moment.

She pulled a mobile from her pocket. She had removed it from the dead man's pocket while Peter had gone up the cliff to get the police.

She turned it over and over in her hand but couldn't bring herself to open the menu, even though it was still switched on. For a moment she wondered at humanity and its ability to adapt. She had never stolen anything in her entire life, and here she was with a dead man's phone in her hand. Perhaps this was what survival felt like: you existed in a frozen zombie land. Other rules applied here. She wondered if that was true for Peter Boutrup as well.

She left the room, locking it behind her, and put the mobile in the kitchen drawer. On her way back to the sofa, she had to clutch the back of a chair for support. She was tired. But she wasn't too tired to wonder what it was he had survived.

8

STINGER'S SISTER, ELISABETH Stevns, had, to put it mildly, gained a lot of weight since Peter had last seen her. Fat bulged through the grey track suit; the top seemed too short and the trousers too tight. Blonde hair and dark roots were arranged in a messy pile on top of her head. When she bent down, he could see the tattoo on the small of her back, a psychedelic design a few centimetres above her bum crack, which was also revealed. But her face was pretty and her smile forgiving in face of life's unpredictability, which included a useless brother with a criminal past and future.

'Here. Go on, take it all! I'm done with him! He can stay with you, can't he?'

She rummaged around for Stinger's few belongings scattered around the flat in Teglværksgade in Århus: T-shirts, dirty underpants, jogging bottoms, a belt, a couple of porn mags and a pouch of tobacco. As she located the items, she stuffed them into a yellow Netto bag. Finally, the whole bag was shoved into Peter's arms.

She was panting from the effort, and brushed the hair from her face. There was a packet of crisps and a half-empty tub of Haribo's Matador Mix on the coffee table. She took a couple of crisps from the bag and ate them noisily.

'I've done everything I could do for him. Two months! And not a bloody *øre* from him. The moment he lays his hands on some cash, he's out of here. He only came back for a quick shower.'

Peter took the cash to be the five hundred kroner he'd given Stinger with his coat, beanie and gloves.

'So where is he now?'

'Where do you think?'

She sent him a knowing look.

'Anholtsgade? Lulu and Miriam?'

A smile flickered in her eyes. She shook her head at her incorrigible big brother and took the Netto bag back from Peter.

'That's a pretty good guess.'

The financial crisis was having an impact, and Lulu's half-days at the massage parlour had been reduced to once a week because people were short of money. She and Miriam spent most of their time running the brothel in Anholtsgade. The two of them serviced the customers, and they – the customers – didn't grow on trees, or queue around the block, these days.

'They're not exactly lining up,' as Miriam said, letting him in. 'We may have to do some retraining.'

Peter kissed her on the corner of her mouth, which was red and heavily pencilled but capable of affection when the mood took her.

'Happy New Year! You'd make great nurses or French maids.'

Miriam pulled a face at him.

'I'm looking for Stinger. You know, the tattooist.'

Miriam adjusted the lipstick at the corner of her mouth with her finger.

'He's down at the massage parlour with Lulu. They'll be here later.'

She examined his face.

'You look tired. Why don't you stay and have some chicken with us?'

She pulled him in from the stairwell. He relaxed the moment he crossed the threshold, as if someone had helped him remove a heavy rucksack from his back. This was how it always was with Miriam. She had been his occasional bedfellow for years, even though the frequency had diminished recently. Miriam belonged to his past, the life he had once lived surrounded by prostitutes and pickpockets. She was still a part of his life, but it had become complicated. He was no longer sure what they expected of each other.

Everything about Miriam was well groomed and desirable, from the radiance of her skin to her breath, which was fresh and inviting. She had a sense of beauty, especially her own. He thought about Felix. He found her beautiful, too, but he was unable to explain to himself why. She had no curves and didn't dress as sexily as Miriam. But she had a fire inside her.

He let himself be led into the living room with its soft furniture as Ramses' dead body drifted further and further into the distance. Stinger was in good hands. There was nothing left for Peter to do but sit back and wait.

'So? What's new with you?'

She placed him in one of the deep chairs. As always, Kaj was on the rug under the coffee table.

Miriam kicked off her heels, stretched her feet and warmed them on the dog's coat.

'Ooh, it's cold today. And there's a draught from the window.'

She massaged Kaj's flank. Peter rose and held up a hand to the six-pane windows, which were old and crumbling. There wasn't much to stop the wind. Some of the panes were cracked and blots of condensation had spread outwards.

'They need replacing.'

'Try telling Lulu that. She says we can't afford it until the recession's over.'

'I'll get them for you at cost price and fit them myself. Got a tape measure?'

She fetched one; he took the measurements and jotted them down in his notebook.

'You should have told me earlier. Is there anything else?'

She flopped back on the sofa again and patted the seat next to her, and he sat down.

'Are you going to tell me what happened or am I going to have to guess?' she said.

More than anything else he wanted to forget, but there was no stopping Miriam.

'Perhaps I can help you.'

Perhaps she could. He tilted his head back and started talking: about his new neighbour; about Stinger turning up; about Ramses' body.

'That's so like you.'

She shook her head.

'You're so scared of having anything to do with the police you make things much worse for yourself. What a mess! You'll have to tell them you know him.' But there was a smile on her face as she spoke and she got up at once. 'Today's my day off. We could have some fun.'

He hesitated and she noticed.

'Consider it payment for the windows.'

He shook his head.

'What about a New Year's present then?'

'Nope.'

She made it sound so simple. But in his mind another face kept appearing, one with dark eyes and a voice that called him a liar.

'Thanks anyway,' he added. 'Some other time.'

She shrugged and feigned indifference. She went into the kitchen and started cooking, with her back to him, banging and slamming things down, but she soon recovered. She produced a bottle of champagne and filled two glasses.

'Seeing that it's New Year. And we haven't seen each other for ages. *Skål!*'

It was three weeks since he had last been to Århus.

'Ramses,' he said after the first mouthful. 'What do you know about him?'

37

She swirled the champagne around in her glass, making the bubbles rise.

'Not an awful lot more than you do,' she said. 'One for the ladies. Thought more with his dick than most men.'

She leaned against the worktop and looked at him. 'That's what makes a man careless.'

'Do you have anything specific you can tell me?'

She shrugged again. Lulu and Miriam knew a great deal, women in their line of work often did, but they were discreet and guarded their customers' secrets the way fairy-tale dragons guard treasure.

'I think he was having a dangerous liaison. There was a rumour.'

'A woman?'

'A woman whose husband was unhappy about this liaison,' Miriam said, locating a roasting tin in the cupboard under the worktop.

'Who should I be looking for?'

He knew he was pushing it. He also knew he would only get a hint by way of an answer. She rinsed the chicken and dabbed it dry with kitchen towel. From a packet in the fridge she took a big blob of butter and slapped it in the roasting tin, then she turned on the cooker and warmed the tin.

'You've got to go back in time, Peter,' she said, standing next to him.

She waited until the butter had browned before placing the rinsed chicken in the tin, making the fat sizzle. She looked at him while sipping her champagne.

'If you want an answer, your own past is where you'll find it. And deep down you know that, don't you? Stinger, Ramses and Brian.'

She put down her glass.

'The whole thing reeks of Horsens.'

Horsens Prison. Peter stared into the distance. He didn't want to look back; he had made a promise to himself. He wasn't interested in revenge or hatred. He wanted to live his new life, go hunting with Manfred and talk about great literature, play with Kaj, put a roof on the pig farmer's barn, do his paintings and dream about the future.

He was done with demons. But it didn't necessarily follow that they were done with him.

Later, when the food was ready, Lulu came in from the cold, wearing more clothes than he had ever seen her wear, and alone.

'Stinger? He ran into someone he knew and he was gone.'

She offered him a cheek to kiss, pushing out her enlarged breasts and sniffing the aroma of roast chicken. 'Yummy, I've been looking forward to this all day.'

9

MARK BILLE HANSEN turned up at Århus police station early on Saturday morning. No one had told him to do so. No one expected him. But he had decided it was the right thing to do. Århus was leading the investigation into the disappearance of Nina Bjerre, and it was also Århus and Anna Bagger who were investigating the death of the man under the cliff. Anna sat there now with a straight back and alert morning gaze, leading from the front and allocating work for the frogmen from the mine-clearing division of the FKP, the Frømandskorpset, with whom the police had a regular contract. She briefly met Mark's eyes, and warmth suffused his body, along with the irritation of having to watch from the wings.

He concentrated on the divers. He had seen their equipment when he parked outside the station at twenty minutes past seven. They had arrived from Nykøbing, Sjælland, late on New Year's Day in three vehicles: a blue pick-up, a green diving truck the size of a house and a towing vehicle with a black, one-tonne fibreglass boat and a small inflatable with an outboard motor on the back. Attending the meeting this morning were the commanding officer, Allan Vraa, as well as three young divers in green sweaters and army trousers, two dog handlers and a couple of police pathologists.

'Nina Bjerre went to a New Year's Eve party with some friends at the new development by the marina. She left the party at around two a.m. A witness saw her in the area near the fishing boats, so we were thinking of searching the harbour, with dogs and with you.'

Anna Bagger spoke to the commanding officer. 'What do you think? How long would it take your team to search the harbour?'

Allan Vraa unfolded a map on the table.

'Grenå Harbour is a dump. There's zero visibility and fish waste scattered around. It covers the seabed up to a depth of a couple of metres.'

'So what do you do if you can't see anything?'

He looked up.

'We use a progressive seabed search technique. We put out one hundred and twenty-metre lines and divide the harbour into a grid. The divers feel their way around.'

'Through fish waste?' Mark asked.

Allan Vraa nodded.

'It's not a pleasant job, but it can be done and it'll take about twenty-four hours, I would guess, but that means we'd cover one hundred per cent of the harbour. We work with two divers at a time.'

'Will you be diving yourself?' Anna Bagger asked him.

He hunched his shoulders.

'I do sometimes. But we happen to have a diver on standby. She lives just outside Grenå.'

'She?'

Even Anna Bagger seemed surprised.

Vraa nodded.

'The only frogwoman in the FKP. She's good. She did her training at Kongsøre and got top marks at graduation five years ago. She was the one who found that body in Vejle Fjord a couple of months ago, if you remember.'

One of the young divers nodded emphatically.

'Kir's good.'

Everyone remembered the Vejle case, of course. A woman

had gone missing after a night out. Witnesses had seen a man sailing in the fjord and dumping something mysterious.

'Vejle was straightforward once we had the witness statement,' the commander said. 'But for that, it would have been impossible. An entire fjord. It would've taken us over a month, and besides, bodies have a tendency to drift.'

'The current in Grenå can be strong,' Mark said. 'I heard about a man who fell into the harbour and was found in Norway.'

The commander nodded.

'When you're dealing with dead bodies anything is possible.'

'But surely they surface at some point?'

This was the dog handler asking.

'Depending on the temperature of the water, the body will sink during the first seven to ten days – in our case possibly longer due to the cold. Then it'll surface for one day before sinking again. It's the gases that cause the body to float.'

'If Nina Bjerre fell into the marina, she won't be surfacing any time soon,' Anna Bagger concluded. 'Which gives us even more reason to start looking for her today.'

'What about all the fish sludge you mentioned?' asked Martin Nielsen, Anna Bagger's colleague. 'Won't the body just sink into it, so you won't be able to find it even by feeling your way?'

The commander shook his head.

'Even if the seabed is very soft and the body has sunk, a submerged body doesn't weigh enough for it to sink right to the bottom. The divers will have their arms in the sludge all the way. If she's there, we'll find her.'

He cleared his throat.

'I understand you found a body in the area yesterday. I was just wondering if the two cases might be related.'

Anna Bagger shook her head.

'No obvious link, but of course we're looking into the possibility.'

'Do you know who he is?' Vraa asked her.

'He's been identified as a petty criminal who was in East Jutland Prison until last spring for handling stolen goods and assault. His name's Ramses Bilal and he was born in Egypt. The post-mortem is being carried out as we speak.'

Mark had seen his share of post-mortems during his time in Copenhagen. He didn't envy the police officers watching the process. Anna Bagger followed up on Vraa's previous question.

'It's hard to see how Ramses Bilal could be involved in the disappearance of a nineteen-year-old woman from a New Year's party. The two of them move in completely different circles, and anyway Gjerrild Cliff is at least ten kilometres from Grenå Harbour.'

They set off in a procession, but without flashing blue lights. Mark thought that if this had been Copenhagen, the media would have been ready and waiting the moment they left the police station. In any case, TV and newspaper journalists would turn up at some point. They needed to agree a press strategy, but perhaps Anna hadn't even thought about it.

His mobile rang as he followed the green diving truck. He could tell from the display it was his mother and felt no desire to reply. When he did so, despite his better judgement, he regretted it immediately.

'You've moved back to Grenå, and yet we hardly ever see you.'

He could have told her it was precisely because of reproaches like that he rarely visited them. But he had no time to reply before she moved on: 'I hope you haven't missed any of your check-ups?'

He would rather be investigating the death of a woman and losing himself in a good case than confronting reminders of his own mortality. He gritted his teeth and replied as amicably as he could that he was at work right now and besides he didn't have his headset on. A man had been found dead at the foot of the cliff and they were searching the marina for a young woman.

'Poor Nina.'

'Don't tell me you know her?'

His mother tut-tutted down the telephone.

'You forget this is a small town. She was in the same year as your cousin.'

'She went to school with Sanne?'

He didn't know his cousin very well.

'Sanne's been here lots of times with Nina.'

'We're on our way to Grenå. If you're at home, I'll stop by in a while, OK?'

Of course she was at home. Where else would she be? The roles were clearly defined in his parents' marriage. His father was first officer on the Grenå–Varberg ferry. His mother had always been at home with their two children and, when money was tight, had worked part-time as a dentist's secretary. They were his parents and he loved them. He also loved living at some distance from them and not having to conform to their expectations of an older son. Not even the events of recent years had caused them to lessen their demands.

He drove through the town to the residential area in the hills feeling that his life had come full circle and he was now back where it had started, and furthermore that he hadn't made any progress. He drove past the school where he and his brother Martin used to go; he passed houses where his friends used to live; streets he used to cycle up and down and where he played; fields where he and his friends had played football. Familiar and yet so alien. The prodigal son had returned. In a film this would be the end and the credits would start rolling. In real life things were very different.

'She's a pretty girl,' his mother said, putting the cups on the table. 'She and Sanne were very close when they were twelve or thirteen. Nice parents. In those days, they lived over in Myntevej.'

'Do you remember if she had any brothers or sisters?'

'A younger sister, I think.'

'Happy New Year, Mum.'

He raised his coffee cup. She angled her head.

'Did you have a nice evening? We tried calling you at midnight.'

'A very nice evening. I was out.'

He drank his coffee, recalled the taste of bought sex and took another sip to get rid of it.

'I hope you're not drinking too much?'

'No.'

He had cruised the town with the world's biggest erection. He hadn't been drinking but knew that he had to take things to the limit and then collapse, knowing he was still a human being. A man.

The girl had been standing on a street corner near the harbour with a couple of colleagues, clearly on the game, even in the cold. Though these days you needed a trained eye to tell the difference between the pros and the tarted-up young women going to New Year's Eve parties in sub-zero temperatures wearing high heels, short Puffa jackets and buttock-short dresses. He had stopped his car and opened the door, and she had jumped in after they had haggled briefly over the price. Young. Not pretty, but not ugly, either. To be honest, he didn't want to remember her face. Or her body, either. Only the function it had in relation to his.

Afterwards he had driven home. He fell asleep just as the bells on the Copenhagen Town Hall clock chimed twelve times and Danmarks Radio Choir sang '*Vær Velkommen*'.

'What do you remember about Nina Bjerre, Mum?'

Sitting at the kitchen table, his mother lit a cigarette.

'She had a brace on her teeth for a while.'

'That must be a long time ago.'

His mother sucked air in with the cigarette. Then she got up.

He heard her rummaging around in the living room and followed her.

'Here. I don't know if this helps. This is Sanne's twelfth birthday.'

There were five photos. The girls – seven of them – were in the garden sitting on the patio eating birthday cake. Most of them were slim, still without women's curves. It was summer. Shorts and skimpy dresses.

His mother pointed.

'That's her. That's Nina.'

It was a full-length shot. She was standing next to Sanne and a couple of the others on the slope in his aunt's garden. They were all posing, pretending to be models.

'She was a little gangly, don't you think?' his mother said, pointing at the photo again. 'Nice, slim body, but a bit knock-kneed. Not something you really notice, and not at all if she wears trousers.'

She looked at him.

'They can fix crooked teeth nowadays, but I've yet to hear of anyone fixing knock knees.'

10

IN THE MORNING Peter called in on Stinger's sister, Elisabeth, on his way home to Djursland, but she hadn't seen a sign of him and had no idea where he was.

'The earth must have swallowed him up,' she said. 'You said he met a woman?'

Lulu had described how a masculine-looking woman dressed in black, with a square face, had gone up to Stinger and persuaded him to skip the roast chicken in favour of something that was evidently more interesting. Elisabeth shook her head. The description didn't match anyone she knew in Stinger's circle, but it sounded just like him to be tempted by the offer of a night out.

'I bet he went pub-crawling with her until closing time and found someone to go home with,' said Elisabeth, who had a visitor and didn't have time to talk.

They stood talking in the doorway and Peter caught a glimpse of her guest sitting in the living room pressing an ice pack against one cheek. She was a tall, skinny girl with a ponytail. She had clearly been beaten up because she had black eyes and bruised cheeks.

'She's run away from her boyfriend. I have to help her,' Elisabeth whispered. 'If he finds out where she is, he'll kill her.'

Peter wanted to ask what the boyfriend would do if he found his girlfriend at Elisabeth's. Would he kill her, too? But he said nothing. He had the feeling he and Stinger's sister had more in common than might be thought at first glance. He knew only too well what it was like to invite in every waif and stray and not know when to say stop. He felt like saying to her: think about when and how to say no. But it was none of his business, so he opened the back of the car for Kaj and drove to Djursland, thinking he would go to the police station and tell them he knew Ramses. But he had promised Manfred to be at work first thing and it was already nine-thirty, so instead he decided he would use his lunch break to do the honourable thing.

The carpenter's workshop was in an old barn opposite the main house, which Manfred was doing up as and when he could find the time; a Sisyphean task, as he called it. When Peter arrived he was standing by the trestles and sanding turquoise paint off a door for his and Jutta's bathroom.

'Great day yesterday.'

Peter shouted his greeting through the noise from the sander. Manfred looked up and switched it off. He ran his hand across the surface of the door and seemed satisfied with it, for the moment.

'Thank you. We did well.'

'How many in total?'

'Three stags and two does. Plus some bits and bobs: two pheasants and a fox.'

Peter whistled.

'Not bad.'

'We displayed them in the yard. What a shame you couldn't stay. I'll e-mail you a couple of photos.'

Manfred looked at him closely.

'I hear you've been busy under the cliff.'

Peter told him about finding Ramses. He should have known the story was already doing the rounds.

'I said I didn't know him.'

No further elaboration was necessary. Manfred patted him on the shoulder and met his gaze with his small intelligent eyes.

'I'm re-reading *Of Mice and Men*,' he said after a pause.

Peter was well acquainted with Steinbeck's story about two

48

friends, George and Lennie, and their hopeless dream of freedom and something better than the hard life of a migrant worker.

Manfred looked at him with his ever amiable expression. But behind his amiability Peter could read the question: was he, like George and Lennie, going to end up sabotaging his chance of a new life through his own stupid actions?

'I made a mistake,' Peter said. 'My plan is to go to the police today and rectify it.'

Manfred merely nodded, and Peter was grateful that things could be discussed between them without doing them to death. As he started on his work he thought about the *Of Mice and Men* analogy. You had to be careful not to destroy your dreams, and his reticence could easily lead to that consequence. But he wasn't like George and Lennie. He had fought too hard for his freedom to let it slip away.

'The police are rushed off their feet today,' Manfred said the next time he switched off the sander. 'You'll probably have to queue.'

'Don't tell me another body has been found.'

Manfred leaned forward and deftly flipped the door resting on the trestles.

'Do you remember me telling you about Jutta's friend whose daughter hadn't come back from a New Year's Eve party?'

'Is she still not back?'

'They're searching the harbour for her today. A team of divers has come over from Kongsøre. That's where they train divers, you know.'

Peter thought about his walk back from the New Year's party and the sub-zero temperatures as he was lying on the balcony in his sleeping bag with the dog huddled against him.

'Poor girl,' he said, knowing these weren't the right words because the right words didn't exist.

Manfred nodded.

'Poor girl. And poor parents.'

11

Kir got the call just as she had surfaced from her dive and was sitting in the boat, dripping wet. It was Allan Vraa calling. Could she get ready to search the harbour in Grenå asap?

'Of course. What are we looking for?'

'A young woman, Nina Bjerre. Does the name mean anything to you? She failed to return from a New Year's Eve party on the seafront.'

Kir was a Grenå girl born and bred, but she didn't recognise the name. Nevertheless, her spirits fell at the thought that someone had ended their life at the bottom of an icy harbour, on New Year's Eve of all nights.

'Where are you?'

'Out walking in Polderrev Plantation,' she lied.

'In this cold?'

She hoped he couldn't hear the waves. What would he think if she told him she was two nautical miles out from the harbour?

'I needed some fresh air,' she said.

'You'll get plenty of that when you're down here helping us, I can guarantee you that,' said her old commander. 'It's minus bloody ten degrees. Snowstorms are forecast. Go home and have a hot drink before you leave.'

She told him not to worry and ended the call. She felt like a complete idiot. No one must know about her hopeless little venture, least of all Allan Vraa, who had professional respect for her as a mine clearance diver – respect which could soon be lost if he knew that she'd gone out on her own to search for a body which had in all likelihood been fish food long ago.

She just had time to stop by her summer house on the outskirts of Grenå. It had been a struggle to scrape up the money to buy it – not surprising, really, considering how much she'd spent on diving equipment over the years, she thought, as she drove up Hasselvej. The summer house was in an enclosed field south of the town, near the old summer house area, and technically she wasn't allowed to live here all year round. It was old, wooden, painted black, with an asphalt roof, and should have been demolished and rebuilt ages ago. But she didn't have enough money for that, and besides, she liked it the way it was. She felt at home here and that was what counted.

She had planned to throw some logs on the fire and sit in front of the wood burner with a mug of hot tea, a woollen blanket and one of the muffins she had baked the day before in a fit of domesticity, but she would have to put that off until later. She parked her car outside the garage, hauled her gear inside and started her post-dive routine. She had changed her clothes when she docked in the harbour, and had – with a selective sense of order which only manifested itself when it came to her diving equipment – carefully returned every item to its respective box. First she switched off her diving cylinder, emptied the tubes of any remaining air and disconnected the regulator from the cylinder valve. She checked the cylinder was properly closed before emptying the tubes again. When she had completed the first stage, she blew on the dust cap and filter to dry them, replaced the cap carefully and rinsed the regulator again before hanging it up to dry in its usual place.

The equipment box also contained her custom-made neoprene drysuit. In addition to that, there was an inner suit for extra insulation; then came the neoprene gloves and the hood, the compensator vest with the integrated weighting system, which could increase or reduce buoyancy – she released the lead weight pockets and laid them out in front of her – the fixed diving cylinder with a compressed air, depth and air pressure console – the compass and everything else needed for safe leisure diving.

She checked her watch. It was ten o'clock. She didn't want to delay the search for the woman in the harbour, so she quickly rinsed every item, cleaned the vest and emptied it again by turning it upside down. Then she re-inflated it so it would dry quickly. She gave the rest – knife, scissors, torch, marker buoys and signalling equipment – a quick once-over before closing the garage door.

In the kitchen she grabbed a rye bread sandwich and glugged down a glass of milk before locking the house and, filled with a mixture of nervous excitement and sadness, drove to the harbour to meet her colleagues, whom she hadn't seen since the search in Vejle Fjord.

They had assembled in the cold outside the big green diving truck, which stood near the harbour's middle basin, holding cups of hot coffee and discussing the day's strategy. Allan Vraa briefed her and handed her a steaming plastic cup.

'She went to a party over there.'

He pointed in the direction of the flats by the marina. The people who lived there probably wouldn't see the attraction of an old wooden summer house, she thought.

'But a witness saw her at around two a.m. by this basin, so that's where we're going to start. Niklas and Karsten have set up the poles.'

Kir had dived in Grenå before. There were three basins in all. The largest industrial basin was furthest away, with a depth of ten to eleven metres. The middle one was where the big trawlers were moored, and it also contained sorting and pumping facilities for industrial fishing. And then the last basin was for the net fishermen and small trawlers. In the middle basin, the depth was around seven metres and visibility was always poor.

The basin lay next to the scrapyards where redundant ships were decommissioned and cut up.

'That was quick,' she said, still cold from her earlier dive.

She drank her coffee. She had swum around where old Hannibal used to take her fishing, but she hadn't found much, except for sand, seaweed and a couple of gawping fish in the sub-zero water. Soon she would have to get this silly idea out of her head. Hannibal was dead. More than likely he had fallen overboard by accident, because his boat had been found later, washed up on Fjellerup Strand. She didn't understand why it continued to haunt her; everybody else appeared to have accepted this explanation. So why couldn't she just let it go?

'. . . mind diving with Niklas?'

Allan Vraa looked at her quizzically.

'Kir?'

She pulled herself together. She'd been looking forward to working with her colleagues again. She was going to make the most of it.

'No, not at all.'

'Good,' Allan Vraa said, crushing his empty plastic cup and throwing it into a bin. 'Get your gear. Let's get cracking.'

12

FELIX KNEW ALL about befriending insomnia.

She had learned something from all those women's magazines she'd ploughed her way through over the years after all: the trick was to embrace your insomnia, welcome it like an old friend.

The only problem was that it didn't work. She'd tried. It always ended up with the old friend outstaying her welcome.

So she walked around in a daze, as if the world was stage scenery and she an extra in a play with a large cast. But she could do nothing else.

She sipped her tea and tried to force down a cracker, pretending to herself that she had slept. She collected the newspaper from her mailbox and in the process let the cold in. The front page told the story of the young girl who had disappeared on New Year's Eve and the discovery of a man's body. His name was Ramses Bilal. Egyptian. An ex-convict.

She looked out of the window, towards her neighbour's house. Who was Peter Boutrup? And how did he come to know a violent criminal?

Boutrup hadn't returned yet. He hadn't been home since he'd left the house the day before. She presumed he'd taken the dog with him. You didn't leave a dog alone for so many hours, and he was clearly a man who loved his dog. Felix wondered if there were people he loved, too.

She looked down the lane that led from the cottages on the cliff towards Gjerrild. The postman had been and gone long ago. Right now there wasn't a soul to be seen. She got up but was overcome by a coughing fit and had to sit down again to recover. This wasn't good. She was ill. She didn't care about the illness, but she did care about the flashbacks, which had troubled her all through the night. Ramses Bilal had triggered it: snippets of stories, intruding, urging her to address them; faces; fragments of conversations. Pieces of jigsaw from the day her world had exploded. She fought them. But they surged like a tsunami against oblivion and demanded she let them in.

Peter Boutrup. She must try to concentrate on him. Perhaps he could force the jigsaw pieces out of her mind.

She put on her coat and boots and went to the car port, where she found a shovel. It took her a few minutes to dig down to the stone Peter Boutrup's guest had unearthed on New Year's Eve. Once the stone was exposed, she quickly found the key. She stood holding it in her hand for a long time, trying to talk herself out of it, but a stronger voice drowned out the warning.

She unlocked the door and went inside.

It was clean and there was a smell that reminded her of something. At first she thought it was the boat: they had painted it a couple of years ago, just before it put to sea after the winter. She didn't remember the details, only the sense of companionship. Erik and her together, sharing a project for once and enjoying it – or she was, at least.

She moved noiselessly through the house. Wooden floors. White walls and white furniture. Austere. There were landscape paintings on the walls. Several were pale winter scenes in blue and white shades and she recognised her surroundings: the cliff, the sea, the lane. She walked up to one of them. Sniffed it. The smell came from them. It was fresh paint. She looked at the initials: PAB. Then she found an easel and paints in another room which apparently served as a studio. Several more paintings were leaning against the wall. She flicked through them. Many of them were part of a series. Just as the ones in the living room had a winter theme, these had a recurring subject: a big, burning tree. Here she noticed the initials were of an older vintage.

She tried to draw some conclusions about the occupant of the house as she moved from room to room, but she kept finding new things that contradicted what she had just deduced. The paintings suggested he might be a cultivated man behind the brusque exterior. But then she looked at his music collection: dreadful canned music, rap, hip-hop; black men wearing layers of gold jewellery, probably with previous for drug dealing and violence, graced several of the CD covers. The same went for his DVD collection: brain-dead action movies and – God help us – a pile of porn. No sophistication there.

She scanned the bookcase, expecting more of the same. But apart from books about dog training and wildlife, she would not have predicted what she found. The majority of the space was given to classics and they looked as if they had been read: Tolstoy, Dostoyevsky, Dickens, Steinbeck, Flaubert, Dumas, Hugo, Cervantes and several others. Robinson Crusoe was so worn and dog-eared it was falling apart. Danish writers were present, too: Johannes V. Jensen, Karen Blixen, Martin A. Hansen, I.P. Jacobsen. She recognised the names, of course, and might well have read some of them at school, but she wasn't much of a reader herself.

She went into the kitchen, expecting his culinary interests to match his literary predilections, but didn't find very much – just expensive dog food from the vet, some bags of porridge oats, a large supply of baked beans, tinned tomatoes and pasta, as well as eggs, milk, bacon and white bread in the fridge. And the remains of a beef joint.

She found the bedroom. It was cold and reminded her of a monastic cell; there was no linen on the bed. She went upstairs, which was one big room. On the floor lay a mattress, a sleeping bag and two thick fleeces. Apart from that there was an old sofa and a small coffee table with a lamp on it. The French doors led out to a balcony overlooking a partial view of the cliff and the town. It was from here she first heard the sound and saw the car coming down the lane, struggling to get through the snow.

She wanted to make a quick exit, but froze. She heard the car engine being turned off. Then a window was smashed. She stood very still while someone started trashing the ground floor. She heard things being pushed over, items splintering, books falling off shelves and landing on the wooden floor with a thud. There was nowhere to hide and she had no weapons within reach. Yes, she did. The lamp on the table. She yanked it out of the socket and pulled off the shade. The base was ceramic. As heavy as lead.

Then she heard the sound of boots on the stairs.

13

K<small>IR</small> <small>FOLLOWED</small> <small>THE</small> line from the red buoy and dived seven metres down to the bottom of Grenå Harbour, right next to the wharf. Visibility was zero. Even when she held a gloved hand to her face, she couldn't see it. She found pole one, grabbed hold of the search line and swam twenty metres across the basin holding the wire in one hand. Along the way she felt the sludge with her other hand for anything that might be a dead body, but found nothing. At pole two she turned around and repeated the process until she was back at pole one with the carabiner an arm's length from the pole, and then swam the twenty metres back to pole two. All the time she kept one hand deep in the fish sludge. After a few minutes, she could feel something bothering her, so she was forced to remove her mask, drain the water out and put it back on. During this manoeuvre she got polluted water in her face, and the stench of fish waste reached her nostrils and made her gag. It was like swimming in fish soup. She appreciated all the more her suit, her gloves and the full mask that kept her dry, and the body heat that was generated by moving around in water that was three degrees Celsius.

She concentrated on her work, her hand groping and touching bottles and scrap iron on its way. And so the first twenty minutes passed. She had almost got used to the smell and the thought of the sludge when something quickly wrapped itself around her fingers. She stopped and examined it more closely. Grass? Hair?

The cold began to penetrate her drysuit now that she was no

longer moving. Images rushed in from the job in Vejle Fjord: the long hair floating in the water. It was the hair she had felt first. She had pulled at it to free her hand and been scared the head might follow.

She tugged gently at whatever it was she had got hold of. It gave and her arm recoiled in an arc, still holding the tuft. It wasn't hair, much too coarse for that, she concluded. More likely old, frayed rope. She forced herself to breathe calmly until she was back to normal. No one must know that she had reacted like this. It would pass, she was sure of it. It always did.

She breathed in and out. Slowly, but regularly.

She started moving forward again, concentrating on being systematic. Routine was her salvation. She swam back and forth, back and forth between the poles in a steady rhythm. It was important not to think too much.

It worked. Her focus returned and she could dismiss the episode while her hands worked away once more and she felt the current pulling at her body. It was strong, but the poles had been anchored firmly and evenly across the seabed and were held down by weights, fixed, so they couldn't move. There was an eighteen-kilo weight at each end, and a seven-kilo one in the middle. In addition, a rope was attached to each pole leading up to a buoy on the surface. The poles weren't going anywhere. Bodies were another matter. They had a tendency to drift in strong currents. She hoped they weren't chasing a body on the move around the harbour.

Time passed quickly, and yet it didn't. Suddenly she felt a double tug from above on the line connecting her to the surface. Then a single tug and then another double tug: Morse code for 'k', which meant it was time for her to surface. She hadn't finished this line so there had to be another reason to break off. She rose to the surface, annoyed. She had found a variety of things: bicycles, shopping trolleys, tyres, oil barrels and bottles. But she hadn't found Nina Bjerre.

'There's a fishing boat coming in,' Allan told her as soon as she grabbed onto the dinghy. Niklas, too, had been asked to surface. They waited in the water until the boat had entered the basin. It was pointless to summon the divers all the way up only to send them down again immediately afterwards. If you did, they would have to start all over again, adjusting the equipment at the bottom. Even so, she had lost her momentum when Allan Vraa finally did send them down again, and when the time was up and the diving was over, she felt dissatisfied.

She sat on the gunwale of the inflatable, her teeth chattering, drinking from a Thermos of hot coffee as they were taken back to shore. The others were wrapped up in one-piece diving suits and wearing caps and gloves. There was always water in the bottom of the rubber dinghy, but today it had almost frozen to ice. There was also a layer of ice over all the equipment. At the mouth of the harbour yet another fishing boat was on its way in. Allan lightly punched her shoulder.

'Remember the saying: a proper sailor is never cold . . .'

She couldn't even finish the saying, her teeth were chattering so much. Allan did it for her: '. . . he just turns blue and dies.'

They quickly reached the quay, and it was only now that she noticed several cars parked there. People were wandering around, some with TV cameras on their shoulders.

A couple of the cars had press logos on their sides: TV2 News was there, *Ekstra Bladet* as well. There was also a van from Private Eyes, another TV company. The cameramen followed them and filmed her and Niklas going ashore. They also shouted out questions.

'Did you find anything?'

'What will you do if you find her?'

She shook her head and held up a hand.

'Don't film my face,' she said to the TV2 News cameramen who had come up to her. 'Speak to my boss when he gets ashore. Allan Vraa. I can't comment.'

They were naval officers and sometimes they were deployed in anti-terror operations. Their faces were not allowed to appear in the media, and this was usually accepted and understood. It would be fatal if enemies – Danish as well as foreign – could identify and possibly attack them.

Before Kir had reached the warmth of the diving truck she caught a glimpse of a man with black, shoulder-length hair talking to a blonde. He raised his eyes and she felt them on her for a brief moment. Police, she thought. He exuded a kind of authority.

Niklas and Kir quickly helped unzip each other so they could get out of their drysuits. Her teeth were still chattering despite the oil heater in the truck. They hung up their suits in the drying cabinet and sat on the bench with another mug of coffee.

'In a way I wish I'd found her,' Niklas said. 'Then at least I would've known what it was like.'

She got up and put on her army trousers over her merino wool bodysuit.

'Finding a body isn't much fun. It's worse when the visibility is like it is here. When you practically swim into it,' she said.

He warmed his hands on the mug.

'But if I had, then I would've experienced the worst that can happen.'

'Have you been to the Morgue and seen the bodies there?'

He shook his head.

'You should ask to go and visit it. It helps. Once you've seen a dead child, nothing else is really that bad.'

He'd been with them in Vejle when they found the body of a woman during a dive at night, but he wasn't in the water when it happened. He could blow up mines and defuse bombs. He could dive down a hundred metres into a shipwreck lying upside down and out again. And yet what scared him most was encountering a dead body.

'They won't hurt you. You need to tell yourself that when it happens. The dead can't hurt you.'

What she didn't tell him, however, was that they might haunt you for months. They could wreck your sleep and they could creep into your subconscious and lodge there like parasites.

In very bad cases, they could fill you with a black fear of everything beneath the surface of the water.

14

Neither Anna Bagger nor Mark Bille was anywhere to be found at Grenå Police Station, so Peter left a message at reception and asked one of them to call him. But he heard nothing for the rest of the day and concluded they probably had other things to think about. Never mind. At least he had shown willing. Driving home after work, he knew immediately that something was wrong. The window in the back door was smashed, and the front door was unlocked. Irrationally, his first thought was that the house would be freezing cold now, and he would have to light the wood burner quickly to warm the place up. Then he realised there were more important things at stake than wasting heat.

He entered cautiously. Kaj followed him, whining and keeping low on his front paws. He immediately embarked on his own search of the crime scene and sniffed around, from the sofa to the overturned bookcase to the cushions lying on the floor, the drawer that had been emptied onto the wooden floor, the paintings that had been snatched and cut up. Peter put the cushions back where they belonged on the sofa and sat in the middle of the chaos. He surveyed the wreckage.

'This is not good, Kaj. Not good at all.'

The dog understood him, he knew he did. Kaj, too, enjoyed having a system and a routine, what other people might call a humdrum existence. Days when you were allowed to do your own thing and maintain contact with the world outside, without anyone getting too close. He patted Kaj on the head when he came back from a recce with frown lines etched into his forehead.

'Good boy.'

It was all because of Ramses and Stinger, Peter thought. Someone had trashed his place looking for information about their miserable get-rich-quick scheme, of that he was certain. The timing of the break-in couldn't be a coincidence. Miriam was right: it was all about the past. It was about Horsens. About everything he wanted to put behind him.

The dog tore itself from his grasp and soon afterwards he heard the click of claws on the stairs, as Kaj decided he would explore the first floor. He started to bark and Peter's immediate thought was that the intruder was still upstairs. He got up and grabbed the poker from by the wood burner to protect himself before going upstairs.

A body in a black Puffa jacket lay across the fleece. The ceramic lamp from the table was lying on the floor, broken in half.

'Felix. Can you hear me?'

He shook her gently. She groaned. Opened her eyes, closed them again. Then she opened them again and stared at him.

'What happened? What are you doing here?'

He helped her into a sitting position, then leaned her against the yellow sofa, which had come with the house when he bought it. Her nose was bleeding and one eye was swollen. Her hair was matted with blood. Her small figure seemed even smaller and thinner than he remembered and her eyes were filled with frightened anger. He took his clean handkerchief and dabbed at some of the blood. Then he held his hand in front of her face and hid his thumb.

'How many fingers am I holding up?'

'Four.'

'I'm calling an ambulance.'

'No. Don't.'

Her head slumped against her chest, as if out of her control. He started to sweat. What if she died here? What would he say to the police?

'Give me a hand,' she said. 'The sofa.'

He helped her to her feet, laid her on the sofa and put cushions under her head. She waved her arms in the air, and moaned.

'I just need a little rest,' she managed to say. 'No police. No ambu . . .'

He went downstairs and put the kettle on, then rummaged around in a kitchen cupboard until he finally found a packet of instant soup and stirred it into a mug of hot water. He took the mug, a glass of water, some painkillers and a blanket upstairs. She didn't seem keen, but he ignored her and put the tablets into her mouth one at a time and held her head so that she could drink. He tried to get a little bit of soup down her, but she pressed her lips together like a stubborn child and he gently released her.

She opened and closed her eyes. The second she looked at him was like a glance all the way into her soul, and he was drawn in, feeling oddly that this was only happening because she was weak. Again, she waved her arms about. He glimpsed some scars stretching from her wrist to under the sleeve of her jacket. He wanted to ask what she was really doing here, in his house. And, not least, who had been here at the same time. But she'd already closed her eyes and was evidently asleep.

He picked up the shattered glass and found a couple of pieces of wood in the outhouse, cut them to size and hammered them across the broken window in the back door as a temporary fix. Then he started clearing up. He was well into his stride – he'd put the bookcase back and filled it with books, organised drawers and cupboards – when he heard noises from above.

He went upstairs. She was sitting upright, still wearing the black Puffa jacket and lying on the sofa in her winter boots.

There was a misty look to her eyes and he wondered whether she might be psychotic, existing in a different reality to his. She could be on drugs, but she didn't look like a junkie. She just looked like someone who couldn't cope with life.

'I've got to go home,' she said.

'Not before I have an explanation.'

'I didn't do it,' she muttered. 'I just wanted to see how you lived.'

'And so you took the key?'

'I saw the man take it the other night.'

'Stinger? New Year's Eve?'

She nodded.

'He borrowed my shovel. I wanted to find out who you were.'

He sat down on the coffee table.

'And did you?'

She shook her head and pulled a face as though it hurt.

'No.'

'Here, drink some soup.'

He handed her the mug, which was still lukewarm. She averted her face.

'When did you last eat?'

She didn't reply.

'You have to eat. Have you got any food in your house?'

She ignored the question and explained she'd been on the first floor when someone had arrived by car and smashed the window in the door. She'd been scared and had taken the lamp to defend herself while the man was ransacking the house below.

'What did the car look like?'

'It was a four by four.'

'Colour?'

She couldn't remember. Grey or black. It was covered in snow. She told him about the break-in and the noises coming from the ground floor.

'Afterwards he came up the stairs and in here.'

'Who was he? What did he look like?'

She shook her head and coughed. The cough didn't sound healthy.

'He was wearing a black balaclava. Like the ones you wear under a motorbike helmet. I think he was just as surprised to see me. I hurled the lamp at him, but he ducked and it hit the wall. Then he took one half of it and knocked me out.'

She pointed to the two pieces.

'I'll pay for the damage.'

A cautious smile appeared on her lips. 'I hope it wasn't a priceless heirloom. Ming dynasty or something like that.'

He'd bought it at a flea market in Ebeltoft.

'This is about the dead body, isn't it? Someone broke in here because you knew Ramses.'

Peter pointed at her arms.

'Were you in a fire or something? Is that why you've stopped eating?'

She carefully pulled down her sleeves. Then she raised her hand to her throat as if to check her jacket was buttoned all the way up.

'Where do you know the dead man from?' she asked.

'From prison.'

She blinked. If her throat had been visible, her gulp would have been more obvious.

'I was in an accident,' she said. 'I was the sole survivor.'

She gave him enough time to think she had been lucky before adding: 'You don't decide if you'll survive or not. Had it been up to me, I'd have chosen differently.'

15

Mark Bille Hansen had seen the woman diver before. He recognised her red hair and inquisitive eyes. He had also noticed her smile when she spoke to her colleague. It was a wry, elfish smile and revealed a big gap between her front teeth. He took all this in before she and her colleague zipped each other up at the back and worked together donning their diving hoods. A yellow neck ring had to be attached and then a rubber hood was folded over it – to prevent water from seeping in, he guessed. The only diving he had ever done was snorkelling, and that was in the Mediterranean on holiday in Malta, in somewhat warmer waters.

He could see they were getting ready to go back out after their break in the diving truck. They climbed into the rubber dinghy and were taken out to the basin, where even the fishing boats appeared to be frozen solid. He stood with his hands buried in the pockets of his jacket, freezing and desperate for some coffee, as the two divers in the boat fell backwards into the icy water. Mark shuddered. It wasn't often he counted himself lucky because of his job, but this was one of those occasions.

'Coffee?'

Anna Bagger proffered a double-wall cup, with hot steam rising from it like a pillar.

'Thank you.'

He took the cup and raised it to his mouth. The contrast between the freezing temperature and the hot coffee was like an electric shock to his lips.

'So you were transferred here from the Copenhagen Homicide Division. Why?'

He looked at her through the steam.

'It's a long story.'

He'd previously thought one single misplaced stroke in the portrait of Anna Bagger would have tipped the balance. Seen in isolation, her jaw was a little too square and her face a little too long, her eyes a little too big and her lower lip a little too full. And yet she was an attractive woman, possibly because she wanted to be and did something about it, with make-up, clothes and the way she moved. This was how some women could create an illusion.

'It's a somewhat unusual career choice,' she said. 'So you know a lot of people around here, do you?'

He nodded. He probably did.

She tilted her head.

'You've lost weight since I last saw you. Are you all right?'

In a recess of his mind he wondered whether she bore him a grudge, whether in her heart of hearts she was his friend or his enemy.

'I'm fine. And you?'

She straightened, as if bracing herself. He didn't know what for.

'I don't suppose divorces are ever much fun. Mine certainly wasn't.'

She'd never referred to her marriage with much enthusiasm, but that probably wasn't the done thing with potential lovers. Mark didn't want to pry, so he returned to the case.

'Did you find that Boutrup?'

She stood for a while scrutinising him, as if she had X-ray eyes, he thought. Then she shook her head.

'As you know, we had to start looking for a body here in the harbour, so he was given a bit more slack than planned. But I've checked him out.'

'And?'

'He's an ex-con. Like Ramses. They were in prison together.'

She looked across the harbour, to where the dinghy was skirting the edge. Two handlers and their dogs were busy searching the buildings leading down to the dock itself. The dogs looked keen, but neither of them seemed to have a scent.

'But you don't think he's the killer?'

'Take it easy, Mark. We're not eliminating anyone or anything at this stage.'

He drank some more coffee, this time with more care.

'What was he in for?'

Her blue eyes blinked in the cold.

'I thought you were the local cop with your ear to the ground.'

'Give over, Anna.'

'Involuntary manslaughter. A trespasser shot his dog. Boutrup shot him with a hunting rifle.'

Mark sighed. He was a detective, too. He'd learned everything he knew during the Copenhagen gang wars, even though he was only thirty-seven. How had he ended up in a situation where his ex-student and lover was his boss?

'Let me have a word with him,' he heard himself say. 'I imagine the investigation is understaffed as usual.'

Any hint of anything personal was purged from her eyes.

'No offence, but questioning murder suspects is not part of your job description.'

That smarted, like a resounding slap in the face, but he controlled himself and assumed an impassive expression. Above all, he was annoyed with himself. The plan had been for him to take it easy. That was the whole reason for the transfer, but sod that. He'd been here for six weeks and he was bored rigid, in a way he'd rarely been during his entire life, and already he was acting up.

He looked across the icy harbour, where the seagulls were screeching with hunger and rage. He might be dying, but he wasn't going to die from boredom. Anna Bagger wasn't going to dictate what kind of policing he did on his own beat.

'So what do you want from me?' he asked, his thoughts already at the cliff in a confrontation with the two neighbours.

Her gaze was still probing, but perhaps it had softened a touch.

'I imagine your own patch is keeping you busy.'

'Come on, Anna, give it a rest. There are questions I can help you answer. I could speak to Boutrup.'

He held up one hand and used his fingers to count the questions: 'What's his relationship with Ramses, apart from the fact that they were in prison at the same time? Why didn't he say he knew him? Why did he run? There must have been something important he had to do. What was it? What do you even know about him?'

She looked him straight in the eye as she replied.

'He isn't local. He bought the house seven years ago and did it up himself, I've been told. Apparently he worked in the region as a carpenter before he went to prison. That's what he does now. He seems to be respected both professionally and generally.'

'What about before? Any other previous convictions?'

'Not documented. But they could be so old that they've been wiped.' She looked at her watch. 'Got to go.'

She left and he stood for a moment watching her. Then he took a sip of his coffee, which had grown cold, tipped out the rest on the tarmac and crushed the cup. He went to chuck it in the bin and passed the diving team on his way. Some of them were standing by the tow truck chatting to the dog handlers, who had evidently finished searching the seafront.

He asked the men standing in a group: 'The local diver, the woman. What's her name?'

'Kir,' said one of her colleagues, a fit young man in army green from top to toe.

'What's Kir short for?'

They looked at each other. Kirstine, they thought, but they weren't sure. It could have been Kirsten. At FKP headquarters in Nykøbing, Sjælland, she had only ever been known as Kir.

'Kir Royal,' said one of her colleagues, with a warm smile.

'Royal?' Mark asked.

'Her surname is Røjel. So we call her Kir Royal. She doesn't mind.'

Mark nodded. Kirstine Røjel. The short form, Kir, must have been something she'd started using as a teenager or an adult. Back at school she was only ever known as Kirstine.

16

KIR QUICKLY REDISCOVERED her rhythm, ploughing back and forth between the poles. In the harbour, Niklas was about to fix another pole in place. They were on track to finish searching the whole basin before dark.

As she felt her way through the fish sludge on the seabed, she thought about the police officer, Mark Bille Hansen. She remembered him from school. He had been in one of the higher classes; three to four years above her. She used to think he was cool. He did a lot of sport and was a real tearaway, but she'd never exchanged as much as two words with him.

At school she had always been a very physical girl. She was good at sport and her body was built for it, agile and strong. She loved athletics. She relished it when her body exploded into life off the starting blocks and she could control it, down to the nearest millimetre, until she crossed the finishing line. But interest in athletics was limited in the small provincial community. Usually people played only handball or volleyball. She didn't love ball games in the same way, but they came easily to her. Anything physical came easily to her.

Books were another matter. She hated books. She hated all of it, all the sitting still, concentrating on words and letters which danced in front of her eyes. It wasn't until she was in year five, and lagging hopelessly behind, that it was discovered she was dyslexic.

It had seemed like a catastrophe. Overnight, she had gone from being the strong, sporty girl to someone in need of help.

She was put in a remedial class, and she had wished the ground would swallow her up in shame. She desperately wanted another life. She wanted to be like her father's brother, Uncle Hannibal, who was a mine clearance diver and a bit of an alcoholic, and could tell blood-curdling stories about bombs he'd detonated underwater or bodies he'd salvaged from dangerous shipwrecks. Her parents had resented her admiration for Uncle Hannibal. Her dad was quite the opposite to him: regular in his habits, traditional, married to his childhood sweetheart, father of three and the heir to a pig farm. According to him, Uncle Hannibal had deep dive syndrome resulting in white spots on the brain. In other words, he was an incorrigible liar.

Kir smiled behind her mask. Her father hadn't been entirely wrong. Hannibal was an old salt and yes, a liar, too, when the mood took him. On more than one occasion she'd hidden in the basement when her father had been looking for her, and she'd heard Uncle Hannibal insisting vehemently that he hadn't seen her for days. After they had quickly hidden her bicycle in the outhouse and lowered his vodka bottles in a bucket down the dry well, of course. No one, least of all his big brother, was going to catch Hannibal red-handed with a stash of bottles and reeking of booze.

She turned around at the pole and attached the carabiner an arm's length across, remembering the summer she turned twelve. For her that summer represented a turning point in her life. It was the summer she decided to become a mine clearance diver. It was the summer her brother Tomas fell overboard and would have drowned if she hadn't dived four metres down under the dinghy to rescue him.

She had come to the end of the wire and was about to give up hope of finding anything when she felt something nudge against her. At the last moment, she managed to move out of the way, otherwise she would have literally found herself face to face with the dead body. As it was, her hands found the body first. She knew immediately what it was. She recognised the soft feel of bloated flesh. Her heart was galloping, but she managed to stay calm. She mustn't panic now. If she kept a lid on everything for long enough, it would go away.

She prodded with gloved fingers. The body was naked and it was female. Legs, torso, neck, head. Hair floating in the water, like a mermaid's, a different, finer texture than the frayed rope from earlier. Matching the description of Nina Bjerre. Some of the hair came out as Kir disentangled herself, and she had a sense of the whole body flopping about, like a flower in a vase. She dug down in the sludge. The dead body was in fish waste up to the ankles. She could feel that the legs had been tied together with a rope. At the end of it was a ship's anchor, resting at the bottom of the sludge. She dived down further and located the anchor, which must have weighed around fifteen kilos. The rope was looped through the eye of the anchor and ran from the ankles, up the calves to the hands, which were tied behind the back. From there, it went up to the neck and was tied tightly around it.

She could see very little, but a strange instinct made her move close to the face. The head had felt peculiar, even through the gloves. Now she strained her eyes to catch a glimpse, but it was too difficult in the light conditions, and for much of the time all she could see was darkness.

In the end, she gave up, marked the spot with a buoy and signalled to the dinghy that she'd found something and was coming up.

'Is the press still there?' she asked, as she was pulled into the boat.

'The place is crawling with them,' Allan said, looking towards the seafront. 'Can you bag her? If Niklas helps you?'

'Yes. But she's tied to an anchor. I'll have to cut the rope, won't I?'

He nodded.

'Just tie another rope around the anchor and we'll salvage it later.'

He looked around and directed his gaze at somewhere on the horizon. She knew what he was thinking before he said it.

'It'll be dark soon. We'll have to hurry. We'll mark the spot, recover the body and the anchor and carry on looking tomorrow for the rest of the evidence.'

With calm professionalism, Allan Vraa radioed the police on shore that the body had been found. The crew noted the time and position, took photographs and measured some distances from the quay and outwards, so that it could all be reconstructed in their report. Then they set off to collect Niklas.

17

PETER WAS TROUBLED. Upstairs, Felix had gone back to sleep. He had no idea where he stood with her. She had seen through him when he lied about Ramses. She had broken into his house, where she had been attacked and was now in a bad way. He should be angry. Who was she? What did she want from him?

But there was something about her pulling him in the opposite direction. She seemed so abandoned and he wondered what her story could be. She had a way of looking at him, hostile at first sight, but underneath there was an element of pleading, as if with one hand she was telling him to go to hell while with the other she was begging for help. He thought about Stinger's sister and her guest: 'I have to help her.' Perhaps he was just like Elisabeth.

He stared out of the kitchen window while he did the washing-up. Outside, it had started to grow dark, but the snow and the moon would shortly take up the baton, and daylight would be transformed into pale reflections of night. On the Kattegat, there were only a few lights to be seen from vessels plying to and fro. Peter had personal experience of people imposing their help and he had protested just as Felix had. Helping was no simple matter. Ultimately, who was helping who?

After washing up, he wandered around the house followed by Kaj. He finished tidying up after the break-in and concluded that nothing had been stolen. Whoever had burgled his house hadn't found what they were looking for. Nor had the intruder known that Peter kept a key under the white stone. It narrowed down the field of suspects considerably.

He made coffee and sandwiches for dinner and gave Kaj a bowl of biscuits. He had just made up his mind to go to the police in the morning, if they hadn't contacted him, when he heard the sound of a car coming down the lane. Soon there was a knock on the door and Mark Bille Hansen appeared outside with his pained expression and a haircut that would have looked more credible on a man holding an electric guitar. Faded designer jeans, smart biker boots and a short shearling jacket completed the impression of a modern badge-less sheriff. His gaze was pure Wyatt Earp: stern, no-nonsense.

'Can I come in?'

Peter stepped aside, pleased that he had managed to clear the place up. The dog growled softly and withdrew after sniffing the policeman, who went down on his haunches and held out a hand.

'Nice dog.'

Mark Bille Hansen straightened up. They were the same height and their eyes met. The word 'police' flashed in front of Peter's eyes and he felt every shutter come down. Lies he didn't want to tell started to force their way to the surface.

'Perhaps we could take a seat?'

Mark Bille Hansen pointed to the sofa where Stinger had been snoring. Peter remembered that he had just made coffee. He also remembered that Felix was asleep upstairs. Neighbours who had claimed not to know each other, and now she was lying on his sofa with a bloody nose and a headache. He hoped she would stay where she was.

'Of course,' he managed to say after a slight hesitation, which the other man picked up on. 'Would you like some coffee?'

He didn't wait for a reply, just put the coffee pot on the table and fetched two mugs.

'I think I owe you an explanation. I left a message at the police station today . . .'

'I've just come from the station. No one said anything.'

'Then she must have forgotten. Dark-haired lady. Short hair and glasses. Mid-forties, I reckon.'

It was already going from bad to worse. Mark Bille sent him a sceptical look.

'You knew Ramses. From prison. Why did you lie?'

Peter sat down, looked at the policeman and tried to assess what he saw. He guessed that Mark Bille Hansen was in his late thirties. There was something local about his accent, but it was mixed with a distinct hint of Copenhagen. He was well dressed in a casual way Peter rarely saw in Djursland, where a shirt from Føtex and a pair of jeans from Bilka constituted dressing up. But there was also something else. He was pale, as if he suffered from anaemia, and his clothes seemed a tad too big. There were visible marks on his hands, by the veins. He was the new man in Grenå Police. Peter had heard that the old Chief had retired. His best guess was that the man sitting opposite him had been through some sort of illness and had been transferred from a stressful police post in Copenhagen to a cushy number in the provinces. He was dealing with a sick man. And this was his way in.

'Most of the time I was in prison I was ill. I would've died if I hadn't been given a new kidney,' he began.

'Touching.'

The interest was there, even though Mark Bille Hansen was shaking his head.

'It's hard to explain,' Peter continued. 'I was sure I was going to die. I was mad at the whole world. I just wanted to be left alone and I didn't want anyone to feel sorry for me or interfere.'

Mark Bille Hansen scratched his hand. He looked around uncomfortably, as if half-expecting to see a hospital bed in the corner.

'I was like that until a kidney suddenly became available. I hadn't been expecting it,' Peter said. 'Perhaps I hadn't deserved it, either. I was in prison. I was the lowest of the low. No one said anything, but I could tell from their faces. That kidney could have gone to a more deserving person.'

Peter eyed Mark Bille Hansen.

'Who can say who gets to live and who gets to die? Both sides are terrible experiences, I can vouch for that.'

The other man's eyes were now burning with intensity.

'But that's how you got to know Ramses.'

Peter nodded.

'From a time I don't have the energy to remember. After the operation and when I finally got out of prison, all I wanted was to be alone. I decided to retreat to this place. The past was the past. So when I found Ramses' body, my first instinct was to deny I knew him. He was everything I didn't want to be confronted with.'

Peter leaned forward.

'Some people call it living on the margins of life. I think you need to have been there to know what it means.'

Mark Bille Hansen rubbed his hand as if he wanted to erase the marks. It took a while before he cleared his throat and said: 'Let's say I understand you. Let's say I accept why you ran. But I'm interested in your opinion.'

He drank some coffee and put the mug back on the table.

'Why do you think Ramses had to die? And why here? Who had any reason to kill him?'

Peter considered his reply. He couldn't get Stinger mixed up in this mess, nor could he talk about the break-in without dragging Felix into it. It was a balancing act, because he had to throw Mark Bille Hansen a bone.

'I don't know. But Ramses didn't hang around with saints. In those circles you tend to resolve matters in a pretty uncomplicated fashion.'

'So he'd upset someone?'

'I presume so. Has the post-mortem been done?'

'He died from the gunshot wound.'

Peter nodded.

'I can ask around a bit if you want me to.'

Mark Bille Hansen said archly: 'I thought you had put the past behind you.'

Peter could have kicked himself.

'I think it's best if you leave that to us,' Mark Bille Hansen said.

'So you haven't questioned anyone in prison yet?'

Mark Bille shook his head.

'We wanted to talk to you first. What kind of man was he?'

No long deliberations for Peter this time.

'He wasn't the sharpest knife in the drawer, if you know what I mean, and he was vain.'

'What do you mean?'

'The Ramses I knew was only interested in women and money. I don't think he ever opened a book.'

Mark Bille looked around the living room before his gaze landed on the bookshelf.

'You like reading?'

He walked up to the bookcase, read the titles and whistled to himself.

'Where did the interest come from?'

'I went to school. They teach you to read there.'

He didn't say the school library had saved him. It was none of Mark Bille's business that his childhood had been spent at Titan Care Home, run by sadistic tyrants, and with brothers and sisters for whom he had felt responsible.

The policeman held up two hands in defence.

'I'm impressed. I never managed to get further than cowboy comics.'

'Then it must be irritating to meet a carpenter who knows his ABC,' Peter said, his shoulders relaxing.

'You can say that again,' Mark Bille laughed.

It was only a moment, but enough for Peter to sense that they had made a connection. In a different life they might have been friends.

'But apart from that, Ramses was a nice enough guy,' he said. 'And that chain around his neck. It had nothing to do with religion. It was a present from a girlfriend.'

Mark Bille Hansen nodded and got up.

'Well, at least we don't have to worry about that. Do you know if he had a regular girlfriend when he died?'

'No idea. Until the dog found him dead, I hadn't seen Ramses for over a year.'

Mark Bille buttoned up his jacket and looked out of the window. It had started to snow in the deepening twilight.

'The forensic examiner estimates that he died on New Year's Eve some time between six and ten p.m. Where were you in the twenty-four hours leading up to the discovery of the body?'

A policeman had to ask such questions, otherwise he wasn't doing his job properly. Peter suppressed his irritation and gave Mark Bille the name and address of his carpenter friend in Gjerrild who had given the New Year's party.

'All the guests arrived in time for the Queen's New Year speech and spent the rest of the evening together. I was back here by two, I'm certain about that. Felix Gomez saw me, and she can vouch I didn't leave the house until the next day when I went hunting with my boss. The light's always on in her place and I have the impression she never sleeps.'

'Hunting? Do you have a gun?'

'Of course not. I'm not allowed to have a gun licence after my conviction. I only go for the company.'

'And you never borrow one?'

Mark Bille scrutinised him. Peter was briefly reminded of the moment he had held the rifle in his hand.

'Manfred does any shooting that needs to be done.'

'Your boss?'

Peter nodded.

'And he would be able to corroborate that?'

'All of it.'

The policeman looked across to Felix's house, where the light was indeed on. He held out his hand to Peter and his handshake was firm and long.

'I'll drop in to see her. We'll probably meet again.'

Seconds later, Peter saw the policeman ring his neighbour's doorbell. He waited for a couple of minutes, then rang again and pushed down the door handle, which was locked. He walked around the house and looked through the windows. Then he gave up, got into his car and drove off.

18

THE BODY BAG was water- and airproof. It was black, made from rubberised canvas and fitted with two solid canvas handles. It rustled in Kir's hands as Allan Vraa handed it to her.

In the past they had used a different kind of bag, Kir remembered. They were green and she couldn't remember anything good about them. They weren't strong enough and the welts had a tendency to burst if the body was too heavy.

'At last I'm going to see one,' Niklas said with enforced bravado.

They were sitting on the gunwale of the inflatable in their drysuits with pressured cylinders on their backs, ready to dive. She slapped him with the bag.

'Boo!'

Niklas's smile was strained.

'Remember now: she can't hurt you. Explosives, mustard gas and true love are dangerous. But not her. She can't even wriggle her big toe.'

He nodded repeatedly as if trying to convince himself. Kir had faith in him. He was a brilliant diver and a skilled mine-clearing expert. Once he had recovered a couple of bodies, death would become a natural part of his work. The navy divers' Explosive Ordnance Disposal division had a standing contract with the police, and when the police didn't use local Falck divers, who were called in mostly to search lakes and streams, they would deploy the mine clearance divers, who had more advanced equipment and greater expertise. Niklas was sure to get more work recovering dead bodies from the seabed.

'Ready?'

The red buoy bobbed up and down on the surface of the water. Light snow was falling. Kir bent forward and squeezed air out of her suit. Niklas did the same. They gave the signal, fell backwards and dived. On her way to the bottom she thought about the summer when she had jumped from the rowing boat and forced her body down to a depth of more than one metre for the first time. The water had been completely clear that day, and she remembered what it felt like when she opened her eyes after jumping in, trying to get her bearings and to find Tomas. For a moment she almost panicked because the seabed was bare and the rays of the sun were making the water and the sand sparkle all sorts of colours. But then she saw the body and fought her way down as the pressure built in her ears. Finally she reached him and manoeuvred him upwards, weightless in the water, with only one thought: to resurface before it was too late. She was twelve years old. Tomas was eight. And in those few seconds she knew she had just looked straight into her own future.

Niklas and Kir had to grope their way around and she was glad to have the line to the buoy. They had agreed Niklas would cut the rope to the anchor. Visibility was still zero, not improved by the fact that now there were two of them muddying the water around the body. But together they managed to shift the lifeless body into the bag without mishap and Kir rose to the surface with her as if they were two dancers clinging together in a strange, intimate dance.

Once on the surface, she was helped and the bag was hauled into the inflatable. Allan unzipped it a little so that some of the water could seep out and reduce the weight of the bag. He did it with great care so as not to destroy any potential evidence.

DNA could be intact on the body, even after several hours in the water.

'Can I have a look? There was something about her face,' Kir said when she was sitting on the gunwale again.

At that point Niklas appeared with the line he had tied to the anchor. Allan Vraa raised the anchor slightly and Niklas dived down to put a bag around it to prevent potential evidence from being washed away when they lifted the anchor out of the water. Shortly afterwards it appeared above the surface and they dragged it aboard the inflatable. Followed by Niklas.

'OK. Did you want to have a look?'

Allan was about to unzip the body bag. Kir shook her head.

'It's probably nothing. The forensic examiners can deal with it.'

Niklas, however, clearly felt a surge of confidence after a job well done.

'I'd like to see her. I couldn't see properly down there so it doesn't really count, does it?'

Kir pulled off her hood and wiped her nose with her fingers. She reached out over the gunwale and rinsed her hand, repressing a premonition that had just gripped her.

'OK. Let's take a look.'

It was starting to get dark, so she switched on her torch as Allan undid the zip. Niklas let out a cry and froze as he stared at the body in the bag. Kir wanted to shine the torch elsewhere, but her hand refused to acknowledge the impulse from her brain. What she saw sent shockwaves through her whole body.

'Oh, shit,' Allan mumbled. 'Who's eaten her face?'

Only then was she able to point the torch at the water. But the image had seared itself on her retina. Nina Bjerre's face was blood and pulp with no skin. In some places white bones stuck out. It was as if someone had taken a very sharp knife and carved a mask.

Kir put down the torch and bent forward to zip up the bag again. At that moment she saw the Falck hearse pull up on the quay.

19

'JUST STAY HERE. You're not well.'

'I'm fine.'

Peter could clearly see the effort it took Felix to stagger downstairs and head for the front door. He blocked her path.

'Don't be so stubborn. You were weak even before you were attacked.'

She tried to shove him aside. Her strength was no match for the effort required and he barely felt her push to the chest.

'You can't keep me locked up here. Get out of my way.'

She refused to look him in the eye. He guessed she couldn't. She was incapable of focusing and in far worse shape than he had at first thought.

'I'm not going to lock you in my house. But you need help.'

He put out a hand as she wobbled and reached for the door handle.

'That burglar gave you a real bang on the head.'

She shook him off.

'My life's none of your business.'

'But my life appears to be yours. You invited yourself into my house.'

'So now you're in charge, are you?'

The duality returned. Her mouth pushed him away with words, but her gaze and her trembling body were begging for his help.

'I'm going home.'

She pushed him again with strength she didn't have and

consequently tired herself even more in the process. She opened the door and stepped out into the cold. He knew she wouldn't make it home and quickly put on his boots. It was completely dark now, but the snow and the moon made it possible to see across to her house.

'Here. Take my arm,' he offered as they crossed the yard in the snow covering the ice. She stubbornly continued to refuse his help. A moment later she slipped and fell, then lay in the snow, exhausted, lifeless.

'Felix? Can you hear me?'

There was no reaction. She remained there, very still, as if asleep. A naughty child, a defiant teenager, a haughty woman; he didn't know which was worst. He lifted her up and carried her back to his house. He put her on the sofa and covered her with a blanket. She half-woke and he managed to get two spoonfuls of soup down her. She looked at him through blurred eyes.

'Ramses,' she mumbled.

'What about him?'

'I knew him.'

'You? *You* knew him?'

'Yes.'

She said nothing more, just closed her eyes again. Peter called the doctor, Johannes Holm, who lived in Grenå, but who arrived forty-five minutes later. He took his time over the examination while Peter looked for some liquids to tempt her with.

'She's malnourished, her blood pressure is far too low, she has a chest infection and she's concussed.'

Johannes Holm packed away his stethoscope and put it in his medical bag. He peered at Peter over the rim of his glasses and looked exactly what he was: a provincial doctor with plenty of experience and common sense. He was wearing sensible boots and had arrived wearing a green loden coat and a stripy scarf. He had hung his outdoor clothes over a chair, and now he was sitting on a stool next to the sofa, in corduroy trousers and a practical sweater, gentle blue eyes behind his glasses.

'It's quite straightforward. She either needs to be admitted to hospital or looked after by someone who'll ensure she eats, drinks and gets plenty of rest. She's lost a frightening amount of weight. Has she got any family?'

'No idea. I don't know her.'

'Then I suggest we admit her to hospital, eh?'

A hand shot out and grabbed the doctor's arm.

'No hospital.'

They were her first words since the doctor had been there. Peter could see her fragile fingers clinging to the sleeve of his sweater.

'No hospital,' Felix repeated, her eyes open and looking straight at Peter.

Dr Holm looked at Peter, too. Peter nodded, even though something inside him protested.

'OK. What do I need to do?'

The doctor rose and took him to one side.

'She seems traumatised. Has she said anything?'

'She told me a little about an accident. She was the sole survivor.'

'Make her talk, tell you about herself. And above all, get some liquid inside her. Soup, milk. Something nutritious. No coffee, tea or alcohol.'

He took his medical bag and removed a flat box containing a small blister pack.

'Antibiotics. Two tablets three times a day, preferably taken with some bread and milk. And here's a sedative – as and when it's needed. I'll be back tomorrow. Can you cope?'

They went back a long way. Dr Holm knew his history and all about his kidney disease. Peter and Manfred had built the doctor's new conservatory and were also acquainted with Mrs Holm, a friendly lady who suffered from sclerosis.

'Try to find out the names of family or friends so they can take over.'

'What about substance abuse?' Peter asked. 'Any sign of that?'

The last thing he needed was a junkie in the house. He had experienced that once too often.

'None at all. I think for some reason she has gone as far as she can. Her system has broken down. Keep her sedated with the tablets and be there for her. Fluids and food, little and often. As much as she can keep down.'

'Is this anything to do with her scars?'

The doctor looked across at Felix, who seemed lost to the world.

'I think the worst scars are internal.'

He patted Peter on the shoulder on his way out. 'Good luck.'

He cast a final glance at the patient and said in a low voice: 'If there's no improvement by tomorrow, I'll hook her to a drip.'

It was a long and restless night. Felix slept most of the time, but now and then she would wake up or seem to have some sort of hallucination.

Whenever she opened her eyes, he tried to get some soup down her. He had found some more sachets of soup and had added an egg. The first time she vomited everything up again, all over his trousers and herself. He had washed her, taken a mattress upstairs and put fresh linen on the duvet and pillow. He would sleep on the sofa.

He watched her as she slept, curled up like an exhausted child, her skin glistening, her eyelids and mouth quivering. Presently she woke up, raving and sweating so profusely that he had to change the bed linen and remove her clothes again. Her fragile naked body revealed that her stomach was slightly bloated, a sign of the malnutrition the doctor had diagnosed. She looked like a Third World child. He managed to get a little more soup down her, then carried her to the toilet, where she swayed as she relieved herself. Afterwards he washed her again, wrapped her in a bath towel and carried her back to the mattress, where she instantly went back to sleep, but soon woke up, her teeth chattering, shaking with fever.

He found her a T-shirt from the wardrobe. It seemed seven sizes too big, and she stared at him with her dark, round eyes, and he didn't know whether she hated him or was grateful for his concern. In any case, she was too weak to react, and at length he lay down next to her on the mattress, holding her in his arms, aware now, if not before, how thin and weakened she was.

In the morning she was sleeping soundly, temperature-free at last, and he let her sleep while he drove into town to buy some groceries.

On his return, she woke up and he fed her tomato soup and noodles. For the first time she seemed both lucid and hungry.

'What's going on?'

'You're ill. The doctor's coming back today.'

'There's nothing wrong with me.'

Obediently, she opened her mouth for a spoonful of soup and swallowed with a visible movement in her throat.

'He says you're traumatised. What happened in the accident?'

She tightened her lips. Her eyes widened with panic.

'Felix?'

She pushed the spoon away and hot soup splashed all over her. She started to sweat and shake, as if her fever had returned. Her head whirred from side to side.

'Nothing. Nothing,' she repeated.

He put his arms around her and pulled her close. Her heart was pounding; her entire body was in overdrive. He fumbled with his hand and found the blister pack with the sedatives and pressed out one tablet.

'Here. This'll help.'

She shook her head.

'Come on. Open wide.'

She looked at him with wild eyes, tears streaming. He cradled her as she sobbed, then he tried again.

'Here.'

This time she dutifully opened her mouth and he put the pill on her tongue and passed her a glass of water. She drank all of it and looked at him through blurry eyes.

'Nothing,' she repeated.

He stroked her hair. It was smooth and sweaty.

'It's OK. We'll talk about it later.'

The panic returned to her eyes. She tried to get up, but fell back into the duvet again. Beads of sweat were forming on her upper lip. Could he really cope with this? He hoped the pill would take effect quickly and Dr Holm would soon be here to take over.

'I want to go home.'

'You can't manage on your own.'

'I don't care.'

'I can't just let you give up. I should take you to hospital.'

'No hospital,' she mumbled.

'They can take care of you much better.'

'Please let me stay here.'

She was begging now. This was his chance.

'Only if you promise to do as you're told and eat. Food and pills,' he said, trying to sound strict.

She stared into space for a long time, then nodded, and he could see how much strength this simple movement cost her. She was a wreck. A lovely one, but a wreck all the same. He discovered that he no longer wished her gone.

'Food and pills,' she repeated.

'And you have to talk to me. The doctor says it's good for you to talk about what happened.'

'No . . .'

She started to grow limp in his arms.

'I can't . . .'

'What is it you can't do, Felix?'

She shook her head. Her eyes seemed to become more and more vacant.

'What about Ramses? You said you knew him?'

She tried to say something, but failed. Her eyes stared wildly round the room, then up at the ceiling, before closing completely. Her head slumped against his shoulder and he carefully leaned forward. He let go of her, and her thin arms flopped to the sides. He placed them on top of the duvet and sat for a while holding her hand in his. It was warm, moist and fragile.

He stroked her cheek.

20

PETER CALLED MANFRED to say he wouldn't be turning up and explained he had to look after his neighbour, who had fallen ill, but that he would try to get to work on the following day. Then he sneaked the keys out of Felix's jacket, checked she was still fast asleep, put on his coat and went over to her house.

He had told himself that he needed to get her some fresh clothes. Underwear, socks, hopefully some warm cotton nightclothes and a couple of sweaters. He let himself in and recognised her scent immediately, the distinctive perfume that had lingered in his nostrils since he first met her on the cliff. The scent mixed with other smells: sweat, sea, seaweed and the normal fug.

He looked in the fridge and kitchen cupboards and found only a packet of crackers, some mouldy rye bread, tinned food and salami well past its sell-by date. There were also some porridge oats and pasta, but there was no sign that anyone ever used the pots and pans, which hung from hooks on the wall, covered in dust. Ironically, a large cookbook was lying on the kitchen table. Spanish cuisine. There were plenty of photos of delicious dishes, as if she had been trying to tempt her appetite with the sight of air-dried ham, olives, prawns in garlic, various types of paella and a range of delicious cheeses.

In the sitting room, her duvet was on the sofa and there were biscuit crumbs on the coffee table and also on the duvet when he lifted it up to carry it back to her bedroom. It smelled of her, of her body and her hair.

In the bedroom, he pulled out drawers and opened cupboards,

then packed some clothes into a bag that had been flung into a corner. Then he stopped and looked around. The place was far too impersonal – it was as if she didn't want anyone to see anything other than a blank canvas.

He returned to the sitting room. But then again, she had only lived here for a month. She must have come from somewhere. She probably kept her personal things elsewhere; a flat in town, possibly. And, he assumed, she must have had a job of some sort.

He noticed a door he hadn't opened yet. It was locked. He took out her keys and tried several until he found one that fitted. The lock clicked open and he pushed the door.

It was a small boxroom, shrouded in darkness. He fumbled for a light switch but couldn't find one. Then he spotted a lamp on the desk, turned it on and recoiled in surprise.

It was a kind of shrine, he thought. A room to commemorate the past, perhaps her history, the one she had forgotten or was trying to forget.

Dazed, he looked around. All four walls were covered in photos stuck randomly one on top of the other, along with newspaper and magazine cuttings. There didn't appear to be any overall system. The photos and the texts were intended to speak for themselves, as if they had been put up precisely to help jog someone's memory.

Felix had said that she didn't remember anything about the accident, but everything that could prompt her memory was here. He read the headlines, one after the other in bold black print above columns of text and the same photo of a small girl with plaits and a big smile, again and again.

'Famous businessman and six-year-old daughter killed in helicopter crash,' one headline ran.

'Erik Gomez Andersen, 44, and his six-year-old daughter Maria were killed yesterday in a tragic accident when Andersen's company helicopter crashed over the Kattegat,' he read. 'The family of three were on their way to the island of Samsø for the weekend. Flying conditions were perfect, the helicopter had just undergone a major service check and Erik Gomez Andersen was known to be a competent pilot. Only Andersen's wife, Felicia Gomez Andersen, survived the accident, though with serious injuries . . .'

Peter stood gawping for a long time. Gomez Andersen. The double-barrelled bit must be both of their surnames.

There was a chair, and he sat down on it. He leaned forward to look at the wall above the desk, which along with the chair was the only furniture in the room. Some business cards had been taped to the articles where the people in question had been quoted. The two most prominent ones were Police Inspector Erling Bank, and a man from the Danish Air Accident Investigation Board by the name of Arthur Sand. All the other names seemed to be professional contacts.

He pulled out a couple of the desk drawers and finally found some personal papers. In the top drawer was a beetroot-coloured Danish passport from which Peter discovered that Felix had been born in Seville on 13 November 1976. He also found a pile of unpaid bills stuffed higgledy-piggledy into a large envelope: everything from a TV licence to water and heating for an address in Højbjerg. There were also tax demands and bank statements – all in the red. And then there were letters from banks and solicitors, which revealed that Erik Gomez Andersen had left no money. He had apparently been the MD of a large construction company and the family had lived at the desirable end of Århus. What had Erik Gomez been up to? Where had all the money gone?

Peter looked up and returned the papers to the drawer when he heard the sound of a car outside. It was the doctor in his bottle-green Nineties Rover. Peter went out to greet him and quickly updated him on events overnight and this morning.

Dr Holm was wearing driving gloves and stamping his frozen feet on the ground. Peter showed him the bag he had just packed.

'I went in to fetch some clothes. But now that you're here there's something you need to see.'

'In there?'

'I think it'll help us to understand her better.'

Dr Holm nodded and together they went inside. Peter pushed open the door to the boxroom. Dr Holm moved around with reverence, as if he had entered a chapel. He looked at the walls, making indecipherable grunts. Often he seemed lost in his own musings as he examined a photo or a text. Then he came to.

'This confirms exactly what I've been told. I took the liberty of asking around. Felix Gomez is, after all, a rather unusual name.'

'What did you find out?'

Holm turned to Peter.

'It was her scars. I thought she must have been registered somewhere. I contacted a couple of colleagues and ended up at the Department of Neurology in the old Århus Kommunehospital.'

Again he looked at the photos and newspaper cuttings on the walls.

'She's suffering from post-traumatic amnesia. Her memory is protecting her from remembering the accident and the ensuing period.'

'Memory loss?'

The doctor looked at Peter and nodded.

'Exactly.'

'She said she wished she'd died in the crash.'

'Perhaps that's not so surprising. Her husband and her child were killed.'

Peter thought about Felix's duality. About her anger and resistance and his sense that despite everything she was asking for help.

'You said her amnesia was protecting her. Doesn't she want to remember?'

Holm hesitated.

'Now this isn't my area. But the doctor I spoke to thinks her memory is right under the surface. And that a single event or piece of information could cause everything to come flooding back.'

21

FELIX DRIFTED IN and out of a bright, happy dream. The moment she left it, she wanted to return, but something kept bothering her and dragging her away.

'Come on. I know you can do it,' the voice said.

The hands were there again. At first she didn't want them and flapped her arms to make them go. But they persisted and held her tight and suddenly they were the only thing protecting her against the world and she let them do whatever they wanted: support the back of her neck, stroke her hair, lift her up so they could feed her hot soup. Eventually she let go of the dream.

'Good girl. I knew you could do it.'

She blinked and swallowed some more. She realised she liked the taste and she was hungry. She couldn't remember when she had last felt hungry.

She watched. And listened. Now who was he again? Where was she?

'Felix? Can you hear me? Look here. How many fingers am I holding up?'

She moistened her lips and tasted blood and cracked skin.

'Three. Who are you?'

But she knew. She couldn't remember his name for the moment, but she remembered his voice, which was soft and deep, and the eyes, they were blue-green, and the square jaw, which now bore day-old reddish stubble. His blond hair was the kind that turned completely white in the summer. He could have been a Viking in the old days, she thought. Thickset, bordering on muscular, not so much from the gym as from working in or with nature. Eyes and cheekbones that merged and ended in fine laughter lines, and skin that was accustomed to wind, rain and snow. A warrior, a hunter, the son of a chieftain. There was something lonely about him.

'The doctor was here. He says you're better. You've been ill for two days.'

She didn't remember anything about a doctor, but she believed him. Now his name came back to her.

'Peter.'

'Mmm?'

He ladled another spoonful of soup and she opened her mouth and swallowed it.

'Your name,' she said.

He grinned. Everything in his face seemed to brighten and open up.

'That's me. Peter. Like my namesake in the Bible, who denied Jesus three times.'

He winked at her. 'You're not usually so pleased to see me. Would you like a piece of toast?'

She did want a piece, but she couldn't find the strength to say 'yes, please'. She could feel herself falling, but he didn't let go of her. She slipped into a soothing, restorative sleep.

When she woke, she was lucid. Far too lucid.

He was still there, as was the dog. He was standing in the corner behind an easel holding a brush; there was an acrid smell of paint and turpentine and she was reminded of the boat which she and Erik had had.

Erik. Maria. The images hovered inside her and lifted her upwards, as if she was floating from a sandy seabed up to the surface, up towards the sun. Someone made a noise. A pitiful lament. Maria's fragile body; the innocence that had been snatched away. Her child. She summoned all her energy to try to block the memory and stifle her own outburst, but Peter was already looking at her searchingly. He put down the paintbrush, went over and sat down beside her.

'You're awake. Are you hungry?'

She nodded.

'Toast? Soup? Fillet steak? Oysters?'

She had no practice in smiling and surprised herself when the corners of her mouth lifted and she felt a lightness she thought had been lost.

'Toast, please.'

'Coming up.'

He got to his feet.

'I'd like to go to the loo, please.'

She started the laborious effort of swinging her legs on to the floor.

'Here. Hold on to me.'

He helped her to the bathroom.

'Give me a shout if you need any help.'

Two whole days. She stood supporting herself on the sink. She looked in the mirror and saw a scrawny ghost, with sockets for eyes and dark, lank hair against white skin. She had a hurried pee and staggered back to the mattress. He had made toast with butter and honey, and there was also a glass of milk.

'How . . .?'

'You were attacked and received a blow to the head. Afterwards you slipped on the ice outside. You're as stubborn as a mule.'

That was exactly what her mother used to say. It was nothing new. She wondered how much of her he had seen. She lowered her gaze and her fingers ran across the familiar spotted material. Someone must have put her in her pyjamas.

'I went to your house for some clothes. I saw your secret room.'

He could have asked about Maria and she would have

screamed. He could also have asked about the accident and she would have said that she remembered nothing.

'Tell me something about Erik. Anything you can remember.'

'I was married to him. I loved him.'

As she said it she had doubts.

'What was he like?'

'He had affairs.'

He clearly expected her to say more. At that moment she wished her memory loss would protect her. But her memory had already started to return when they discovered the body at the foot of the cliff.

She looked at him. Something inside her wanted to tell him everything. But another part of her made her hold back. She didn't tell him about the high life they had lived, she and Erik. A privileged life. A house in Skåde with a view of the sea and the woods, a daily cleaner, their own yacht at Marselisborg Marina – Erik had named it *Felix* – and one well-behaved six-year-old child whom she had loved to dress in the latest fashion. She was the manager of a shop in the centre of Århus: skincare, spa, exclusive brands of make-up, well-groomed, fit employees. She had worked her way up from the bottom; she had literally started as a cleaner and five years later she was in charge. This was what she was good at: working her way up and doggedly sticking at it.

Erik was the managing director of one of the country's largest construction firms and received a salary appropriate to his status. The company, Kjær Entreprise A/S, had its own helicopter and Erik, who had held a pilot's licence since he was young, had flown it both for business and pleasure.

'How did you meet?' Peter asked.

It was a trick, to make her open up. To make her pour out intimate details about how Erik had been at the beauty clinic in Bruunsgade one day to buy a gift card to pamper his wife. Although he was handsome enough, he was nothing special. It was his attitude she fell for. As if he took it for granted that the world existed for him.

She sold him the most exclusive package and he invited her out. They fell in love – yes, they had been in love, hadn't they? – and he divorced his wife.

Peter handed her a glass of milk and tried to make her drink some more. He had kind eyes and nice hands. But could she trust him?

'I didn't grow up with money,' she heard herself say. 'We left Spain when I was six years old. My mum was on her own with my brother and me. She worked as a cleaner, but then she met a Dane.'

She saw he was interested. Talking about this particular subject seemed harmless enough.

'We moved to Denmark. I promised myself that one day I would have a lot of money. I thought money would give me a nice, free life.'

He smiled.

'That's what you think when you haven't got any,' she said. 'I loved Erik, and I loved the security his income gave me.'

Peter broke off a piece of toast and held it up to her mouth. She chewed and drank from the milk he held out for her.

'You're looking better.'

She shook her head.

'You're beautiful,' he insisted.

She didn't have the strength to blush, but, quite absurdly, her body suddenly felt different. It was only brief, but it was there, like the memory of a life she no longer had.

'You're also very private.'

She remembered the trip that summer. They had talked for ages about flying to Samsø some day. Everything was planned around the weather forecast, which promised a week of sunshine. They would fly from the company's helipad. The four-seater helicopter was reserved and checked, the helipad on Samsø had been alerted and a table had been booked for lunch at Ballen Marina. After lunch they intended to spend a couple of hours on the beach, so bags were packed with swimming costumes, snorkels and towels, suntan lotion and baseball caps.

She remembered all of this without difficulty: the planning, the sense of anticipation. But there were still gaps around the accident itself. Perhaps they would always be there. Perhaps this was how she wanted it, but she could hardly tell him that. She was private, yes. There were aspects even she didn't want to confront, so why share them with others?

'I found the room with the newspaper cuttings,' Peter said. 'Is it an attempt to remember what happened?'

He had sat her on the sofa with pillows and the duvet. He focused his attention on her, so much so she felt as if she was under a microscope.

'They kept asking me questions. The police and the Air Accident Investigation Board. So I tried to create a system.'

She took the glass of milk from the tray and drained it.

'You said Erik had affairs?'

She made do with a nod while remembering the signs: text messages from mistresses, which she found when she checked his mobile; his shirts smelling of unfamiliar perfumes; a packet of condoms in his jacket pocket. She had known about it and still closed her eyes. She hadn't wanted to know and she had managed to suppress it.

'What about Ramses?'

'What about him?'

She wriggled down under the duvet. She didn't have the energy. What was he really doing here, this strange man? What did he want from her when it came down to it? Was he friend or foe? She wished her tiredness and dreams would come back. Now she was getting agitated.

'I've seen him before,' she said at length. 'I can't remember where or how.'

'Try.'

'That's easy for you to say.'

'I know.'

He could be irritating, but right now he was all she had. Him and the dog, which had reclined on the floor within patting distance. And then there was the doctor he had mentioned, but he might have invented that.

'I saw him with Erik. They were up to something. What, I don't know.'

22

Most of the eight hundred pigs had long since been sent to the abattoir, and those that had died when the barn collapsed had been destroyed. The roof had been ten years old and the present work consisted of clearing up the mess before a new roof could be built. It was hard going. The weather was against them, but the farmer was keen to get started with a new herd.

'Nice of you to show up,' the pig farmer said sarcastically. 'We know you've had other things on your mind.'

Christian Røjel was a man who was used to being in charge and Peter could clearly hear the censure in his voice. Røjel was tall and lean with a long face that reflected his life as a farmer: ruddy-cheeked and weather-beaten, with hands the size of shovels, protected today by rough working gloves. He wore a cap and an Icelandic sweater under his padded overalls. Wellies and a permanent smell of pig completed the picture.

Peter nodded, but he didn't apologise or elaborate. Everyone had heard about the discovery of Ramses' body and possibly about Felix as well. When you lived in the country you didn't need a radio or a television. Rumours were much quicker, and gossip spread without let or hindrance from village to village.

'And then there's little Nina,' Røjel said in a milder tone of voice, still spoiling for a fight.

'But they've found her, haven't they?' Peter said. 'Didn't Kir recover her?'

It was possibly not the most propitious thing to say. He knew

Christian Røjel had never approved of his daughter's choice of career. Diving to the bottom of the sea, looking for bodies, it was not a suitable job for a woman, but Kir was a rebel and did exactly what she wanted. The family's history was well known locally; every family's was.

'Ye-ah,' the pig farmer said, spitting. 'She was there with them. They found Nina in Grenå Harbour yesterday. They're saying they'll open her up today.'

Peter decided to change the subject.

'So how far have you got?'

He scanned the collapsed barn. Røjel took in the destruction with a sweep of his hand.

'Falck was here and supported the structure so that we could get the animals out. The insurance company says the rafters cracked under the weight of the snow.'

'Will they pay up?'

'Too damn right they will! The roof was built according to the regulations in place at the time.'

Together they walked across to the group of helpers, who greeted them amicably. The group included Claus Dam, who still lived with his mother at the age of forty-five; Birger, the grocer's son Hans, and Røjel's younger son, Tomas.

'How do, Peter,' Claus Dam said, straightening up. 'Some New Year's Eve company you're keeping. We hear you found a dead body washed up on the beach.'

'And a happy New Year to you, too, Claus,' Peter said.

'Well, it could happen to anyone,' Hans said.

'What? Ending up dead on the beach or finding a body?' Peter asked.

The mood lightened. Everyone laughed.

'With all that walking you do by the cliff it's a wonder you haven't found one before,' Birger opined. 'My wife says you're there all the time.'

'Not when I'm here,' Peter said, and bent down to drag away

a smashed rafter. 'So, Christian, has the insurance company said it wouldn't have happened if the roof had been newer?'

'If my aunt'd had bollocks, she'd have been my uncle,' Røjel muttered, grabbing hold of the rafter. 'They say they're checking the building regs. Eight roofs in total have collapsed after the snowstorm here in Jutland alone.'

'The problem occurs when it thaws,' Claus chipped in. 'Then the snow is too heavy, and if it's more than half a metre thick, the roof can't take it.'

'A riding hall collapsed,' Birger said. 'One girl was injured.'

'What is it about girls and horses?' Claus said, and left the rest of the sentence hanging.

They carried on working in good-natured silence. Peter observed them from time to time as they struggled with the heavy beams and the snow creaked from the weight of their boots.

The doctor had dropped by for a third time to check on Felix. He was satisfied with her progress, even though her concussion was still causing concern and she remained very weak. The main thing was that she had started eating, although she was still taking only small amounts. They had agreed that Peter could go to work, no problem.

'You can't put your whole life on hold,' Dr Holm said, and he was right. It was important that Peter maintained his everyday routine. Felix could disappear from his life at the drop of a hat. He had already let her in too far.

When he first moved to the area, Peter had been aware of the locals' scepticism. He had sensed that they talked about him behind his back, and he knew his prison sentence was common knowledge. But in some weird way he had managed to gain their acceptance, even though he would always be an outsider. He kept a low profile in Djursland, and that seemed to be the norm for everyone. He didn't stick his nose into anything or into anyone's lives. He let people get to know him. He let them talk and doggedly maintained a friendly attitude. He had only a few friends, but they were precious. They accepted him as he was and came to terms with the fact he wasn't always sociable. He needed space. Emptiness. He needed his own company, but he also needed theirs.

He hadn't moved here with a dream of becoming like them, but nor was he trying to change anything. They were the way they were. They had their secrets, and in all probability he knew only a fragment of what was going on. Many of them drove around in expensive cars, but where did the money come from? Several were on the dole or some other kind of benefit and still did odd jobs. Others lived off their parents and had never left home – Claus was by no means the only one. It was a kind of Klondike: a land beyond the rule of law. Everyone minded their own business. That suited him fine.

'Give us a hand, will you, Peter?'

Peter helped the pig farmer with a roofing sheet while his thoughts continued to churn.

He was no saint, either, when it came to tax. He worked loyally for Manfred of course, and this job was an insurance claim, so the paperwork would have to be in order. But occasionally a cash-in-hand job came up outside working hours, and Manfred was perfectly happy to turn a blind eye. In this way, life here suited him fine: have as little to do with the authorities as possible and when they turn up, don't give them more than absolutely necessary. If there was any kind of creed he would sign up to, then this was it. He'd had too many bad experiences with everything else.

He let go of the roofing sheet and went over to help Tomas, who was struggling with a beam. Of the three siblings, Røjel's younger son was the most difficult to talk to.

'Canny lass, your sister, eh?'

He asked this as they were carrying the beam over to a heap in the snow. Tomas nodded and glanced over at his father. He was sniffing. Peter could see from his eyes he had a cold.

'It was her who found that body yesterday.'

His voice was flat and monotonous. Tomas was lean like his father but didn't have his brute strength. With his delicate appearance and careful movements he seemed far too refined to work on a farm.

'How are things with Red and the pub?'

Tomas's older brother, Red, had an Irish pub in Grenå called the Bull's Eye.

'All right, I think.'

'I might drop by some time.'

'It's a great pub,' Tomas said proudly.

Everyone knew the story of how Kir had dived into the sea and saved his life. They said it was a miracle he had survived. There were also rumours that this might be the reason why Tomas was a little odd.

'So you'll be taking over the farm in due course?'

An indeterminate expression spread across Tomas's face.

'I think so.'

They carried on working in silence. Peter thought about Stinger. He ought to do something to find him, but he had run out of ideas. He couldn't stay off work, and then there was Felix, who was undoubtedly feeling better, although she still needed him. He had called Elisabeth several times, but she had no news for him. Stinger had vanished into thin air, and his mobile was dead.

When it grew dark they stopped work and went their separate ways, and Peter went home. Felix was sitting on the sofa cuddling the dog. He fried a couple of steaks and made some mashed potato, which he served for her on a tray. While they ate, he made yet another attempt to get her to talk about the accident and her past, but she reacted so badly that he gave up.

He stayed awake until she fell asleep, covered almost

completely by the duvet and with her head sunk into the pillows, looking very small indeed. He thought about lying beside her and holding her, but decided she was probably so well now that she would regard it as taking advantage of her. So, as usual, he put a mattress outside in the cold and slipped into his sleeping bag with the dog snuggling up against him on the fleece. For a long time he lay there looking up at the sky and the stars and listening to the waves rolling in, while the dog breathed regularly by his side. Everyone had something they had to do, he thought. Something they couldn't do differently. Just as he had to sleep under the open sky, he knew he also had to find Stinger. And however much he had wanted to live without getting mixed up in other people's lives, this was now impossible. His isolation had been broken; he might as well accept it. Beneath him, on a mattress, a woman lay asleep and she was his responsibility because that was what he wanted.

He was deep in a dream without any meaning when a persistent sound slowly brought him back to the surface. It took him a while to work out that it was his mobile ringing, and that it was already morning. When he finally managed to press the button, he could barely recognise the voice of Elisabeth Stevns through her sobs.

'You've got to come. Stinger is asking for you. Come right now. It's bad.'

23

Mark Bille Hansen preferred the old police station in Grenå he remembered from his childhood. However, changing requirements and times had caused the council to build a more spacious, modern version on Vester Skovvej, east of Ringgaden on the road to Århus. It was on the outskirts of Grenå, hidden away like an unwanted child, behind tall trees with only a small, discreet 'Police' sign to show citizens where to go.

Parking spaces were at a premium this morning. Someone had already taken his personal spot, so he slowly circled all the unfamiliar cars a couple of times, then left his car blocking the entrance to the adjacent green, which at this moment was an icy white. Anna Bagger and her numerous colleagues were camped out on half of the first floor. He noticed that her new company car – a Renault Scenic with sunroof and trendy aluminium wheels – was parked right in front of the main entrance. Apart from the Århus cars, the divers' vehicles occupied the rest of the space. Local coppers were well down the pecking order.

He had only just said good morning to his colleagues and sat down behind his desk to switch on his computer when there was a knock at the door. Anna Bagger entered without waiting for a reply. Her entire appearance, from the pale blue blouse and dark trouser suit to the light-coloured glossy lipstick, exuded an aura of calm and gentle forbearing, but he sensed at once that it was a front. There was something hectic about her movements, which were normally so gracious, and her eyes sparkled a thousand shades of blue.

And he knew why. He had been expecting it.

'Good morning, Anna. What's new?'

She drew breath audibly.

'I'll tell you what's new. I went to see Peter Boutrup, our man on the cliff, the other day, but he wasn't there. So I rang him to summon him here for an interview, and do you know what he said?'

Rhetorical question, Mark assumed.

'He said you'd already spoken to him.'

He nodded.

'That's right. So?'

'Yes, so?'

She turned her back on him and paced up and down his small office, then spun round to face him again. Her voice was rising in pitch, even though she was very obviously trying to control it. A big part of him felt like ignoring every rule and regulation and telling her to sling her hook, but a very small part wanted the exact opposite. The small part wanted to undo her hair, unbutton her blouse and relax her with drink. It was the same part of him that wanted to have sex with her.

'I thought we had an agreement,' she said. 'This is a murder investigation. Interviews fall under In-ves-ti-ga-tion. That was what we agreed, wasn't it?'

He watched her. She could be frightening when she was angry, but she didn't frighten him.

'I'm the local police officer in the district where the murder took place,' he said with a calm he knew would provoke her. 'I was the first officer on the scene and I had some questions for a man in my area. I was only doing my job.'

He splayed his palms with a smile that had once been enough to disarm her. He was far from sure of its effect now.

'If that's illegal you'll just have to lead me off in cuffs.'

She rested her knuckles on the desktop and leaned over.

'Don't you play the clown with me, Mark. I know you. And I know perfectly well this isn't about the case. Let's be honest.'

'I don't have a problem with honesty. Do you? Don't you think we owe it to everyone in this building to let them listen in as we exhibit our relationship in all its splendour? I'd be quite happy to leave the door open.'

She retreated slightly and blinked, as if she had been on the other end of an attack. He got up and walked over to the door, where he placed his hand on the door handle, then let go.

'There was no interview,' he said. 'I made no notes and I haven't filed a report. You're free to interview Boutrup. I had a chat with him, that's all.'

He sat down behind his desk again. She went over to the window and looked down at the car park. He couldn't help himself: 'And in future please remember that you're our guests. There needs to be room for everyone in the car park, and you would make a better impression if you didn't hog the spaces near the entrance.'

She turned around. She was smiling.

'The alpha male reduced to playing second fiddle, eh? You can't handle that. You never could.'

He nodded.

'You can interpret it any way you like. If that makes it easier for you.'

Since their last meeting, Mark had done some research: she was a young and inexperienced leader. It was exactly a fortnight since she had been transferred to Århus as chief investigator from a more junior post in Esbjerg because the legendary John Wagner had requested leave of absence. She wanted to assert herself in front of her staff and an ex who had humiliated her by losing interest and thus provoked her into dumping him. Why, she couldn't know, nor would she ever find out if he had anything to do with it.

'But you could also choose to see it as a helping hand.'

He was looking for a crack in the facade, but none was forth-coming. She had her strengths and weaknesses as a detective. One of the latter was her obstinacy when the mood took her. She could sink her teeth into a case – but this could also lead to a wild goose chase. Her stubbornness often produced results, though. In Esbjerg, she had a high clear-up rate which you ignored at your peril. But she didn't have his sense of the psychology behind a murder, they both knew that. A killing triggered vibrations, and he had always been good at picking up on the ripples.

'You'll get the credit, of course,' he said.

Finally a crack. He could see her making mental calculations and knew now was the time to strike.

'Is Nina Bjerre's post-mortem finished?'

She checked her watch automatically.

'Yes. Cause of death was strangulation.'

'Any photos available?'

She nodded.

'Her face is gone. The skin was peeled off, simple as that.'

'I heard the rumour. When?'

He held his breath.

'After she was dead, thank God.'

Mark slowly let out his breath

'How are you going to identify her? You're not going to bring in her parents, surely?'

She shook her head.

'We're not savages. We'll find a way, dental records or DNA. Unless the parents insist, of course.'

'They won't. I've spoken to them.'

She looked shaken, wanted to say something, but he beat her to it.

'May I see the photos?'

'It's against the rules.'

'Screw the rules.'

Her lips opened and her mouth took on the form he had loved: soft with a full lower lip; it was sexier than anything he had ever known.

'Then come with me.'

On the first floor, the divers were assembled for the briefing. He caught a glimpse of red-headed Kir with the elfin face, and his mood took a turn for the better, without his quite knowing why. Anna strode, heels clicking, into their improvised command centre. Martin Nielsen and four other detectives greeted him somewhat hesitantly and Mark surmised they had heard about his interview with Boutrup.

Documents relating to the two cases were being put up on a big noticeboard. In one photo Ramses lay at the foot of the cliff staring at him with his one eye. In the other, the naked body of a woman lay on a stretcher. Her face was one big lump of raw meat.

Mark studied the dead woman. She was tall and slim, skinny even. Her legs were splayed. He moved a step closer and had another look before addressing Anna Bagger.

'I'm not sure that's Nina Bjerre.'

'Come on, Mark. Height and build point to Nina. It has to be her.'

Anna whispered in his ear, 'Please don't complicate matters for no reason.'

Was that what he was doing? He scrutinised the photo again. She might be right. Perhaps Nina Bjerre had outgrown her knock knees. It was one possibility. Because if it wasn't her, who was the woman the divers had fished out of the harbour?

24

STINGER LAY CONNECTED to a drip with several metres of tubes coming out of every orifice. Over his nose he had a CPAP mask feeding him oxygen.

He looked tiny in the hospital bed, his sparse strands of hair and bald patch reminiscent of Fethry Duck. His scabby, tattooed hands moved restlessly across the duvet as if trying to tell a story. Apart from that, he was barely recognisable. He had been beaten black and blue and left in the stairwell. Elisabeth had found him early that morning; driven by anxiety and a power cut she had taken a flashlight and gone down to wake the janitor.

'He said your name. It was the first thing he did. So that's why I called you.'

She looked at Peter, her eyes shiny where her mascara had run. With her rotund figure and otherwise pale face, she looked like a very concerned panda. 'He hasn't said anything since.'

Peter felt he ought to comfort her, but he didn't know how. She was so big and so well concealed behind her mountain of fat that it was difficult to find the part of her he wanted to contact.

'He can't,' he said. 'If he could talk he would.'

They had been told to wait, so they sat by the bed whispering. Over by the window Elisabeth's friend from the other day was sitting stiffly in a chair, still with a black eye and swollen lips, still with a defiant vulnerability in her eyes and a long ponytail down her back. Peter looked at Stinger and wondered if he would ever say anything again.

'I'm glad you called,' he said.

Otherwise they said nothing, and in the silence he reconstructed his early morning start, being woken by the sound of his mobile and Elisabeth's panic-stricken voice. He had got dressed quickly and driven to the hospital after leaving a note for Felix and ringing Manfred, but by then Stinger had already been taken to intensive care and was about to have a scan to identify probable internal bleeding. Peter had waited in reception with Elisabeth and Anja, her injured friend, who really should have taken up residence in a crisis centre.

'No places available, and her boyfriend was looking for her. He's in a gang,' Elisabeth whispered, and Peter recalled that Elisabeth herself had once had a biker boyfriend, careered around on a motorbike and allowed herself to be bullied. Even in his addle-brained state, Stinger had always been very annoyed by it.

'Did he say anything else?' Peter asked.

She shook her head as they sat looking out at the snow, which gave the impression it was never going to stop. Once again tears welled up and ran down her fat cheeks like meltwater from a glacier.

'He was almost completely covered by snow. He must have been lying there a long time, possibly all night. His pulse was very weak, they said.'

Peter rose and fetched coffee for all of them from the cafeteria. He also bought three cakes. Halfway through her cake, Elisabeth seemed to recover her memory.

'Oh yes. He did say something about a tattoo.'

'What?'

'He said: "That tattoo." Or something like that. It was hard to make out. The bastards knocked out most of his teeth.'

She shook her head. 'I thought he was delirious and he was talking about it because it was his work,' she said, and added 'Kind of' with a little smile.

At that point they had been waiting in reception for close on three hours. Finally they were approached by a nurse, who was able to inform them that they had operated on Stinger to treat the internal bleeding. They had put him into a medically induced coma so that his body could recover from the trauma it had suffered. They were welcome to sit by his bed, if they kept their voices down, but they shouldn't expect him to wake up. Later, a doctor arrived to update them. He had done his best and would see if he could bring the patient out of the artificial coma in a couple of days. But he couldn't make any promises, the doctor said, and didn't really sound particularly interested in the patient or the next-of-kin. The patient might not survive. In addition to the bleeding, his liver was dangerously enlarged. It looked like alcoholism. Was that a possibility?

Peter said nothing, but thought about the times he had seen Stinger knock back a bottle of vodka plus a few chasers. Elisabeth nodded quietly. Yes, it was. The doctor looked at her and Peter saw what he saw: an unkempt mountain of blubber, indicating excessive intake of fat and sugar and hence – the doctor might have erroneously concluded – stupidity. Perhaps he lumped her and Stinger together: patients whose illnesses were self-inflicted to the point where treating them was a matter of debate. If he had examined their circumstances more closely, he would also have discovered that they were both on benefits and consequently not making a contribution to Denmark's gross national product.

Sitting on one side of the bed with Elisabeth on the other, Peter could still hear the doctor's strained neutral tone:

'He might not survive.'

He saw Stinger's eyes twitching nervously behind the eyelids as if he could still feel the blows raining down on him. In the hospital, Stinger wasn't known as Stinger. He was Lasse Stevns, aged forty-five, an ex-offender and one of society's losers. He smelt of filth, smoke and booze, and God knows what other infections he carried. In the doctor's eyes, there was nothing charming about him. The doctor had never personally spoken to Stinger or laughed at his pranks, or seen in his eyes the tenderness he had for animals and children, or his roguish interest in the fair sex, always tempered with his insight that beautiful, clever women were beyond his reach.

'Just give me one with a bag over her head,' he used to say. 'False teeth, glass eyes, I don't care. Just as long as there's something to get my hands on.'

He would then pick up a cushion and dance an intimate tango or something resembling it.

His tattooed hands were active again. Peter suddenly remembered what Elisabeth had said: *That tattoo*. Was it important, or were they just the delirious words of a man who had been subjected to a battering? Was it about Stinger's work and identity?

'It meant a lot to him, didn't it?' he said. 'Doing tattoos?'

He suddenly realised he had spoken in the past tense, but Elisabeth didn't appear to notice. She nodded.

'It was his thing. And he made a bit of money doing it.'

Not much, Peter thought. He remembered several offers of free tattoos from a semi-plastered Stinger. He had always refused politely. On principle. He wasn't going to subject his body to any more pain than he already had done.

He smiled wryly. Stinger had always been proud of his craftsmanship and yet his work had been appalling.

'Do you think he was trying to tell us something important? Something about a tattoo?'

Elisabeth shrugged.

'What would that be?'

'What about Stinger himself? Has he had any new tattoos recently?'

She considered the question for a moment.

'A number, I think. On his bicep. I don't know what it means.

Perhaps it's a telephone number. I saw it when he came out of the shower one day.'

'Do you think we could have a peek?'

She nodded. They glanced around. They were alone in the side ward and there were no nurses around. There was only Anja. They told her to keep a lookout and cough if anyone came down the corridor. Elisabeth carefully held the sleeve of the white hospital gown and rolled it up. Stinger's arm was thin and the gown far too big, so it was an easy job.

The tattoo was clear. He must have got someone else to do it. There were six digits, like a telephone number without the area code: 561562.

'Whose number is that, I wonder?' Elisabeth said. 'Do you think we should call it and say Stinger's here?'

Peter shook his head.

'I don't think that would be a very good idea.'

25

Something didn't add up, but Kir couldn't put her finger on what.

It was early in the morning and the search had been resumed with dogs, mine clearance divers and teams of police; SOC officers and EODs – the Explosive Ordnance Disposal division – filled the part of the quay that had been sectioned off with their vehicles. She was waiting. While she waited she went for a stroll around the harbour, to the ice's favourite haunts. It had covered the entire marina area, where the modern flats now had a view of a frozen harbour, and the few big motorboats still there were held in the freeze's grip. The wooden gangways were encased in ice and snow, and only around the mooring posts could you see any pockets of black water. On the open balconies, pots of herbs and bushes were buried, and only a few brown branches or evergreens poked through the snow. In the corner of one balcony, a lonely Christmas tree stood stripped of its decorations.

Kir tilted her head back and looked up. She wondered which flat Nina Bjerre had been in for the New Year's Eve party. There was no sign of life now behind the big dark windows with the best view that Grenå could offer. The whole residential development was protected from the public by sheets of black metal fencing with a solid chain looping from fence to fence. The message was clear. This is a private area: no trespassing. But people lived here. She had also seen police officers coming and going through all the entrances. Nothing was private during a murder investigation.

Were the people behind the windows sitting on information? Had someone seen something or were they accessories? Was the killer to be found in one of the flats? Who knew?

She turned around and walked the other way, towards the fishing harbour and the ferry, and passed restaurants boarded up for the winter. In the summer, there was festivity, noise and high spirits; yachts were moored and used as holiday homes. Now everyone and everything shivered in the freezing temperatures. She wasn't the only person waiting.

As she walked, her initial misgivings returned: something didn't add up. About the body she had found. About how she had found it. It wasn't as she had imagined, but then again, when had it ever been?

She watched the inflatable on its way out to the buoy with the two divers. She would have to wait a little longer. That was how the job was, and it was the least attractive part. The best was being chosen for an operation. She saw the two divers fall back into the water. They had found the body, but they needed to search for more. Much more. She would get her turn today.

The harbour had changed a great deal over the years. She remembered the summers when she had come here with Uncle Hannibal, him chatting with fishermen or making arrangements for a dive. In those days Grenå was a major fishing port and smacks lay shoulder to shoulder when they weren't at sea. There had also been more ferries, but the crossing to Hundested had been closed down long ago and now only the route to Varberg in Sweden still functioned, mostly for freight, she thought. Whenever the ferry docked, there was a queue of heavy goods lorries waiting to embark, but she never saw very many ordinary passengers with suitcases and rucksacks, prams and buggies. In general, the harbour no longer bustled with life as it once had. Many people had lost their jobs and several businesses in the area had had to close. Some were still there, though.

Three women appeared with bags and white plastic trays from the staff entrance to the fish factory, the biggest employer in the harbour. Many of the vehicles parked in front of the building carried the Thorfisk name. Some were white saloon cars with the characteristic blue fish logo; others were large cooling trucks with the same logo. These vehicles transported vacuum-packed fish to the supermarkets, where they would end up in consumers' shopping trolleys.

'Ah, Thorfisk. The essence of our childhood town, eh.'

She turned around and discovered the black-haired policeman. The sun had appeared in the frosty weather, and snowflakes glistened in his hair and on the shoulders of his jacket. He came up to her and extended his hand in a slightly formal manner, which contradicted his long-haired look.

'Mark Bille Hansen. Weren't we at school together?'

She nodded and felt awkward under his scrutinising gaze.

'Yes, we were.'

She withdrew her hand, not knowing what to say next.

'You found the body, didn't you?'

She nodded once more. Here she was on more familiar territory. He started to walk and automatically she followed. He flapped his arms to keep warm as he walked.

'You need to keep moving in this cold. What do you reckon about it all? What do you think happened?'

He had homed right in on her inability to make sense of the killing, she felt. She would have liked to say something clever, but as so often happened she couldn't find the right words and wasn't even out of the starting blocks before he continued.

'She was tied up. Very thoroughly, I understand. And weighed down by an anchor?'

He looked at her while they walked, as if waiting for

confirmation. The thought occurred to her that he wasn't a detective on this case. He was the local policeman, but he didn't seem like one. He seemed to have the detective's customary right to turn every stone.

She limited her response to a nod.

'But why?' he said into the frozen air. 'Why mutilate her face?'

His voice became more insistent: 'And why not just dump her in the sea? She must have been held somewhere before she was dropped into the water. How could there have been enough time? And what about the anchor, and the rope?'

That was one of the words she had been casting around for: time. He was right. It didn't seem logical, but killers often weren't.

'He must have had a car,' she thought out loud. 'Perhaps he transported her in the boot. To a place where he could do whatever he wanted without disturbance. Afterwards he must have had a boat to dump her.'

'So, a car. A boat. Quite a few things.'

He mulled this over.

'And then there's the anchor she was tied to,' Kir continued. 'If it's not from his own boat, he might have stolen it. Perhaps someone's missing one?'

He nodded, with a look suggesting she had said something clever. If only he knew how images of the faceless body had floated around her head all night.

'Did you know her?' he asked suddenly. 'Nina Bjerre?'

She shook her head.

'How old are you?'

'Thirty-two. Nina was nineteen.'

He smiled.

'Of course. You wouldn't have known each other. My cousin was at school with her.'

She didn't know what to say, so she stood there feeling

inadequate, as she often did. She was good at many things, but casual conversation with strangers wasn't one of them.

He seemed to snap out of a reverie, as if realising he was talking to the wrong person. She was just a diver, after all. What did she know about murder?

'Right, I should be going,' he said. 'See you later probably.'

'Something doesn't add up,' she burst out, surprising herself. 'It seems too planned.'

He nodded.

'I think you're right.'

He turned his palms up.

'Oh, well. We found her. We have a body. It's a start.'

He left her, and she watched him go, feeling just as she had at school when she had watched him unobserved. Yes, he had spoken to her. But he hadn't noticed her. 'We', he had said, not 'you'. But so what? Since when had she been a little girl craving praise from her teacher?

To avoid attracting attention, she carried on walking along the harbour towards an area she had dubbed the 'cemetery': where the bodies of old fishing vessels and other clapped-out ships were dismembered and converted into valuable scrap. The breakers' company had started up after her childhood and stood as a testimony to the way the town had developed: it had gone from being alive to something that resembled death; it was definitely heaving to, at any rate.

She looked at the rusty ships crammed together side by side and stacked on top of one another. Workers in winter overalls operated cranes and loader tractors, swallowing up pieces of iron, metal and wood like giant scavengers, but taking care to remove any useful components: engines, trawl nets, freezers, pumps, pulleys, propellers and compressors. Everything that made the ship's heart beat.

A feeling of death and destruction spread through her. Perhaps the whole place was cursed.

She turned around and went back to the diving truck and the quay. Allan Vraa had returned in the inflatable. One of the detectives walked gingerly down the icy gangway to take a bag that had been held up to him. It was a transparent plastic bag, and as she came closer, she saw it contained a mobile telephone.

26

THERE WAS NOTHING more they could do for the time being. Stinger was stable. The nurse said they should go home and get some rest. They would need all their strength soon enough, she said.

Elisabeth sat for a while, slumped and passive, just staring into space. Anja was still sitting in the chair by the window, her eyes intermittently darting around in a panic-stricken way. She seemed subdued and bruised, as if the encounter with her ex-boyfriend's fists had also affected her ability to speak.

'Perhaps she's right,' Peter suggested at last. He was also thinking about Felix and Manfred, whom he owed an explanation. 'They'll call if there's any news.'

Elisabeth wiped her nose on her sleeve.

'Can we be sure of that?'

'I don't know. But you can't possibly stay here day in, day out, can you?' he said. 'You've done everything you can.'

He wanted to add that she should be proud of herself, but it wasn't his business to grade other people's qualities.

A sharp intake of breath came from over by the window. Anja had got up from her chair and was moving back into the room.

'It's him!'

Elisabeth went to the window and looked out.

'It's his car. I recognise it!' Anja gasped.

Elisabeth leisurely scanned the car park.

'You mean the Volvo?'

Anja nodded. Peter, too, could see the white Volvo, an older model, parked at an angle by the postbox.

Elisabeth shook her head.

'Can you read the number plate, Anja? Please tell me what it says.'

Anja's voice was trembling.

'ZJ something.'

'And what did we agree Klaus's car was?'

'Something beginning with A.'

'There you go. It's just one that looks like it.'

Anja stood very still, staring down at the Volvo. Peter followed her eyes. The car appeared to be empty.

'A lot of people drive those old Volvos,' Elisabeth said. 'I can see why you got scared, but it can't be him.'

Anja shook her head as if trying to convince herself, but she continued to look doubtful. Elisabeth put a hand on her arm.

'You'll have to get used to this. You'll have to get into the habit of combating your fear with common sense, see? It'll happen so many times. Believe me. I know what I'm talking about.'

Anja nodded again and swallowed. Elisabeth continued: 'There are three of us. Peter is with us. We'll all leave together and nothing will happen to us, you'll see.'

She looked at Peter, a new, determined expression in her eyes.

They said goodbye to Stinger, who didn't react, and started walking down a long corridor towards reception and the car park. Anja walked between them. Her anxiety was palpable. She looked behind and to both sides, and blinked with fear every time they met someone, whether it was a nurse, doctor, patient or visitor.

'I can drive you home,' Peter said. 'If you wait at the entrance I'll just go and get the car.'

He had taken the car key from his pocket, and they had just emerged from the door when a gruff male voice shouted in a loud, ringing voice: 'You fuckin' bitch. You're coming with me right now.'

Peter turned, as did Elisabeth. The man, who looked like an angry bull, his head lowered between burly shoulders, came charging from behind them, and he had someone with him. They were heading for Anja. His henchman looked the same type. He moved like an armoured tank on slow caterpillar tracks. His broad boxer's nose had undoubtedly been broken more times than he could count. Both men were wearing leather and heavy boots and had gang insignia fore and aft, as if they welcomed being identified as thugs. The leader grabbed Anja in a stranglehold and started dragging her along the pavement despite her screams and resistance. Boxer Nose crashed into Elisabeth, sending her flying into a snowdrift, where he pummelled her with his fists.

Peter's instincts were aroused and old routines took over. The most expedient moves and blows flashed up in his brain, like springs from a well-worn mattress, as he grabbed Elisabeth's attacker from behind, spun him around, rammed a knee into his groin, rabbit-chopped him as he doubled up and dumped him into the snow. The man seized his legs and Peter felt iron fists tear the ground away from beneath him and a pain in his back as he landed with a thud. Then the enemy was on top of him, his hands around his neck, using gravity to hold Peter down. But Peter was both faster and lighter, and he wriggled free from under the dead weight and got in a crunching upper cut to the boxer's nose. The man tumbled to the deck, leaving his flank exposed. Peter slipped on the ice, but managed to stand up again and launch one kick into the man's liver and then a second, until the guy was curled up in pain.

Peter straightened up. In another world, in another place, he would have finished him off with a couple of kicks to the face, but he restrained himself. Instead he went after Anja's ex-boyfriend, who was now close to the white Volvo with Anja in tow. Her ponytail bobbed up and down wildly. She had lost her handbag.

He had almost caught up with them when an old silver 4x4 pulled up on the pavement and two figures jumped out. He registered their faces and the fact that they were wearing black. They were both women. One was wielding a baseball bat. The other had a gun. The first was big and sturdy in a muscular way, like a female wrestler; the other slender and quick. The woman with the gun had a boy's haircut, short, black hair that stood up, and piercings in her nose, eyebrow and lips. He knew he had seen her before.

The operation went like clockwork: the larger woman rained down blows on Anja's ex while the smaller one led Anja from the battlefield and into the car.

Speechless, Peter stared after them as they left Anja's ex bleeding in the snow, piled into the 4x4 and roared out of the hospital car park. A hand touched his arm and he swivelled round.

'Let's get out of here,' Elisabeth said. 'Where's your car?'

Peter pointed to the two men.

'What about them?'

She pulled at him.

'Forget them. They could hardly be in a better place, could they?'

'Shit, shit, shit.'

'What are you going on about?' Elisabeth asked when, fifteen minutes later, Peter was in her flat, where Anja's few belongings were neatly organised next to the sofa: a book, a wash bag, a jumper, a pair of flat shoes, a bottle of perfume and a box of tampons.

He looked at her and abandoned any attempt to explain.

'Nothing.'

She was proud of him and the fight he had put up. She had

talked of nothing else all the way back from the hospital, sitting next to him, shaking with excitement, her eyes gleaming. 'It was amazing! You floored him, just like that!'

The more she spoke, the worse he felt. He had promised himself never to get involved with anything like that ever again. He had promised himself never to use the combat techniques he had learned in the past and refined in prison. Yet that was what he had done. Elisabeth had no truck with this kind of moral hangover, though, he was certain of that. However, she was strong on TLC and fetched an ice pack for his lower back, found some crisps and made them a cup of tea.

'Who were those women?' he asked.

Elisabeth crunched a crisp.

'No idea.'

Her face had assumed a neutral expression.

'I think I recognised one of them,' he said. 'The one with the pistol and all the piercings.'

'Did you?' Her voice seemed indifferent.

He studied her.

'You recognised her, too, didn't you?'

She shook her head vehemently.

'Yes, you did. You've seen her before. What are the two of them up to?'

Elisabeth shrugged and her mighty bosom heaved.

'I don't know. But Anja went with them willingly.'

He nodded. He had noticed that, too. Anja had given a hazy little smile before letting herself be pushed into the car.

'I think she knew them,' he said. 'Perhaps it was planned.'

They sat for a while in silence. He tried in vain to remember where he had seen the girl with the gun before, but every time he came close to an answer, it eluded him.

'Ramses,' Elisabeth said at last, still munching.

'What about him?'

She averted her eyes.

'One of the women,' she mumbled. 'I've seen her with him.'

He slung the ice pack on the coffee table in irritation.

'How hard was that to say? Perhaps it'll help us find out what happened. To Stinger, I mean.'

She shrugged and sulked.

'What could that bitch have to do with it?'

'Did Stinger bring Ramses here? To your flat?'

'What do you think? It's not like he had any other places he could take him.'

Her wounded gaze touched him and he saw the hurt in her eyes. Of course. She'd had a soft spot for Ramses, like so many other girls who had fallen for his macho looks.

'He always had one skinny model after another in tow,' she went on, looking down. 'But he was really keen on this one.'

'What's her name?'

Elisabeth muttered something inaudible.

'Sorry?'

'Lily,' she said in a voice thick with contempt. 'Lily Klein. And the name suited her, she really was klein. Small, that is.'

'Lily Klein. Where have I seen her before?'

Again she shrugged. She looked sulky, hurt and sad, all at the same time, trapped in her enormous body, dreaming perhaps of being just as skinny and pretty as Lily.

'How should I know?'

27

According to *Yellow Pages*, there was a Lily Klein living in Brammersgade in Århus.

He called Felix to check she'd eaten and ask how she was doing. She assured him she'd had some cheese on rye and drunk a cup of tea. The doctor had been round. He was satisfied with her progress, she thought.

'I'd better move back to my own place.'

He put on his voice of authority.

'You're staying right where you are.'

'But I have a place of my own. I'm in your way.'

'You're not in my way. Besides, you're looking after the dog.'

'I could do something,' she said. 'I could clean your house.'

He wasn't crazy about the idea of her in a smock with a headscarf, mop and bucket.

'Save your strength. I'll be back soon. I've just got to do something.'

'How's your friend?'

He told her about Stinger's condition. He didn't mention the incident with the four women after they had left the hospital, but when he had ended the call, he couldn't get it out of his head. Ramses' murder, the girl in the harbour, the attack on Stinger and now a rescue operation straight out of a Hollywood movie, in broad daylight outside Skejby Hospital. What – if anything – did all these things have to do with each other?

A big part of him screamed forget it, concentrate on your

own life. But Stinger was in a coma in hospital. Who had attacked him? And why? The key had to be the treasure hunt he and Ramses were planning. And Lily Klein had known Ramses.

He drove to the address in Brammersgade and rang the bell. A plump, grey-haired woman opened the door wearing an apron over a floral dress and a long cardigan on top of that. Peter reckoned she must have been around seventy.

'Could I talk to Lily Klein?'

'She's moved. She left months ago.'

'Do you know where she went?'

The woman shook her head. She smelled of food and the same smell was wafting through the half-open door – fried onions and beefburgers, he guessed.

Peter put on a smile, and it was easy to do. The woman seemed friendly enough; there was something wise and yet playful in her eyes.

'You wouldn't happen to be the owner of this building, would you, Madam?'

It might have been a cheap trick to address her as madam, but showing a bit of respect never did any harm.

She buttoned up the cardigan over her apron to protect herself from the cold.

'Come in,' she said.

Peter entered the hall. The door closed on the snow blowing down the street. She led the way up to her door.

'I was born in this house. On the second floor. My family has owned it for decades.'

She tilted her head and patted the wall. 'If walls could talk, eh? Oh, the stories they could tell. This house has seen a little of everything, including a World War. Makes you wonder, doesn't it?'

'Fascinating,' Peter said, and he meant it. He had often had the same thought himself. Houses. They had a life of their own, and the walls absorbed the lives and the stories that were played out within them.

The woman pointed up the stairs.

'She lived up there, Lily did. The attic room. The room hasn't been rented out yet.'

'I don't suppose I could have a look, could I?'

She looked him up and down.

'You don't look like someone in need of a room. Are you a private detective or the police?'

He smiled.

'Why would you think that?'

'I saw her boyfriend's photo in the paper.'

'You should be a detective,' Peter said. 'And, yes, Ramses said he'd left something for me here.'

'Here?'

She examined him carefully, and at length reached inside the door, took a key from the cupboard and led him upstairs. At the top, she opened the door to a sparsely furnished room with sloping walls and stripy blue wallpaper.

'See for yourself. Neither of them left anything behind. No information. I've got some post lying around, but that's addressed to her. What did you expect?'

He decided honesty was the best policy.

'Actually I was hoping to talk to her. One of Ramses' friends has just been beaten up.'

She shuddered.

'So much violence. Will it never end?'

He touched his neck, where Flat Nose had squeezed, and thought about all the punches and kicks he had dished out himself.

'What was she like?' he asked, scanning the room.

'Lily? Difficult to work out. Clever girl. Always had a ready answer. Pretty, too. And helpful. But what she was doing mixing with that lot God only knows.'

'Was there anyone apart from Ramses?'

He knelt down and looked under the bed as he spoke. Further back, he saw a small shiny object.

'A few women. Rough-looking types with nose, mouth and eyebrow piercings. Just like Lily.'

He stretched his arm, but couldn't quite reach. He got up and pulled the bed out. Among all the dust bunnies there was indeed an object. He grabbed it and held it up.

'Oh, did she leave that here?' the old lady said. 'I don't suppose she'll be back for it.'

It was an earring, silver as far as he could judge. In the shape of a flower. A fleur-de-lis.

'You keep it. You can always give it to her when you find her.'

28

Felix had fallen asleep again in the late afternoon after a day of minute but nonetheless notable progress: a slice of buttered toast, some porridge oats with full-fat milk, a shower on wobbly legs and a short walk in the frost, well wrapped up in a Puffa jacket, with the dog running around. Finally the tiredness overcame her and she fell asleep again.

It was dark outside; she awoke to the sound of grinding organ tones and an oppressive melancholy, like a weight on her chest. For a moment she thought Peter had come home and was playing music on the CD player.

Then she realised the organ was playing inside her head.

She wanted to sit up, but it was an unequal struggle, so she gave up and fell back on to the pillow. Her eyes and her head ached, and the ceiling was a blur. The weight on her chest spread to every nook and cranny of her body; a sob burst forth from deep inside and engulfed her.

Crying was both a curse and a liberation. She realised it was the music that was causing her reaction. The organ notes wound themselves in and out of her insides, sending tentacles to the places where her grief lay encapsulated. The music teased out, penetrated and opened up the hardness in her, and the magnitude of her loss suddenly cut through her with merciless force.

She struggled into a sitting position, racked with sobs.

'Maria.'

She said the name and tasted it again. She called out, knowing full well there would be no reply: 'Maria? Sweet Maria . . .'

The organ ground on inside her head. She suddenly remembered they had played this tune at the funeral. Now the words came back: 'Sleep, my child, sleep for ever more.'

How could she have forgotten? How could she have repressed this final farewell, the sense of the bottomless pit in which she found herself? How could she have mislaid the memory of two coffins, one big, one small, side by side in a church filled with flowers, the suffocating scent?

Maria. Maria. Maria.

How could she ever have gone on living without Maria? How could she have drawn breath without constantly thinking about Maria, without grieving, despairing and picturing her daughter's cheery face, Maria's body in a close embrace with her own?

She knew the rational answer. Her memory had protected her after the crash. She had woken up at the hospital, her memory wiped clean, and not even the funeral or being told about it all could evoke feelings or memories. Her brain had wrapped itself around a few days of her life. But now they were seeping out. From the day they found Ramses at the foot of the cliff they had begun to trickle and now they were in full flow. Grief contorted her insides and sent her into a maelstrom of emotion. It threatened to crush her.

A high-pitched whine intruded into the music, forcing its way through. The dog was staring at her, bewildered. She put out a hand, and it rested its big head on her knee. The touch of a living being comforted her.

Some time later she heard a car arrive, and Peter entered carrying shopping bags and whistling. The whistle froze on his lips when he saw her on the sofa, her body convulsed with sobs and the dog's head in her lap.

'What's happened?'

She dried her eyes, but the tears kept flowing. It was like a flood she couldn't stop. He sat down next to her and put his arm around her shoulders.

'It's silly,' she hiccupped. 'It won't do any good.'

'Of course it will.'

'She's gone. Maria. She's not coming back.'

'But it feels good to remember her, doesn't it?'

He was right. How could he know?

They sat in silence for a long time. Slowly her crying subsided. He held her hand. He gave her warmth, and it felt good to be with someone. She had been alone for so long.

'I remembered the funeral,' she said. 'The hymns, the flowers, the coffins and . . .'

She stopped.

'You can do it,' he said.

She took a deep breath.

'It was August. Late summer. Five months ago.'

Suddenly the words flowed. She told him about Maria. She told him what it had been like to have a daughter, about the ties that bound them tighter and tighter, ties she never thought could have existed between two people. Unending love. The precious moments of pure happiness.

She told him about the life she had lived. About Erik. About the boat he had named *Felix*. About their first meeting and her desperate need for financial security, which meant she never questioned the wealth that became a part of their lives. She talked about his affairs. But most of all she talked about the child she had lost. Maria, lying in the small white coffin while the organ played 'Sleep, my child, sleep for ever more.'

He got up a little later. He put away the shopping, made her a cup of tea, came back and sat down.

'Who organised the funeral?' he asked. 'Were you involved?'

She shook her head.

'Erik's secretary and my parents arranged everything. I was ill.

I was in a coma for I don't know how long and then I was in a wheelchair.'

'Was Ramses there? At the funeral?'

She looked at him in surprise.

'Why would he be?'

'Because he knew Erik?'

'I don't think they were friends.'

'Why don't you think so?'

'Ramses wasn't Erik's type. I think it was about something else.'

'Money?'

'Possibly. Probably.'

She studied him as he sat there, leaning back, legs apart, jeans, a coarse wool jumper puckered up, still wearing boots. What was the real reason he was doing so much for her? Why was he so keen to help?

As though he had read her mind, he said: 'I'm on your side, Felix. I'm not trying to hurt you.'

'But you're also using me.'

She felt ashamed, but not enough to stop herself. 'My story's your story, too. Or, at least, some of it is.'

He shrugged.

'Perhaps.'

She noticed that the pain lessened when she concentrated on him, on the colour of his hair and its composition – it was like looking at a million grains of sand on the beach, and together they made a whole – on his expression, a smile, close behind the seriousness, ready to jump in.

'Tell me about you,' she said. 'You know so much about me now. But what do I really know about you?'

She saw him retreat. Not physically, but mentally.

'What if I said that learning something about you might help me?' she said.

'It's not a very happy story. It won't make you feel any better.'

'Try me.'

He gave her an abridged version, and she soon realised she had only been given a tiny snippet.

It was a bitter snippet, growing up in a care home, a sadistic manager handing out punishments to the youngest children for the slightest offences. He described instruments of torture as though they were old acquaintances: the Box, the Horse and the Rings. He explained their individual function and told her how the children had been terrified of isolation and pain, but most of all the darkness in the Box. And yet there wasn't a trace of bitterness or hatred in his voice and she wondered how anyone could have survived something like that.

'It's a choice,' he said in response. 'You can choose not to hate, not to want revenge. I made that choice, but it took me time.'

He added with a smile: 'Four years behind bars puts life in perspective.'

She couldn't do the same. She needed the hatred and the desire for revenge and she told him so. It kept her alive: her rage at what had happened was all-consuming. He said he understood and that for the time being she had to hang on to it; perhaps later she could let it go.

'Perhaps we should try to work through what happened,' he said, as though suggesting they should paint the house together or shovel the snow from the drive. 'It'll probably help you to recover. We could start with Ramses. See if you can remember any more.'

She mulled over his suggestion, then decided the time had come.

'I've got something you need to see,' she said. 'It's in the kitchen, second drawer down. A mobile phone.'

'And you'd like me to get it?'

She nodded.

He did as she asked and quickly returned with a mobile in a plastic bag.

'Is this it?'

He took out the mobile.

'Yes. I think it's still charged.'

'Is it yours?'

She shook her head. 'It's his. Ramses'. I took it while your back was turned.'

He gaped at her. He had not expected this.

'You stole a dead man's mobile? A man who had just been murdered?'

She looked at him but said nothing. He shook his head as though he still didn't believe her.

'And yet you accused me of betraying him because I said I didn't know him?'

He had raised his voice. The dog, which had been lying on the rug, pulled back its ears and pretended to be invisible.

She looked away.

'You were the one who suggested we could start with him. You knew him. I've seen him before and I just want him identified and out of my life.'

Peter got up. He took the empty carrier bags from his shopping and stuffed them into a drawer. Pushing them down, with his back to her, he said: 'It's too dangerous. You should have given the mobile to the police on the first day.'

'I had to take it. He haunts me,' she said. 'Ramses is the key to everything that ruined my life and I have to find out how it all fits together.'

As she said it, she knew it was true. She owed it to Maria and she owed it to herself.

'I'm sure the mobile could be of use to you, too,' she said.

He turned around and leaned against the kitchen drawers.

'To me?'

'Perhaps it's all connected,' she said. 'You knew Ramses. I've seen him before. Now he's dead. Perhaps it's got something to do with both of us.'

She nodded towards the mobile. 'Perhaps the answer's there? If we can get it to work.'

He sighed and picked up Ramses' mobile.

'I'm not trying to be a saint, but the police already have their eye on me,' he said. 'We'll have to hand it in.'

'And we will.'

'It's working,' he said, pressing a key. 'The battery's still charged. Full.'

For a moment, a silence fell between them. They looked at each other.

'I need to think about this,' he said.

'OK.'

It was better than an outright rejection. It was a partial victory.

He checked his watch.

'It's half-past six. Are you hungry?'

She felt hollow inside, and not solely from hunger. Even so, she nodded.

He reached down, took her hand and pulled her to her feet. Her head still hurt, but the room had stopped spinning.

'Do you think you can manage a drive?'

The thought of getting out was tempting.

'We can try.'

'Come on then. Let's get a bite to eat in town.'

29

The restlessness set in late at night. It was like pent-up energy, like a boxer before a big fight that had been cancelled at the last minute. His blood was in ferment, his muscles tense. He was sweating like a pig. He needed a release.

Just after ten o'clock Mark Bille Hansen left his flat near the railway station and the meandering river which gave rise to the town's name of Grenå. The water looked black as it ran between the snow-covered banks parallel to the railway. In the station car park, he started the engine, gunned it to the roundabout and drove the three kilometres from the town centre down to the harbour. Thoughts were pounding in his head. Anna Bagger was still insisting the body in the harbour was Nina Bjerre – age, build, long blonde hair – it all fitted. But her face was missing. And even though Anna was certain she was right, his doubts had clearly shaken her. They would know for certain tomorrow when the dentist submitted his final judgement, but Mark was sure that Anna was lying in her bed now or sitting in her living room pondering the obvious question that followed: if it wasn't Nina Bjerre they had found in the harbour, then who was it? And where was Nina Bjerre if she wasn't in cold storage at the Morgue?

The latter question was no less pressing because earlier that day the divers had found a mobile in the harbour. The insides had obviously been destroyed by the water, but it was a Nokia and it matched the model that Nina Bjerre had had.

The night was freezing cold and dark. With the shops behind

him, he glided past homes where people sat behind their windows with the blue glow of the television for company. There were very few people around on a Monday evening when the outside temperature was well below minus ten. But as he approached the harbour, strangers started appearing in the streets – black people, who looked as if they belonged beneath the African sun rather than wrapped up in thick coats for a Danish winter. There was a refugee centre just outside the town. They had to be from there. It was hard to see what had attracted them to the harbour. But wasn't it the same story with harbours everywhere? A motley assortment of people from the fringes of society, just like the waters of a river, found their way to the harbour, making their way to the bars and hotels traditionally located by the well-worn paths of seamen and fishermen. And didn't the same apply to restless men, their blood in ferment, didn't they follow the same stream, in a downward spiral, a whirlpool of desire, which could crush human destinies as easily as the current could carry a body to Norway?

Mark scanned the pavement as he drove. She worked in this area. He didn't remember her face clearly or even her name. And yet he would be able to recognise her, he knew that.

He had driven all the way down to Havnevejen and turned right when he saw her standing with a fellow prostitute. They were close to the entrance of the Strand Hotel. The tip of her cigarette glowed in the dark when she took a drag, and even though he didn't remember her face or her name, he remembered her body: petite with jeans fitting like an extra layer of skin, a short white Puffa jacket and an imitation fur hood. High-heeled boots to above her knees.

He stopped the car and didn't have to wait long before she appeared outside. He rolled down the window.

'Are you busy?'

She looked as though she was considering his question. He was half-expecting her to produce a diary.

'Same as last time?'

He nodded. What had she been expecting? Dinner for two followed by a marriage proposal?

'Price has gone up. It'll be another three hundred kroner.'

The haggling gene asserted itself in him.

'You can't just hike your price for no reason.'

'It's not for no reason,' she said solemnly, and now he could see her face, possibly for the first time. Pale and narrow. There was caution mixed with greed in her eyes. 'Most girls refuse to go out. Ever since they found the body of that girl Nina.'

Of course. He hadn't even considered the consequences for the girls on the street. He felt like an idiot.

'OK. Jump in.'

She turned around and said something he couldn't hear to her friend. Then she took a final drag, flicked the cigarette and got in on the passenger side. She had make-up plastered over her young face and her cheap perfume filled the car.

He headed towards the summer house area before doing a U-turn. He made a decision.

'Why don't we go back to my place? It's too cold in the car, don't you think?'

She thought about it, then nodded.

'How old are you really?'

The question hadn't troubled him before, but the words were out before he knew it. He had slept with her once and he hadn't given her name or her age a thought. Where had this interest crept in from? He didn't like it.

'Twenty-two.'

Other questions stacked up, but he kept them back. He could have focused on whether she had a family, if she had a place to live, if there was a pimp in the background who took most of her money. But he didn't. Instead his blood was in ferment again, and he cast a sidelong glance at her thighs in the tight jeans and remembered what it felt like to run his hands up them. His erection stirred, and reaching the car park and walking up to the flat together, he felt as though he would explode.

She looked around quickly when he switched on the light in the passage. There was a guarded look in her eyes behind the thick kohl and clumps of mascara.

'I don't bite. Don't worry,' he said, hearing his own impatience.

She walked through the flat with a feigned lofty air. Every now and then she would touch objects. He knew he was walking a fine line here. A dangerous line. He was a police officer. He should be living a comfortable family life, not cruising the streets to pick up hookers. If he really had to, he should be doing it in a different town. Århus. He should have gone to Århus, but this was easier. It was quicker. And quick was what he needed.

'Come on. Sleeping quarters are in here.'

'Who said anything about sleeping?'

She had already started to undress. Small breasts jutted out at him beneath a thin jumper. 'I'd rather have a drink,' she added. 'And seeing that we're back at your place, how about some music?'

He poured a little whisky into two glasses and put on a Coldplay CD. Clit music, as one of his friends had called it. It was a crude but apt expression. Most women loved Coldplay and its lead singer. Personally, he couldn't imagine why they would have wet dreams over such a morose guy.

She stripped for him in time to the music. Smiles wreathed his face. They would probably be added to her bill.

'What's your name again?' he asked while cupping her breasts from behind. She wriggled against his erection.

'Gry.'

'You're sexy, Gry.'

She rotated her hips to the rhythm of the music. She was wearing only a G-string. He pulled her down on to the sofa, on top of him. She took care of the rest. Along the way, they haggled a little, until she opened her hand and showed him a condom. She rode him with professional lust in her eyes, and he cascaded inside her, with a variety of female faces appearing in his head in a multi-coloured fan. Afterwards it annoyed him that his guilt would rear its ugly head, as it always did.

She quickly got dressed again.

'Can you give me a lift back?'

It wasn't a part of their deal, but he could hardly say no. He looked at her and felt disgust, mostly with himself. He couldn't get rid of her quickly enough.

'Come on then.'

In the street, she lit a cigarette. The smoke followed her, along with her frozen breath, as they crossed the car park.

'You're a cop, aren't you?'

The question hit him in the solar plexus. Now what? How much did she know? That he was a randy bastard who, like all the other randy bastards, had made a fool of himself by paying for sex? She most definitely knew that. Also, that his work was linked to the body in the harbour and the body at the foot of the cliff? She probably knew that, too, and he wasn't pleased about it. So he made no reply, merely unlocked the car from a distance of twenty metres and heard a promise of liberation in the click of the lock.

'Right, get in.'

She took the cigarette with her inside the car. He pressed the button and rolled down the window on the passenger side.

'Chuck it out.'

She sent him a provocative look.

'Or what? Am I going to be arrested?'

'Or you can walk.'

She flicked away the cigarette with a grin. She had brown stains on her teeth. Why hadn't he noticed that before?

'I hope you catch the guy who did it.'

'Did what?'

'Threw that Nina in the water, of course. What else?'

He deemed it wisest not to say anything. He drove as fast as the speed limit would allow, and then some. She continued: 'Are you sure she's the one you found?'

He nearly drove into the kerb. He straightened up and had to concentrate on steering through the residential area down to Kattegatvej, where he turned right and stopped outside the Strand Hotel. Her colleague was still standing under the street light and the neon sign. He turned to her.

'What made you say that?'

He kept his voice neutral, but inside he was seething. What did she know?

'No reason. Thanks for the lift, cop.'

She got out. He opened the door on his side and followed her. As she was about to cross over to see her friend, he reached out and grabbed her arm.

'You owe me an answer.'

'Let go of me.'

She writhed, but he held on. Out of the corner of his eye he saw the hotel door open and two people come out. The woman was petite and dark, her contours blurred; the man's blond hair and square features, by contrast, were clear in the light from the neon sign. He knew who they were and that he should let go of the girl's arm, but he was enveloped by a red haze and his rage washed away his common sense.

'Not before you give me an answer.'

'OK. There were three girls.'

All of a sudden, she seemed to calm down. The two people from the hotel nodded to him by way of greeting and disappeared into a car. Gry carried on.

'They hung out with us for a while, but then they, like, vanished. We talked about the killer who was at large, the one in England, the guy who killed all those girls. People like that exist.' She sent him a challenging stare, and she was right, he thought. People like that did exist. So why not here?

'What were their names? The three girls?'

She shrugged.

'I can't bloody remember. They were only here a couple of days.'

'When?'

'Around Christmas. And just before.'

'Where do they live?'

She shook her head. 'How should I know? Somewhere. They weren't local.'

'Describe them.'

'They looked tough, leather, studs and all that. They put us a bit on edge.'

She spat on the pavement. 'They'd fucking got it sussed.'

'Appearance?'

Her eyes took on a sly expression and she opened the palm of one hand.

'Soon going to owe me something for all this info, aren't you?'

He looked at her fragile body. How would she defend herself if she was confronted by a thug?

'Don't forget, this is in your own interests,' he said. 'What if a killer really is at large, looking for girls like you?'

He nodded in the direction of her friend, who was bent over a car, leaning inside and apparently negotiating with the driver. He stoked up the threat.

'What if it's the guy in the white Toyota? What if your friend doesn't show up tomorrow? How would you feel if you'd held something back?'

She fumbled in her jacket pocket for an almost empty pack of cigarettes. She lit one and blew a puff of smoke into his face. Then she turned away and looked after her friend, who was now getting into the Toyota.

'That's what I mean,' she said pensively. 'I saw a photo in the newspaper. Of that Nina.'

She looked at him. He had to look hard, but thought he could detect fear behind her defiant gaze.

'One of the three girls. She looked like Nina. Spitting image.'

30

THEY WERE NEARLY home when Felix said: 'Do you think he had sex with her?'

'Perhaps,' Peter said, steering the car through the snow over the home straight.

He didn't doubt for one moment that Mark Bille had something going with the prostitute.

Even so, he said, 'Or maybe it was something quite different. It could be work.'

She looked unconvinced. He parked by the house and they emerged into a winter night so bitingly cold it made her shiver and a gust of wind nearly knocked her over.

'Come on. Let's get you inside. I'll take the dog for a short walk.'

'I'll come with you.'

He recognised her first day's stubbornness and took it to be a good sign, but she was clearly tired so they didn't stray too far from the house. She had eaten almost all her dinner at the hotel and the change of scenery had done her good. She had even sipped some beer while he told her about Stinger, Brian and Ramses, the treasure in the sea and the number they had found tattooed on Stinger's arm. He omitted his role in the story about the women and the rescue of Anja.

The dog enjoyed its brief freedom, scampering about and chasing after the snowballs he threw. The sea lay shrouded in darkness and Peter wondered where Brian could have scuttled his boat. The Kattegat was deep. If you planned to retrieve goods from a sunken ship, you probably wouldn't dump it at the deepest point. But Brian had known the sea like the back of his hand. He would have known where the best place was.

When they came back inside, Ramses' mobile was waiting for them. Peter had expected Felix to go straight to bed, but she seemed to get a second wind when she picked up the mobile.

'I know we should give it to the police,' she said. 'But there's no harm in looking, is there?'

She started scrolling through Ramses' contacts.

'There's probably nothing here,' she said. 'Not as far as those coordinates go. Or the mobile wouldn't have been left behind.'

She was right. There was no harm in looking and they might discover something the police wouldn't pick up on.

He looked with her. Contacts were listed by initials or first names.

'Why don't we copy them down?' she suggested.

He looked at the names. There were several numbers and initials he could put together and make sense of. Old friends, prison contacts. Stinger's number was there, too.

'This is illegal. You know that, don't you? This is evidence in a murder case.'

Her eyes narrowed. Her fingers worked away.

'I'm not a criminal,' she said. 'But I'm beyond rules.'

He shook his head at her logic, and yet he understood her. He used to be like that and perhaps he still was. They had both been there, where only a thin membrane separated life from death. It changed you.

'That probably won't stand up in court,' he said.

'I couldn't care less.'

She reached for a notebook on the table and meticulously wrote down the names and numbers. It was slow going.

'Why don't you dictate?'

He did as she asked. Ramses' list of contacts was fairly short and contained no surprises.

'And what do we do if we find the place?' she asked. 'Hire a diver and send him down?'

The thought had already crossed his mind.

'It depends how deep it is. Perhaps we can have a word with Kir?'

'Who's Kir?'

'Christian Røjel's daughter. The pig farmer whose roof I'm rebuilding.'

'Kir.'

She tasted the sound. 'Funny name.'

She asked, almost in the same breath: 'Why do you always sleep on the balcony?'

The question took him by surprise. He attempted a vague answer, about how he loved nature and the open sky, but he could tell from looking at her that she knew there was more to it than that.

Later when he had dragged the mattress outside and was lying with Kaj beside him, he thought about the range of answers he could have given her. The terror of the Box at the care home still gripped him and he broke out in a cold sweat at the thought of being trapped indoors, for one. All the children from Titan Care Home had developed a touch of claustrophobia and his case was far from the worst. Or that the four years in prison had taught him what locked doors could do to the human mind and he had always sworn that, for the rest of his life, he would sleep outside so that he could breathe freely.

He turned over in the sleeping bag and found a comfortable position. Perhaps he should have suggested that she keep him company. She had told him about her insomnia. Bed was the worst, she said. It was a reminder that she was chasing sleep. Sleep and peace of mind were closely connected; he knew that only too well.

And what about his peace of mind? He'd thought he'd found

it and had hoped to keep it. He'd thought he'd made peace with his past and found contentment on his cliff. But then Felix had appeared and triggered something inside him. Ramses was dead and Stinger had been beaten to pulp; a police officer had come sniffing around his home and Anja's ex-boyfriend had forced him to be violent again, causing two ninja girls to appear out of thin air. All this had sent him straight back to a place he had promised himself he would never go again. Back. Back to what smelled and tasted of violence and crime and the sound of his cell door when the lock clicked shut.

He didn't want to go back to that life. He wanted to move on, but right now he didn't have a choice. He stared into the night, at the stars. It was another clear and frosty night.

In the midst of everything that had happened there had been something else. He couldn't put it into words, and he didn't know if it was good or bad, but it felt as if something inside him had been moved. As though something which had been frozen solid for years was now starting to thaw.

He heard a sound. Could it be a creak on the stairs? Was she coming to him? Would she suddenly be standing there in her thin T-shirt? Would she slip into his sleeping bag unbidden and give him something she thought he might want, out of gratitude perhaps? And did he? How could he accept a payment for something else?

He listened. He hoped he would have the strength to resist and send her away. But the noise had stopped and he fell asleep, disappointed deep into his bones.

31

KIR MANOEUVRED THE Toyota up the long, snow-covered gravel road leading to Konkylien, hearing Uncle Hannibal's voice in her ear: 'No two ships sound alike under water.'

Konkylien had an uninterrupted view of Nederskov forest, and Kir had been a frequent visitor as a child. Now she could see the whitewashed house, the flaking plaster and the roof, which had so much moss growing on top it almost looked thatched. The moss was mixed with smudges of snow and in a few places you could see that underneath it was an ageing felt roof badly in need of replacement. The ridge of the old barn sagged like an overburdened sofa.

The *For Sale* sign had been taken down. There had never been any buyers, possibly because the family hadn't taken the trouble to do the place up. Besides, Red used the barn as a depot for the pub he had opened in Grenå. It was a bad time to open a pub, everyone knew that, but Red had managed to make it happen with his usual determination. Kir had a strong feeling that her father had lent him the money for the venture and possibly also for his flat down by the river. Red was the first-born and had a special status purely for that reason. She and Tomas accepted it. Tomas still lived at home and would probably take over the farm one day. She had her summer house but she had always thought of Konkylien as her house. Here she could breathe freely and feel welcome.

She got out of the car and slammed the door. Then she put

her key in the lock and let herself in. She wanted to check the heating during this icy winter. Pipes might burst and water could leak in the wrong places. You had to keep an eye on old houses, but she knew perfectly well this wasn't the sole reason she had come here.

She walked from room to room. The doors stuck and creaked. The floorboards groaned under her weight. She slipped deeper and deeper into a world she loved, and it was as if the events of the past few days evaporated into thin air. The body in the harbour, the fear that had overpowered her, the shock at seeing the mutilated face in the body bag – it all vanished and was replaced by the sounds and smells of her childhood. There was the red velvet sofa with its threadbare upholstery and embroidered cushions from an age when women – her great-grandmother, apparently – would sit at home in the evening with a needle and embroidery yarn. There was a standard lamp in the corner, its base a mass of intertwined brass snakes; there was the old-fashioned diving suit, standing like a suit of armour with hinges on the visor and heavy shoes that made it look like a Martian; hanging on the wall was a lifebuoy from the old fishing vessel, *Malene*, of Grenå. There were photos, black and white and colour, from various diving expeditions in Denmark as well as abroad, strong young men waving from the surface of the water, their diving masks pushed right up their foreheads, or snorkelling in reeds by a lake or cheering from an ice hole some-where in Northern Norway. There were divers standing next to mines covered in algae and seaweed, corroded gas flasks and other dangerous materials. As Uncle Hannibal used to say about the mines in Danish waters: 'The Germans laid theirs neatly and systematically so that you could find practically every single one of them. The English just dumped theirs from the air with no system at all.'

The house was cold even though they had decided to leave

the heating on low. She found an old rug which she wrapped around herself, sat down on the red velvet sofa and tucked her feet under her.

She reached down to the newspaper holder and picked up some of the old magazines. *Familie Journalen*. *Ugens Rapport* from some time in the Nineties. Diving magazines such as *DYK* and *Sportsdykkeren*. She flicked through them, remembering the feeling of Mark Bille Hansen near her when they had stood together in the harbour. If anyone had asked her, she would have been able to describe him exactly. His height. His gestures. His tone of voice. The snow on his hair and in his dark stubble. His eyes searching out hers as though he believed she held the answer to every riddle. Blue, green, brown – the colour didn't matter, and she couldn't remember it anyway. But she did remember the intensity. It had sent her reeling and she didn't like that.

She dropped the magazine she was holding when she heard the sound of a car in the drive. A second later she saw Red's black Honda stop outside the window, and shortly afterwards he appeared in the doorway.

'What are you doing here?' he asked.

'Hunting ghosts.'

It was a standing joke going back to their childhood. Hannibal's house had always echoed with strange noises that had fired their imagination when they were children. They had formed a club to catch every ghost in the house.

Red grinned, drawing the big birthmark on his cheek up to his eyes. It was dark red and had given rise to his nickname. His real name was Mogens.

'And have you found any?'

'Nah.'

He entered the room. Red was both broad and tall, and his size made the low-ceilinged room look like something out of a cartoon. He sat down in the old stripy wing chair and looked around.

'It's almost as if the old boy was still here.'

He grinned. 'In a moment he'll come in and tell us about the time he recovered a body from a cabin at a depth of forty-five metres and pulled off its leg.' Red made a pulling motion. He could imitate Hannibal's facial expressions and voice to a T: 'Blooooody hell! Shiver me timbers!'

Hannibal had been the very cliché of an old salt, and he knew it only too well. Red held up the imaginary leg and squinted short-sightedly at it.

Kir laughed. She remembered it vividly. Hannibal had thought he had accidentally twisted off a leg, but it had turned out to be a false leg.

She looked at Red and missed her childhood, when they had done things together, her, Tomas and Red. It had stopped suddenly. From the day she saved Tomas from drowning, Red had turned his back on their little group. It had never been quite the same again, which made this shared moment even more rare and precious.

'What do you think happened to him?'

Red leaned back in the tall chair, and the sinews in his neck stood out like thick ropes.

'I imagine he was legless, and he was having a piss over the side. And then: splash!'

'I've been looking for him,' she admitted. 'I've been diving in the places where he used to fish.'

'Forget it,' Red said. 'It's like I said. He went over the railing. The old boy got the death he'd have wanted.'

Kir was far from sure about this, but lots of people believed Hannibal's death must have been an accident. And perhaps they were right. Hannibal's motor boat had been found on Fjellerup Beach two days after he went missing. No one had seemed terribly surprised. Most felt it was only a question of time before something like that happened. Their father, in particular, had been certain – a certainty that had turned to anger when he discovered that Hannibal had left everything to his nephews and niece and not a krone to the pig farmer.

'Right. I've come here to collect some casks.'

Red launched himself out of the chair. He turned around in the doorway, about to say something, when Kir's mobile rang. The display showed Allan Vraa's number.

'Work,' she mouthed to Red, and then said into the mobile: 'Hi, what's up?'

'I just wanted you to know the latest,' her boss said. 'The forensic odontologist has just confirmed the body you found isn't Nina Bjerre.'

'If it isn't her, then who is it?'

She heard a hiss as Allan Vraa heaved a deep sigh.

'God only knows. But the mobile we found was definitely hers, so I think we'll have to get back down in the sludge and keep looking. It appears we may be talking about two bodies.'

32

POLITI.

The sign looked as signs did at police stations all over Denmark. But this new police station also had an idyllic location in the middle of a public park which was usually green but was now white with snow. Piles of snow had been cleared away for access, but even so, he had to overcome his reluctance to enter. In the end, however, he managed to push open the door, with his brow perspiring and his knees wobbling, to his immense irritation.

All the car park spaces had been taken and he'd had to leave his car some distance away. He recognised the detectives' cars from the day by the cliff. The team from Århus had probably set up camp here, where all the action seemed to be. It was as if all roads led to Grenå.

Peter asked for Mark Bille Hansen at the counter.

'Do you have an appointment?'

'No. But he knows who I am. Tell him I've got something for him.'

He waved a plastic bag in front of the receptionist's nose. Ramses' mobile was inside.

A few minutes later he was shown up to Mark Bille's office by a uniformed officer, who knocked cautiously at the door.

'Now what?'

The voice issuing from the office did not exactly have that fresh-as-a-morning-daisy feel. The policeman opened the door slightly, but didn't poke his head too far in.

'Peter Boutrup for you.'

'Oh, all right,' came the not terribly enthusiastic response.

The officer quickly stepped aside to let Peter in. The office looked tidy – and austere. Impersonal was possibly a better word, he thought, wondering about the best way to greet Mark Bille Hansen. Formal or informal? He hated the sense of being on unknown territory. The day the policeman had turned up in his home had been easier.

'Morning.'

Mark Bille Hansen muttered something by way of reply, but it wasn't enormously welcoming. He was clearly not a morning person. His hair looked a mess and thick stubble darkened his winter-pale face. He wore a light blue shirt but looked as if he would have preferred to relax in a T-shirt. There was a Thermos and a mug on the table in front of him.

'They can look after themselves, those girls can,' Peter said and knew at once he should have kept his mouth shut.

Mark Bille gawped at him.

'Girls?'

'Last night, I mean. Down at the harbour. They'll have you by the nuts, if you're not careful.'

'I was working.'

It was a defensive answer, and it came far too quickly. They both knew it. Mark Bille examined some papers lying on the blotter on his desk.

'Is that what you came to tell me?'

Peter placed the bag on the desk.

'We thought this might interest you. We decided to give it to you rather than Århus.'

'We?'

'Felix Gomez and me.'

A glint of interest appeared in Mark Bille's eyes.

'Whose is it?'

'Felix found it at the foot of the cliff, a short distance from where Ramses was lying.'

'That area was fingertip searched by CSIs. When did she find it? Why didn't she bring it in herself?'

Peter shrugged.

'Perhaps the snow had covered it. She found it when she was out for a walk.'

Mark Bille looked at him with undisguised scepticism.

'And I thought you didn't know each other.'

Peter looked at the man in front of him. He looked under pressure.

'You get to know each other quite well when you find a body together.'

'I've been going through some papers and asking around,' the policeman said, shuffling some documents. 'You're a man with an interesting past.'

Of course the officer had done some research on him. Peter should have known.

'Not just your time in Horsens Prison,' Mark Bille said. 'Your childhood at Titan Care Home. Punishments, sadism. And a girl called My.'

Mark Bille looked up at him. 'Tell me about her.'

Peter looked out of the window and down at the snow-covered vehicles in the car park. Suddenly he needed some fresh air.

'She's got nothing to do with this case.'

'That's for me to decide.'

Mark Bille glanced at some notes.

'Autistic. Twenty-six years old. Murdered. Found hanging from a tree. You were close friends? You took her dog in when she died.'

'What if I did?'

Mark Bille lowered the paper and looked at him.

'I'm just asking myself how involved you might be in recent

events – Ramses, the woman in the harbour – I'm wondering what your agenda is?'

He nodded at the mobile in the plastic bag. 'And now this. I keep learning new things about you, Peter Boutrup. For instance, what happened in your house the day Hans Martin Krøll was shot? You went to prison for manslaughter, but what happened prior to that?'

Peter tried to look indifferent, but inside he was seething.

'I don't think the police reports tell the whole truth,' Mark Bille said. 'You're clearly holding something back. You keep holding something back. What is it?'

Peter desperately wanted to leave, but he couldn't. He tried to be casual. There had been a new development, he was certain of it. Something that had made Mark Bille smell blood.

He pulled out a chair and sat down. As if Mark Bille had read his thoughts he said: 'The body in the harbour wasn't Nina Bjerre.'

'Then who was it?'

The policeman shrugged. 'She has yet to be identified. But it's possible now there might be a connection between her and Ramses after all. Nina Bjerre was clean. She lived with her parents. She was still at school. She had no known links to criminal or suspicious activities. She was an A-grade student: pretty, hard-working and intelligent.'

He turned his palms upwards. 'The case has changed. Now we're dealing with a mysterious dead girl and Ramses. Now it seems more likely the two deaths might be related. And if they are, she might also be someone you know. Seeing as you knew Ramses.'

Peter swallowed some saliva. He hoped not. Christ, he hoped not.

'Then let me see her.'

Mark Bille got up.

'One moment.'

He darted through the door. Peter waited. Shortly afterwards Mark Bille returned and asked him to follow. They went up one floor and down a corridor. At the end he could hear voices. In a large, airy room the detectives had set up their headquarters. There were seven of them and they sat at separate desks, with computers and telephones. Mobile whiteboards had been pushed together by the end wall and the scene reminded him of a class-room. On one whiteboard the teacher had scribbled words in a blue marker pen. Hastily drawn arrows connected one keyword to another, joining all the words in a chain. Little round magnets attached various photos to the whiteboard and together with the words, they made up an ingenious pattern, which might or might not have made sense.

The female officer from the day by the cliff came up to them and shook hands. She was wearing jeans and a grey silk blouse. Her somewhat square face and the glide of her hips made her seem both masculine and feminine.

'Anna Bagger. We've met.'

Peter nodded. His gaze was attracted by the photographs on the whiteboard. The detectives must be desperate, he thought. Otherwise they'd never let an outsider see how they worked.

Anna Bagger nodded towards the whiteboard and the area where the photos of the dead woman were displayed. She was lying on a steel table. There were close-ups of details, but also of her in full figure. Her face was gone.

'She's impossible to recognise,' he said.

Anna Bagger pointed to a close-up.

'Look at this. It's a detail we've held back, but now we'll have to release it.'

He peered at it. At first glance, it looked like a complicated scar.

'What is it?'

'She's been branded,' Anna Bagger said, as much to Mark Bille as to him. 'A very specific brand.'

A brand. Like the ones they used to burn into the hide of longhorn cattle in Texas to show they belonged to a specific ranch. He looked at it more closely. Now he could see the symbol.

'A fleur-de-lis,' Anna Bagger said. 'In case you didn't know.'

He did.

'It's on the inside of her right thigh, quite high up,' Anna Bagger said. 'It's roughly three by three centimetres, and the interesting thing about it is that this brand has been superimposed on a matching tattoo.'

She pointed to the edge of the pattern. He saw it now. Under the brand which had drawn the skin together into a red scar he could make out blue lines almost following the same shape, but not quite.

'I'd say you'd have to know a girl quite well to know about those marks,' Anna Bagger said. 'I don't suppose you've seen them before or heard about them?'

Peter straightened up after studying the mark. He looked at Mark Bille.

'The Three Musketeers,' he said.

'What about them?'

Peter was tempted to say they were like the Magnificent Seven, minus four – three, if you included D'Artagnan – but he restrained himself.

'In the novel by Dumas, *The Three Musketeers*, the villainous Milady de Winter has a fleur-de-lis branded on to one shoulder.'

Anna Bagger's eyes zoomed in on him.

'In the book, it means she's a harlot and a murderess.'

33

Mark stood in his office watching Peter Boutrup cross the road and walk back towards his car. He walked taller now than when he'd entered the office, as though he had just cast off a burden. As Mark himself had to do: unburden himself. Stop thinking he could or indeed should make a difference to this shithole of a town.

There was a knock at the door and Anna Bagger entered.

'You could have told me about the brand,' he said.

She straightened her fringe with two fingers.

'Forensics wasn't sure. We only found out today it was a tattoo and a brand.'

'And what are you going to do about it?'

'So far we've spoken to every tattoo parlour in the district. No one recognises it.'

She perched on the corner of his desk.

'Or they're not prepared to admit it.'

She fidgeted with the pen on his blotter. He took that as a kind of professional come-on. He pulled out his chair, sat down and leaned back as he pushed himself a little further away from the table.

'Branding is the new tattooing,' he said. 'It's the next step up the ladder if you want to show how tough you are. You have to endure metal heated to one thousand, one hundred degrees being pressed against your skin for five seconds. You have to be one tough woman to handle that.'

She shifted her gaze to the wall, to some modern art he hadn't asked for and didn't understand.

'Was it voluntary, I wonder?' she speculated.

He took a deep breath.

'Do you really want to hear my opinion?'

'I wouldn't be asking if I didn't.'

He sat for a while looking at her. He was irritated, but he was also a police officer and the case was more important than personalities.

'OK,' he said. 'I don't think it was voluntary. I think you need to distinguish between the tattoo and the brand. The tattoo might have been her choice and it might be significant. The brand looks like someone was mocking her, perhaps someone using their power to mock the tattoo.'

She looked as if his words had made an impression and nodded to indicate that he should go on.

'But this brand is a pro job,' he said. 'You should see some of the things we came across in Copenhagen. Home-made. Infected, misshapen, leaving hideous scars.'

She shook her head.

'If she'd been branded against her will, who would do something like that?'

'Her owners,' he said. 'Or rather, her self-appointed owners.'

'Brothel owners?'

'Or gang bosses.'

'What does it mean?'

Again one of her fingers sought out the fringe.

'That you're one of the herd,' he said. 'You brand horses. And cattle.'

'So it's about belonging to a group,' she said. 'Someone's group?'

He nodded. 'Seems logical to me.'

She crossed her arms, looking as if she felt cold.

'Do you think there are any more branded women out there?'

'Who knows? You need to get her identified.'

He started reeling off the checklist: 'Who else was reported missing? Does the odontologist's report give you anything to go on? Other identifying marks? And tell the press about the brand and see what info comes back.'

She took his coffee mug and wound her fingers around its handle.

'Do you think that Boutrup knows any more?' she asked.

'Maybe.'

'Do you think he did it?'

'It's a possibility. But no, I don't think so.'

'Why not?'

He thought about how the girl had died. Bound, humiliated and disfigured. Whoever had done this had wanted to display his power.

'He's not angry enough. Or stupid enough.'

'Anything else?'

He had been annoyed with Peter Boutrup for turning up, even though he'd given him the mobile. Boutrup had seen him in the harbour with Gry. He had felt pathetic. He felt as though someone had taken a 1,100-degree hot iron and branded *him*. But Peter Boutrup had shown solidarity. 'They'll have you by the nuts if you're not careful,' he had said and turned it into a man versus woman thing.

'He's all right,' he said.

She got up, nodded and walked towards the door.

'Thank you, Mark.'

'You're welcome.'

That was all. She pressed the door handle. He wanted to tell her they should quickly check the mobile to be sure it really had belonged to Ramses. Then they had to track down all of Ramses' contacts and their contacts again, if at all possible. A released repeat offender shot in the chest and a young girl branded, bound and submerged in the sea with a face like a piece of raw meat: he was becoming increasingly convinced that the two killings were connected. But she hadn't asked him about that, so he hadn't told her. He paced up and down his office, his mind turning over the information Gry had given him by the hotel. The sudden arrival of the three unknown women. One of them had looked like Nina Bjerre.

He took a piece of chewing gum from the packet on the table and sat for a while shuffling sheets of paper back and forth. He had to concentrate. Others could deal with the routine workload: a spate of robberies in town. His thoughts returned to the previous night. He had to find Gry again. And this time it wasn't to have sex with her. Or not only.

34

STINGER'S CONDITION WAS unchanged, and there wasn't a doctor in sight. There was just the skinny man in the bed with arms like matchsticks and tubes all over the place. It made a strange contrast to Elisabeth's enormous body perched on the edge of the bed, which was perilously close to capsizing. She was heavy-hearted, despondent, lost to the world; her eyes drooped and her fleshy cheeks were swollen with grief. All she and Stinger really had was each other.

'What's going on, Peter? What's he mixed up in?'

Peter shook his head.

'I don't know. He's in way over his head.'

He had called Manfred again and asked for time off. He felt bad about it, but Manfred was a friend and he understood. He had called in another carpenter to work on Røjel's roof, and Peter was free to return to work whenever he was ready.

'Sounds like you've got enough on your plate,' Manfred remarked.

'And Jutta?' Peter had asked. 'How's her friend?'

He had called Manfred when he got to the hospital and he savoured the whine of the workshop chainsaw in the background. Hospital sounds were the last things he wanted to hear, but he felt obliged to visit Stinger. Stinger wasn't just his friend; he also held the key to the riddle of everything that had happened, and Peter had to get his hands on it.

On the telephone he heard Manfred switch off the chainsaw.

'They're still hoping, I suppose, now that they know it wasn't Nina's body in the harbour,' Manfred said. But Peter could tell from his voice it was a very faint hope.

'By the way,' Manfred said. 'I hope you're looking after yourself.'

Was he? Perhaps he should drop everything.

'Have you finished the Steinbeck?'

'Yes,' Manfred said. 'Not a happy ending. But you already knew that.'

'Remember, it's only fiction.'

'Of course,' Manfred said. 'Real life is different.'

'I'll be back at work tomorrow,' Peter said. 'You can count on it.'

He still had Manfred's voice in his ear when he returned to Elisabeth. Again he saw what he had seen on the day he had been looking for Stinger: her obesity and her shapeless clothing, but also her form of vanity – her tattoos. On her arms and the small of her back and in other places too, no doubt. Not Stinger's workmanship.

'You were a biker chick once, weren't you? Didn't you use to hang out with some sort of club?'

She nodded, but he could see she was on her guard.

'Do you still see them?'

'Nope. They were a bunch of wankers. But getting out was tough.'

'Like it is for Anja?'

She didn't reply, but he could see he had hit home.

'Those are some impressive tattoos you've got. Are they from back then?'

She smiled as though he had said she was beautiful.

'We all had them. It was part of the whole thing.' She giggled like a teenager. 'Stinger went ape.'

'Where do girls like you go to get your tattoos?'

He told her about the dead girl in the harbour and her fleur-de-lis.

'Rollo's Kennel in Vestergade. He's the best. I'm going there soon to get another one.'

Peter eyed Stinger in bed.

'Watch out, he might hear you.'

She smiled through her tears.

'What has he got himself mixed up in this time?'

He wished he could help. But what would it involve? Deep down, what he really wanted was to stay out of it.

'What a pile of shit,' she said.

What could he say? He looked at her without speaking and she reached across the bed and touched his shirt collar, as if she wanted to hug him but didn't know how.

'Stinger's not a bad person,' she said. 'He's all right.'

'I know that.'

He owed Stinger that. Perhaps she was expecting it, too. Everyone expected it, including Felix, who had hooked him with her boyish little figure and eyes like My's, which saw straight through him.

'I'll try to find out,' he promised and cursed his sense of responsibility.

Elisabeth held out her hand, and when he returned her hand-shake, he knew he was sealing his own accursed fate.

After leaving the hospital he went to see Miriam in Anholtsgade and told her about the fleur-de-lis.

'Some African prostitutes are branded,' she said. She had pulled him down to her on the sofa, but he stayed put on the edge.

'In Denmark?'

She nodded. 'As far as we're concerned they're the competi-tion, but many of them aren't here of their own free will. Someone has trafficked them, like they traded slaves in the old days. Sometimes the owners brand them. Barbaric, isn't it? Like putting a barcode on consumer goods.'

'Barbaric, certainly. Great line of business you're in.'

She looked upset and he regretted his remark.

'Sorry.'

'What's up with you?'

She reached up to his face and a finger traced the line around his mouth. He sat very still. She removed her hand.

'Is it Felix?'

He couldn't say yes or no.

'What's going on?'

He realised he couldn't say it out loud. He didn't want to hurt her, but even so it was as if every sentence he uttered diminished her.

'You're suffering from Stockholm syndrome,' she said at last. 'You've heard about that, haven't you?'

He knew what it was. The term was coined after a bank robbery in Stockholm. The robber's hostages became so attached to him that, later, they defended him.

'Perhaps it works both ways?' she suggested. 'Both for the kidnapper and the kidnapped?'

'No one has been kidnapped.'

She arched her eyebrows.

'You're practically living together. Feelings grow.'

He made an attempt to change the subject.

'Her husband was the managing director of Kjær Entreprise,' he said. 'A big construction company in Højbjerg. Erik Gomez Andersen. Does that name mean anything to you?'

Miriam was puzzled by the name but only briefly.

'No, not off the . . .'

She clicked one fingernail against another.

'Perhaps you could ask around?' he asked her.

She nodded and picked at a seemingly perfect nail.

'I don't suppose that could do any harm.'

She looked at him.

'You're saying she doesn't remember anything?'

'So she says. But I think her memory's coming back.'

Again she caressed his cheek, this time scratching him with her nails.

'You take care,' she whispered. 'Don't forget you've got enemies out there.'

He drove home to Felix and Kaj. That evening they sat talking, Felix curled up in her chair with her hooded eyes resting on him. In one way they were alike, he thought. She had lost her old life. He had never really had one.

Yes, he had enemies, he thought, as he took the dog out for the last walk of the night. The snow glinted in the darkness while the waves crashed down over the ice on the beach and against the cliff. But how could his enemies be connected with recent events, with Stinger's hospitalisation, Ramses' death and the young girl in the harbour? Was the whole thing just chance, here, where he lived, on his doorstep? Or was there a pattern, a plan? Surely that was what Miriam had been hinting at – that somehow everything was about him. But if that was the case, what could it be?

'Come on. In you go.'

He got the dog inside and followed. It was going to be another cold night. The stars were out. The forecast said the temperature would be down to minus fourteen.

Lying in his sleeping bag on the balcony with Kaj by his side, he discovered what was troubling him. It had been bubbling just beneath the surface. He thought about Ramses' mobile and the names and numbers it contained. He knew from Elisabeth that Ramses had been close to Lily Klein. He wriggled out of his sleeping bag and went downstairs to find the note he had written with the names of the contacts. No Lily. No name or number.

35

FELIX STEPPED OUT of the shower and reached for the towel. Then she got dressed and went into the kitchen. She made tea, ate some toast and a banana and ignored the temptation to lie down and let tiredness take over. She thought about the endless days she had spent without food or any inclination to do anything but float off into nothingness. Those days were gone. She knew when the turning point had been: waking up with the organ music in her ears and the sobs that had overpowered her, the tears that had flown freely.

It was as if they had washed away her self-pity and her guilty conscience at having survived. What remained was the burning desire to find out what Erik had been up to and what had caused the accident that cost Maria and him their lives. That was the difference: she was no longer thinking about herself. She was thinking about Maria.

Well, a little bit about him too: about Peter. As she ate, she slipped the dog titbits, knowing full well it would annoy him. He was strict with the dog. He was also strict with her, and with himself, she guessed. He was quite different from any other man she had ever known. Unyielding, persistent. He had seen her in the most pitiful of all situations and he had treated her with respect.

'Here, boy.'

She threw a piece of cheese to Kaj, and he caught it in mid-air, his eyes glinting with mischief.

'We won't tell anyone, will we?'

She scratched him between his ears and felt envious. Kaj was alone in being allowed to share his bed. She had considered it one night when lust had started flowing through her veins and sent thoughts of him racing to her brain. She had wondered how he might react if she went upstairs and slid into his sleeping bag, just like that. But her courage had failed her and she had ended up relishing the fact of her lust and the feeling that her body wanted something the rest of her might not be quite ready for yet.

But the lust had been there and that in itself was a triumph. With that and the previous day's events at the back of her mind she felt ready, even though her body was still weak. She let the dog out and watched it running around on the cliff before letting it back in. Then she walked to her car and drove off with a squeal of tyres.

As she drove, she let back in the memory of the day that had turned her life upside down.

It had been a beautiful summer's day. The sun was baking hot and Maria's school holidays had started. They walked around the house in shorts, sleeveless tops and sandals, and Erik had put on a mint-green short-sleeved polo shirt. There was a sense of anticipation running through the whole family, or at least that was how it felt to her. Perhaps she was happy.

They flew in the helicopter across the sea towards the island of Samsø. She remembered her own impatience. She wanted Erik to fly faster, just get them to Samsø and land the big metal insect as Maria described it: 'It looks like a dragonfly, Daddy, can't you see?'

But Erik didn't land the helicopter. Instead he found a spot, a specific spot, it struck her, where he circled over the water at a very low altitude. He checked the instruments and entered numbers into the GPS. He said something over the noise which she couldn't quite hear because Maria was chatting away in a loud voice, pointing down at the ships, the yachts and the water skiers. They were close to an island. Hesselø, probably. And then the summer's day, the idyllic scene, the blue sky and the even bluer sea was transformed into panic, death and destruction. The helicopter started to spiral downwards.

Felix gripped the steering wheel tightly as she recalled the vortex and the crash. Sweat began to pour off her. Her heart was pounding. She had to use all her energy to turn the picture off. It was the past. She was in the future now. She was on her way.

On reaching Højbjerg, she turned into Oddervej. The road was a slushy brown, but on the verges the snow was still virgin and surprisingly white. Trees and bushes in the gardens were heavily laden and clad in white, and the traffic moved up the hill at a snail's pace. She indicated, turned left and parked by the church. Then she got out, opened the cemetery gate and went inside.

She remembered the place exactly – just as well, because everything was hidden under snow. Only the tops of headstones protruded, and she had to brush snow off the red stone so that she could see the inscription:

Erik Gomez Andersen 23/11 1965–22/7 2009
Maria Gomez Andersen 1/5 2003–22/7 2009
Loved and missed

She stood gazing at it. Loved and missed. Sally, Erik's secretary, had suggested the wording. She had thought it was fitting. Was it really, though?

The loss of Maria had only just begun to make itself felt. What about Erik? Was he loved and missed? She stared at his name and tried to remember him, his skin, his voice, the way he moved. She tried to miss him, but her anger was stronger.

Something inside her screamed at him that everything was his fault. Why was he circling? Why did he have mistresses? Why didn't he put his family first?

'What made you do it?'

She said it and it felt good. She wanted to scream it out loud. She had never felt like this before.

She looked around. She was the only person in the cemetery. She sank to her knees. Maria's name danced in front of her eyes and Felix remembered her sweet smell when she was a baby, sleeping in her arms, warm, her pale, delicate skin and her thick, black hair. Tiny hands moving as she slept, reaching out for a comforting finger to hold on to. A tiny rosebud of a mouth, red against her pale complexion.

She leaned on the headstone for support. For the second time, sobs took hold of her and shook her body until she noticed she was so cold her fingertips were numb, even inside her gloves. She wanted to stand up, but a sudden impulse made her run her hand across the headstone once more. From there it was no great leap to remove the snow around the stone, and she uncovered a tiny moss heart and a nightlight in a closed glass cube. The truth hit home. Of course. She wasn't the only person to love Maria and Erik. She had hidden herself away, but other people also felt grief and pain. Others were left with the loss, and there were so many questions unanswered.

She struggled up and walked back to the car. Behind the wheel, she had to lean against the headrest and relax for a couple of minutes. Then she drove down Oddervej, to the other side of Højbjerg, until the red buildings of Kjær Entreprise A/S emerged from the winter mist.

She hadn't been there since Erik's death. Where had she been? She didn't remember. Had she buried herself at home, in a dark room? Who had looked after her? What had really happened in the weeks and months following the accident?

She parked and went into reception, where the girls sent her smiles of recognition and let her take the lift to the second floor. But someone else was sitting in Erik's old office now, of course. A man by the name of Mads Bendtsen, according to the sign. He must have been brought in from outside, she thought. He wasn't anyone she knew, but the secretary's name was still the same and she was in the front office, or so the sign said: Sally Mortensen. Except that she wasn't.

Felix entered. Everything was neat and tidy.

'Oh, hello!'

Sally rushed in like a whirlwind. She was wearing a smart black trouser suit and a cobalt-blue T-shirt with some kind of print motif.

They hugged and Sally held her at arm's length. Questions came flooding out of Felix.

'What happened, Sally? How did I get through the first period? Were you there? You were, weren't you? You made things happen.'

Sally nodded.

'Of course I was there. I dealt with most of the practicalities.'

'Erik's office things. Where are they?'

'I've had them all packed for you. They're boxed up in the basement.'

'Could you show me? Then I can take them with me.'

'But . . .'

Felix was propelled towards the door on a burst of energy.

'Come on. We might as well do it now.'

Sally followed. 'I'm not sure I've got a key.'

'Oh, we'll just get it from Olsen in reception,' Felix said. 'Perhaps he could give us a hand carrying them to my car.'

Afterwards, she wasn't entirely sure how she had managed to organise it all. But with Olsen's key in her hand and Sally's help, they went down to the basement and found the storage area. Erik's name was on three boxes, which Sally pointed out.

'I could help you go through it all,' Sally offered.

'That's very kind of you.' Felix hugged her and inhaled the scent of her perfume. 'But I think I can manage.'

When she got home, she managed to lug the boxes inside the house. Afterwards she had to sit down and catch her breath as realisation set in. This was just the first step. There was no way back now; on the contrary, there would be more. She had no idea what was happening to the house in Skåde, which she had literally fled. Maria's room, Erik's personal papers and belongings. The family home. How would she ever bear to unravel the past? But in time it would all be there.

She got up and made a pot of tea. Then she made herself comfortable on some cushions and opened the first box.

36

Late in the afternoon, Kir and Niklas were lifting weights at the gym. Down in the harbour a team of divers was still searching, but soon it would be dark and the search would be suspended. After the news that they were still looking for Nina Bjerre and after a long day searching practically the entire harbour, their mood had hit rock bottom. Sitting in the diving truck and drinking coffee, Kir had suggested to Niklas they take out their frustrations on the weights in the gym and he had agreed.

'Another five. You can do it!'

She knew she was a good instructor. Niklas was lying on the bench grappling with the iron bar. Sweat poured from his face and his expression was one of grim determination. Slowly he raised and lowered the weight and exhaled.

'And again!'

He sent her a pleading look. He had hit a wall.

'Yes, you can do it!'

He clenched his teeth and pushed the weight up again. The muscles in his upper body tensed, accompanied by a roar of pain this time.

'No more.'

'Just one. Come on! We'll go for a beer afterwards.'

He managed to raise the bar again and held it for a quarter of a second before lowering it. His arms were glistening with sweat.

'One more and I'll buy you dinner.'

He grinned.

'We're on expenses.'

'Oh, that's right, I forgot. I'll buy you another beer then.'

'I don't drink and you know that very well.'

Of course she did. Mine clearance divers drank only in moderation and often not at all, certainly not during an op. She drank only the occasional glass of wine or beer, rarely more than a unit or two, and never if she was going to work the next day. She looked at Niklas. He was a man and there was nothing wrong with his body, but in her eyes he was still just a boy and an innocent in so many ways. Sex briefly crossed her mind, but she wasn't going to get involved in anything that could become complicated. So what could she bribe him with?

'A Coke, then! At my brother's pub. And I'll wipe the floor with you at pool.'

'Coke,' he repeated, pushing the weight up with everything he had in him. 'But I'll thrash you, you know that.'

This was after he had lowered the bar and was gasping for air. She slapped him with her towel.

'OK. See you after the shower.'

She had always been a tomboy. Dolls interested her only to the extent that she could encase them in rubber, put a mask and flippers on them and lower them into water. She had lost count of the number of dolls she had destroyed in various sinks and bathtubs.

Kir turned off the shower and reached for the towel to dry herself. The desire for physical intimacy returned. It had been a long time since she broke up with Kasper. At the age of thirty-two, she still considered love an unfathomable concept.

She stepped out of the shower, wrapped a towel around her hair and started getting dressed. Possibly, she wondered, not for the first time, it might be easier to fall in love with a girl who understood her lifestyle rather than throw herself into doomed relationships with men who were unable to grasp the idea that you could be a woman and a mine clearance diver at the same time. She had, in all honesty, met men who, when told what she did for a living, had reacted with the same shock as if she had announced that she was a serial killer. Romantically speaking, she hadn't done herself any favours with her choice of career.

She dried her short curls with the towel and looked at herself in the mirror. It wasn't that she didn't care about her appearance, and if needs must, she could even wear a little make-up. A discreet day cream to match her very pale skin, a dab of brown kohl around her eyes and brown mascara. On her lips a little pink gloss. Nothing major, nothing loud. That wouldn't complement her chestnut hair and freckles. It had to be subdued and downplayed, just like her style in clothes. Jeans and a smart shirt and she was happy. It worked for her. Simple, easy and quick to put on and take off. She loved the feel of the tight-fitting diving suit under water. Paradoxically, however, she hated the sense of feeling trapped in clothing.

They had bubble and squeak – Niklas's choice – at a small café in town, then went in her car to the harbour and Red's pub, the Bull's Eye. Niklas had cheered up after the workout and seemed quite jolly.

'Christ, you know how to motivate me. Why don't you come over to Kongsøre to train us?'

She grinned.

'You wouldn't be able to handle it. You're all a bunch of sissies.'

'What was it like the time you were there, when you started at Kongsøre? I guess you were the only girl?'

She nodded and blinked.

'I enjoyed it. All those men.'

'Weren't you bullied?'

She shook her head.

'No. I don't think so.'

He smiled. When he did that, she could really see the boy he still was.

'No, I doubt you were. You'd just have told them to put another five on the weights and then stick them where the sun didn't shine.'

Red was behind the bar. She introduced him to Niklas and they ordered a couple of Cokes. The financial crisis was biting here and had done ever since the pub opened. A couple of lovers were sitting at a corner table; she had a glass of wine, he had a large draught beer. Apart from that, there were only a couple of young men playing darts. Niklas and Kir found a table a little further away. His question had started the film inside her rolling and she began to tell him about her early days.

She could remember everything from the very beginning, her first day at Kongsøre Torpedo Station, where the frogmen and mine clearance divers were trained. There had been four of them in this latest intake and, yes, she was the only girl. There had been other female recruits on the mine clearance diver course before, but not this time. Few women had the stamina for the job or were interested in the combination of diving and explosives. But she had not only listened to Hannibal's stories, she had also seen every film in existence and read every book she could get her hands on about high-risk mine diving. She already knew a fair bit about a variety of mines in Danish waters. She knew what mines reacted to: magnetism, acoustics and pressure – and she knew that during their training they would be issued with the best, most expensive equipment, especially designed down to the tiniest detail without a hint of magnetic material. Everything from zips to diving packs, and the weights that held them down, was made to their own exacting specifications. These packs cost 300,000 kroner. You would usually see bubbles on the surface of the water when an ordinary diver breathed, but you could barely see where a mine clearance diver was. The oxygen apparatus reused the air six to seven times and released only tiny bubbles – not because it was necessarily essential for them to be invisible, but because the tiny bubbles made hardly any sound when they burst. For the same reason the rubber dinghy was low-noise and non-magnetic.

It was all this and a whole lot more that had kept her dream alive. As a girl, she had read comics handed down to her by Red: *Superman*, *Batman* and *Spiderman*. She had loved them, but felt she was missing an underwater hero. She imagined herself as a silent protective dolphin gliding through dark waters, quiet, calm and confident. Being a mine clearance diver was the closest she could get to being a superhero in her imagination.

Niklas grinned from ear to ear after she'd told him this.

'Super Kir!'

'Don't you dare tell anyone!'

They played pool and she gave him such a drubbing that she started to feel sorry for him and let him win. They drank more Coke, more customers began to turn up, and little by little the pub started to feel as it should: a place where you could hide in the crowd, drink what you wanted and then make a discreet exit.

Niklas had gone back to his hotel and she was in the bar chatting to Red when she saw Mark Bille Hansen walk through the door. Her initial thought was that he had come to question Red about something, but then she realised that even a police officer might need a beer, because he sat down on a stool by the bar. Red pulled a large beer for him and exchanged a few words before addressing another customer. She stared, knowing it was wrong, but she couldn't help herself. Mark Bille was like an exotic stranger here, surrounded by provincial dreariness. She was fascinated by what he did, the way he drank his beer and sat at the bar without displaying any insecurity. He stood out. She recognised that quality from herself.

He looked up and caught sight of her. There was no time to

withdraw her gaze, so she merely blinked and kept staring. He nodded and raised his beer. She took a sip of Coke. They looked at each other. Then he got up, came over and stood beside her.

'Are you on your own?'

'It's my brother's pub.'

She nodded towards Red, who was pouring foaming beer from the barrel.

'I was here with a colleague, but he went home,' she explained and added, 'I'm working tomorrow.'

He nodded.

'So you didn't find anything today?'

'Nope.'

'You were right,' he said then. 'Something didn't add up.'

She blushed. She did this easily and it had been a torment all her life.

'It doesn't make things easier,' she said. 'Now there might be two dead women.'

He nodded. There was something unabashedly hungry about the look he sent her, and she sensed his presence all the way from her hands and feet to the skin under her hair.

'They must have been similar,' she said, mostly to keep the conversation going so that he wouldn't walk away. 'Could it be a coincidence?'

He shrugged. He seemed tangible and distant at the same time. It was as if something needed to be released, but couldn't find a way out.

'Young blondes. Almost identical height and build. That could be a coincidence, of course.'

'How long was she in the water?' Kir asked.

'Pathologist reckons a couple of days.'

'So New Year's Eve fits?'

He nodded. They looked at each other and suddenly she knew they'd had exactly the same thought and were thinking it for the first time.

'Nina could have walked by and seen a girl being thrown in,' Kir said. 'She was a witness, so the killer grabbed her and threw her in as well.'

She sensed her own excitement and started talking faster.

'He didn't have time to do to her what he did to the other girl: tie her up and weigh her down. That's why she's not there. The current would have taken her.'

His eyes had narrowed to slits. He leaned over to her. Her heart was pounding madly.

'That's what I'm thinking. You're good, Kir.'

His lips tickled her ear. When he straightened up again, his eyes were telling her quite a lot more than she wanted to know. But then there was a rumpus outside on the pavement and he turned to look out of the window, to where a young girl in a buttock-skimming dress and a bum-freezer jacket was having an argument with an older man. No prizes for guessing what the drama was about.

Mark Bille forgot all about his beer and went outside. Kir watched him break up the quarrel between the punter and the prostitute, who either hadn't been paid or was annoyed about something. Shortly afterwards, the customer drove off in his car, but Mark Bille stayed behind to talk to the girl, who lit up a cigarette and waved it around in an agitated manner, making patterns in the darkness. Their frozen breath mingled to form bigger clouds that rose and dispersed in the pub's neon light above the entrance. Mark Bille nodded and even smiled. Then he took the girl by the elbow and led her across the road into the hotel. Kir waited, not sure what she had just witnessed, expecting him to return at any moment. She stood by the window for a quarter of an hour, then another. But he didn't come back.

37

WHEN PETER CAME home after work, his arms weighed down with shopping bags, Felix was sitting on the floor rummaging through boxes. Her cheeks were glowing and her eyes sparkling in a way he hadn't seen before. There was an almost manic intensity to her movements as she picked items out of the boxes, only to throw them back in again.

'Nothing!'

She reached for a mug beside her on the floor. Tea, he guessed. She was an inveterate tea drinker and as such belonged to a tribe of people he didn't understand.

She stood up. She was wearing jeans and a dark blue T-shirt. Her breasts were pushed up by her bra, which he hadn't seen her wear before. Her clothes hung loosely and her trousers were gathered in at the waist by a tight belt, but her voice was energetic.

'Are you busy at the moment?' she asked.

'No. I thought we were going to cook dinner together?'

'Would you mind coming with me to the house in Århus?'

'Now?'

'Yes, now! I have to know what happened. Why Erik and Maria had to die.'

She moved closer to him. Her perfume wafted into his nostrils and he recognised something he'd felt about her from the day they first met – her willpower and ability to latch on to him.

She tugged at his jumper.

'I'm ready now.'

He knew that feeling only too well. You reached a point where you had to know. Even if the truth was grim and painful. 'OK.'

He put the shopping bags down on the kitchen table.

'When we've cooked dinner and I've seen you eat half of it.'

It was a part of town he knew only from the surface. No one he knew had ever lived in Skåde, and the further they entered the complex of steep, winding residential roads, the more he understood why: people like him didn't own this type of house. Some of the residences resembled Gothic castles with towers and spires. He and his friends lived in badly maintained flats in the city centre, in social housing ghettos, or paid 500,000 kroner for a derelict cottage on Djursland, which they then did up.

It was nine o'clock when Felix and Peter parked outside the house set back behind a tall hedge at the end of a cul-de-sac. It was a dark night, but street lamps and the snow lit up the area, showing where responsible house owners had cleared the pavements and shovelled the white mounds to the sides. The snow also weighed down the branches of the tall spruces surrounding the three-storey house. The sounds of suburban living reached their ears as they got out. Excited, happy voices. Somewhere behind the undulating terrain there had to be a hill where you could go tobogganing. In next door's garden they could see the outline of a snowman. Somewhere a dog was barking and a female voice called out into the night.

Felix rummaged around in her bag for the key and he could tell from her deep breaths that she was trying to summon the courage she had felt before they left Djursland.

'It's been a long time. It feels very alien and yet at the same time . . .'

They walked up the garden path to the front door. A security light caught them in its beam halfway there. Felix entered a code, pushed open the door and they stepped inside a hallway with a high ceiling. The house reminded Peter of the English country manor in Cluedo.

'Erik loved this house,' Felix practically whispered as they moved from room to room.

Peter was no expert, but he thought everything looked seriously expensive. In prison he had worked in the carpentry workshop. The furniture here was of quite a different calibre and most certainly came from the house of one of the renowned Danish furniture designers: Børge Mogensen, Arne Jacobsen or Hans Wegener. He knew the names. He had studied them in books at the prison library. Fiction or non-fiction, he had devoured both with equal hunger. At school, a teacher had encouraged him to read. Sebastian Warming was his name and he had a big black beard. One day he had put *Robinson Crusoe* into Peter's hand and told him it was a story about survival against all the odds. After that he had read *Treasure Island*, then *Oliver Twist* and *David Copperfield* and other stories about boys or men who overcame life's trials and tribulations. This was how books had become an indispensable part of his life.

Felix held an office chair and rotated it. It made a soft creaking noise.

'I think I was always a little frightened by all the money it cost us to run this place. I was scared we wouldn't be able to pay the bills, but Erik always dealt with that side of things.'

She sat down on the office chair and swivelled around. Her face hardened.

'I was an idiot. Look at this. No one can afford a house like this, even if they're a managing director on a good salary, unless they've got other sources of income.'

'What sources would that be?'

'That's precisely what I'm asking myself.'

She got up. 'The police took away a lot of stuff, but they've returned most of it. They were obviously looking for a cause for the crash, because they failed to identify a technical fault.

We had plenty of fuel and visibility was good. Come on, let me show you Maria's room.'

They went up the staircase and down the landing. Maria's room was a typical girl's bedroom with several Disney posters of characters he didn't recognise on the walls. There were teddy bears on the pink bedspread and the curtains were also pink. Felix stood for a brief moment without saying anything. Peter searched for some suitable words to say, but all he could manage was a brusque, masculine presence.

'Maybe we should have a look at Erik's study, if he had one. I don't think we'll find where the money came from here.'

Looking hurt and vulnerable, she sat on the bed, took one of the teddy bears and hugged it.

'This was her favourite teddy. She called it Toben.' She held the teddy at arm's length. 'Perhaps it should have been in the coffin with her.'

Her voice was thick. Peter looked away, at the flower tendrils on the wallpaper coiling up towards the ceiling and around the white bookcase.

'I wasn't there to make the decision. I was in hospital.'

At length she got up. He would have liked to say or do something kind. Something more than kind. But the moment passed and she walked on to the landing still holding the teddy.

Downstairs, she showed him Erik's study. If Maria's bedroom had been typical of a six-year-old girl's, Erik's room was typical of a man with a top job and a high level of self-esteem.

Here, they found themselves in veritable Cluedo territory: the room was like an imitation of a gentleman's study, with a massive mahogany desk, a high-backed swivel chair in black leather, floor-to-ceiling bookcases in dark wood and what looked like a Persian rug on the floor. The walls were painted ox-blood red and there was a lamp with a green glass shade on the desk. In the middle was a laptop.

'Perhaps you should take it with you?'

She shrugged.

'I could, but the police confiscated it, so if there was anything on it, they'd probably have found it.'

Peter looked around. The books were packed spine to spine. Many were bound in leather, the majority biographies of industrialists and thick tomes about economics and politics.

'What are we looking for?' he asked. 'If we are looking for something, that is.'

He perched on the edge of the desk. Felix flopped on to the chair and swivelled from side to side with the teddy bear on her lap.

'I don't know how thorough the police search was,' she said. 'Don't forget Erik wasn't a suspect. He was killed in the crash. They never found a cause, and I suppose there wasn't really anything suspicious about him.'

'So you don't think they did a detailed search of his study? Took all the books out? Discovered secret compartments in the desk?'

She shook her head.

'Why would they? They might have done a superficial search, checked his diary and computer to see if he had any enemies.'

She started opening desk drawers and pulling out piles of paper from them.

'Anyway, what would they be looking for?'

They rifled through some of the paperwork without finding anything to attract their attention. There were tax forms, receipts, old diaries, notepads and folders containing contracts and covering letters. They flicked through them, but found nothing of interest.

Felix pulled out a notebook, black moleskin held together with a black elastic binder. She removed the elastic and opened the book. Inside it Erik had kept scraps of paper – a receipt from the dentist, various private telephone numbers and a couple of business cards from restaurants and a hairdresser.

A folded piece of paper fell out and Peter picked it up. 'What's that?'

He unfolded it and showed it to her. She frowned.

'East Jutland Prison,' she read, sounding baffled. 'Application to visit.'

She looked at him: 'Who would he want to visit there?'

38

MARK DRAGGED GRY over to the hotel room window.

Her face was devoid of expression. Her jaws were working without cease on a piece of chewing gum and the fingers of her right hand kept twisting locks of hair.

'Can you see it? Can you see the water in the harbour? Salt water freezes at minus one-point-eight degrees. The entire marina is covered in ice. If you fall into that, you'll be dead within a few minutes, if not seconds.'

He shook her, but not nearly as violently as he wanted to. Her fragility, defiance and the slight fear in her eyes caused his lust to swell. It didn't make him feel proud and he tried to ignore it.

'You walk around down there every night. It's pure chance that separates you from Nina Bjerre. You could've ended up in the freezing water. You still can.'

'Let me go. You're hurting me.'

'And for what? For some loose change, for the next packet of fags or the next joint? You're bloody pathetic. Get a life.'

She tore herself loose. His blood was pumping hard.

'You get a life.'

'I'm trying to find the killer.'

'You're sick in the head, do you know that?'

'He's out there.'

Mark grabbed hold of her again and pushed her up against the window pane. He pointed out of the window.

'He might kill again. In a provincial dump like this, who are the easiest victims? Girls working the streets – and you know it. No one wants to know about them. No one will miss them because their parents don't really know what their daughters are up to.'

She recoiled. He carried on: 'Does your mother know where you are? Does she know what you do? When did you last speak to her?'

She sniffed. Possibly because she had a cold or else because she was on the verge of tears.

'Now tell me about the three girls who turned up. What were their names? What did they look like?'

She sat down on the bed and crossed her legs. She would have looked young and innocent had it not been for the far too worldly gaze skulking behind the heavy eye make-up. She was neither innocent nor naive. She took a cigarette from her small bag.

'This is a non-smoking room.'

'Stop me if you can.'

She lit the cigarette with a plastic lighter, her hands shaking. Her voice was, too.

'Her name was Tora, the girl who looked like Nina.'

'What else?'

'I don't know her surname.'

'And the others?'

She shook her head.

'Lily, I think. Or Lilian. Something like that.'

'Describe her.'

'Short and dark with a lot of piercings. I've never seen so many before. Short, spiky hair.'

'And the third one?'

Gry sat for a while rocking her leg. Suddenly her face cracked into a childish grin.

'She had a mullet,' she said. 'Layered at the top and long at the back, you know. It looked like a train wreck, but she thought it looked great. And she was a big girl.'

'Fat?'

'No. Just . . . big.'

'Why did you let them join you? Were they allowed to make money here?'

She shook her head.

'They weren't on the game. They had their own cash. They just hung out with us.'

'Hung out?'

'It was like they were waiting for something. They were dead cool. We only saw them a couple of times.'

She took a long drag of her cigarette and exhaled.

'I don't know where they stayed, but we may well have had some shots together or done a few lines.'

'Coke?'

She smiled and pulled him closer.

'You won't tell anyone, will you?'

He wondered if she was high on something. She probably was.

'What about men? Did you see them with any?'

She seemed uninterested in the question.

'Men. They're always there.'

'Can you describe them?'

She made no reply.

'What happened to the girls?'

She stubbed out the cigarette in a small bowl on the bedside table and rubbed up against him. He wanted to push her away, but his body refused to obey.

'One day they were just gone. It happens,' she said, putting her hand on his crotch.

Her mouth was half open. He pushed her back on to the bed and put his hand up the short skirt. Her snatch was wet. Images rolled around inside his head, of Anna Bagger's stern face and Kir with her gappy teeth and red hair. He pushed them all away and buried himself in meaninglessness.

Afterwards, though, his moral hangover returned and he cursed it and himself roundly. Why did he constantly have to prove that he could do something most men in the world took for granted? Why was the casual encounter – the faceless fuck – so important to him?

Afterwards he took a shower, got dressed and zipped up his trousers. So much had been destroyed, that might be why, he thought. Everything was hopeless. It was tempting to finish the job and just screw everything up.

He paid her. She looked at him with dull eyes now.

'Will you order me a Coke?'

He left her on the bed with the TV blaring. In reception he asked them to send a Coke up to her. It wasn't until he was on the way back out in the cold that it struck him: perhaps this was how you had to think to kill. Perhaps you just had to be as indifferent as he was.

The thought still lingered as he sat in the hospital waiting room fifteen hours later. As always the scan had been pain-free. The worst was still to come.

As usual, he involuntarily started to take stock. When in his life had he ever been happy? The answer wasn't when he married Helle, he was absolutely sure about that. The marriage had been a mistake from day one, and she would undoubtedly agree with him. He had needed someone to show TLC and she had needed to give it. It hadn't been a question of infatuation or even love, but selfish needs on both sides. Helle was the nurse in his GP's practice. She was young and pretty and the first person to reach out to him when he'd been diagnosed two years ago. She was by his side after the op. From then on it could only go one way: into mutual dependency.

They had agreed she should stay in Copenhagen to keep the job she loved when he moved to Grenå, a tacit agreement that they were going their separate ways. The care and understanding had been exhausted. His illness had eaten it all up. Including what they'd never had.

Before Helle, there had been Anna. He took a random magazine from the stand in the waiting room. An old one, creased, with models in bikinis and swimsuits. One of the models seemed to him to have Anna Bagger's oval, angular face, her expression that was both provocative and prim. Anna could embody everything from frostiness to passion. Had he been happy in the time they had spent together, in the stolen moments when her husband was unaware, on a course, or when they were working together?

He had started getting symptoms, even then – at first without realising. His desire disappeared and more importantly his potency. He was ashamed and he retreated from her. He got the diagnosis the day before she broke off their relationship with an iciness that didn't touch him, because nothing did any longer.

'Mark Bille Hansen.'

The door had opened and the nurse had called him in.

Fifteen minutes later he drove back to Grenå and went straight to Anna Bagger's temporary office where she sat with her eyes glued to the screen and her mobile pressed against her ear.

Mark ignored her conversation.

'Her name is Tora. The woman in the harbour. She and two other girls were pulling punters in Grenå a month ago.'

Anna Bagger ended the call and put down her mobile.

'How do you know that?'

'Does it fit in anywhere?'

She nodded, her fingers tapping away on the keyboard like castanets.

'We've been contacted by a couple from Mors. They haven't had e-mail contact with their eighteen-year-old daughter for a week. Her name is Tora.'

She turned her laptop so that Mark could see.

'They thought she was staying with a girlfriend in Århus,

but it turned out to be a pack of lies. For six months she was sending false e-mails and photos of herself and her friend.'

A picture emerged from the screen of a young blonde. She was quite pretty, Mark thought, but she still looked like so many other teenage girls: blue eyes, straight nose, full lips and regular features. A small birthmark on her right cheek appeared to be her only distinguishing feature.

'So where was she really? For those six months?'

Anna Bagger shrugged.

'Who knows? The girlfriend says she has no idea. They only met a couple of times at a café and she couldn't understand why the girl had to take photos of every meeting they had. She didn't think they were that close.'

'And the brand? Anything about that?'

'Nothing.'

He pulled out a chair and sat down.

'You look pale. Are you ill?' she asked.

He nodded at first, but then shook his head. It didn't matter now.

'So we're talking about a girl who has actually been missing for six months. There have been signs of life in the form of false e-mails and photos, but no one really knows where she has been or what she's been doing, is that right?'

Anna Bagger laid both hands flat on the desk.

'Looks like it.'

39

ICE CRUNCHED UNDER the soles of Peter's boots. It was minus seven.

The fishing boats lined the jetty on both sides, ropes connecting them to their mooring posts like umbilical cords. The day was cloudless and the sunshine made the sea sparkle like blue silver and the piles of snow glisten. Hopeful gulls screamed out their hunger and circled close to the smell of fish on decks and in trawl nets. Otherwise all was quiet.

He walked along the jetty, his woollen hat pulled over his ears, and stopped at the end. He could see down to the empty ferry berth and the low grey buildings of the fish factory, and further to the left the ship cemetery where old vessels were scrapped.

A fisherman in an Icelandic sweater and rubber overalls was standing on the deck of his boat stacking crates. Peter greeted him, raising two fingers to his hat.

The fisherman nodded to the harbour entrance where the divers were working. Everyone in town now knew that the body they had found wasn't Nina Bjerre.

'Wonder if they'll find her today.'

'We can only hope,' Peter said.

'So you knew her, did you?'

'My boss did.'

The fisherman shook his head.

'I dread pulling in the net at the moment.'

Peter could well understand why. Nets didn't always catch just fish.

As if he had read Peter's thoughts, the fisherman said: 'Old mines and flotsam and jetsam, if you're lucky.'

He wiped the back of his glove under his nose.

'And wrecks?'

Peter was thinking of Brian's boat.

'Nah, we sail around them. Most of them are listed on the charts. Or at least the commercial vessels are.'

'But an ordinary motorboat might not be?'

The fisherman shook his head as he patted the railing of his boat.

'No, only boats like this one. And bigger ones. Small wrecks usually go undocumented.'

Peter was frozen. He turned his face to the light, but the sun still didn't have the strength to warm him. He really should be back at work, but restlessness and the many questions on his mind had driven him down to the harbour in his lunch break.

'What about if the water's shallow? Couldn't you get your boat torn to shreds, or the propeller caught on something?'

'No problem for dinghies or such like,' the fisherman said.

He stacked a crate on top of the others and looked as if he, too, had work to do.

'The Kattegat's deep.'

'Not everywhere, surely?'

'There are shallows, of course.'

The fisherman took another crate and started hosing it down. His voice rose over the noise: 'Out near Hesselø. Hastens Grund and Lille Lysegrund. You want to watch yourself there.'

Peter walked back to the car. He needed to get hold of a chart. If Brian had scuttled his boat in the hope of returning to it to retrieve a cargo, he wouldn't have done it in very deep waters. He knew the sea like the back of his hand. He would have picked the right spot for it.

He walked past the harbour office and found a shop selling ship's supplies. An old-fashioned bell rang when he pushed open the door and stepped into the warmth. From the back appeared a man of around fifty with glasses and unkempt grey hair, as though he had been pulling at it. He was chewing a matchstick.

'We're closed during the winter,' he said. 'I'm just doing a stock-take.'

'I'm looking for a chart.'

'Go on to the K&M homepage.'

The man took out the matchstick.

'Do you know how to read a chart?'

'No, I don't suppose I do,' Peter said. 'Do you need to?'

The man chuckled.

'Well, it helps. What are you looking for?'

'The shallows around Hesselø. Hastens Grund and Lille Lysegrund.'

'Then you'll want chart one-two-nine. Number five-zero-three, B and D.'

'I'm impressed.'

'Let's say I've got a head for numbers.'

The man returned the matchstick and held up a finger to indicate that Peter should wait. Then he opened a large drawer and rummaged around under the counter until he reappeared with a rolled-up piece of paper.

'No charge. We're such nice people here in Grenå.'

Peter unrolled the chart when he was back in his car. Stinger's six-figure tattoo matched one of the coordinates for Lille Lysegrund.

40

Kir didn't want to get mixed up in anything to do with the investigation. She didn't want to get caught between the local police and the detectives from Århus, and she most definitely didn't want to do anything that might bring her into contact with Mark Bille Hansen.

She left the group of divers and the depressed atmosphere at coming up empty-handed. Allan Vraa had ordered the big fibreglass boat in the water and they had dived in the deeper waters at the harbour entrance, but in vain. They had found nothing apart from tyres, a couple of bicycles, a pram and two shopping trolleys. The time was approaching when Århus Police would call off the search and pack them off home. It was expensive for a financially pressed police force to engage mine clearance divers plus equipment day after day.

She crossed the harbour and headed for town, dressed in camouflage gear and heavy boots. It was twelve hours since she had been in the Bull's Eye with Mark Bille Hansen and suddenly seen him rush out of the door and then disappear inside the hotel with a girl in tow. And there it was, right in front of her. The Strand Hotel. The building looked different, much more modest in daylight than when it was lit up at night. It irked her. Of course she was curious, and her pride was hurt, too. Of course she wondered why he would rather go to a hotel with a hooker than gaze deep into her eyes over a glass of beer. But c'est la vie. Anything was more feminine and sexier than a highly trained mine clearance diver with red hair and murder theories. Even a mini-skirted prostitute with a body like a beanpole could do more to ignite a weary police officer.

The hotel, painted in traditional warm Skagen yellow, stood bathed in the low sunshine. Icicles dripped from the gutter on to the pavement while the snow on the tiled roof held the building in a tight grip. It looked empty and indeed there were few cars in the car park. Winter in the provinces, Kir thought. Many hotels and restaurants simply closed down, and those that stayed open were marking time. There were only a few cars in Kattegatvej as well. They drove slowly on a surface of dirty slush and sleet. Opposite the hotel, she saw one of Red's staff moving chairs and tables about inside the Bull's Eye. She saw him take out a bucket and mop, then she turned around and started walking back.

But she didn't get very far. From the open windows on the first floor of the hotel she heard the sound of a Hoover starting, followed by a scream.

Reacting automatically, she ran around the corner to the entrance and pushed open the door to the lobby. There was no one around, so she darted up the stairs to the first floor. Halfway down the corridor she found an abandoned trolley loaded with clean linen and detergents. Then a girl came running towards her. She was wearing a pale blue uniform and her black hair was pinned up. Her eyes were wide with shock. Another girl, also Asian, and in a pale blue uniform, followed.

'What's going on?'

Kir took charge. Perhaps it was her camouflage gear that did it. The girl in shock pointed to the door of Room 103. She didn't say a word, just stared at Kir with big eyes.

Kir looked around. There was still no one else around. No receptionist. No one to take control. She pushed open the door. At first glance she saw nothing. The bed was messy, the bed linen crumpled, there was an empty bottle of Coke and a half-full glass on the bedside table. The window was open and it was freezing cold. Even so there was a strange, sweet smell.

The body lay in a corner, a ghost of the body from the harbour. The face was gone. Someone had ripped off the skin. A scarf had been pulled tight around the girl's neck. Her tongue hung out. It was blue. Her short skirt had ridden up around her hips; her panties had been pulled down around her ankles and the body lay exposed as though ready for more humiliation.

'What's wrong?'

An authoritative voice cut through the shock. But authoritative as it was, and deep, it was still shaking. Kir calmly introduced herself to the man.

'I'll call the police,' she said, taking out a mobile. 'Nobody touch anything. Leave the room exactly as it was. What's your name?'

She looked at his badge: Morten Hansen. Reception. 'Morten. I'll stay here outside the room. No one is to leave the building. The police will want to talk to anyone who's been here in the last twenty-four hours.'

She nodded to him. 'Could you contact guests who left last night?'

At first he looked dubious, but then he did as he was told. Ten minutes later she heard the sirens and soon after footsteps stomped up the stairs.

'Tell me it's not true.'

Mark Bille Hansen and another local police officer stared at her. She glared back. Mark Bille's normally dark face was pale. 'And what are you doing here?'

She met his gaze and saw his anger and panic in one confused expression. She attempted a composed answer: 'I was just passing.'

The policemen went inside. Kir went to follow them, but bumped into the junior officer's back as he was brought up short.

'Bloody hell!'

The officer covered his mouth and his body went into convulsions. Mark Bille turned around and looked at his partner.

'If you're going to throw up, then please do it outside. We don't want any more DNA here than we already have.'

The officer staggered past Kir and out of the door and they heard him double up in the corridor. Mark Bille looked at her.

'How much do you know?'

Her mind raced to sort through what needed to be said and what should remain unsaid. But it was no use. Everything came out in one single sentence.

'You were with her.'

Suddenly he looked tired, as though he might decide to lie down on the floor next to the dead woman.

'I didn't kill her. You do believe me, don't you? Whatever else I've done, I didn't do that, OK?'

She nodded. The other officer returned. Now there was also an acrid smell. Mark knelt down by the body of the dead girl and his eyes took in the mutilated body.

'Stupid little girl,' he muttered and got up. 'Stupid, frightened little girl.'

He rummaged in his pocket for his mobile, tapped in a number and asked to speak to Anna Bagger, East Jutland Crime Division. Then he took a jar of pills from his jacket, swallowed two without water and slumped down on a chair.

41

'Gry, you say?'

Mark nodded.

'Let me make sure I've got this right,' Anna Bagger said, training her laser-eyes on him.

She pulled him to one side so that the SOC officers could enter Room 103. A maid was mopping up Jepsen's vomit. Anna's voice struck Mark like an ice pick.

'You booked and paid for the room? You were with the girl here last night at around ten o'clock?'

'There's no need to shout it from the rooftops,' he said in a muted voice.

'Yes or no?'

He nodded.

'Answer me!'

'Yes.'

'And you left the hotel when?'

'An hour later. More or less. There must be witnesses.'

She took notes. If she had used a pencil it would have snapped long ago, so hard was she pressing against the paper.

'Is there anything else I need to know?'

She looked at him again. 'DNA? What can we expect?'

Christ, he could have done without this. The pain was throbbing in his head and his whole body was soaked in sweat. But there was no way out; he had known that from the moment Kir called. He knew it would all come out and at this moment he couldn't even begin to imagine the consequences. He looked at Anna. His world had already collapsed around his ears, like the walls of Jericho, so what did a few more bricks matter?

'A condom left in the bin in the bathroom. If the maid hasn't already emptied it.'

Her lips became a straight line. She lowered her notepad.

'And I had a shower.'

'I presume she was your secret informant?'

'Anna . . .'

'And that the whole exercise was your style of police work, undertaken solely for the purposes of obtaining information?'

The sarcasm was obvious. Kir hadn't exactly been over the moon, either. He'd developed a new ability to piss women off, or perhaps he'd always had it, he reflected.

He sat on a window sill. He would have given a lot for a bed and a darkened locked room right now, and yet he didn't want it. Deep down he didn't want to be alone with himself. Anything but that.

'Who saw you leave?'

'The guy in reception. I told them she could stay in the room. I ordered her a Coke.'

She nodded, unconvinced.

'Let's hope he can be bothered to save your skin.'

At that moment he realised he didn't care. He ran the film of his meeting with Gry on an internal channel and heard his own warning to her again and again. The irony was that he might have brought her to the very place she was meant to die.

'I don't think she knew very much,' he said. 'But she was nervous.'

He told Anna about the three girls who had appeared from nowhere and then disappeared.

'She knew something was wrong. There was something wrong about them appearing from nowhere. And there was something wrong about them disappearing. She was scared.'

'But she carried on working.'

'She probably didn't have any choice.'

'Was she on drugs?'

He shrugged.

'Did she have a pimp?'

'Possibly. What do I know?'

'Yes, what would you know? You only had sex with her.'

She laid on the contempt with a trowel. He would have smiled if he hadn't been in such pain and feeling so tired of it all.

'Safe sex,' he corrected her, and was relieved that Gry had produced a condom from her pocket and insisted on it.

Anna Bagger stood opposite him, legs apart, as if conducting an interrogation. There was a strength, a professionalism and a vulnerability about her, but he didn't have the energy to deal with it.

'We'll probably find your DNA elsewhere, in the shower at any rate. You were the last person to see her alive until the contrary can be proven. We're talking a possible suspension and investigation by the public prosecutor.'

Perhaps she really did think he was guilty. Perhaps he would have thought the same if the boot had been on the other foot. He sighed. It was all as messed up as it could be.

'I'm ill,' he said.

'Agreed.'

'I've got cancer.'

He avoided looking at her this time.

'They took one of my kidneys last year. There's a tumour in the other, and one in my liver. I had a scan this morning. Both tumours have grown in the last three months.'

She took a step backwards. Not forwards, he noted. Disease terrified people. In his experience, most people wanted to distance themselves from it.

'How long have you known?'

He knew what she was thinking. She would do the maths

now and he cursed himself. He should have kept his mouth shut.

He got up.

'Don't worry. It's not contagious. I just want to leave.'

But she didn't let him go. He could see it churning around behind her eyes. The face, the perfect/imperfect mix of hard and soft features.

'Did you know back then?'

He nodded.

'But you were too cowardly to tell me?'

He took no pleasure in her reaction. There was sorrow in the anger. He preferred the latter to the former, but he didn't have a choice, and besides, everything was complicated enough. He preferred to talk about the case.

'Listen.'

He nodded towards Room 103, where an officer appeared at that moment with a brown paper bag. 'Forensic evidence' it said in clear red letters. It could be anything: bed linen, pillows, the girl's jacket which had been lying on the floor.

'It's Tora all over again.'

He could see she was slowly turning her thoughts back to the case.

'Another case of mistaken identity? Is that what you're saying?'

'I'm talking about the killing,' he said. 'What does he want with their faces? Is he a serial killer?'

He slipped off the window sill and sat on the floor in the corner. He placed his elbows on his knees and ran his fingers through his hair. She crouched down on her haunches opposite him. Like an expression of solidarity.

'Are the faces trophies in his cupboard?' she asked.

'It could be a copycat killing,' he suggested. 'The first one was well organised. The second one was hurried.'

'Perhaps it's just revenge, pure and simple,' she said. 'Because she spoke to you.'

He pulled at his hair. It dulled the other agonies.

'I pressed her. She might have died because of a name.'

She put her hand on his shoulder.

'We have something to go on now,' she said. 'We discovered Tora's story.'

He pulled his shoulder away.

'It wasn't in vain, is that what you're saying? As long as you help to solve a murder, then your death isn't pointless?'

She got up.

'Perhaps you should go home and rest.'

That was the last thing he needed. He looked at his watch. Kir had called him at 3.15 p.m., it was now 5.20 and in the meantime night had fallen. He crossed the road and pushed open the door to the pub where ten customers or so were having a drink after work. Kir was sitting at the bar with a Coke. He walked up to her.

'Perhaps you shouldn't be alone?'

'I'm not alone,' she said.

She was a soldier. He forgot that when he saw her, despite the camouflage gear. He sat down on a bar stool and ordered a beer. There was country music playing on the stereo. In a corner sat a couple of muscular men with some obscure club insignia on their backs. There were more couples than he could face. Some of them were kissing; he felt like walking up to them and separating them.

The song was the deathless 'Achy Breaky Heart'. Mark leaned forward slightly towards Kir.

'How many country musicians does it take to change a light bulb?'

She looked at him blankly.

'I hate country music.'

He didn't know why. The situation was completely absurd, but she cheered him up.

'Three. Two to change the bulb and one to sing about how much he misses the old one.'

The miracle happened. She laughed and he saw the gap between her teeth. Only briefly, of course, then she grew serious again.

'I didn't see you leave the hotel last night.'

'Then you probably didn't wait long enough.'

He took a sip of his beer, inwardly cursing his actions that night.

Kir shrugged.

'She, Anna Bagger, must have believed you. Or you wouldn't be sitting here. Did you check in as Mr and Mrs Smith?'

He owed her a smile and she got it, but it was hard to keep it up.

'Two girls without faces,' Kir said.

He nodded.

'Two girls, same killer?' she asked.

It wasn't her business, but even so he told her what little he knew: what Gry had told him about the three women and a first name she'd given him which had helped them to identify the dead body.

'I'm sure she knew more.'

'And that's why the two of you had to take a room?'

He shook his head, ready with his defence, but she clearly didn't want to hear about his moral qualms.

'Someone must have seen something,' she said. 'Don't they have CCTV at the hotel?'

'Not at this time of year.'

The provinces. No one expected anything out of the ordinary to happen, and certainly not in the winter when the cold kept people indoors.

'You can see everything from the pub,' she persisted. 'Red didn't close until late. Try asking him. Someone must have seen something.'

'What about him?'

'I've asked him.'

She looked away and he sensed a distance between brother and sister. Mark waved to Red, who nodded.

'There were a couple of guests I didn't know. But I can get you a copy of their credit card receipts.'

He sent his sister a look. Soon afterwards he put a couple of beers in front of them.

'On the house. You look as if you need them.'

The beer glasses were dewy. Outside, in the glow from the street lights, a Falck hearse pulled away heading for Århus and the Morgue? The dove-blue SOC van was still there, with two police vehicles and Anna's and the pathologist's cars. At the entrance to the hotel, red and white police tape fluttered in the winter breeze.

'I hope they check for prints on the window in the room,' Kir said. 'He could have jumped out. It's only one floor up.'

He nodded.

'I'm sure they will.'

'And then there was that customer she was arguing with. The man who was the reason you went outside.'

She didn't miss a thing.

'You saw him close up,' she said. 'You must be able to give a description.'

And added: 'You being a police officer.'

He was, but a bad one, because he'd forgotten all about that row. He was fairly sure the customer had nothing to do with the killing, but of course they should talk to him. He called Anna Bagger on her mobile, outlined the incident and described the man.

'Was he in a car?' she asked.

'Yes, but I didn't see the model and I didn't get the number, either. I've given you everything I've got.'

She sighed.

'Your mind was probably on other things. We'll look into it.'

He drained his glass and it struck him how quickly death could strike when it wanted to and how it could prolong the agony at other times. He hoped Gry's death had been quick. He was all too familiar with the fear when it dragged on and he knew what he would prefer – if he'd had a choice.

42

'I should go back to my place,' Felix said.

'You're not going anywhere.'

He held her by the shoulders. He could still feel her bones, but a protective layer was forming around them even though she was still very thin.

'Not until we know what all this is about,' he said. 'Have you found anything in the boxes? Remembered anything?'

She shook her head.

'I'm going round in circles.'

He made meatballs for them, with stewed white cabbage. That would put some more weight on her, he thought. After they had eaten, they sat on the sofa with tea and coffee like an old married couple and switched on the television.

He had never owned a TV and hadn't missed it, but his neighbour on the farm had bought a flat screen and given him his old one. TV2 was showing local news now. He sat up when he heard that a girl had been found dead at the Strand Hotel in Grenå. They showed footage of Kattegatvej; the hotel from the outside, parked police cars and officers carrying bags and boxes from the building. A detective, Anna Bagger, said a few words to a reporter. The girl's identity had yet to be established, but she was young and had checked into the room the previous night with a man who had now been identified. The police thought there might be a connection with the body found in the harbour, which had now been identified as an eighteen-year-old girl, Tora Juel Andersen from Nykøbing, Mors.

'Strand Hotel. That's where we had dinner,' said Felix. 'We saw that policeman.'

She looked at him with dark eyes.

'What does that mean?'

He couldn't give her an answer.

'Listen.'

She tucked her legs beneath her and listened. The first gust of wind took hold of the woodwork and howled around the house corners. The predicted snowstorm had arrived. Peter turned off the TV and got up to fetch the chart. He unfolded it on the coffee table and she leaned over and studied it.

'This is where we crashed.'

She pointed to the area around Hesselø. 'That's why I'm living here,' she said. 'I wanted to get away, yet I wanted to be close to where it happened. Does that sound like a contradiction?'

He smiled.

'It sounds like a tricky exercise.'

But he understood her. After he'd been released from prison, his first move had been to return to the woods around the care home. He had imagined he was looking for a future. But he had merely been seeking out his past.

He pointed to a line on the chart crossing Lille Lysegrund.

'I think the boat must be near that. Brian's *Molly*.'

'We need the other coordinate. We need to know precisely, otherwise we won't find it.'

'And what if we do find something? What do we do with it?' she asked.

He was in no doubt.

'We hand it over to the police.'

That was possibly what they should be doing now – just giving them everything they had. But there were too many loose ends and too many people he felt responsible for and whom he couldn't betray. Most of all her.

For the umpteenth time he wondered how it was all connected

and in particular what Erik Gomez's role had been, if indeed he'd had one. Why would a man like him contact East Jutland Prison? She reckoned he'd known Ramses. But the date was wrong. At the time Erik had applied for a prison visit permit, Ramses had already been released. So who was he keen to visit? And why?

He had spent two years in the new East Jutland Prison after the closure of the old Horsens Prison. Cold and damp and outmoded though it had been, it was a lot less frightening than the new, modern, escape-proof facility where everything was so impersonal and computerised that even the warders seemed like robots. He had hated the place. He had hated the hierarchical separation into strong and weak prisoners that was allowed to flourish. He had hated seeing gang members recruit new disciples and make them run errands for them, and hated the fact that highly dangerous prisoners were allowed to serve out their sentence at a prison of their choice, where they had a substantial measure of control over their lives, could go shopping, cook meals and keep slaves. Whereas others who wanted to leave the gangs and provided the police with information were kept in the old remand cells for their own protection, with no other facilities than a loo and a hard bed. He had survived as he always had. Survival was his speciality. But he had never hated anywhere more than that prison and had sworn never to return.

He drank the last mouthful of coffee and put the mug on the table. With everything that had happened, including the killing they had just learned about on the television, it was now an oath he would have to break. But it wasn't the only one. Once he'd also sworn his weeks as a kidney patient in hospital would never return and gain a hold over him. He hadn't lied to Mark Bille Hansen: there had been a time when he only wanted to be left alone and either die – or if there was a miracle – learn to live with someone else's kidney. And when he'd left the hospital a healthy man, he'd had no desire to look back.

But you had to be careful with the promises you made, he realised that now. As a kidney patient he had met people who had changed his life. He hoped the reverse was also true as he picked up his mobile and called the ward to make an appointment with his old nurse.

43

FELIX KNEW THAT Peter hated leaving her on her own. It was as if he feared a relapse and was scared the memory of the crash would weaken her. She was starting to remember more and more.

She watched as he drove off in the morning. She would have liked to stop him worrying, but she couldn't find the right words. Whenever he looked at her there were so many other things queuing up to be said, and underneath it all was the urge to cling to him. She fought it as best she could.

She sat down with the boxes from Erik's office. She knew perfectly well what had happened to her brain; she had learned the clinical terms during her hospital stay. She had suffered from both retrograde and anterograde amnesia. Which was simply a nice way of saying that she didn't remember what had happened in the time leading up to the accident, nor the accident itself, nor the time that followed. Her memory had gone into protective mode and had tried to shield her from what had happened by tricking her into forgetting it. But she had known all along, of course. And she had also, on a purely intellectual level, known how to jog her memory. In a half-hearted attempt to help the Air Accident Investigation Board and the police she had put up the cuttings on the wall. But in truth she hadn't wanted to remember. Not until now.

Her rage helped her. The papers, the boxes from the office and what she had seen in her house would be her tools. Every little scrap of information, whether a taxi receipt or the sight of

Erik's handwriting, would press a button which evoked a fragment of her memories.

She knew from her stay in hospital that it was a balancing act deciding how much you should delve into the past. For some people their experiences were so dreadful that reliving them would be more than they could bear. One of her fellow patients had had a breakdown and tried to commit suicide. She had fled from Sierra Leone where she had been tortured. The thought of reliving the memory of her torturers and what had happened in the torture chamber had been too much. Sometimes you had to accept that the brain knew best.

At other times a post-traumatic amnesia patient could find it a release to recover their memory, the psychiatrist had told her. As painful as it was to remember, it might help them to move on, possibly into a grieving process, which might later result in their returning to normal life.

Her memory loss had postponed her grieving. She hadn't started to grieve properly until she had woken up to the sound of the organ that day and afterwards sitting by the grave. And now she needed it like she needed sleep after countless sleepless nights. Grief would help her move from her zombie existence among survivors to a life among the living with her eyes open.

She emptied the last box on to the floor. Erik had worked for the company for over ten years so he'd accumulated a great deal: diaries, notebooks, folders, books. The company had, of course, retained all the commercial documents.

Felix flicked through Erik's 2008 calendar. His handwriting was elegant, with confident strokes and a slight slant. It had energy, as he'd had, and she remembered the love letters he had sent her over the years – little vignettes with affectionate or suggestive turns of phrase, but always with style. Those letters were probably still lying in a chest of drawers in her room, but she hadn't given them a thought in years.

She went on rummaging and checking everything in detail:

shaking books upside down to see if they contained hidden notes, rifling through boxes of paper clips, staples, reams of paper and boxes of matches and Post-it notes. The items from the notice-board were in a separate bag. She remembered Erik's noticeboard in his study and lingered over the familiar photos of Maria and her and Erik together. He had loved her once, she was sure. When had it stopped? What kind of life was it that he had kept hidden from her? He'd had mistresses, she knew that. But had there been anything else?

She thought about the expensive house. Two expensive cars. The boat. Numerous luxury holidays. Where had the money come from?

Erik didn't come from a rich family. He came from a family where you took chances, and once it had fascinated her. His father had run his construction company into the ground when she and Erik met. But they'd both lapped up the father's stories: stories of entrepreneurial daring, crushing your rivals without scruples, balancing on the edge of credit with banks as willing collaborators and living the high life. Exclusive wine, caviar, silk sheets at the Grand Hotel, a waiter waiting on you hand and foot at the Oriental Hotel in Bangkok, poker tournaments, women with voluptuous figures and red lips: sun, sex and non-stop champagne. He had made it sound so exciting. She and Erik had dreamed of life in the fast lane. And suddenly it was there. From one day to the next they frequented more and more expensive restaurants. The Toyota was replaced with a BMW, Erik's suits were now made by Armani, holidays were no longer taken on European beaches, but at the world's most exotic resorts and at legendary hotels. Armed with Erik's Platinum card she would go clothes-shopping and take her pick of expensive designer shops. Her childhood in Spain with a constant lack of money had left its scars. She'd sworn she would be rich one day. Now her dream had come true and she loved it. So much so that she swept all her doubts aside.

Felix sipped her tea. She had been naive in so many ways. Here she was in jeans from H&M and a sweater from Kvickly supermarket in Grenå. All her designer clothes hung in the wardrobe in Skåde and she no longer cared about them. It had turned out that Erik owed money to everyone. The bubble had burst, with the financial crisis. But it didn't matter any more. It had been there and now it was gone. And here she was in a cottage on a cliff at the end of the world, with a neighbour who was quite unlike anyone she'd ever met.

Peter Boutrup. On the surface he was an ordinary man with a house, a job and a dog. But then there was everything you didn't see at first glance. It was under his skin like an extra layer which no one else had penetrated, with the possible exception of herself. There was still a lot she didn't know, but she sensed this much: they might be different, but they were also alike in many ways. They were both struggling to survive, climbing back to the life they had once had, at the edge of the abyss where nothing can grow except for hatred, impotence and fear. But it was hard. You didn't jump out of the pit you had landed in just like that. It required a superhuman effort and sometimes the cost was extraordinarily high. She knew it and feared it: the price she would have to pay for certainty about what had happened. Peter had already gone much further than she had. What price had he paid? she wondered. What had he given up to get his new life?

She rummaged through the boxes. Her grief had started to slop around in her brain again, making her almost seasick, as she flicked through Maria's drawings of Mummy and Daddy, of the house and the cat, of happy people with no worries.

Then she remembered the moleskin notebook in her bag. Something had made her take it with her, like the teddy bear. She found it and leafed through it, scrutinising the scraps of paper for the first time. A neatly folded piece of green paper attracted her attention and she unfolded it. She read it twice but she still didn't understand it. There was beginning to be so much she didn't understand about Erik.

She wondered about the letter and looked at the date: 20th July. Two days before the fatal helicopter trip. 'Århus Chief of Police' the letterhead said. It was a receipt from a lost property office, issued to Erik, who would never in his life – or at least not in his new luxury life – have considered catching a train. But, black on green, it said he had handed in a briefcase he had found on the intercity train between Århus and Copenhagen.

Felix carefully put the receipt in her purse. Erik was far too busy and selfish ever to waste time handing in someone else's briefcase to a lost property office.

She started repacking the boxes. Little by little, her mind all a-whirl, she managed to close them and stack them on top of one another, and then she made herself another cup of tea. There was only one possible explanation for why Erik would have handed in that bag: it didn't belong to someone else. It belonged to him.

44

After visiting Stinger, Peter said goodbye to Elisabeth and went down to the hospital cafeteria, where he had arranged to meet someone.

Ingrid Andersen waved from a table where she was sitting with a cup of coffee. She was in her nurse's uniform, but with a blue cardigan hung loosely over her shoulders and sensible shoes that could tolerate long walks up and down hospital corridors. She was in her late fifties, a little on the motherly side, and the nurse who had got closest to him during his admission. A kind of mutual understanding had developed between them. Some of the staff kept him at arm's length because he arrived flanked by two prison officers and with a conviction for manslaughter, but Ingrid had always treated him as the person she thought he was: a young male patient who could benefit from a little TLC plus some strictness and a healthy dose of humour, which, as far as she was concerned, was perhaps the most important weapon in the fight against all disease. To repay her humanity he had turned on the charm and listened to her talk about her marriage to a violent man, whom in the end she had kicked out, and her love for a dog that had hovered between life and death after cutting its paw. The dog, Bella, meant everything to her. It was a sentiment they shared.

'How's your friend?'

'Not very well. I've just been to see him.'

The doctors had brought Stinger out of the medically induced coma, but it was Peter's impression that it hadn't made much difference. Stinger simply lay in bed staring vacantly at the ceiling without saying a word.

'And it's because of him you want to know something about that other patient? Brian? You know we take an oath of confidentiality, don't you?'

She had lowered her voice and he pulled out a chair and sat down opposite her.

They had to go through it, of course. He was prepared for that. He would have to beg and she would be reticent and insist on sticking to the rules. But eventually she would give in, he knew that. Just as he knew she'd already enquired about a close colleague who worked in the cancer ward. He knew her too well.

'So what's it like to be a free man?' she asked. 'And healthy?'

She sent him a critical but affectionate look.

'You seem to be thriving,' she added.

He smiled and told her about his first year. About working for Manfred, restoring the house after four years of neglect due to his imprisonment, about the dog, the cliff, the countryside around him and working out with weights, jogging and trying to keep in shape, which he'd never done before.

'And you don't smoke?'

'I don't smoke, no.'

'So have you found yourself a girlfriend yet to keep you on the straight and narrow?'

'You know very well you're the only one for me.'

She smacked him with the back of her hand.

'You're just as silly as you always were. I keep telling you: you need a woman in your life.'

He told her a little about Felix, and not just to satisfy her curiosity. Afterwards he told her about Stinger, Ramses and Brian while she sat erect in the chair, drinking coffee and listening attentively.

'Alliances are formed in prison and, indirectly, Brian is the reason why my friend Stinger is now close to death and Ramses was found dead. So I need to know more about Brian's last days.'

'I hope you're not getting yourself into trouble again?'

She sent him a stern look. He could have wasted hours telling her he'd never seriously been a part of the criminal fraternity, but it would probably have disappointed her, so he did what she hoped he would do: vehemently shake his head.

'I've just been released. I've no intention of sabotaging my future.'

'Good,' she said, seemingly satisfied, and readied herself to tell him what she knew. He could tell from the way she collected herself, pulling the cardigan more tightly around her shoulders, pushing the coffee cup slightly to one side and placing both palms on the table.

'It's not often we have the honour of caring for patients from prison,' she said. 'So, of course, my colleague could remember Brian. And I've asked her the questions you wanted me to.'

'That's really very kind of you. I owe you a favour.'

She waved her hand dismissively.

'Nonsense. Neither of us will be on the slippery slope for lack of a favour.'

He was about to express his gratitude again, but she interrupted him.

'Wait and listen to what I've got to say.'

She looked around as though afraid the walls had ears. But the visitors in the cafeteria were busy eating and chatting, and all the sound was swallowed by the ceiling and the large room. Ingrid Andersen said: 'You wanted to know who visited Brian and how he felt during his last days. Let's start with the latter: Annemette, my colleague, says he believed right until the last moment that he would survive and his cancer was something he could fight.'

Peter nodded. Ingrid continued.

'As regards his visitors, she said, and I quote: "You would have to be an idiot to suppose they came from the Salvation Army."'

Peter could vividly imagine the kind of clientele that had been at Brian's bedside. Ramses and Stinger were a couple of them and were probably among the most subdued.

'According to Annemette, they needed their ears boxing,' Ingrid said. 'But they got nowhere with her. Rules were rules. When one of them started smoking in the ward, she grabbed him and threw him out and confiscated a bottle of vodka while she was at it.'

'The two of you could be twins,' said Peter, who had been caught smuggling in cigarettes himself. Ingrid had been furious and subjected him to a long lecture on the damaging effects of tobacco.

Her eyes sparkled with humour.

'You can't pull the wool over Annemette's eyes. Anyway, she also told me that someone had been after Brian. One day when she entered the ward his face was all blue and there were bruises on his neck after an attempted strangulation.'

'That sounds serious,' he said. 'Attempted murder of a dying man.'

She nodded.

'Annemette called security and they tried to find out who had been in the ward, but to no avail. Too many people coming and going. From then on, they were very careful as to whom they let in to see him, and staff were always present.'

She removed an imaginary speck of dust from her white uniform.

'So that's how Annemette was able to tell me about what you call Brian's plan. That's what you wanted to know, wasn't it? What his plan was?'

Peter nodded. He was increasingly convinced that Brian had planned everything and that Stinger and Ramses were merely a means to an end. The treasure in the boat, if there ever was any, was never meant for the likes of them.

Ingrid looked at him. 'You were right. He had a plan. He wanted revenge.'

'On whom?'

'Annemette had the impression it was whoever had grassed on him and sent him to prison. Whatever it was he was inside for.'

'He robbed a security depot,' Peter said. 'But it probably wasn't the only thing he'd done.'

She grabbed his arm.

'Sometimes dying patients do something with the final strength they can muster. They shout or spit, or even get up to leave the hospital.'

She squeezed.

'Annemette says Brian grabbed her by the arm like this. And then he stared at her, broke into a grin and said: "I'll have the last laugh!" And then he drew his final breath.'

45

'WE'VE GOT TWO young women, killed in almost identical fashion, and a man fatally shot through the chest.'

Anna Bagger tapped her pointer on the whiteboard where photos of the three victims were displayed.

'The women were strangled before their faces were removed. The pathologist describes the latter as primitive and brutal in its execution. The weapon could have been a sharp knife, but the killer isn't a professional.'

Mark wondered what line of business qualified you to be professional in this context. Surgeon? Butcher? Fur trapper?

'The forensic psychiatrist describes the killer as callous.'

Anna Bagger switched the pointer to her left hand while taking a marker from the ledge under the board with her right. She drew a straight line from the name of one girl to the other with such force that Mark could hear the tip of the marker squeal against the surface.

'Gry Johansen gave us Tora's name. She and two other girls hung out with the local prostitutes in the weeks leading up to Christmas.'

She circled the name of the faceless girl the divers had fished out of the harbour.

'Tora Juel Andersen. Aged eighteen. Left school with average exam results and had been working in Føtex supermarket in Nykøbing, Mors, ever since. She lived at home with her parents, Anemarie and Ulrik Juel Andersen, until the summer of 2009 when she went to Århus, supposedly to share a flat with a girlfriend and start further education in Viby. Her parents have described her as a bright, unruly girl who felt trapped in Mors and wanted to be where the action was.'

'Can you blame her?' one of the detectives said loudly.

Mark looked across the room in Grenå Police Station which the Århus team had commandeered and increasingly reminded him of a command centre in a war zone. He counted nine detectives in total, all sitting like attentive students. Plus Mark himself, who had been summoned at the crack of dawn. He didn't know what to make of it. Anna Bagger had, it seemed, completely changed her tune after learning about his illness, and he didn't like that. He preferred to be free of any sort of clinginess and just wanted to work on his own, but it wasn't going to happen today. She appeared to have decided that he would be coupled to the team, like an extra carriage for awkward passengers.

'We're still awaiting Gry's autopsy report, but we've compiled witness statements which we need to review. In the meantime, there's enough to do with Tora.'

Bang, bang. The pointer hit the board again. Anna Bagger was wearing jeans and a cream silk blouse, and her eyes were a gleaming blue, without a trace of sentimentality. She explained: 'Here we have some happy photos showing Tora with her friend Ida. But it's all a big fat lie. Listen to what Ida said when we interviewed her yesterday.'

Anna Bagger pressed a button. The hesitant voice of a young girl could be heard on the tape recorder: 'I don't know where she lived. She never said. She was so secretive and in the end I just didn't care.'

The detective's question followed: 'Are you aware her parents thought she was living in your flat?'

There was a silence. Mark Bille imagined the girl was nodding. The detective said: 'You need to reply with a yes or a no.'

'Yes.'

The girl muttered something inaudible. The detective asked her to speak louder.

'She paid me five hundred kroner a month not to tell anyone. She said she wanted to be in control of her own life and that her family wouldn't understand.'

'Do you know where she really lived?'

'No. But she lived with her boyfriend.'

'Do you know his name?'

'She called him Swatch. I think she'd met him at a concert.'

'What else do you know about him? Have you seen any photos of him?'

'No.'

'Didn't Tora ever talk about him?'

'Not much.'

'What nationality is he, do you know? Danish? Foreign?'

The girl was clearly giving the question some thought.

'Tora said he had a pal called Ibrahim. She was scared of him.'

'Why?'

'Something about Ibrahim lording it over Swatch or something like that. I didn't really ask. I didn't want anything to do with it.'

'When did you last see her?'

Another pause for thought. They could hear the girl taking a drag of a cigarette.

'Three, four weeks ago, I think.'

'December the tenth?'

'That sounds about right.'

'The last photos her parents got via the Internet were taken that day. They show you and her at a café in town. Who took the picture?'

'Tora got the waiter to take it. We were in Bruuns Galleri. In the coffee bar.'

'Didn't you wonder why you didn't hear anything from her?'

'Nope.'

There was another silence, then the girl said: 'She came straight from the gym that day. I think she worked out at fitness.dk up in Banegårdsgade. I think her boyfriend was a member there, too.'

Anna Bagger pressed stop. She scanned the assembled officers.

'We need to find Swatch and Ibrahim. We can start at the fitness centre. We also have to show photos of Tora at the kind of cafés and restaurants in the centre of Århus where young people go.'

A couple of detectives were assigned to the job and packed their things to go to Århus.

Anna Bagger pointed to the photos of Gry.

'They're all connected. As previously mentioned, Gry knew Tora as one of the three girls who came from nowhere and spent time with them. One of the others might have been called Lily. She was short and dark with lots of piercings. The third girl is vaguer and described as tall, with a square face and a mullet haircut, as it's known, layered at the top and long at the back. Someone must have seen those girls. They must have been staying somewhere.'

She looked at Mark and he knew what was coming.

'Mark, we need your local knowledge.'

There wasn't a hint of irony in her words, but even so he detected an obvious unrest among the other officers, although he wasn't able to say who was responsible. They knew everything, of course. They knew he had been one of Gry's punters. Fortunately, they also knew that the receptionist at the hotel had confirmed his story about the Coke. He wasn't the last person to see Gry alive, but he had acted irresponsibly. It wasn't something people respected.

Anna Bagger cleared her throat.

'See what you can dig up. What do Gry's colleagues have to

say? When did they last see Tora? Under what circumstances? Who else was she seen with?'

She pointed to two officers in the back row.

'Go and talk to Gry's parents. They live in Rønde. What kind of girl was she? Who were her friends? What was her life like?'

'Where did Gry live?' Mark asked.

Anna Bagger flicked through some papers in a file likely to include a list of the contents of Gry's handbag. She held up a yellow health insurance card.

'Fredensgade twenty-seven. We went there last night, obviously, and it has been cordoned off, but why don't you go and see what you can discover.'

'What kind of property is it?'

'Private landlord,' she said. 'A small flat. There are four flats in total and the landlord lives in one of them. The other three are rented out to young girls who might be in the same line of business as Gry, but we need to determine that. Their names are . . .'

Anna Bagger looked down at her notes and straightened up again: 'Helle Bjergager and Iben Bank. We've interviewed Iben Bank but we didn't glean very much. She says she was in Århus visiting a sister all of December and the sister has confirmed that. But we still need to speak to Helle, who wasn't at home last night.'

'Anything else?' Mark asked.

Anna Bagger hesitated.

'We haven't found any receipts for rent paid anywhere. I guess it's probably cash in hand. But perhaps the landlord and the tenants had come to a somewhat different arrangement.'

Ten minutes later he was shown into a dilapidated old house in the northern part of the town by a middle-aged man with a beer belly, a stained jumper and days-old stubble covering several chins. His trousers were old-fashioned men's slacks in an inde-terminate shade of grey, held up with a piece of red string, not a belt. Under the camel-coloured jumper he wore a red checked shirt in heavy duty cotton.

'Asger Toft?'

'The police again?'

He eyed Mark from head to toe. Mark nodded.

'Is there some place we can talk?'

The man shook his head, but opened the door for Mark to pass into the dark hallway. There was a smell of filth and damp. The plaster was flaking off the walls.

'Are you the owner?'

They entered a sitting room with furniture jammed in so close together you had to navigate around it with great care. The place looked like something from a car boot sale. Asger Toft explained that he'd inherited the property from his mother, who had died in 1997. Gry had lived there for six months, the other two girls for nine months.

'Did they know each other, the three tenants?'

'Of course they did.'

'Are they in the same line of business?'

'I wouldn't know anything about that. They just live here. Lived.'

Something inside the man's mouth made a clicking sound as he spoke. Mark wondered if it came from his teeth.

'Did they ever have visitors in their rooms?'

The man shrugged.

'I didn't keep track of that. But they weren't allowed to have anyone staying over. Unless they paid extra.'

'How much was the rent for Gry's flat?'

There was a brief hesitation. Then the mouth clicked: 'Three thousand kroner.'

'Can I see the rent book, please?'

'She was in arrears.'

'If she was in arrears, why was she still living here? Or perhaps she paid you in some other way?'

The man looked at him. Small eyes hidden in pouches of fat.
'Is that illegal?'

Mark nodded.

'It's procuring. Good as. You accepted sex as payment. Did you also take a share of her earnings?'

'I don't know what you're talking about. Like I said, guests cost extra.'

There was a noise from the stairwell. Mark quickly got up and opened the door. Outside stood a girl who was just as pathetic and skinny-looking as Gry.

'Is your name Helle?'

'Who wants to know?'

He recognised her as the girl who had been working in the harbour alongside Gry. Then he nodded and introduced himself. Reluctantly she agreed to invite him in and he left Asger Toft to his own devices. The flat was small, possibly twenty-five square metres. The furnishing was austere, a sitting room-cum-bedroom. The bedspread was burgundy, distressed velvet, as were the curtains. There was a circular table with a white embroidered tablecloth and three square black candles of varying heights on a small metal tray. There were two high-backed chairs that could have belonged to his grandmother.

'You know Gry is dead, don't you?'

She nodded. They had sat down on the chairs facing each other. She sat with her legs together like a schoolgirl. Her face had been made up to look tarty, but underneath the make-up she might have been beautiful. She had a small, delicate snub nose and her lips were full in a sulky sort of way, yet looked as if they could easily break into a smile. Her hair was blonde and cut very short to reveal a finely shaped head with small ears close to her head.

'How old are you?'

'Twenty-three.'

He sat for a while without saying anything. She just looked

at him with a gaze which was so direct he struggled to return it.

'What do you want to know?' she asked.

'Did Gry have any regular customers?'

'You.'

A quick smile flitted across the face and a dimple appeared. But then she grew serious again.

He had deserved that.

'Do you know anything about the three girls who were here right before Christmas? Such as where they lived?'

She shrugged. 'Sometimes they stayed here. Either with Gry or with me. Otherwise I don't know where they would . . .'

'What were their names?'

'Tora, Lily and Lena.'

'What else?'

She didn't know.

'Why did you let them stay here?'

She shrugged, uninterested.

'They had money and they were fun to hang out with.'

'Where did the money come from? Did they have jobs?'

She looked as though he'd asked her an obscene question. She shook her head.

'Drugs?'

'A bit. Some coke and so on. Nothing major.'

'Did they have friends in town? Do you know what they were doing here?'

Her face took on an expression that didn't suit her. She was far too young to look like that, Mark thought.

'They hung out with all sorts of people,' she said, vaguely studying nails that looked too perfect. They'd probably been bought in some cheap salon.

'The three of them had a plan,' she said, apparently testing the strength of the nails by clicking them against each other. 'They wanted us to help them, but Gry and me had to work.'

'How were you meant to help them?'

The girl shrugged her shoulders.

'Sometimes they would get on their high horses. Talk about standing together, that sort of thing.'

'What were you supposed to understand by *standing together*?'

Helle chewed at a nail and eyed him.

'It's important,' he said, urging her. 'Gry's dead. She lived a life exposed to all kinds of dangers. Like you do.'

She looked down and concentrated on picking at a cuticle, then she sighed.

'OK. They needed help to find a treasure. They promised there would be money in it for us.'

'Where was the treasure supposed to be?'

She squirmed.

'Somewhere on the seabed, they said.'

Mark thought about Ramses and about the body of Tora recovered from the harbour. Could this really be about a treasure?

Helle quickly added: 'Of course we didn't believe them. They were usually drunk when they talked about it.'

46

Enner Mark, aka East Jutland Prison, near Horsens, was situated in a barren and hostile icy landscape. A glacier where no life could grow.

But there was life here. Peter knew that from personal experience. Not a happy life, but a life, one that fitted the place the way it looked today, with the wind howling and the snow blowing in Arctic gusts across the open terrain. Low yellow buildings lay like oversized rectangular Lego bricks, abandoned in the middle of a snowstorm by a petulant child and surrounded by a 1,400-metre perimeter wall and two fine-meshed metal fences. The homepage promoted the prison's numerous facilities as though it were a five-star hotel you could book for a holiday in the Mediterranean sun. However, a stay at Enner Mark guaranteed no sunshine; on the contrary, it meant an impersonal sojourn in the shadows.

He was examined at close quarters and asked to identify himself by the guard, who was new and fortunately didn't recognise him. He was processed through security as though he was a dangerous terrorist at a high-tech airport. No mobile, no bags. He had brought two packets of Camel as a gift. They, too, were scanned and treated as though they contained explosives.

Normally he would have had to apply for permission to visit the prison and various letters would have gone back and forth. But Peter's old friend, Matti Jørgensen, had used his influence from his past life as a prison officer. Matti had also grown up at Titan Care Home and Peter had been very surprised to meet him again when he was sent to Horsens Prison. Big, good-natured Matti, who had been such a frightened child, had been the one person who made his last months in prison bearable. He was the reason why Peter was now following hard on the heels of a prison officer who opened various doors simply by running a finger across the fingerprint scanner. No heavy bundles of keys here. Everything was just how spacecraft were conceived in the Nineties: silent apart from digital clicks and beeps. Artificial, sexless and claustrophobic.

He was led through long corridors to the visitors' section, where the pale wooden furniture was upholstered in blue, which brought him back with a bump to his time in the carpentry workshop. Naturally enough the interior was furnished with its own products and the result was a clumsy, autocratic, institutional attempt to create cosiness.

He was told to wait. The room was much too hot and he could feel sweat starting to trickle down his forehead. His whole body itched and he had to force himself to breathe in and out calmly, more calmly than he felt.

There was a Thermos flask of coffee on the table and a couple of cups. He poured himself one purely to keep himself busy and noticed that his hands were shaking slightly. He was locked inside, but kept telling himself that he could get out. This time he could get out. All he had to do was call the prison officer and say he had changed his mind and a few minutes later he would be back outside in the cold, feeling the wind on his face and sucking it into his lungs.

He put down the coffee cup, closed his eyes and could almost feel the wind and frost. In this way he fought against the walls closing in on him. He was able to push against them. He wondered how Cato, who was now serving his sentence in this place where Peter had once been, dealt with his claustrophobia. All his brothers and sisters who had grown up at Titan Care Home suffered from a fear of enclosed spaces. He himself had managed, Peter thought. He had a system. If he felt he was on the verge of suffocating and if he was mentally back in time, trapped in the Box, he thought about the *family* and disappeared into a fantasy of a happy life. He could handle his fear and had done so during the four years he was in prison. But My would never have survived here. They would have found My hanging from her sheets one morning, he had no doubt about that.

He heard footsteps coming down the corridor and the door opened.

'I thought I must have misheard,' coughed Cato, who, as always, looked like a living skeleton. 'I told them it had to be a mistake. You're the last person I expected to show up here.'

Peter half expected to hear bones rattle when Cato flopped on to the chair opposite and carried on coughing.

'It's the smoking ban. All that clean air is killing me.'

His tone of voice was more cheerful than his appearance suggested. He had obviously been subjected to brutal treatment by someone stronger than him, and perhaps this someone had rearranged his lungs and airways. His face was blue and yellow and swollen behind the death mask. He had black stitches to repair a split eyebrow and there were burst blood vessels around his eyes.

'You've looked better,' Peter said, pushing the two packets of Camel across to him. 'I hope you can find somewhere to smoke them.'

Cato nodded and fidgeted with the cigarette packets.

'So what do you want?'

Peter leaned back and folded his hands behind his head.

'Just wanted to see how you were doing.'

Cato hawked and spat a yellow gobbet on to the tiled floor.

'Since when do you care about that?'

'We're brothers, aren't we?'

Cato laughed. Peter could see this caused him physical pain. Cato's body had always had strangely contorted movements.

Now an electric current seemed to be running through him, and his arms and legs twisted convulsively.

'It's freezing cold in here. It's always cold.'

'I think it's hot.'

'The old prison was worse.'

Cato shivered. His cough started again. He looked as if someone was shaking him from the inside, like when you shake a fruit tree and the overripe fruit falls to the ground.

'So what do you want?' he asked for the second time. 'They record everything, you know that, don't you?'

'The tape recorder's broken.'

Cato rolled his eyes, until he twigged. Normally the prison would record every conversation between prisoners and visitors, but Matti had once again proved to be a true friend. It was sorted, he had said. The tape recorder was temporarily out of action so they were safe to speak freely.

'It must be something important.'

Peter nodded.

'I've got a problem. I thought you might help me to solve it, seeing that you're here, at the centre of the world.'

'Why would I want to help you?'

His cough exploded in a splutter. Another gobbet landed on the floor.

'Perhaps I can do something for you in return,' Peter said, pushing the buttons all weakened prisoners could be bought for.

'Perhaps I can get you something you want.'

Cato looked neutral, turning a packet of Camel round and round, on its end, then on its side. For a long time it was the only sound in the room.

'How could you do that?'

The voice was curious. A new thought was forming in Peter's mind.

'I know this place. Trust me.'

The cigarette packet was laid down flat.

'What do you want in return?'

Peter told him selected snippets of what had happened since New Year's Eve: Ramses, Stinger, the disappearance of Nina Bjerre and the body in the harbour, which wasn't her.

'I know all of that.'

Peter knew from Matti that Cato was victimised in his block. He was no beefcake and had come to prison without any allies on the inside. The strong prisoners had a hold over him and could make him do anything they wanted when the prison officers turned their backs. Cato knew all about hierarchy and the price you paid for being at the bottom.

'Is Grimme still running the place or has he got a rival?'

Grimme, a biker gang leader, was inside for drug dealing. Approximately five years ago, when he'd been serving the last part of his murder sentence, he had ordered his henchmen to beat up the new prisoner in the shower simply to set an example. Oh no, not just for that reason, Peter thought. There was another reason as well.

He sat for a while looking at Cato and remembering the price he had paid for standing up to the self-elected leader of the prison.

Cato was his brother. They'd grown up together at Titan Care Home and they had been friends. They had roamed the woods around Ry, on the rare occasions that they escaped surveillance and punishment. With his long, bony arms and legs, Cato looked like a lean scarecrow with cheekbones that always seemed to be threatening to burst out of his skin and eyes rolling around in their sockets. Cato had desperately hoped for a miracle, as they all had. They had trusted each other then. They no longer did. But they could use each other for a variety of purposes.

'Matti?' Cato asked. 'Is he OK?'

'Fine. He says hi.'

'Say hi back.'

For a moment this happy family scenario felt completely absurd. Cato smiled a shadow of a smile.

'And Ing-Kistine?'

Inger-Kirstine was Matti's big-breasted wife. Matti struggled to pronounce his 'r's.

'She's put him on a diet. Salad. No bread.'

Cato's mouth split open in a fleeting grin. Then he grew serious again.

'So we're not being recorded?'

Peter slowly shook his head. Eventually Cato nodded.

'Grimme's still running the place,' he said.

He raised a hand to his face and carefully touched the skin. 'But Urban did this. He's Grimme's second-in-command.'

'What will it take to stop it?'

Peter knew the answer. Cato shrugged his skinny shoulders. 'Drugs. Money. Power.'

Peter couldn't get any of that, or at least not in large quantities. But right now he couldn't afford to admit it.

'OK. I'll try. With Matti's help, we'll get you moved into better conditions. Possibly even with a telephone.'

They no longer trusted each other, but Cato's eyes still hung on his with an expression that resembled desperation. Peter leaned forward.

'A man by the name of Erik Gomez Andersen applied for permission to visit the prison back in July. I want to know who he was visiting and why.'

Cato regarded him blankly. His lean fingers dug into the cobalt-blue armrest of the chair. His skull turned on its own axis.

'I also want to know what is being said on the jungle telegraph. Who has Grimme got his nails into outside the prison?'

'In Grenå?' Cato asked.

'Yes.'

Peter inhaled.

'And then there's Brian. Why would Stinger and Ramses stick their necks out for him?'

The prison officer came back. Visiting hours were over. Cato rose with a nod.

'Was that all?'

He stood for a moment watching Peter from a distance and scratching his hair. His fringe hung in long thin strands while the hair at the back was gathered in a crude ponytail.

'You want the dimensions of the biggest chopper inside as well and the name of the person who gets it daily?'

He turned his back on Peter, who called out to him: 'See you under the clock.' It was an expression from their childhood. You never knew when a child would disappear off to a foster family, move to a different institution or simply vanish into thin air. No one had ever met underneath the clock. It was a pathetic joke among boys and girls who had elevated a lack of hope and certainty to a non-existent agreement.

Cato held up a hand, still with his back to Peter, as he was led away. Peter breathed a sigh of relief when he was finally outside. He tilted his head back and looked up into the air, which was heavy and grey with falling snow.

47

'THAT'S A REALLY long time ago.'

The woman behind the lost property counter looked worried. A vertical crease had made its way down her otherwise smooth forehead, but Felix had an inkling that she might always have looked like this. Perhaps she was born this way. One of life's worriers.

In addition, she was pretty overweight, dark-skinned with a hint of a moustache and generally reminded Felix of one of the more sluggish bureaucrats in her home country.

'I know. I should've come much earlier.'

Felix dusted snow off her jacket. Her cheeks were tingling with the transition from the wind and snow outside to the damp heat in the lost property office, where snow and ice trudged in by the customers had formed small puddles on the floor mats. She did her best to look rueful. A man might have been more receptive, she thought; however, the woman did actually look as if she might want to help her.

'As I said, I've been travelling for a couple of months and the contents in the briefcase are of minor importance. The briefcase is what matters to me. It was a wedding present from my sister in Barcelona.'

The woman tapped away on her computer, her glasses perched on the tip of her nose. She wore a tight-fitting green-patterned blouse made from some artificial material. A faint smell of sweaty armpits emanated from her body. She looked determined now, like a bloodhound on the trail, and Felix got the impression she wasn't one of those people who would give up at the first obstacle.

'What did you say the date was?'

'July the twenty-first. On the train I met a very nice man and we had a long conversation. We said goodbye without exchanging names, but it struck me later that he might have handed in the bag when he realised that I'd left it behind.'

Felix was racking her brain so hard you could almost hear the cogs. She had been to the house in Skåde to look for Erik's burgundy briefcase and had been unable to find it, though she had searched the house from top to bottom. She had decided that the briefcase must be what he had handed into lost property. She didn't even dare think about why he might have done so, or what it might contain.

'Any distinguishing features?'

Was this a trick question? Felix tried to remember what the briefcase had looked like. She had given it to Erik for Christmas one year. She didn't remember the brand, but it was bound to have been expensive. He had lost his temper one day when Maria had knocked a mug of hot chocolate into it as it lay open on the table. It was a few days before the helicopter trip, she remembered.

'There's a stain on the inside. Hot chocolate. It has a pale fabric lining.'

The woman nodded and beamed as though Felix had just given the right answer to a question in *Who Wants to be a Millionaire*. Then she grew serious and her worried crease returned as she read the information on the screen.

'I'm afraid it's been auctioned. I thought it might have been after such a long time.'

She forced her eyes from the screen and peered at Felix from above her glasses.

'From time to time we auction unclaimed items. It was sold less than a week ago.'

Felix didn't like the sound of that. There had to be something in the briefcase Erik had wanted to hide, something he didn't want anyone to know about.

'Do you know what happened to the contents of the briefcase? I don't suppose they were sold as well, were they?'

The woman frowned.

'It doesn't say here. Oh yes, wait. It says here that the briefcase was empty.'

Her eyes scrolled down the screen. 'We always open briefcases and bags to see if we can identify the owner and find an address. It appears that it was opened, but nothing was found. Do you remember what you had in it?'

Felix lied effortlessly: 'Some documents and a newspaper, that kind of thing. Nothing important and nothing anyone would benefit from, I think. I always carry my purse and my credit cards in here.'

She patted her shoulder bag. Even so, the woman looked uncomfortable, as though Felix had personally suspected her of stealing the contents of the briefcase. It gave Felix the courage to launch another foray.

'I don't suppose you could put me in contact with the buyer, could you? I could offer to buy it back.'

The woman slowly shook her head. Not allowed. She wasn't at liberty to reveal any names.

'It means a great deal to me.'

It wasn't hard to shed a solitary tear. So many emotions were demanding to be released and sheer physical exhaustion itself was frequently enough to make her cry. The woman behind the counter looked horrified when Felix started sniffling.

'There, there. We'll find a way. We're not very busy right now.'

She nodded in the direction of a bench in the far corner.

'You sit down over there and I'll call and ask the buyer if they're prepared to talk to you. I promise I'll explain everything.'

Felix dabbed her nose with a tissue and duly sat down while her new friend sprang into action. There were no other customers and no one arrived while she waited. Working here must be seriously dull, Felix concluded. Perhaps it was nice to do something different for a change.

Five minutes later she left with an address in Hjortshøj. She fought her way through the wind and the lashing snow down to Toldboden, the customs house by the harbour where she had parked her car. It was the only remnant of their past splendour, she thought, unlocking it with the remote: a black BMW 4x4 registered in her name, now almost covered by snow.

As she approached the car, she suddenly had a strange feeling she was being watched. For the first time it dawned on her that what she was doing might be dangerous. People had died. If someone had been prepared to kill once, they might do so again. As long as there was something worth killing for.

She stopped several times and turned round to see who was nearby, but she saw nothing suspicious. Only random passers-by: an older man also going to his car and some builders who had started unloading a van across Kystvejen. She scanned the area, but visibility was poor and she got snow and wind in her eyes, which started watering. The red Toldboden building looked like something off a Christmas card; the railway tracks were almost hidden by snow. The cathedral spire soared above the town's rooftops. Cars moved at a snail's pace along Kystvejen and had to stop in front of the level-crossing barrier that came down for the train that slid past.

The snow also seemed to calm her nerves, and her pulse started to drop. Life went on. Right here, close to her, people were living their usual lives, shopping, going to work, taking their children to and from nursery, helping them out of their snow suits. Everyday events. The town was normal and it seemed ridiculous to her that a moment ago she had felt frightened that someone was following her. She dismissed it as the result of months of sleep deprivation and parts of her brain that had jammed. She got into her car, entered the address in Hjortshøj on the satnav and joined the slow-moving traffic.

48

IN THE SUMMER, Marselisborg Marina was a jewel as it lay by Tangkrogen and Strandvejen, near the large, palatial villas in Skåde and Højbjerg. Peter had only ever visited it on a summer's day to eat pancakes with Matti and Ing-Kirstine. The weather had been good and the place teeming with people. Restaurants and ice cream stands here had had their balmy days.

Today was probably not one many would choose to come here.

He slammed the car door shut and pulled up his collar to shield himself against the swirling snow. He had driven here after Horsens and in this way exchanged one icy location for another.

He kicked his way through the snow and walked up to the closed restaurants and past a few boats shivering in the water. There was ice on the masts and railings, and the wooden jetties and pontoons were very slippery. The fronts of the buildings looked cold and hostile. He walked around to the car park behind the hotel where numerous boats were stored in cradles on dry land for the winter, like stranded seabirds.

Erik Gomez Andersen. The name of Felix's ex-husband kept buzzing round his head. There were all sorts of loose ends, but he had no doubt that Erik was connected to Ramses and thus with his own wretched past, from which he was struggling to free himself. Who was Erik planning to visit in prison, and what was the nature of his involvement with Brian, Stinger and Ramses?

Peter stopped, flapped his arms to get warm and pulled his woollen cap further down over his ears. Hadn't he nursed Felix and listened to her story and seen in her eyes that she had loved Erik despite his affairs? The man was a poser who had splashed money around and had what some called style, a chancer who had deceived his wife and left her with nothing but debt.

He circled the boats, barely able to see in the gusting snow. He kicked his way through the snowdrifts and crunched through frozen puddles. Some people appeared to be pillars of the community. No one had suspected Erik Gomez of doing anything other than holding down his job and providing for his family. Others were automatically suspect. Especially if they'd served four years for manslaughter and one of their friends had been found dead at the foot of a cliff. This was how it was and he accepted it. But there was something rotten about Erik Gomez, of that he was sure.

He reached up and tried to scrape snow from the bow of one of the boats, but he couldn't find its name anywhere. Felix and Erik had kept their boat moored here. It might already have been sold or confiscated, but there was always a chance he might find it. The boat was the only place left, now that they had gone through the boxes from the office and searched the house in Skåde.

The problem was that he had no idea what he was looking for. He couldn't remember whether it was a motorboat or a yacht, but he guessed the latter. Nor did he know its make or size. He only knew the name: *Felix*. Of course that might have been changed – a new owner could have changed the name as soon as he bought her. But he might be in luck.

He looked up at the boats and tried to make out the names behind the ice and snow. Finally he went back to the car and fetched a shovel from the boot and used it to scrape away the snow from each bow in turn.

He had cleared the snow from perhaps twenty boats and his arms had started to grow leaden when he finally found it. It was a beautiful, stylish wooden boat. He didn't know very much about yachts, but he knew good craftsmanship when he saw it. It was painted navy blue and the paintwork was flawless, like the name, when uncovered, which was painted in beautiful white looped letters: FELIX.

He put down the shovel and looked around. There were only a few people nearby, an elderly couple out walking their dog by the restaurants. Two or three cars were parked in the area, but he saw nothing suspicious. He found a suitable toe-hole and quickly swung himself up on to the cradle and the deck of the boat, where a tarpaulin effectively denied access to the cabin. He worked quickly to loosen the ropes and flick aside the tarpaulin so that he could pick the lock and open the hatch. It was dark. He switched on his torch.

The inside of the boat was well maintained, just like the rest of it. All the cupboards, drawers and tables were made from beautifully varnished, exotic dark mahogany and the bench surrounding the fixed dining table was upholstered in leather. As in most boats, space was at a premium, but effective use had been made of what was available and there was a small, but fully equipped galley with a stove and an oven – he could have been in a tiny bungalow. The sleeping accommodation was the same – compact luxury in mahogany and leather. Everything seemed new and unused.

He moved around quickly, searching the empty cupboards and drawers, and concluded that the boat had either had very tidy owners who hadn't left behind so much as a hairpin or a can of shaving cream, or it had no owners at all. Felix hadn't mentioned whether the boat had been sold. She probably didn't even know.

After a superficial search he started looking more thoroughly. He loosened carpets and looked under them; he lifted the mattresses off the bunks and moved anything that could be moved to explore every nook and cranny.

He heard the sound just as he found the small plastic card wedged in between the leather cushions on the bench. Was that footsteps? Someone walking round the boat and then stopping? A rattling of the hatch he had closed behind him? Or was it merely the wind catching the boat and causing something, possibly his shovel, to fall over?

For a moment he froze, then he quickly retreated to the fo'c'sle. He squeezed behind the door, trying to keep his pulse under control. The footsteps on the deck were louder now. Someone came down into the cabin and moved around. Soon afterwards the door to the fo'c'sle was kicked open and a black-clad Lily Klein appeared, pointing a pistol at him like some latterday Lara Croft. She was small and black in the darkness, multiple piercings in her face which flashed like glow worms. Her eyes matched the muzzle of the pistol.

'Hands up.'

Peter raised his hands. Adrenaline was making his heart pound. Lily tossed her head and now he could see her pit bull from the hospital: the big woman with the broad face and the mullet came down the ladder and shone her torch. The eyes came closer. He could smell garlic on her breath. She knelt down in front of him and heavy hands patted their way down his body and up again, along his sides and in between his legs until she shook her head.

'Nothing.'

Peter's fear gave way to rage.

'What did you expect?'

'What are you doing here?' Lily's question rang out like a gunshot.

'What are *you* doing here? What are you up to?'

'I don't have to tell you anything,' she said.

'What are you looking for?' Peter asked. 'Who are you, Lily Klein?'

'Who do you think I am?'

'I've seen you before.'

'What do you know?'

'About what?'

She flung out an arm.

'About Gomez? His role? The whole operation?'

'What operation?'

She pushed her face into his.

'What do you know?' she asked again. 'What did Stinger tell you?'

'You bitch! Was it you who beat Stinger to a pulp?'

The big girl lashed out with her torch, but Lily raised her hand.

'It's all right, Lena. Let him talk.'

Her voice was calm, but the pistol was still pointing at him.

'Just because you're waving that penis extension about, you think you can do whatever you like,' he said. 'Where are your baseball bats this time?'

'You're starting to bore me,' she said. 'For the last time, what are you doing here?'

'Are you looking for the boat?' he asked. 'The one at the bottom of the Kattegat?'

He saw her interest in her eyes, like a surge of greed.

It could be them. They were certainly involved, he was sure of that. But were they acting alone or did they have someone behind them?

'Fuck you, you bitch.'

Lily stood weighing up the situation.

'You really don't know anything?' she said at length.

'And Ramses,' Peter said. 'I thought the two of you were friends.'

'Ramses was an idiot.'

'And that was why he had to die?'

She nodded to her friend. Lena commenced a search similar to his own. Lily gave the pistol another wave upwards.

'What were you doing in Horsens?'

He was at a huge disadvantage. She knew more about him than he knew about her. He would need to change that if he got the chance.

'I'm sure you already know.'

'Cato,' she said. 'Why him?'

'We're old friends.'

She nodded.

'Let me give you some advice,' she said. 'You never saw us. You never met us. Stay at home and get on with your life. Forget Horsens, forget your past and everything else.'

She didn't look as if she expected a reply. Instead she cast a glance at her friend, who shook her head and held her palms up after searching the boat. Lily nodded towards the hatch and Lena climbed up the ladder.

'Horsens,' Peter said as something returned in a flash. 'I saw you in Horsens Prison once.'

She started walking backwards, still pointing the pistol at him.

'Drop it.'

49

FELIX KEPT HER eye on the road to Hjortshøj, but she couldn't see anything unusual in the rear-view mirror. She looked at the clock in the car. It was a quarter past two. Which meant she would be doing the return journey in darkness.

She drove along the small roads as the snow closed off the landscape and reduced the number of cars both in front of and behind her. She could see their headlights through the curtain of snow tumbling down from the sky and wondered whether it might not be wiser to turn around and go home. But she was so close now and the car continued to plough its way through the snow like a faithful dog. She knew it was either Hjortshøj or another sleepless night.

She found the address and rang the bell, glad that the woman at the lost property office had done the spadework for her. The nameplate on the door said Østerby. They knew she was coming. And they knew why.

A man opened the door. Late thirties, at a guess. Blond hair, glasses, the spitting image of her financial adviser. Behind him, a medium-sized black dog was barking and he tried to control it. She took its wagging tail to be a good sign.

'I'm so sorry to intrude. I'm here about the briefcase . . .'

She could feel the man sizing her up, but she must have looked safe enough for him to let her in because he nodded to indicate that she should follow.

'Don't mind the dog. It's harmless. Let's go into the living room.'

A girl the same age as Maria was watching television. The man asked her to turn down the volume. She was still at the age when she obeyed without sulks.

'I'm so sorry about this,' Felix said again. 'I was abroad and haven't been able to get along to the lost property office until now. The lady who works there was really kind and helpful.'

The man nodded sympathetically.

'It's quite all right.'

'Of course I'll pay you whatever you paid for it. Plus a little extra.'

She had stopped on the way and taken out 2,000 kroner from a cashpoint. They agreed on 1,000 kroner. The briefcase had been sold for 500 kroner at auction, but the Østerby family had also spent money on petrol driving to Århus, and then there was the time they had spent at the auction. Felix made the offer.

'Ah, well, in that case.'

Østerby got up. 'I'll get it straightaway.'

They completed the transaction discreetly and with friendly smiles. Felix thanked him and repeated the story about her sister in Barcelona. The dog, which had calmed down, came over to sniff the leather.

'Dreadful weather,' she said as the man and the dog accompanied her to the door. The girl in the living room had turned up the volume again. 'I'm heading for Djursland. I hope I'll be all right.'

The man opened the door for her. Dusk was approaching.

'I'm sure you'll be fine in that,' he said, looking at the BMW, which she had driven all the way up the drive to avoid having to walk through the snow. The sky and the ground were now one, and the falling snowflakes were the size of cotton wool balls.

She put the briefcase and her bag on the passenger seat and started the engine. She turned on the satnav, reversed out and let it take her out of the maze of residential roads. As she drove, she noticed a black saloon behind her. She decided it was probably a coincidence. She hadn't noticed when exactly it had first appeared. It stuck close to her rear bumper. She could see that the driver was wearing a hoodie or a headscarf, but not whether it was a man or a woman. The car looked smart and new.

She joined the main road and the black car was still in her wake. They drove like this for a long time while she debated with herself how best to tackle the situation. The other car might not have been following her. It might just be going the same way. Finally she decided to deviate from her route. She indicated left and was soon in a narrow lane. The black car duly followed. Now she was absolutely sure it wasn't there by chance and her heart started beating wildly as she drove further and further from the main road, approaching what looked like a forest. The road twisted and turned and the tyres ploughed their way through virgin snow and whatever was hidden beneath. The other car was still following, but it had started to lag behind. Occasionally it would swerve then straighten up again. She realised the four-wheel drive gave her an advantage and accelerated even though it was risky. As she manoeuvred the car round the bends, she tried to read the number plate of the black car in the mirrors. It was difficult. She had to give up on the numbers, but she thought she could see an X and possibly a D. She couldn't see what make of car it was.

As she drove into the forest, the road narrowed even more. She had to reduce her speed dramatically when a car came towards her and the black car seized the chance to close the gap between them.

She didn't see it before it was too late. The road was even narrower now. A tree lay across it. She slammed on the brakes and felt a bump as the black car hit her from behind. She acted so quickly her brain nearly overheated. She drove forward.

Reversed and manoeuvred in a frenzy. The door of the black car opened and a second later someone was pulling at her door. In the darkness she caught a glimpse of a man with a hood over his head. Surreally, he was pointing a pistol straight at her, but she ignored it and revved the engine. He grabbed hold of the door handle, but only with one hand. It swung open. She quickly pressed the accelerator and drove in between the trees with him hanging on. Eventually he had to let go when a tree got in his way. She ploughed the BMW back on the road and drove the way they had come, her pulse racing through her entire body and the passenger door still wide open. She heard a shot ring out. Then another. But the car continued undaunted and she started doubting whether she had heard any shots at all.

Back on the main road, she had to pull over to close the door while keeping an eye on the rear-view mirror. Her hands shaking and the blood throbbing in her veins, she put the car into gear and drove on. As she drove, she took her mobile from her bag and called Peter Boutrup, but there was no reply.

She headed for Djursland and kept checking her rear-view mirror to see if the black car had returned. But she couldn't see it. She turned off at a sign on the left to Tirstrup Airport and pulled into the short-term car park. She stopped near the taxi rank and let the engine idle while she watched the traffic. Once she was certain that no one was following her, she took out the briefcase and opened it. It was empty, but there had to be something concealed inside it. She patted it. The lining was indeed stained and she remembered when Maria had spilt hot chocolate and Erik had told her off. Had he already hidden whatever it was he wanted to hide inside the briefcase? Had he already planned at that stage to hand it to lost property so that no one coming to the house could find compromising evidence? Because that must have been what all this was about, she guessed. The briefcase had to contain something valuable or incriminating. And it didn't have to be very big.

Her fingers explored every corner of the briefcase. She looked for a concealed bottom, but found nothing. She turned the briefcase upside down and shook it; she explored every nook and cranny, and all the pockets. Still nothing. It was empty. Completely and utterly empty.

50

PETER CLAMBERED OUT of the cabin, but Lily and her friend had already gone.

Horsens Prison. Something rang a bell, but he couldn't say what. Had she been an inmate in the women's prison? Or on the staff? Whatever it was, he was certain she was part of his past.

It was getting dark. He struggled to close the boat in the snow; his fingers were frozen as he reattached the tarpaulin and he stood for a moment watching as the snow covered all traces of the uninvited guests. Then he grabbed his shovel and walked back to the car. He took a detour around the areas of Højbjerg and Skåde until he rejoined Kystvejen and headed for the town centre. At Hotel Atlantic he pulled in, parked and sat for a moment scouring the area to see if he was being followed, possibly by a battered, silver-coloured 4x4, like the one the girls had used at the hospital when they rescued Anja. But there was only the snow falling like a blanket over the town and the traffic, which was almost at a standstill. On the road a snowplough drove past scraping the tarmac and spreading salt.

It was only then that he removed his woolly hat and eased the plastic card he had found between the boat's leather cushions out of the folds in the hat. It was a Hotel Atlantic key card. Room 422. He got out of the car, bought a parking ticket and placed it by the windscreen. Then he went inside the hotel, which was furnished in retro style, like something out of the

1960s, with functional furniture and a plain, light wood reception area.

There were no problems walking through the lobby and
taking the lift up, nor inserting the key into the door of Room
422 and waiting to see if the lock would click open. But nothing
happened, and that was when his mission grew more problem-
atic. He thought for a while before taking the lift down again.
He went to reception and joined the queue. When it was his
turn, he leaned against the counter and gave the female receptionist his most charming smile.

'Hi. A friend of mine used to stay in Room four-two-two and
I haven't seen him for a long time. Erik Gomez Andersen. Do
you know if he still comes here?'

He saw the confusion on her face. She frowned and her smile
took on a sympathetic expression. '*The* Erik Gomez Andersen?'

'Yes, what about him?'

'He's dead, I'm afraid. An accident.'

She trained her gaze on him as though expecting him to faint
from the shock and thinking she would need her first-aid
training. Peter adapted his facial expression to a suitably shocked
one and muttered something about having been out of town for
a long time.

'There you go,' he said. 'You should never put off seeing your
friends. One day it might be too late. But am I right in thinking
that he used to come here often?'

She lowered her voice to signal she was speaking in
confidence.

'He booked Room four-two-two for weeks, but he rarely
stayed here.'

Peter thanked her and turned to leave when he recognised a
pair of long red boots and a head of dark hair, sitting in a chair
with her back to him. A middle-aged man in a suit and white
shirt with no tie sat next to Miriam.

Peter walked across and sat down in a chair nearby. The

surprise on Miriam's face, when she saw him, was palpable, but she quickly shifted her gaze to the man in the suit.

'Shall we go upstairs?'

The customer got up. They left two drinks on the table and crossed for the lift. Peter stayed where he was until she came back down again half an hour later and hesitantly approached him. She had probably been hoping he would have gone away in the meantime. She was in her work clothes: a short dress, long boots, dolled up for a party.

'Before you start . . .'

She sat down and crossed her legs. He knew her. Her whole body was in defensive mode.

'I don't owe you an explanation or an apology. You know what I do. Times are hard, work comes first.'

Her reaction saddened him. He had always expected her to carry on working. That was how they had got to know each other. There had to be another reason for her annoyance, he thought.

He handed her the card. She took it and he heard her click her long nails against the plastic.

'What is it?'

'You can see what it is. It's a key card for Room four-two-two.'

'How did you get it?'

He told her and watched her face at the same time. Miriam was frowning and starting to look angry.

'Four-two-two,' she said.

'You've known all along, haven't you? You knew who Felix was. You knew what her husband was.'

He could tell from looking at Miriam that he was right, and he also saw the slight regret as she closed her eyes and massaged her temple.

'Never mind all the things you haven't told me,' he said. 'I'm sure you've got your reasons. We're here now.'

He looked around the lobby, at the guests coming and going through the revolving door, trundling their cabin cases after them.

'And you clearly know this place much better than I do.'

He could see she was scared. He felt sorry for her, but also strangely hard inside.

'Was Erik Gomez one of your punters?'

She made no reply.

'Tell me about him.'

'Peter . . .'

Her voice was swallowed up by noises from reception where guests were checking in and out. He waited while she scanned the room for someone. Who, he didn't know.

'They called him MD,' she said at last, almost whispering. 'He came here a lot.'

'With women?'

'And men.'

'He was into men as well?'

She smirked. 'It's not what you think.'

'Then what? What kind of man was he?'

Miriam stared at the ceiling.

'Nice man, good job. Wife and child.'

'And the men?'

She pressed a nostril with one finger and sniffed with the other.

'Drugs?' he asked.

Miriam's eyes became slits and her voice a hiss.

'What's going on around you, Boy Scout? How do you think Lulu and I can stay in business?'

The realisation hit home.

'You're working for someone.'

'You work for someone.'

'A biker gang?'

He could feel cold sweat on his forehead. For him biker gangs had a face.

'Why do you think I'm here?' Miriam asked.

'You've never told me.'

'Would it have made a difference?'

'I thought we were friends. I thought we had something special.'

There was disappointment in her eyes. Then she straightened up in the chair and rearranged her legs, her face firmly set.

'We did,' she said.

'You've changed.'

'Has it ever occurred to you that you might be the one who has changed, Peter?'

She said it quietly, but it hit the mark. He shook his head. He didn't want to spend time analysing himself now, but he knew it would catch up with him later.

'And if you think I'm going to give you any names, you're dumber than I thought,' she said.

They sat for a while in silence glaring at each other. Then he took a box of hotel matches from a bowl on the table and stood it on its side.

'OK. I'm going to say something. If what I say is correct all you have to do is knock over the matchbox.'

It was a while before she nodded.

'Erik was a drug dealer. He was in charge of distribution. He knew people who could afford it.'

Peter held up his hand. He hadn't finished. She remained silent as she looked straight at him and then down at her lap. He carried on: 'But other people supplied the goods. Grimme was in charge of imports.'

She looked at him. It felt like an eternity. He could have sworn she blinked away a tear, but afterwards he wasn't so sure. Then her arm quickly shot out and her hand with the long red nails knocked over the matchbox. Then she got up and left.

It wasn't until he had sat for a moment composing himself

that he remembered he hadn't switched his mobile back on after his visit to Horsens Prison. He took it out and saw there was a message from Felix. Her voice sounded frightened, but when he rang, there was no reply.

51

Kir squinted, but it was six o'clock and so dark that she couldn't see the new roof on the pig barn.

She felt tense the moment she opened the door to her parents' house. Her airways started to close up in the porch as soon as she saw her mother's clogs and her father's wellies and was hit by the smell of pigs that always lingered on the clothes hanging from the coat stand. She went inside to the big kitchen. They were all there: Mum, Dad, Tomas and for once, Red, as well. It wasn't necessarily the recipe for a pleasant and relaxed dinner, but they had to have dinner together once a week, like it or lump it; her father insisted. Even if it only amounted to half an hour of grim silence until everyone could breathe a sigh of relief and go their separate ways. Of course they could choose to say no, or they could choose not to go, but Red was the only one who got away with that.

In her family they didn't go in for physical greetings, not even a handshake, it was just a nod and a 'hi'. She had only ever hugged her parents once. It had been the day she appeared with a rucksack on her back ready to go to Kongsøre, thrilled at having been accepted for mine clearance diver training. They had frozen, both of them, as though she were a carrier of a contagious disease. It wasn't the done thing. The only creature ever to receive affection was Zita, a rough-haired pointer her father went hunting with. And the dog was the one Kir lavished her love on now as Zita politely came to greet her, again the only one.

'Smells nice, Mum.'

'The roast is a bit overdone. The meat's falling apart.'

Her mother made a quarter-turn while Kir squatted down and patted the dog. Her mother cut the crackling off the thick pork joint she had roasted in the oven with prunes and apples. There would be gravy and home-made red cabbage with boiled and caramelised potatoes, and under normal circumstances Kir would love nothing more than to tuck into a massive plateful, but today was different. Today the discovery of Gry's body lingered on her retina, and the smell of blood from the hotel room mixed with the smell of pork and forced bile up her throat.

'So, not satisfied with finding a dead body washed up on the beach,' grunted her father, 'this time you've gone and found a body at the hotel.'

He was sitting at the dinner table, holding a newspaper open, freshly showered, grey hair combed back, clearly emphasising the long, pointed shape of his face. His skin was weather-beaten, and his eyes were filled with scorn.

'What were you doing there?'

She always had to defend herself. It had become a habit, so nowadays she barely gave it a thought.

'She wasn't washed up on the beach.'

Her father lowered his newspaper and looked straight at her. No one ever came to her rescue, she thought. Either they were too scared or they thought she had only herself to blame. She usually played along. She usually gave him a detailed, polite reply, simply to keep the peace and ultimately perhaps for the sake of her mother. Possibly also a little for the sake of Tomas, even though he was too much in their pocket to speak up for himself. But today felt different and for the first time in ages she had seriously considered absenting herself.

'And the hotel?' asked her father, who never missed a thing.

'I was just passing,' she said, hoping that would suffice, but knowing full well that it wouldn't. She had called in advance and told her mother the story, to prepare them for the newspaper headlines, but fortunately she hadn't been named in the article.

The newspaper rustled as her father put it down on the table. He took a deep breath.

'Just passing, were you? I can see how you would pass a hotel. But as I understand it, you just had to rush in when you heard something from an open window. Why do you always have to go and stick your nose in other people's business?'

She stood very still. It wasn't going to go away. She looked at her mother, who turned her back on them and started carving, at Tomas, who was leaning against the window sill scratching his chin and avoiding her gaze, and at Red, who was taking the cap off a beer, apparently revelling in the entertainment. She considered her strategy, as she had done so many times before. And she asked herself why she didn't just give up. Why was it so important to her to pretend they were really a happy family? Why did she keep hoping that they would be blinded by some light and suddenly see what was wrong? She was thirty-two years old. Things were never going to change.

She chose a third option. She walked across to her mother.

'Can I help you with anything?'

'You can set the table.'

It was the closest she would ever get to helping her, being asked to do something. She made a big fuss out of looking for plates in the cupboard – she knew exactly where everything was kept. Ditto cutlery in the drawer and glasses from the vitrine cabinet. Tomas and Red didn't move, but talked in muted tones about the new roof on the barn and the new herd of pigs. Her father watched as she cleared the table, including the newspaper, which she put in the kitchen window. Tomas sent her a small, secretive smile, or at least that was her impression.

'Right, I think we can eat now.'

It was her cue to put the food on the mats. After all, she was the girl in the family.

Her mother handed her a bowl of boiled potatoes. She looked at Kir, but didn't see her; that was how it felt, and it was her mother's speciality. Kir had to remind herself that her mother was caught in the middle. This was the only life she knew. Her daughter's lifestyle with no boyfriend or children but with a job she loved was a constant threat to a more traditional way of life. Kir knew that only too well, yet still it hurt.

'Why couldn't you have walked on past the hotel?'

Everyone had sat down, the dishes were being passed around, and her father's question came like a slap across the face.

'I couldn't ignore a cry for help,' she said.

Her father shovelled caramelised potatoes on to his plate.

'You can't save the whole world. It's rotten anyway.'

No one spoke. She helped herself to a slice of pork, the smallest she could find.

'Perhaps you don't think I'm entitled to ask?' her father continued after the first mouthful, and she knew what was coming next. 'I go about my business every day without both-ering anyone, but my daughter keeps finding one corpse after another and interfering in other people's lives. People are talking.'

Kir put down her fork.

'Then let them talk. I'm only doing my job.'

Her father, too, put down his cutlery on his plate.

'To my knowledge it's not a mine clearance diver's job to find bodies in hotels. Unless we're talking about flooding. A tsunami, perhaps?'

'It is my job,' Kir repeated. 'I was in the area because I was looking for rooms for my colleagues.'

Her father snorted.

'They've probably got somewhere to stay already. And what's that got to do with you? The police are footing the bill.'

'It's my town,' Kir said. 'I wanted to find them a good deal. But now it's too late. Today was the last day.'

This time Red, who was sitting opposite her, chewing a piece of crackling and then holding it between his fingers, reacted.

'Have you only found the one body in the harbour?'

'And a few bits and pieces,' Kir said vaguely. She wasn't allowed to discuss the case with anyone, not even family.

'Bits and pieces?'

Red's eyebrows shot up. Kir shrugged her shoulders.

'I found the body. That's all. She's been identified now. As you know, it wasn't Nina Bjerre, so she must still be out there somewhere. Chances are she's on her way to Norway.'

'Says who?' Tomas said.

She told him her theory that Nina had stumbled across Tora's killer and had been thrown into the sea.

'She'll turn up,' Kir said. 'They always do.'

At least the interrogation by her father had been halted, but this wasn't much of an improvement. During the rest of the dinner she fought off questions to the best of her ability. She knew better than to get up and leave. She knew better than to call them what she felt they were right now: not her family, just four people tied to her by blood and very little else. From experience she knew she would regret it later. It would take months, years possibly, to mend fences because deep down they didn't understand her. She loved them; that was the root of the problem. She longed for closeness and intimacy. In her childhood she had harboured the illusion that it had once been like that, with her siblings and especially with her mother, but she must have been deluding herself. Everything was broken and she knew exactly when it had happened.

She endured it. She answered their questions, stayed for pudding, lemon mousse, and then used tiredness as an excuse to leave.

Back home in her summer house, she was frozen to the bone and lit a fire in the wood burner before sitting down with a whisky. But no matter how close she moved to the fire she couldn't get warm. Her teeth began to chatter and one shiver after another rippled across her skin as though there were ghosts nearby. Perhaps there are, she thought. There was the ghost of Uncle Hannibal and then there were those of Nina Bjerre, Gry and Tora. No matter where she turned something was breathing down her neck and it went back a long way, to the time her path had been strewn with the dead creatures, and not all of them wished her well.

The family. None of them had ever forgiven her. It all started the day she had dived down and pulled Tomas out of the water to a life with brain damage. Two years ago the episode had been raised at a family dinner, just like tonight's. The evening had ended in conflict with mutual recriminations and she had no desire to repeat the experience, but the essence of it was still a bitter pill for her to swallow.

She ran her finger around the rim of her whisky glass. There was a knock at the door. Through the spyhole she could see Mark Bille Hansen outside. She let him in, still holding her glass, and seated him next to the wood burner, with an identical glass.

'What's happened?' he asked. 'You look worse than me.'

She scrutinised him and concluded that, if so, things had to be pretty bad. He was definitely a mess, with bags under his eyes, his jacket and trousers crumpled and his hair all over the place. He apologised for turning up at her home, but he couldn't stop thinking about the case.

'And you seem to have a flair for crime,' he said.

She followed her smile with a sip from her glass, and the whisky burned all the way down her throat.

'That's what my dad says. He thinks I've got a flair for finding bodies and upsetting a small community where everyone knows everybody else.'

He gave her a look which she interpreted as compassion.

'I know what you mean.'

She nodded. She could tell from his face that he understood and before she knew it, she had started telling him about her evening. Normally she was a very private person. She was astonished and possibly also a little annoyed with herself, but the intimacy – or the illusion of it – was so very welcome. She needed it. She told him about that night two years ago.

'We ended up talking about the time I jumped in the water and fished out my brother, Tomas. We don't usually talk about it. That day is taboo.'

'Why?'

'Because it's all about emotions and we've never been good with emotions. Love, gratitude, anger.' She corrected herself, 'Oh no, that's wrong, we can do anger.'

'What were they angry about?'

'My dad was angry that I'd brought up the subject. I did it because I thought we should talk about it; it was a day that changed everyone's lives. We began treating each other differently from that day onwards and I didn't understand why.'

'Your brother was brain-damaged?'

She nodded.

'It isn't immediately obvious, but his short-term memory isn't very good. Nor is his concentration. But Tomas wasn't the problem.'

'Then what was?'

'My dad said it was rather reckless of the guilty party to raise the subject.'

'Guilty party?'

'That's what I queried. And you know what he said? He said everyone knew that it was me who had pushed Tomas overboard.'

'And had you?'

She shook her head. The tears welled up, but she managed to suppress them.

'Of course not. But I realised that everyone thinks I did.'

This was the essence of her life, and there she was, talking about it to someone who was actually a stranger. It was an open wound she was constantly trying to heal. That was why she kept going back for those dinners. That was why she was still living in Grenå. She lived in hope of healing a family that refused to be healed.

Mark Bille asked her: 'How did Tomas end up in the water?'

She hunched her shoulders.

'Perhaps he just fell in. Perhaps the boat listed suddenly, I can't remember. I think I must've been looking away or had my back turned when it happened.'

They sat in silence for a little while. Then he said: 'There's a reason for my visit.'

'Oh yes?'

'Gry. The flat she lived in. Her landlord, a man called Asger Toft, told me he inherited the property from his mother, and that was technically correct. But, just to be on the safe side, I looked into it and it turns out he sold the house a year ago.'

Intuitively she knew something was about to happen and she needed to brace herself. She pressed her knees against the edge of the table.

'Who to?'

He looked at her as though anticipating a reaction.

'Your mother.'

52

'COME ON. DANCE with me.'

Felix put on some music and reached out for Peter, but he shook his head. She just smiled at him, a sad inward-turning smile, and slowly her body started moving to the rhythm of the music. To and fro, back and forth, spinning around, bending her knees and stretching up on her toes in dance moves that looked as if she was improvising, but whose magic had him completely hypnotised. Her body was like a single organic movement: it twisted around itself, it swayed like a flower in the wind, it unfurled and it contracted. He was reminded of his encounter with a stag, with something wild and untamed and beautiful. Something you couldn't change or disturb, but could only watch, although you didn't quite understand what you were witnessing.

All he could do was devour her with his eyes until the music subsided and she collapsed like a rose under the weight of rainwater. Tired. But without the anger and fear that had recently consumed her.

They had swapped stories. Shaking and agitated, she had told him about her escape from the black saloon. Once she had started to calm down, she sat wrapped in a blanket and drank three cups of tea. Afterwards he told her what Miriam had said about Erik's secret life. He felt no pleasure, as he might have imagined he would. Felix's sadness, her anger and fear, had knocked him for six, and he was left wishing he could have spared her the truth.

'He loved me once.'

She had said the words with the usual stubbornness in her voice, followed by the more sceptical: 'He must have done.'

He discovered that he would have liked to eradicate her doubt and replace it with certainty, to see her happy.

'I'm sure he did,' he had said.

That was when she had turned on the music and started dancing with her eyes closed, as though she could dispel disappointment and pain in that way. Perhaps she could.

'One day I'd like to paint you dancing,' he said after she had flopped down on an easy chair and curled up in it.

'I thought you don't paint people.'

'I could make an exception.'

She smiled, a little distracted, and he knew that her thoughts had once again returned to Erik. She took the burgundy briefcase from the table, placed it on her lap and drummed her fingers.

'He must have had enemies. It's par for the course in the drugs business.'

He didn't know what was worse for her: the women or the drugs. But ultimately lying had to be the greatest villain. With lies came doubts about everything she had believed in and trusted. Trusted blindly, or so it seemed.

'I don't think it was an accident,' she blurted. 'Not any more.'

'But the Air Accident Investigation Board didn't find anything, did they?'

She shook her head.

'That was before all of this.'

She was alluding to the briefcase and the boxes from Erik's office. 'They found nothing because they weren't looking.'

'Is the investigation over?'

'No. I'm meeting them tomorrow. I'll have to tell them what I know now, won't I?'

He nodded. He supposed she would.

She got up and started pacing the room, again as if driven by an internal engine.

'The question is who was behind it. Whoever killed Erik also killed Maria.'

In her eyes he could see her thoughts making connections.

'They must be the same people who are after me now. They think I know something. Or they're scared I might start remembering things.'

As though by mutual agreement, they both looked at the briefcase.

'Let's take another look at it,' he said. 'Have you got a knife or a pair of scissors? I think we're going to have to destroy it.'

'Do you think that he slit the leather to hide drugs inside?' She answered her own question. 'Surely you can see there's no room. There can't possibly be any money or drugs anywhere. It would take up too much space, don't you think?'

He agreed.

'It's a wild goose chase,' she said. 'I risked life and limb on a wild goose chase.'

'Possibly. Now get me those scissors.'

He watched her go into the kitchen, a tiny figure in an oversized jumper with ski socks on her feet, gliding across the floor.

'Here you are.'

She passed him the scissors. He took them and started cutting away the lining of the briefcase.

'Your sister in Barcelona will be upset,' he said as the scissors sliced through the silky fabric.

'I don't have a sister. And certainly not in Barcelona.'

He arched his eyebrows.

'I'd forgotten what a good liar you are.'

'Necessity teaches naked women to spin wool, as you say in Danish.'

He looked at her. She was right. That was what she was.

Naked. Despite the jumper, the baggy jeans and the socks. So exposed and naked he could almost see her heart valve flaps opening and closing.

'You're staring at me.'

She sounded very uneasy. He had nursed her and seen her body in every possible situation. He couldn't help smiling as he tore the lining from the briefcase in one piece. There were no banknotes or drugs, but he did find something else. Written in black felt tip pen on the red leather under the lining was a series of numbers: 561562 N 011 34 22 E.

Felix frowned.

'The first bit looks like my dad's mobile number except that he has two-eight at the start and six-zero rather than six-two.'

'That's the number on Stinger's arm.'

'The second half could be my aunt's birthday, except that she was born in 'fifty-four and not 'thirty-four.'

She gave him an almost apologetic look.

'When I did accounts and worked with numbers, I always had to find a system. Is that the location of the treasure?'

He nodded.

'N is for North and E is for East. The numbers are degrees. We should be able to find it on the chart.'

'Erik never could memorise numbers,' she said. 'He could barely remember Maria's birthday. Or our wedding anniversary,' she added.

Peter got up and fetched the chart he had got from the chandler's. He unrolled it, put it on the table and held the corners down with an ashtray, a mug and two apples from the fruit bowl. It didn't take them long to find the spot where the two lines intersected. It was just like the fisherman in Grenå harbour had said.

'Lille Lysegrund. A depth of ten to twenty metres,' Peter said, putting his finger on the chart. 'An hour's sail from the harbour. It's perfect.'

Felix stared at the intersection on the chart. Her lips moved as though trying to memorise the position.

'How did Erik get hold of these numbers?'

He turned to her. He could see her thoughts following his.

'Ramses,' she said. 'He's the link between Erik and the boat. He has to be.'

She slumped down on the far end of the sofa. Her gaze and her whole expression turned inwards. She took the briefcase from him, put it on her lap and ran her hands across the leather, playing with the key and the handle, clicking it open and shut.

'I met him twice. No, I didn't meet him,' she corrected herself. 'I saw him twice. Twice that I can remember. The first time he came to our house and was with Erik in his study. It seemed like an ordinary business meeting, but he did look a little unusual, as though he had made an attempt to dress up. Put on a suit, you know, and possibly a tie, yet it was obvious he wasn't an ordinary business associate.'

'Do you know why he was there? Did he bring anything?'

She shook her head and clicked the lock again.

'I don't remember. I only remember his face. His black hair, the sleepy eyes and the long lashes. He was a handsome man, as you know. The kind of man women notice.'

For a brief moment he wondered what she had noticed about him.

'And the second time?'

She shut her eyes.

'The second time was a few days before the helicopter trip.'

She spoke with her eyes closed as she had done when she was dancing.

'He rang the bell and I let him in. He asked to speak to Erik, but he seemed stressed. Unshaven and scruffy. It was a very brief meeting.'

She opened her eyes.

'He looked like a man on the run.'

Peter reckoned Stinger had been set up big time. Ramses hadn't known just one coordinate; he had known them both. He had known the location of the boat all the time, and perhaps that had been his death sentence.

53

'Shouldn't you be at home in bed?'

Anna Bagger looked hard at Mark. She probably meant well, but her attitude merely served to irritate him. As did her appearance, the blue silk blouse matching her eyes and signalling control, and the fact that apparently she felt entitled to make assumptions about his health.

'I've got cancer. Not flu. Crawling under the duvet and taking paracetamol isn't going to make it go away.'

She blinked.

'What's so urgent?'

The case wasn't progressing as she had expected. Neither was he. She was losing her grip, and part of him felt sorry for her while another part jumped for joy. They had been lovers once and she had left her mark on him. Perhaps he was only trying to get his own back.

He gestured towards the screen.

'I'm watching a film.'

It was the truth. He had remembered the string of robberies carried out in Grenå just before New Year. Corner shops and even a bakery had been robbed by masked intruders who had terrified staff and forced them to empty their tills. It had suddenly occurred to him that the staff in every single case had been female. He had contacted businesses in town and in particular those shops which had been affected. All five victims had independently stated that the robbers hadn't spoken. Each time they had produced a note stating that it was a robbery. They had also been wearing ski suits, which convinced the victims that at least one of them was a man. Each robbery had been carried out by two or three perpetrators, and that was what had made the alarm bells go off.

'CCTV footage? Where from?'

She looked over his shoulder.

'This is from the bank next to the bakery where the robbery was.'

He explained his theory. Three women had arrived in town at around the time the robberies took place. Perhaps they had needed money. Perhaps they were the ones who had robbed the small shops, the ones with only a few assistants and cameras.

'So obviously they wouldn't have risked robbing the bank,' he said. 'But there's a fifty-fifty chance that they passed the bank's CCTV. They must've approached from the left or the right.'

She nodded. He continued.

'The bakery was robbed on the twenty-second of December, just before Christmas. I know it's going to take time, but in my opinion there's a good chance we'll find them on the footage.'

She straightened up. Right now she had no choice but to accept his help, he thought. The case had become so complex that she had to rely on his experience. She had to relinquish some of her control, and he knew she loathed the idea of it.

'Let me know what you find,' she said. 'If we can identify the two others, we have an idea what happened to Tora. We need to find out when she disappeared and why. Who are their enemies?'

He felt a surge of satisfaction. He thought about Tora and Gry, who were dead, and about the missing Nina, who was very likely to be dead, too. As long as he kept his focus on the dead women, his mind was clear. So that was what he intended to do.

'What about Gry's post-mortem?' he asked. 'Can you tell me anything about the time of death?'

'Not accurately, but somewhere between two and six a.m. the day she was found,' she said.

'Have you found the murder weapon?'

Anna Bagger leaned towards his desk.

'No, but the pathologist found quite a lot of DNA. No semen, though. Death was by strangulation. Her face was removed after death.'

Melancholy laid its heavy hand on him.

'Same as with Tora.'

Her voice was, as always, cool and considered, but he detected a slight tremble. Same killer. It had to be.

'I talked to people in the pub,' Mark said. 'No one saw anything.'

She perched on his desk, although she didn't look like she had any intention of staying.

'We're still looking for the man Gry had a row with. But he probably doesn't feel any great need to say he was out buying sex that night.'

'Did you speak to Elise Røjel about the property in Fredensgade?' Mark asked.

'We sent a man out there. Did you know she's the mother of that frogwoman?'

He nodded.

'She sounded almost surprised to learn that she owned the property,' Anna Bagger said. 'I think it's her husband's investment and he just put it in his wife's name.'

She got up and headed for the door.

'We spoke to him as well, but he referred us to his lawyer and said he hadn't been to the property since before Christmas and he had no idea what was going on.'

'Do you believe him?'

She turned and shrugged her shoulders.

'Difficult to tell. But I find it hard to imagine that an old pig farmer would carry out a murder like Gry's. It doesn't really add up, does it?'

He shook his head. It didn't add up. There wasn't much that did. He thought about Kir's description of her family.

Anna Bagger hesitated before pressing the door handle. The moment stretched out and he knew what was coming.

'What are the odds?' she asked.

He nodded towards the screen.

'Same as here. Fifty-fifty, according to the doctors. They're going to give me some alternative treatment. The kind they offer you when traditional methods fail.'

He could tell from her face she thought it sounded dubious. As did he. He said nothing more, and she waved briefly and left.

Long after she had gone he was still concentrating on the screen, fast forwarding his way through the bank recordings.

His back straightened as three girls passed under the camera. And not only that. They came back again and stood for a while discussing something. Then one of them seemed to spot the camera and pull the other two away. He pressed freeze-frame. One of the girls had long blonde hair and was slightly taller than the other two. Tora, he guessed. The other two girls were very different. One was wearing black punk clothes and had short black hair and a petite boyish body. The other had a mullet and broad features.

54

SHE CAME TO him at night, a dark shadow in all the blackness. He lay awake on the balcony listening to her footsteps on the stairs. Without a word, she slipped into his sleeping bag.

She was so thin; her breasts were small, practically non-existent. He had seen her frail and sick, but she had a strength he hadn't previously known and in her ecstasy she held him so tight and gave voice to pent-up lust, both hers and his, with an energy that had to originate from an atavistic past. He entered her in an explosion; she pulled him down towards her and caressed him.

Afterwards they lay stomach to stomach in his sleeping bag covered by the duvet. It almost felt more intimate than what they had just done.

'They're looking for the coordinates, aren't they?' she said out of the blue. 'They're not looking for me at all.'

He didn't quite know how to say it, but thought he might as well be honest: 'I think they want both. The position because there might be valuables hidden in the boat on the seabed. And you because you're starting to remember more than they want you to.'

'But how do they know that?'

He didn't know so he could only hazard a guess.

'You've started to get out and about. You and I found Ramses. You were in my house when someone broke in. You went to pick up Erik's stuff from the office. You went to your house in Skåde. You tracked down the briefcase.'

She shuddered and her nerves spread to him.

'Do you think someone has been watching me all this time?'

'It's beginning to look like it.'

Her body was both hot and cold, just as it was both soft and hard. She snuggled up to him, reminding him of water seeping into every crack and crevice. Harmless on the surface, but with a force and a direction that could be overwhelming. He wondered if he would be allowed to keep her in his life.

'Tell me about My,' she said, as though able to read his mind.

He looked up at the stars and searched for the words.

'She died. She lived and she died. She was twenty-six years old.'

Felix turned her face up towards him. In the darkness all he could make out was her eyes.

'Were you in a relationship?'

'You couldn't be in a relationship with My.'

'But you loved her?'

It was a word he would never have chosen himself. Not because it wasn't accurate, but because it was a word My wouldn't understand. For her, life was concrete. It was about the next meal, going for a walk with Kaj, sleeping on someone's sofa and avoiding her fears of the past, especially the Box. My had been absolutely terrified of the Box at the care home.

'She was like a sister to me. We grew up together.'

Felix pressed herself against him and put her head on his shoulder. It stayed there, as light as a feather. As light as My's, but in an utterly different way he couldn't even begin to describe.

'My was different. She was very . . . innocent.'

They lay very still and he thought she had fallen asleep when suddenly she said: 'What happened?'

'What do you mean? To My?'

'And to you? Why did you go to prison? It had something to do with her, didn't it?'

Her breathing came in short gasps and he could hear the

question had been hard to ask. He supposed it had been like a barrier between them, as was always the case whenever the past and the present collided around him. He lay looking into the night for a long time before speaking.

He cast his mind back more than five years, to a distant day he still cursed for his inattentiveness. He and My had been sitting with his dog, Thor, at a pavement café in Grenå one summer. My drank juice, he recalled. She had been chatting away, enjoying the moment as only she could. He had to concentrate to keep up because My had a habit of speaking in codes and disjointed sentences. Thor was the most handsome and cleverest Alsatian in all the world. They sat there, a small family triangle of their own, unaware of the two men approaching. My gesticulated as she always did, completely at random. An arm would go up, then her bad leg would twitch and kick out at Thor, who shifted position. She was talking about a traffic accident she had seen on her way there on the bus. She was agitated in her usual intense way, savouring the drama.

'She was talking about the cars that had crashed,' he said. 'She knew exactly what make and colour they were. She was really excited about the yellow ambulance.'

He didn't dare ask if there were any casualties or fatalities. My's brain hadn't got that far. She was more interested in tangible facts about the cars.

'Then the two guys entered the café. They were drunk and they sat down at the table next to us. Trouble was brewing.'

Peter carried on in short bursts. My hadn't noticed the men. She was lost in a world of her own, reeling off her impressions. Her excitement caused her legs to kick more than usual and she hit the man sitting closest.

'He glared at her, but she didn't see it. Then he got up and stood right in front of her and shouted: "Shut your mouth, you stupid bitch."'

'My asked him a classic My question. She looked at the man and asked him in a puzzled tone: "Who are you?"'

'She had no sense of danger. The man asked whose business it was and My replied honestly, as she always did: "Mine".'

'The situation got out of hand. The man pulled My by the hair. Thor growled and his hair bristled. The man's friend tried to drag him away. He succeeded, but as they left they threatened to come after us one day.

'I thought it was just an empty threat,' Peter said. 'But two days later they turned up at my house out here and they shot Thor.'

'And then what happened?' Felix asked.

'I had a hunting rifle. I had taken it out because Manfred and I were going hunting.'

The truth was on the tip of his tongue and he was tempted to tell her. But it wasn't an option, so he sighed into the night, knowing she might very well decide to leave him at this point.

'The man I shot was called Hans Martin Krøll. He turned out to be the brother of a gang leader called Grimme. Grimme was already serving a sentence in Horsens Prison for a double murder when I was sent there. As a result it wasn't exactly a mini-break at Lalandia.'

He could feel her heart pounding against his body. It was contagious. Was she about to get up and leave him? Was this when he realised that the door to his new life was well and truly shut?

'Some say you didn't pull the trigger,' she said.

'Who is some? Who have you been talking to?'

'Is it true?'

She might have been talking to Mark Bille. Or she might have worked it out for herself.

'No,' he said. 'No, it isn't.'

She snuggled up to him and muttered drowsily: 'I thought you'd say that.'

They lay for a while without speaking. The dog stirred on the fleece. The air was dry and crackled with frost.

'How did My die?' she asked quietly.

'It's complicated.'

She lifted her face from his chest and simply looked at him.

'Cato killed her,' he said. 'He didn't mean to, but he always had a temper. It was an accident. He whacked her and she died. Then he tried to make it look like suicide by hanging her in a tree.'

'Cato? From prison? Is that why you're no longer friends?'

He sighed. He couldn't begin to describe his wretched life and the ties that bound him to it. He couldn't even explain it to himself. So how would he be able to explain it to her?

He touched her hair. So soft against his skin.

'That's one reason,' he said.

Dawn arrived in cold, purple colours. It had stopped snowing and the fresh snow on the cliff glittered like mother-of-pearl. The sea was the brightest shade of blue. There was a thin layer of hoarfrost on the duvet, but they were warm inside the sleeping bag. They made love again and afterwards she raised a hand to his face to feel his skin, as though she were blind.

'I've been wondering what it would feel like,' she said.

'And how does it feel?'

He held his breath, but sighed with relief when she said: 'It feels good.'

They were interrupted by his mobile beside the dog's fleece. He could see from the number that it was Elisabeth.

'Do you remember me telling you I was going to get a new tattoo?'

'At Rollo's Kennel?'

She confirmed his recollection.

'I asked him if he had ever tattooed a fleur-de-lis on a girl's thigh.'

'And?'

'He had. One day last autumn three girls came in and asked for identical tattoos.'

'On the inside of their thighs?'

'Yes. Exactly. A place no one sees. Or only a few. I just thought you should know.'

55

THE CAT WAS dead. Someone had covered its mouth with gaffer tape and shoved a fat stick up its rectum. It must have been a dreadful death.

Kir only found it because she wanted to go for a walk around the barn to see the new roof from every angle, composing herself to face her mother. And there it was, on the dung heap, half-covered by a load of fresh manure tipped there after the previous day's snowstorm. Its ginger fur stood out against the brown pile. She carefully pulled it out by its front paws and saw the tragic sight. The cat's name was Georg, one of many cats on the farm and as such not irreplaceable. They were inured to cats dying from time to time. But this wasn't an accident and it made her go cold all over, even colder than the outside temperature, which was a biting minus seven.

She stroked the cat's fur as it lay there on the dung heap. It wasn't the first animal she had seen suffer a painful death on the farm, but it was a long time since the last one. Several years, in fact. She didn't like to think about it and had repressed the memory. But sometimes the memories would return, like now, when she remembered how another cat had died: with a piece of string tied around its front paws and another around its hind legs, it had been ripped apart while still alive. And years back – fifteen perhaps – there was the incident with the burned cockerel: someone had taken the cockerel from the hen coop, poured petrol over it and set it on fire. They discovered this when the small ball of fire ran screeching around the yard before falling down dead. Animal cruelty, said Kir, who threatened to go to the police. But her father called it a boyish prank and threw the cockerel on the dung heap with a shrug, making it quite clear that if any member of the family brought the police home, he never wanted to see them again.

Kir had no doubt his response would be the same this time as well. She stood for a while contemplating the cat, which was frozen solid. Then she turned and went back to the house, where she found her mother busy hoovering. For a moment she watched her mother from behind. She was wearing a checked casual skirt and a brown knitted jumper. Her back was broad and short; her arms moved in powerful sweeps; her legs, clad in thick nylon tights, were set in sturdy brogues.

Kir was muscular like her mother, but she had inherited her height and sinewy build from her father. Appearances, however, could be deceptive. From the back her mother looked like a robust farmer's wife, but when she turned around, her eyes revealed what her body was hiding: the permanent nervous twitch in her left eye, which always increased at times of tension; her habit of blinking in fear and beating a hasty retreat like a chastened dog; her expression of distrust, bordering on contempt, in the face of all kindness and love. Kir didn't remember her father ever hitting her mother, but she had often thought that it might have been easier to deal with if he had. Perhaps the threat of violence and humiliation was worse than the act itself. And threats had never been in short supply, both verbal and non-verbal.

'Mum?'

It was the dog that made her mother turn around and notice her when it left its basket and went to greet Kir, wagging its tail. Her mother turned off the Hoover.

'Is that you, Kirstine?'

As always, she sounded frightened. Last night's dinner had exhausted her and now her daughter had turned up two days on the trot. Kir forced herself to continue into the living room and ignore the sensation that the walls were trapping her in a spider's web.

'Have you seen the cat?'

Her mother frowned and smoothed her skirt. For a moment they stood facing each other.

'Is that why you're here?'

Kir shook her head.

'Why don't we go into the kitchen? Where's Dad?'

'He's gone to the DIY store to get some tools.'

Kir persuaded her mother to sit down at the long kitchen table. She put the kettle on and fetched some cups.

'And Tomas?'

'In the pig barn, I think. I don't know. What's wrong with the cat?'

Kir told her about Georg.

'You really ought to contact the police.'

'Your father'll get really angry. And it's too late now.'

That was how it always was. Too late, they'd say. It's already dead.

Kir made tea and left the pot to brew on the table.

'It's not too late for the next cat.'

Her mum shuddered.

'It probably won't happen again. Your dad says these things are just boyish pranks. All sorts of people live around here. It's hard to stop this kind of thing.'

In a way she was right. The farm bordered the forest where schools often went on trips, where, since time immemorial, boys had played cops and robbers or whatever they called their games. She herself had played in the forest with her friends from school. As had Tomas and Red.

'Even so,' she insisted. 'It's not the first time, is it?'

Once her mother had been a beautiful woman, Kir thought. Not film star looks, of course, but she'd had a luxuriant, full-bodied kind of beauty, curves which hadn't yet turned into a staunch, defensive corset. Her cheeks were as round as apples, her face was almost wrinkle-free and her eyes were dark blue like her own. Cut in a short, practical style and shaped like a soldier's helmet, her hair had in recent years gone from salt-and-pepper to completely white.

'You haven't come here to talk about the cat, surely?'

Kir poured tea for both of them, asking herself what her plan really was and why she had come. Was she hoping to help Mark unravel any threads related to her own family? Or was this a final attempt to heal her family, to clear up all the misunderstandings and misdeeds and start afresh?

'I didn't know you'd become a property investor.'

Her mother was startled.

'What do you mean?'

'Fredensgade twenty-seven is registered in your name.'

Her mother looked at her without seeing.

'Have you been speaking to the police?'

Kir forced herself to ignore the implied threat, as she had done most of her life.

'Of course I've spoken to the police. I'm working for the police on this case. And suddenly my mother's name appears on the deeds to a house where one of the victims lived.'

Her mother shook her head.

'It means nothing.'

'Everything in an investigation means something. What do you know? I'm perfectly aware that Dad is just using your name. What does he do with the property?'

Her mother brushed some crumbs from the table.

'You know we hire seasonal workers every now and then.'

'The Poles?'

An eye muscle twitched. The dark blue eyes focused on her. It was a nightmare. She'd dreaded facing a moment like this: having to choose between what was morally right and her loyalty to her family. She had always known the day would come.

'This is a murder case, Mum, and I'm involved. Was it so that the Poles could have fun with prostitutes? Was that why Dad did it?'

Her mother looked away, down to where her wedding ring cut into her flesh on the left hand. There might never have been much love between her parents, but that ring meant more than every law in the whole wide world, and it wasn't just because of her father's regime of terror. It was so much more than that. It was about tradition and tribal identity. For better or worse, they were a farming family, united against the rest of society. You kept to yourself and stuck with your own.

They sat in silence for a while. Her mother's mouth had tightened and Kir knew perfectly well that she wouldn't get any more answers to her questions today. She felt exhausted as she always did after a confrontation. This was followed by a longing for the little closeness they had once shared. This dreadful longing would be the death of her.

'Can you remember the days when we went to the beach in the summer, Mum, the whole family?'

It happened so seldom, maybe once a year. That was probably why she remembered so well and why she cherished the memories of those days as if they were precious stones she had found in the sand.

Her mother nodded.

'We always took the dog with us. And enough bags and cool boxes of food for a whole week.'

'But we had to be home by evening because the pigs had to be fed,' Kir said.

'You children would always find lugworms and fish. You and Dad. And float off on lilos.'

Kir felt a wonderful tingle in her stomach. She was carried away by the memory and the rare warmth in her mother's voice.

'We always argued for the first hour. Red wanted to decide everything and Tomas always had a cold. Dad let us do what we wanted. I hated putting worms on a fishing hook, but Tomas and Red loved it. Later we sat under a blanket when we were cold from being in the water. All of us together under the same blanket.'

Her mother nodded. Kir wondered if perhaps those days were all she had to hold on to as well. Memories of good family life, those few happy hours and the hope of more. The rare days in her life when everything seemed bright and happy had a meaning far beyond time and place. That was what cemented loyalty.

Kir thought of the cat, wondering how long the loyalty would last.

56

PETER COULD EASILY see why people would spend hours in Rollo's Kennel.

The shop was an absolute paradise for any adult children into role playing. The owner himself looked like a fairy-tale character – a giant of a man, heavily muscled, but with a solid layer of fat over the top. He wore a long blue smock with a broad leather belt, brown leather trousers and a pair of equally worn boots. His hair was bright red, as was his long beard. His eyes sparkled and were the darkest blue you could ever see, until the blue changed into black.

'Are you Rollo?'

'At your service, kind sir,' bellowed a deep bass. 'How may I tempt you?'

Peter and Felix looked around the dimly lit shop. A couple of teenage boys in a corner were testing out some very lifelike Viking swords. There were stacks of various games, all with fantasy motifs of dragons and knights or Vikings. There were also costumes and accessories for role play: capes, helmets, swords, knives, armour, chain mail, gloves, coins and leather purses. In another corner, posters displayed images of tattoos in the same style: dragons and orcs, Vikings and elves, and whatever else belonged to the world of role play. There was also a display cabinet with several rings and other gold and silver ornaments clearly meant for piercings in various parts of the body.

'I'm a friend of Elisabeth Stevns, who came here yesterday

for a tattoo. She said you'd had three women here to have lilies tattooed on their thighs, high up. Some time last spring.'

Rollo examined him closely, then shook his head as though someone had insulted his professional honour.

'I thought it was a bloody funny place to have a tattoo. I told them I thought it was weird. Said they wouldn't get much out of it.'

He winked at Felix.

'But then again, what do I know? The customer's always right, isn't that what they say?'

'Can you describe them?'

'The girls? Yes, easily. But who are you?'

At that moment Peter dearly wished he could have produced a police badge.

'Did one of them look like a boy, short with spiky black hair and a lot of piercings?' he asked instead. 'And was the other one very Danish with long blonde hair?'

Rollo chewed on something in his mouth while watching them.

'And was the third one sort of Russian, touch of Asian, with a broad face?' Peter continued.

Rollo nodded slowly.

'It wasn't illegal. Everything was carried out in a clean, responsible way. Has anyone complained?'

Peter made a quick decision. Anna Bagger would probably be furious and so might Mark Bille, but he wasn't going to be put off by that.

'The blonde was found dead in Grenå Harbour on New Year's Day. Strangled, with her hands tied behind her back. She had a fleur-de-lis on the inside of one thigh, with the same image branded over it.'

The shock effect was obvious. Rollo opened and closed his mouth as he stared at them.

'*What?*'

Peter was about to repeat it, but Rollo stopped him.

'No, no, I did hear you. But that's dreadful. She was such a nice girl. She was a bit worried that it was going to hurt.'

Felix had picked up a sword and was waving it around, testing it. It was made from a light material and completely harmless. All the items in the shop were toys of some kind.

'Did they say why they wanted the tattoos? Or did you get an impression of the reason?'

Rollo shook his head, still struggling to digest Peter's information.

'I'm not really sure. It was obviously something to unite them. A pact of some sort. The short girl was in charge.'

'Did they mention a pact?'

Rollo scratched his beard.

'Yes, because the blonde one especially needed persuading. The short one kept saying: "Remember we're better than them."'

'Do you know anything about branding with an iron?' Felix asked, putting the sword back.

He looked at them both with a serious expression.

'It's hardcore. Some people also have horns surgically grafted on to their foreheads or hooks screwed into their skin so they can be suspended from the ceiling.'

He showed with his hand where potential hooks would be sited on Peter's back.

'Some people get off on it.'

'From the pain?' Felix asked.

Rollo nodded.

'I think it's a kind of manhood test for boys who feel the need to prove something.'

'A form of tribal ritual?' Peter asked.

Rollo nodded.

'But they won't get that kind of thing here,' he said.

'Did the women ask you to brand them?'

'No. The tattoos were more than enough for them.'

More customers entered and started looking through the games. Peter and Felix thanked him and left the shop.

They had set out from Djursland at nine o'clock and had constantly checked to see if they were being followed. Peter had noticed that Felix's mood had changed a million times on the way, from intense and talkative to silent and introverted. Now her meeting with Arthur Sand from the Air Accident Investigation Board was an hour away. It was as if she was putting her faith in that appointment, hoping that she could tell him everything she knew and then put it all behind her. It probably wasn't going to be an easy meeting. He was sure she knew that, but even so he didn't dare say it out loud.

They found a café and ordered two coffees and a couple of sandwiches. He could clearly sense her nerves.

'Boys who feel the need to prove something,' Felix said, stirring in sugar and slopping coffee into the saucer. 'Was it someone like that who branded Tora and skinned her face?'

Peter took a bite of his sandwich, mostly to encourage her to do the same.

'It's a possibility,' he said.

She pushed her plate away.

'Men versus women? Is it war? Is that what this is all about?'

It occurred to him that she might just be right.

57

Felix couldn't swallow a bite. The fear was back, and the thought of the black car tailing her was like a chill down her spine.

For a while, being with Peter and feeling his body embrace hers had calmed her. Just like when she danced, she had been able to free herself from the burden she was carrying, from Erik's betrayal and his lies and everything that had happened as a result. She had floated, weightless and carefree, from the moment she set her foot on the stairs to the second they had let go of each other and slept together in his sleeping bag. But reality had dawned with the sun. A reality which told her that she had been married to a drug dealer and was now lying in the arms of a man who had been in prison for manslaughter.

What did that make her? A naive, unintelligent woman who was also a terrible judge of character? Or – in the case of Peter – the opposite: a woman who instinctively sensed there was more to his story than he had told her?

She didn't want to risk further humiliation by letting herself be fooled by a wrong'un again. On the other hand, her intuition was usually sound.

She watched Peter eat first his own sandwich and then the rest of hers with a healthy appetite. She couldn't understand how he could get it down. She was still shaken from her encounter with the man in the black car, a man she had seen and not seen at the same time. She had tried to describe him to Peter, but to no avail. She'd had other things on her mind than getting a good look at her attacker. She realised that she had even been too busy to feel truly scared. But now the fear was getting under her skin again and pushing the night's events aside. The fear could make everything else seem insignificant.

She sipped her coffee. Her hand was shaking, and she hoped he hadn't noticed.

What had happened between them would have to wait. Right now the chill was spreading down her spine.

More than anything else she was tormented by a sense of chaos, and she longed to rid herself of her burden.

After leaving the café they drove to Sødalsparken in Brabrand. The buildings resembled large white boxes and had been situated so they would overlook Brabrand Lake. Felix thought it only appropriate to site SOK, *Søværnets Operative Kommando*, the navy building, here, where there was at least a view of water. The construction was brand new and the architecture modern. Large amounts of glass had been used so that the view could be enjoyed from the maximum number of angles. The Danish Air and Rail Accident Investigation Board occupied some of the offices.

Peter followed her to reception. They agreed she would text him when her meeting had finished and he would come to pick her up.

She giggled when they said goodbye, suddenly feeling playful in the safe surroundings.

'Are we just being paranoid? You didn't see anyone, did you?'

'No.'

No one had been tailing them on the road from Djursland. And now here they were in a sleepy Århus suburb in bright daylight.

'Felix!'

Arthur Sand from the Air Accident Investigation Board came down the stairs. She quickly introduced the two men before Peter nodded goodbye and left.

She had met Sand twice before. First when she had just been discharged from hospital and remembered absolutely nothing, and later when she had gone to live by the cliff and didn't *want* to remember. Both times he had seemed frustrated, but had been enough of a gentleman to try and hide it.

'Let's go this way.'

He walked back up the broad staircase and she followed. He carried on talking to her over his shoulder: 'It's a little more informal than the police station, don't you think?'

'It's nice here,' Felix said, feeling an urge to be friendlier than last time. Sand was a pleasant man in his fifties with a genuinely helpful manner. He always spoke in a soft voice, as though he had grown used to dealing with people who could jump at the slightest noise. He wore dark trousers and a red roll-neck sweater and walked more like a sailor than the pilot he was. The sturdy legs were in harmony with the rest of his compact body as he barrelled along.

He ushered them into a bright room with modern tables and chairs, and large windows overlooking Brabrand Lake. Surrounded by a wintry landscape and snow-covered red roof-tops, the lake was being used as an ice rink. Sand pointed to a few dot-like skaters.

'The ice isn't thick enough. No insurance would cover an accident there. I'm sorely tempted to draw the curtains, but it would be a shame given the view and the light.'

She considered telling him that she had gone skating on that same lake as a child. After her early childhood in Spain, she had grown up in a flat in Brabrand. If she looked out of the windows long enough she would probably be able to pick out the apartment block where her parents still lived. But she didn't say anything. She knew a cautious man when she saw one.

'It's human nature to take risks, isn't it?' she said instead.

He gave her a smile and pulled out a chair.

'I'm afraid you're right. And that's one of the reasons we've asked you to come in. There's been a new development in the case of your husband and daughter's death.'

Sand pushed a file across the table to her.

'We've prepared a preliminary report. Your husband was flying a four-seater Robinson forty-four, a very stable and popular helicopter in Denmark. Its safety record is second to none. The aircraft has been constructed with a safety factor of three-point-five, which means that several components must fail simultaneously before an accident can happen.'

Her mouth went dry.

'Are you saying that we were particularly unlucky?'

He looked at her sympathetically. Then he shook his head.

'No, what I'm saying is we no longer think it was an accident. However, it would require an expert to tamper with such an aircraft to make it look like an accident. It's not something anyone could do.'

Felix moistened her lips.

'But who . . .?'

'That's exactly what we've asked the flight mechanic.'

She fought to regain her voice.

'Do you think he did it on purpose?'

'It would seem so. But we can't prove it. And, anyway, we still don't know why anyone would want to.'

This didn't come as a surprise to her. Not now, not given what she knew about Erik's life. And yet it still felt like a shock.

'The helicopter exploded into a million pieces,' Sand said. 'It's a miracle you survived, but fortunately miracles do happen.'

Only a few days ago she would have disagreed with him. She had wished she'd died in the crash. If he looked, he could probably detect the change in her, she thought.

Sand continued after a slight pause: 'The manner of the crash has always suggested that the tail rotor was at fault. It's almost the only possibility. And if it had been defective, the mechanic would have discovered it during the obligatory pre-flight check.'

'But not if he'd sabotaged it,' Felix interjected.

Sand nodded.

'Exactly.'

'I remember us circling,' she said. 'And I remember Erik suddenly pressing some buttons.'

Sand produced more photos. They showed the sequence of a helicopter in dire trouble; the angles and the rotation of the aircraft made that clear.

'When you lose control of your tail rotor, you need to get it into auto rotation quickly. If you don't, the helicopter will twist in the opposite direction and spiral downwards.'

He held up a picture of the inside of a helicopter engine.

'The tail rotor gearbox is driven by an axle. Our theory is that someone tampered with the drive shaft flex plate – that's the axle mechanism that drives the tail rotor – and loosened a few bolts.'

Felix straightened. It all added up. She'd had her suspicions, but she hadn't wanted to face the truth. She stared right into Sand's brown eyes and saw the pieces of the jigsaw falling into place: Erik and his drug connections. Someone had been out to get him.

'I'm starting to remember much more,' she said. 'And it all fits with what you're telling me.'

He looked hopeful.

'Feel free to tell me.'

She launched into it. They had drunk their coffee and Sand had eaten a couple of sandwiches by the time she'd finished telling him about the briefcase and her suspicion that Erik was involved in drug trafficking. For Peter's sake, she avoided mentioning Stinger or Peter himself, but spoke only about what she remembered or had experienced personally.

After she had finished, he looked at her pensively.

'And no one specific springs to mind? Someone who'd want to kill Erik?'

She shook her head.

'I'm sure it's about drug trafficking. I don't know the names of Erik's associates, but I think he was circling over a place called Lille Lysegrund.'

She had memorised the coordinates, but she had also written them down on the note she pushed across to Sand. He took it, read and nodded. She felt his eyes on her, regarding her with respect.

'They're real enough. It's somewhere in the Kattegat, and Lille Lysegrund sounds about right. We'll check it out and see what we can find.'

He closed the file to indicate that the meeting was over.

'We'll obviously be in touch. I'll contact Inspector Erling Bank of East Jutland Police. We've been working together closely on this investigation.'

Felix nodded. It was done. She had passed her burden on to the right person. The police could deal with it now. She felt as if a weight had been lifted from her shoulders when she rang Peter shortly afterwards to tell him that the meeting had finished and would he please come and get her. There was no reply. She thought he might be driving and couldn't hear the phone, so she left a message.

Sand stood up.

'I have to go. I've got another meeting in two minutes.'

He looked at her.

'I'll contact the police as we've agreed. In the meantime, take care.'

He escorted her down to reception and they shook hands. 'We'll do our best,' he said. 'It would be a relief for everyone to get to the bottom of this and, given what you've just told me, I think we have a good chance.'

She waited fifteen minutes before finally receiving a text from Peter.

58

PETER LEFT HIS car, stuffed his mobile into a pocket and ran to the main entrance of Skejby Hospital. He was still in two minds as to whether he had made the right decision, but Elisabeth had called him, in tears, while he was waiting for Felix. Stinger had regained consciousness and asked after him, but doctors described his condition as critical. All they could do was hope that Stinger would make it through the day.

'Please come, Peter. I think he has something important to tell you.'

He hated abandoning Felix but convinced himself that she was in safe hands. SOK was the closest you could get to a naval police force, so for the time being she was protected by the long arm of the law, an institution he had loathed and detested most of his life. But this wasn't about him. This was about her. He had texted her to wait for him.

Stinger was still hooked up to several machines. Elisabeth was sitting on the bed, flattening one end of the mattress. Her blue and green T-shirt was far too tight and her shoulders were quivering.

'Hi.'

She turned around, tears streaming down her cheeks.

'I'm so glad you came.'

At first he thought the man in the bed had already died. His breathing was so shallow and the movement of his chest so minimal that he could barely see it. There was no light in the eyes staring into the room and if Stinger had been thin before, now he looked like a concentration camp victim: the skin on his face was stretched taut over bones which protruded and threatened to pierce it. The wispy hair couldn't hide the veins clearly visible beneath the thin membrane of skin over his skull, and his arms lay on the bed like stems of withered flowers. His tattoos had blurred because the muscles were wasted.

Peter took Stinger's hand and squeezed it carefully.

'Stinger, you old swinger you.'

It took time. But eventually the hand returned his squeeze, though only weakly. The eyes tried to focus. Peter carried on talking and felt his throat swell around a lump that refused to go away.

'It's Peter. I'm right here.'

Stinger's cracked lips moved, but he gave up. He flapped helplessly with his free hand on the duvet.

'Here.'

Elisabeth handed Peter a cup of water. There was a swab in it, with a small, round sponge on the end. He took it and wetted Stinger's lips. Some of the water trickled into his mouth and he swallowed with difficulty while his tongue searched for more.

'. . . eter . . .'

The sound seemed to come from the grave, dry and feeble.

'. . . eter . . .'

'Yes, Stinger. I'm here.'

He squeezed Stinger's hand again, and this time it grabbed his with greater strength. In the course of a few seconds their friendship flashed before his eyes. He remembered their first meeting: Stinger had found him in the prison showers, battered and beaten, friendless and practically unconscious. He remembered Stinger lifting him up and calling the guard. He remembered Stinger's self-deprecating gesture later when he thanked him. A movement that said saving someone's life was no big deal. He remembered happy hours in Stinger's company; the glint in his eyes when he came up with yet another scheme to improve his life in prison; winding the staff round his little finger and his constant generosity when it came to booze or cigarettes, which he preferred to share rather than keep for himself. This was the essence of Stinger's life: friends meant more to him than all the intoxicating stimulants in the world.

Stinger's colourless eyes focused on him while he tried to raise his head from the pillow, like a dead man pulling himself out of his coffin. The lump in Peter's throat spread to the rest of his body.

'. . . rian . . .'

'Brian?'

'. . . rian sai . . .'

'Brian said?'

Stinger was clearly exerting himself. It was as if all his strength was going into the words.

'. . . rian said you would . . . Grimme . . . lanned it.'

'Planned it? Had Brian planned that I would deal with Grimme?'

Stinger didn't appear to be listening. He mumbled again: '. . . eter will do it.'

Stinger's head fell back on the pillow. His eyes rolled upwards. The exertion had sapped the last of his strength. His chest barely rose and fell now. Elisabeth whimpered.

'What's happening?'

'Call the doctor,' Peter said, but he knew it was already too late.

Old Stinger who had sung and danced and blagged his way through life had danced his final dance. Elisabeth pulled the cord for help, but before it arrived Stinger's chest rose and he let out a sigh. He breathed his last holding Peter's hand and staring at the ceiling.

59

PETER'S TEXT MESSAGE was very brief. An emergency had come up, she gathered. He told her to wait.

She sat down on the leather sofa in reception wondering whether she should be worried. What could have happened since he'd failed to pick her up as agreed? It obviously had to be something important if it couldn't be put off. But perhaps he didn't have to worry about her now. She'd given the coordinates to Sand. It felt good.

She got up and started pacing the floor. The woman behind the counter ignored her and carried on speaking into her headset while leafing through some papers. In the car park vehicles came and went, and people – mostly men – negotiated their way through the piles of snow outside the building. Anyone entering through the glass door stamped their feet on the mat to get the snow off their shoes and hurried up the stairs with briefcases under their arms. A couple of the men, in uniform and heavy boots, were clearly naval officers.

Felix bought herself a cup of hot chocolate from a vending machine and looked at her watch. Half an hour had passed and still there was no news from Peter. What was he doing?

She wandered around the reception area holding the hot cup. She stopped for a moment in front of a large abstract painting, an explosion of colour, remembering how, after the helicopter crash, she had opened her eyes to a white world: the ward was white; the walls, the ceiling, the blinds and curtains were white, the bed linen too. A nurse in a white uniform had called a doctor, who had probably been wearing green. But everything inside her head was white and flickered like an old black-and-white TV screen. There was nothing to hold her attention. Everything merged into an indefinable mass of tingling and bubbling sensations.

She had only slowly realised why she was in hospital. She could understand the words they said to her and she could just about understand the fragments of memory that helped her to cobble her life together. She knew she had lost Erik and Maria. She knew it intellectually, but not emotionally. Everything inside her had died. She felt nothing, no grief, no joy.

She drank the hot chocolate and let it flow through her. Nice and hot. The same feeling she'd had when she went upstairs to Peter. He had guided her to where she was now. He had turned on the tap and opened the floodgates so that she could start to feel something again. The fact that she could feel joy again, despite still mourning the loss of Maria, was his doing.

In that way she was indebted to him, but he wasn't here now and perhaps it was about time she started taking responsibility for herself. They had grown close in the days when he nursed her. They had made love. But she couldn't be his responsibility.

All this time her parents had been waiting in the wings for her to go to them and ask for their help. They would have loved to have her with them until the police and Sand had completed their investigation and she could start rebuilding her life.

She wandered up and down mulling these things over, giving Peter a chance to turn up or send another text. But as neither happened, she called her mother and agreed to go over to their flat straightaway.

She waited a little longer and finished the rest of her hot chocolate. She was about to call a taxi when the absurdity of the situation suddenly struck her. This was Denmark. This was Brabrand of all places. Her childhood town. She could walk there in ten minutes.

The car park was the most peaceful spot on earth. The snow had been shovelled into heaps, some black with dirt, others white and pristine. Some of the cars still had snow on their roofs and their owners hadn't bothered to de-ice the windows. Others were immaculate, no snow or ice, as if their owners were models of virtue in a classroom of badly behaved children. The sun was shining.

She pushed open the door and stepped outside into the fresh air, determined to put the slightly stuffy, unnatural indoor climate behind her. She started walking and, for the first time in a long while, she felt happy, free and independent. The chill down her spine had gone. She had handed over her problems to Sand. She texted Peter. She perceived the world in a new way now, thanks to him. And she wanted to tell him.

Perhaps there was another reason. Perhaps she wanted to talk about their early morning activity. She was pondering this when a black car slid alongside, as swiftly as a shark through water.

Peter hoped Felix would still be waiting for him, but he had been unable to compose a fitting text message. He rubbed his wrist while manoeuvring the car through snow and slush on his way from Skejby Hospital to Brabrand. He could still feel Stinger's grip on his arm.

Brian had thought someone should stop Grimme, and had decided that person would be Peter. Because he could be manipulated. Because he and Grimme had old scores to settle.

With one foot in the grave, Brian had neatly orchestrated his own revenge on Grimme. He had just forgotten to take into account that his remote-controlled avenger might refuse to play ball.

Peter reached for the radio and turned it on. Thomas Helmig poured out of the speakers singing 'Stupid Man'. The song felt like it was about Peter. He had been stupid to think he could put the past behind him. He was stupid to dream of a normal life when parts of his present were still attached to his past, like an unravelling sweater caught in a door.

His mobile beeped – probably Felix. More evidence of his stupidity. He was stupid and soft-hearted. He had taken her in; he had nursed her. And now, as she was starting to recover, he was no longer the focal point; his past was. Had he really killed a man?

He was approaching the SOK building and had signalled to turn when he spotted her in her black Puffa jacket roughly fifty metres ahead. She walked the way she danced and it hit him like a punch in the midriff; the memory of her thin, supple body, her lips, her eyes. Her strength when she held him tight and sent them both into ecstasy.

For a second the memory of Stinger was gone and his sombre thoughts dissolved into thin air. There she was, alive and kicking. His dream come true. Perhaps it would melt and disappear like the snow on his tyres, but it had been there. He'd had a sense of her. That in itself was huge.

He was about to sound the horn to attract her attention when a black saloon car overtook him, slid in front of her and blocked her path. A man jumped out from the back and grabbed her as you would grab a difficult child and make it sit in a pushchair. A few seconds later the car pulled away before the door had even been shut.

With the engine roaring, Peter screeched after the black saloon, squinting to read the number plate. They joined a small suburban road and the car in front of him skidded round the sharp bend, spraying slush and snow from under the wheels. Peter gunned the accelerator. He was gaining and only a few metres behind the saloon. Both cars screamed down several quiet streets before the fleeing saloon took another turn, this time to the left, across a junction, just missing an oncoming juggernaut. It was pure reflex that made Peter hit the brakes and avoid a collision. The truck driver honked his horn angrily, swerved to the side and stopped in the middle of the junction. Peter heard the black saloon racing down the road.

'NOOOO!'

Someone was yelling, a powerful roar from a man in great pain. The truck driver got out and came over to him. Pedestrians stopped and sent him strange looks. One passer-by shook her head.

The man who was yelling was Peter.

60

MARK WATCHED ANNA Bagger walk through the office at Grenå Police Station and head for the interactive whiteboard and the computer. Nine detectives were observing her attentively. His brain was pounding.

Someone had shot Ramses Bilal on Gjerrild Cliff during New Year's Eve. That same night Nina Bjerre had disappeared from a party and two days later the body of Tora Juel Andersen was discovered in the harbour. A few days after that Kir found Gry Johansen strangled, and faceless, in a hotel room. Gry had told him about the three girls from out of town. From the CCTV evidence it looked as if those same three girls had robbed small shops in Grenå to get food and – according to Gry – booze and drugs. How was it all connected, if it even was? Who were the three girls? Why did Ramses and Tora have to die? What was the motive? The girls had talked about treasure in a boat on the seabed. What was the treasure – money? Drugs? Or was it simply a fantasy?

His headache spread to the rest of his body, which ached like a battered punchball, but right now pain was good. It meant he was alive.

He watched as Anna Bagger stooped over her laptop and tapped away on the keyboard. They weren't coming up with enough results; her grim expression told him as much. What else was needed – luck, or skill? Something was clearly lacking in the investigation.

'OK . . .'

She straightened up and clicked the remote control. The whiteboard became a screen.

'Swatch, Tora's boyfriend. His real name is Mohammed Reza. He's twenty-five years old and a second-generation immigrant from Lebanon.'

The detectives turned their attention to the two photographs, one in profile and one full face: dark eyes, black crew-cut with a circular pattern shaved into the scalp; longish nose, long eyelashes and a mouth balancing on a knife edge between sensuality and brutality.

One of the female detectives, Pia Thorsen, whistled softly. Another wolf-whistled.

'Christ, he's hot,' said Pia, who was single, chubby and wore what Mark regarded as unflattering, large smocks to hide what little shape she had. But he liked her. She was straightforward and didn't play games and was one of the few who had looked him straight in the eye after Gry's murder. Pia continued: 'You can't blame her risking life and limb to be with him.'

He was probably the only officer to notice Anna Bagger stiffen. He flashed Pia a friendly smile, then came the lash of Anna's sharp tongue.

'Mohammed Reza is a violent psychopath. He's currently in prison for gang-related violence and has been there since October. I don't think being his girlfriend is a picnic.'

Mark felt sorry for Pia, who bowed her head and focused on her notes.

'However, his sentence means,' Anna Bagger continued, 'that he can't have killed Tora. He was banged up when she died and still is.'

Mark stared at the photo. Anna carried on talking and clicking to show more images. Next came a young, Danish-looking man, as broad as an ox, with a bald head and rolls of fat on his neck. He had a long, strawberry-blond beard tapering to a tatty point and wore a small skull cap on his head.

'Ibrahim Frandsen. Muslim. Danish convert. Friend of Swatch since school. Not a gang member, but on the sidelines.'

Anna nodded and handed over to Martin Nielsen, whom Mark had met for the first time on the cliff when the body of Ramses Bilal had been found. Mark regarded him as a solid, somewhat traditional detective. He was starting to gain an insight into Anna Bagger's team. Some he didn't like, others were OK. It was a set-up he could live with. He'd never been the type to get on with everyone.

'Ibrahim has vanished without a trace,' Martin Nielsen said. 'But we've spoken to his family, who are Danish and haven't converted to Islam. His sister, Paulina, is a trainee with Matas at Bruuns Galleri in Århus. She knew Tora well and had met her a couple of times. She says – and this is the interesting bit – that Tora wanted to end the relationship with Swatch. She'd asked various people, including Paulina, for help, but Paulina couldn't promise to help because her brother would be angry with her. Tora was too scared to go home to her parents because Swatch had threatened to find her and kill her. He'd also threatened to take it out on her family.'

Martin Nielsen scanned the assembled officers.

'The question is: Did Tora die because of her relationship with Swatch?' he said. 'Life as a biker chick is fraught with danger.'

Anna Bagger took up the gauntlet: 'He would have needed someone to kill her while he was in prison.'

Her gaze landed on Mark.

'Could Swatch have made Ibrahim do it?'

'Or someone else,' Mark said. 'He wouldn't have had to do it himself. Gangs are highly sensitive if a bitch – pardon the expression – acts up.'

'Has anyone ever managed to break away?' asked one of the detectives whose name Mark couldn't remember.

'That's a good question,' Mark said. 'We've had several cases in Copenhagen where girls came to us asking for protection.'

'And did they get it?'

Mark shook his head.

'We can't give everyone new identities and new flats.'

He looked around the circle.

'It's not just about jealousy and a macho mentality. The girls are often in possession of information which the gang doesn't want leaking out – to the police or their rivals.'

Anna Bagger nodded.

'We need to look into that.'

Mark didn't say anything, but he wondered how she would go about it. Biker gangs seldom willingly permitted close scrutiny. The immigrant gangs were completely inaccessible. She wouldn't get a word out of anyone.

Martin Nielsen said: 'According to Paulina, Tora had met another girl in the same situation. She hinted to Paulina that the two of them would help each other get out.'

Anna Bagger reacted immediately.

'Do we know anything about the identity of the other girl?'

'No,' said Nielsen. 'She's likely to be one of the two girls Tora was running around with here in Grenå. I understand they were picked up on CCTV?'

Anna looked at Mark, passing the ball to him. Mark pressed some keys on his computer and showed them the reason he'd been asked to attend the meeting: freeze-frames off the surveillance camera. The three girls could be seen clearly.

'We need to have them identified,' Anna Bagger said. 'We've already issued photos to the media. I suggest that you, Martin, take the photos and show them around at the fitness centre where Tora was a member, to Ibrahim's sister and anyone else who might have been in contact with Tora.'

Afterwards he needed fresh air and something to do, so he took the car and drove to the property in Fredensgade. It was late in the afternoon now and night had begun to fall over Grenå. The building with the four flats was squeezed between two taller and wider buildings, and by comparison it was badly maintained, with peeling window frames and graffiti-covered brickwork in urgent need of repointing. The snow had been cleared in front of the other houses in the street, but no one had done anything to shift the snow and ice away from number 27, and he slipped on the icy pavement and nearly fell. This did nothing to improve his mood.

He opened the front door wondering why he had avoided interviewing Christian Røjel. Reluctantly, he had to admit it was because of Kir. There was something in the tone of her voice when she spoke about her family, like a doctor desperately hoping she can heal a sick patient. He understood that they were what kept her in Grenå – a kind of doomed love between a rebellious daughter and traditional parents, where both parties constantly misunderstood each other. He and Kir had more in common than she might have thought.

He walked up the creaking staircase, which was narrow and dark like a rubbish chute. The light didn't work. The steps were made of dark wood, and remnants of varnish suggested they had once been clean and well maintained. Now they were filthy and worn. The raw wood was covered in grime.

Asger Toft, the caretaker, was out, and no one else reacted when he knocked on the doors of the other tenants. He stood for a moment on the top landing weighing his options. Even in the dark stairwell he could clearly see a hatch in the ceiling. He stretched out his hand but couldn't reach it. He went all the way back downstairs. On the ground floor detritus was piled up under the stairs. There were pots of dried paint, old suitcases and a few boxes of books. He opened the suitcases, but they were empty. He dragged them upstairs, stacked them one on top of the other and clambered up. His weight compressed them somewhat, but even so he could still reach the ceiling hatch with his fingertips. He pushed it aside. Then he felt around the edge until he came across something hard.

He dragged the object closer and over the opening. It was a narrow ladder. He pulled it down and saw that it could be attached to two hooks on the wooden opening. However, it didn't reach all the way down to the floor and he had to jump on to it as if mounting a temperamental horse. The ladder swung back and forth, but it held firm. He just managed to squeeze himself through the hole. Once up, he sat on the edge and took out his mobile to use as a torch. It produced just enough light for him to see an attic room which was inhabited, or had been recently. He discovered two mattresses with filthy, crumpled bed linen on either side of the hatch. In one corner was a bucket with a lid. From that direction came the unmistakable stench of an unflushed toilet. There was more rubbish lying around: pizza boxes, burger packaging, foam cups with lids and straws, cigarette packets and a few magazines. He picked one up. The language wasn't Danish; it was something Eastern European. He was practically forced on to all fours to move around. Someone had lived here in desperate conditions, with no toilet, no water, no room to stand up, and on top of that it was freezing cold. Now he could see electric cables pulled up from below, but there was no heater, nor was there a light bulb in the ceiling or anywhere else.

He sat down on one of the mattresses and had to brace himself before searching through the filthy bed linen. He groped with his hand, not really sure what he was looking for. Then two things happened at once: he heard someone on the stairs and his hand closed around a small object hidden in the folds of the sheet. He clutched the object in his hand and speculated briefly whether to pull up the ladder and close the hatch, but before he had time to do anything, he heard a voice he recognised: 'Mark? Is that you?'

He felt like a boy caught apple scrumping. He grunted a

reply, but Kir had already climbed the ladder and poked her head through the hole.

'You found it,' she stated.

'It wasn't difficult. Who lives here?'

She pulled herself up and sat on the edge. She looked concerned and her crinkly smile was long gone.

'Dad's Poles. They do all the real work on the farm.'

Her voice was laden with sarcasm.

'Such as?'

She shifted first one buttock then the other to find a more comfortable position further back in the attic.

'I think they insulated the main building just before Christmas. They were here last year as well to help with the harvest.'

'So your father grows crops as well?'

She nodded.

'There's quite a lot of land attached to the farm and he has to do something with it. We've always had seasonal workers.'

'Why don't they stay at the farm?'

She pulled up her legs and rested her chin on her knees.

'They did for several years. But one day the union came by and started asking questions and Dad found it best to keep them at arm's length.'

'That's when he bought this place?'

She shrugged and sent him an apologetic look.

'I didn't know.'

'I know you didn't. But I'm going to have to talk to your father.'

Kir sat for a while staring into the darkness. He could see the anxiety in her gaze and the nagging doubt.

'Let me have a word with him first,' she said, looking him in the eye. 'He's as tough as old boots. You're not going to get anything from him he doesn't want to tell you.'

She noticed his hand was clenched.

'What have you found?'

He opened his hand. In it was a silver fleur-de-lis with a stud and a butterfly clip at the back.

'An earring,' Kir declared, looking around the attic as though expecting to find the owner. 'Someone has had female company.'

61

PETER PAID FOR the mobile phone, asked for 500 kroner cashback and hurried out of the shop in City Vest. After his failed pursuit of Felix's abductors, he had driven aimlessly around Brabrand and ended up at City Vest Shopping Centre in Gjellerup. After paying he went into Føtex and bought several cartons of Camel and again asked for 500 kroner cashback. He withdrew another 2,000 kroner at a cashpoint outside the bank.

Afterwards he sat in his car to collect his thoughts. His head was still buzzing after the chase and he was desperate to track down the black saloon. But it was hopeless. He couldn't go to the police. They wouldn't understand. They would waste all their resources on him rather than on looking for Felix. He was the last person to see her. He had spent days with her, after claiming they didn't know each other. With his background he would be their prime suspect.

He rolled down his window and let in the frost. A Falck roadside assistance vehicle drove into the car park, to where a middle-aged couple were waving. Car batteries suffered in the frost. Older cars conked out and all roadside assistance services were working overtime.

Watching the couple's old Škoda being given the kiss of life, he wondered if he should have acted differently. Felix had been washed up on his beach like a castaway. Yes, he'd taken her in and nursed her, and yes, he'd tried to prod her memory when he realised that she had recognised Ramses. But if he hadn't done that, she might not have been abducted. Perhaps he should have left her alone.

He leaned back. The Falck mechanic was sitting inside the hapless Škoda now, but no matter what he did, he couldn't get the car started. He went back to his own vehicle to get some jump leads.

Peter almost felt the electric charge as the Škoda was resuscitated with a roar and it also kick-started his own need to act.

He opened the Camel carton, took some cigarettes out of one of the packets and inserted the rolled-up banknotes. He removed a whole packet at the bottom of the carton and replaced it with the new mobile. He closed the carton, took out his mobile and called Matti.

'I need a favour.'

Desperation has never been a very strong basis for negotiation. He tried to hide the tension in his voice, but Matti wasn't fooled for a second.

'What's happened?'

Peter told him about Felix's kidnapping.

Matti sighed.

'OK. What do you want?'

'Fifteen minutes in Horsens. In half an hour's time. No cameras and no recording equipment of any kind.'

'Cato again, I presume?' Matti said.

'Cato,' he confirmed.

A few seconds passed, then Matti said: 'I can't promise anything.'

'That's not good enough, Matti.'

That was all it took. He didn't have to remind him what had happened while they were growing up at Titan Care Home, him and Matti and Cato and My and all the other broken spirits. He didn't have to list all the occasions he had taken punishment for Matti and the others because he was the only one who could cope with being locked inside the Box. He didn't say anything, but he might as well have.

'OK,' Matti said. 'I'll take care of it.'

'Thanks.'

Afterwards he sat holding his mobile while the Falck vehicle left the car park and the Škoda reversed. He had called in favours he never thought he would need and had never intended to use. He had done so without a second thought and without feeling ashamed. He was already slipping back into his old ways.

62

FELIX HAD TRIED to work out where they were going, but they had soon blindfolded her and forced her to lie on the rear seat. As she could no longer see where they were going, she started counting minutes to calculate the distance. But at length she had to give up. It was an impossible task and they might easily have been driving around in circles simply to disorient her. In the end, everything was blurred and she lost track of time and place.

'You won't get very far. I was supposed to be meeting someone.'

She tried to say it with conviction, but the driver merely told the man in the back to shut her up – which he did with deeds, not words, forcing a rag into her mouth. She fought against the urge to retch. She heard him unroll sticky tape. Then he tore it off and slapped it across her mouth. It felt like a tight-fitting mask and she panicked. Her chest heaved convulsively; sobs gurgled in her throat. She lunged at the man, but he grabbed her arms and bound them together with what felt like a plastic tie, the kind the police use to arrest protesters and round them up.

The two men were very different and yet they seemed to understand each other's every move. The driver was the boss. She realised she would have to appeal to him. Even though she couldn't see him, a distinct feeling of authority and solidity emanated from the front of the car. She could hear it in the man's breathing and sense it in his movements, when he changed gear or turned the steering wheel or simply shifted position. He had considerable physical presence.

The other man did as he was told. He seemed smaller, but he was strong. She had discovered that for herself when he tossed her into the car like a sack. He was like a watch spring: he could be at rest, then someone would wind him up and he would perform actions you wouldn't imagine him capable of.

A boss and his gofer. Both parties seemed happy with the arrangement. They formed a united front.

All this was going through her head as her body reacted in shock. She was shaking, inside and out. One moment she would be freezing, the next sweating with fear. She knew she was in the same car that had tailed her from Hjortshøj. She should have recognised it, but it had all happened so quickly.

She wasn't sure whether she had seen Peter's van pull into the car park or not. Maybe she was just deluding herself, or it was wishful thinking. Nor was she sure what the driver looked like, even though she knew she had caught a glimpse of him in the confusion. Dark, she seemed to remember. She had seen something dark. That was all. She had also thought she'd heard a car following them, but she was beginning to doubt herself now. They had driven hell for leather at first, screaming round bends and roaring past cars. The conditions weren't right for such high speeds. She only hoped they were stupid enough to attract the attention of the police. If a patrol car had suddenly switched on its flashing light, pulled them over and asked to see a driver's licence, she would have been overjoyed.

But soon the bends gave way to what must have been a main road, possibly a motorway. After a while, she didn't know how long, they started twisting and turning again, snaking along smaller roads. The car skidded a couple of times and the driver swore and muttered something.

She sensed they were nearing their destination when the car bumped up and down, going down a dirt track perhaps, where the snow had only been cleared in places. She heard the crunch of ice as they drove over holes in the road.

They came to a halt, and the two men got out and slammed the doors. She heard their voices, but she couldn't make out the words; all she knew was that one gave orders and the other obeyed. The car door was opened again; she was pulled out and dragged along like a rag doll. The snow was up to her ankles, the icy wind cut into her and, quite irrationally, she thought she was going to die from pneumonia. Perhaps it didn't matter. Perhaps now she would be reunited with Maria.

She clung on to this thought and her longing for her daughter when a door or a hatch was opened and she was pushed into a dark room. The smell was dank and stale and foul and clammy, and if she hadn't been so terrified, she would have protested as they pushed her further in. Then they sat her on a cold cement floor and she could feel a thin mattress she could huddle up on. Someone took her arms and pulled them apart; her wrists were attached to something in a brick wall, forcing her to sit as if embracing the world. Then they did the same with her legs. She felt ice-cold metal close around her ankles as the shackles clicked into place. Sitting with her legs apart, she felt the cold penetrate and creep up her abdomen.

They left her like that, without a word. She wanted to cry, but couldn't manage to sob without hyperventilating, so she made herself think calm thoughts and visualise a beautiful, blue spring sky above a green meadow, where she and Maria were walking hand in hand. She imagined the fragrance of fresh grass and dandelions and the lilt of a young girl's light, carefree voice singing a song. But the illusion was shattered by the cold setting in with a vengeance and soon she was shivering so much her lips couldn't even form the word 'help'.

63

HORSENS HADN'T CHANGED. The winter seemed endless here as well. The prison shivered in the snow drifts, hoping for warmer weather, and even the strong steel mesh around the perimeter wall seemed frozen in time, as though it might shatter at the first gust of wind.

It was always windy here, but the fence held. No one had the pleasure of slipping away before the end of their sentence from what was intended to be an escape-proof prison. There were very few pleasures here at all. However, some pleasures were held in high regard, as evidenced by Cato's expression when Peter pushed the carton of Camel across the table to him.

'Is it my birthday or do you bloody want something?'

'I just wanted to see you happy for a change.'

Cato feigned a big smile, revealing bad teeth destroyed by drugs, cigarettes and infrequent visits to the dentist.

'Don't open it until you're alone.'

Cato opened the carton and peeked inside. He moved a couple of packets and flashed a genuine smile.

'A mobile phone. Jesus. How did you get away with that?'

'Shut the carton. We've only got fifteen minutes.'

Peter checked his watch. Three minutes had already gone.

'Felix has been kidnapped.'

Cato tore his eyes away from the carton and looked at him.

'I'll do whatever it takes to find her, do you understand? I'm here because of her husband,' Peter said. 'Erik Gomez. Who was he visiting in prison?'

The answer was just one word. Cato whispered it.

'Grimme.'

The name was a kick in the solar plexus.

'Why?'

Cato played with the carton, turning it around again and again on the table.

'Anyone listening?'

His voice was still low. Peter shook his head.

'What were Erik Gomez and Grimme up to?'

Cato slid further down the blue institutional chair, tilted back his head and looked up at the ceiling as if the answer could be found there.

'Ten kilos of heroin. Street value of seven million kroner. Someone tipped off the cops. Grimme and Brian went to prison. Erik went nowhere. Grimme concluded Erik was the mole.'

'So what was Erik doing here in Horsens?'

Cato shrugged.

'He was in fear of his life. Of Grimme's revenge. He came here to clear his name.'

'Because Grimme thought he was the mole?'

Cato shrugged his shoulders again and pulled a cigarette from his own half-squashed pack in his pocket. The cigarette bobbed up and down in his mouth as he lit a match and inhaled the smoke, sucking in his already hollow cheeks.

'I don't think it worked. It doesn't take a genius to figure that out, does it? After all, Erik is dead.'

'And what happened to the stash?'

Cato sat up straight in the chair.

'No idea. Brian, Grimme and Erik had their fingers in lots of pies. Grimme and his henchmen had contacts in Poland who could get them the drugs, Brian had a boat and Erik had become addicted to the high life and owed money all over the shop. He was their link to the dealers and he also sold drugs to people in his own circles – at great risk and for large sums.'

'But then it went tits up? The police found out?'

Cato nodded.

'It really went tits up. Everyone panicked, thinking the others had leaked the network to the cops.'

Cato waved his hand in the air, scattering ash.

'Everyone started blaming everyone else.'

Peter visualised it: three men who had dreamed of the big time in their own individual ways only to see it fall apart. Three inflated egos who thought that together they could acquire wealth, if not glory or honour.

'But if none of them had tipped the cops off, who had?'

'How should I know? Someone who doesn't frighten easily, that's for sure.'

'Can you find out?'

Cato looked uncertain. He flicked ash on the floor and shifted his gaze to where the warder usually stood. But the officer was on the toilet with a stomach bug and in his rush had forgotten to request a replacement.

'I don't know. Something is very wrong, if you want my honest opinion.'

Honesty had never been Cato's forte, but in his own way he spoke the truth. Like now – Peter could tell from his face that he knew nothing.

'What about the ten kilos then? What happened to them?' Peter asked.

Cato squirmed. Peter could see he wanted to make off with his loot.

He nodded at the carton.

'Prepaid phone card,' Peter said. 'And there's more where that came from. But you've got to give me more.'

Cato finally found his voice again: 'How the hell should I know where the drugs are?'

Peter saw his expression change; Cato's face changed like the weather.

'Listen. The men who took Felix think she knows where the ten kilos are.'

Cato took another drag on his cigarette. He seemed nervous. 'And does she?'

Peter studied him. Cato could easily have been working for Grimme. You had to watch yourself around people prepared to sell their own grandmother.

'No,' Peter replied. 'She knows nothing.'

'Do *you*?' Cato asked carefully as though tiptoeing across broken glass.

'Who wants to know?'

Cato didn't reply.

'Who's running this show?' Peter asked. 'If it's Grimme, then tell him I know something. But he has to let Felix go.'

Cato's nervous swallowing had stopped. His only reaction was a twitch in his left eye. Peter breathed out. They looked at each other, he and Cato. Blood brothers with no blood ties.

'If it's not Grimme, tell him he and I have a common enemy. The man who double-crossed him is the same person who kidnapped Felix.'

He got up and squeezed Cato's shoulder. His skeletal body writhed. Peter could smell his fear and his greed. Cato owed him big time and they both knew it.

He felt Cato's eyes on his back as he stood up to leave. Cato's voice dripped with irony: 'See you under the clock.'

64

THE PIGLET IN the corner didn't even have the strength to squeal. It was the runt of the litter. Number seventeen, to be precise. Kir looked into its tiny, blinking eyes, which at that moment seemed to know what was going to happen. There were not enough teats and it didn't have the strength to fight its siblings for the available milk. It was going to die.

Her father made short work of it. With a grunt, Christian Røjel bent down and grabbed the piglet with one hand. Holding its tiny head with the other, he twisted and snapped its neck. The expression of panic disappeared from its eyes, to be replaced by a void.

'What d'you want?'

He didn't even look at her. She wanted to say that an injection was more humane, but he would only retort that he couldn't afford the vet's bill. The piglet should count itself lucky he didn't just let it starve to death. She knew he was right. This was the lesser of the two evils.

'You've been blabbing to the police, haven't you? Who do you think you are?'

Mark Bille Hansen had driven straight from Fredensgade 27 to talk to her father. She'd asked to be the first to contact him, but he'd probably been right. A surprise visit was probably best – no time to prepare answers or put up his guard. He was cunning, the old pig farmer, his daughter could vouch for that.

'What a little shit. Thinks he can come here, poking his nose into our business.'

Finally he turned to face her.

'I don't know why you're after him. Thinks he's something special, he does, the smart-arse.'

He was angry and hurt because she had told Mark Bille about the Polish workers, she knew that. That was why she was there, to make it up to him. To see with her own eyes, to experience for herself, whether there was any basis for mutual understanding or whether it was all over. After all, she was his daughter and that was what always drew her back to him. But now his mouth erupted like a volcano and his words spewed out like molten lava. She tried, to no avail, to remind herself of his background. He was old school. His view of the world differed from most people's. He might be a Christian, but in his actions he believed in neither mercy nor forgiveness. He believed in the soil and the animals and power and his God-given right to exercise it over his own. Pigs as well as people. He was the patriarch. A Djursland version of a stubborn old bull elephant.

'I'm not after anyone. I'm doing my job.'

'Job. Pah!'

He threw the dead piglet into the aisle and spat on the floor. He moved on to the next bay and she had to follow.

'I curse the day you started that rubbish.'

His long fingers closed around yet another newborn piglet. He held it in his hand as though he were an Egyptian god weighing the soul before deciding whether to send it to Heaven or Hell.

Childhood memories flashed through her brain. The image of him standing in the same pose, not with a piglet in his hand but her diving mask. A present from Uncle Hannibal. She loved it. That and the matching snorkel she had hidden under her pillow so that no one would find it. She remembered his long fingers closing around the glass. And the sound of it shattering when he smashed her diving mask with one blow. And then his hand reaching under her pillow, with snake-like rapidity, finding the snorkel and snapping it in half. He had turned around to see her and he hadn't even had the decency to look guilty.

'He's putting ideas in your head,' he had growled, glaring at her, fists clenched. 'Stay away from him.'

The piglet writhed and squealed in his hand. His face was expressionless as he bent down to push it in between its siblings so that it could find a teat to suck. She remembered that this was his life, his whole world. The same way she loved water, he loved working the soil, working with animals. The same way she respected the sea, without an ounce of sentimentality, with no more than a fleeting smile for silly amateur divers, he was equally unsentimental with his passion. He had no time for tree-huggers who wanted to save the world or bleeding-heart liberals trying to save the lives of animals born and bred for the slaughterhouse. 'Most of them are quite happy to sink their teeth into a nice pork joint with crackling,' he used to say.

She knew from Mark that he had been cooperative. He had given him the names of two Polish workers who had now moved on to other jobs. It was winter and there was little work to be had, but he thought they might have gone to a farm in Allingåbro near Randers, to build a barn.

She watched him bend down to study the sow, looked at his back, his long, lean body.

'It wasn't about diving, was it?'

Kir was thinking about the diving mask. Its fate was the entire basis of her rebellion. Obviously, she'd got herself a new one. She had gone snorkelling in secret and practised diving with and without the new snorkel.

'It was about you and Hannibal. The rivalry between you. The older and the younger son.'

There were many things she had never understood, but slowly they were starting to make sense. Recent events, the body in the harbour and her family's reaction. Her mother's rejection, her father's anger. They were scared. Once again their world was under threat.

'Hannibal was younger, but he was also brighter. He was open to the world. He wasn't scared. He didn't need to flex his muscles and bully people. But then again, he wasn't going to inherit the farm. It wasn't his responsibility and you despised him for that.'

He made no reply. She carried on despite wishing she could stop.

'Hannibal was a threat. He saw the world differently. He saw me differently. All you saw was a daughter, preferably one who would stay close to home and be there to look after you and Mum when you got old. Someone who shouldn't aim too high or try to be independent.'

She ran after him as he moved down the aisle, past the bays where the piglets squealed and fought for their mothers' teats.

'The daughter's spirit had to be broken, didn't it? But the sons! Sons were pure gold. No limits for them.'

He straightened up, his hand on his lower back, and turned. The volcano erupted again. Fire flashed from his eyes as he broke the neck of yet another runt and dropped it on the concrete floor with a splat.

'Shut your mouth!'

She was scared of him, but not scared enough.

'I found the cat. Why do you keep protecting him? He keeps doing it. What will it be next?'

He took a step towards her. The crater opened, red and spitting fire.

'I said shut up, didn't I?'

'It wasn't me that time in the boat, Dad. It was Red.'

She had hardly uttered the words before the slap came. But she carried on, the slap singing in her ears and the certainty that this was the end for him and for her, father and daughter.

'Red pushed Tomas overboard. But you said it was me. He

had to be protected. The older son. He always had to be protected.'

'This has nothing to do with Red.'

His voice was trembling; his entire body was quivering with rage. She knew that slap number two was on its way.

She looked at her father one last time. Then she turned on her heel and left.

65

THE HOUSE SEEMED so empty without Felix. Peter wandered around aimlessly, had a cup of coffee, tried a cheese sandwich, but he couldn't concentrate on eating. Even the dog seemed lost.

He had taken Kaj for a walk on the cliff and was back inside the warm house when his mobile rang. It was Cato and he sounded just as nervous as he had done in the visitors' room.

'I haven't got much time.'

The smoker's voice could crack at any moment.

'What have you got for me?'

There was background noise and a gale blowing. Cato was gasping as he walked and his voice mixed intermittently with the crunch of his footsteps.

'Operation Lily,' he said.

Peter imagined him in a corner in the prison yard somewhere. He hoped he was safe. The only problem was that nowhere in prison was safe. You had to watch both the staff and your fellow inmates.

'Operation Lily? What do you mean?'

Peter felt like reaching out and shaking him for more information.

'Grimme's girlfriend is called Lily. She was the mole.'

'Lily Klein?'

He'd known it was about Horsens. He had seen Lily there. She must have been there to visit Grimme.

'Yes, Lily Klein. Do you know her?' Cato asked. 'Small girl with dark hair and more piercings than a Zulu chief.'

The description was apt.

'Why?'

Cato laughed and coughed at the same time.

'Grimme was shagging her sister. Lily walked out, but Grimme beat her up. Then he cast her out, but decided to brand her first so that other men would know she belonged to him.'

Peter heard him cough.

'But she got away and set out to plot her revenge. She started going out with Ramses.'

He spat, and Peter imagined the gobbet landing on the snow-covered prison yard.

'So now what?'

Peter heard Cato light a cigarette and inhale the smoke.

'She's dead meat. Examples are being set. They've got someone helping them on the outside.'

Cato blew out the smoke. Peter saw his face with the sunken cheeks and the thinning ponytail.

'What kind of examples?'

There was silence down the other end while Cato filled his lungs with smoke.

'Well, that girl who lived with the Arab, the girl who ended up in the harbour, if you didn't already know.'

'Arab? How could Arabs be mixed up with Grimme?'

Cato burst into a hoarse laugh, which turned into a hacking cough.

'You can have lots of different types of customer in a shop.'

Peter was reminded of the fleur-de-lis. The branding. It was war. Men against women.

'Are you telling me they've joined forces? Biker gangs and immigrants?'

'A bitch is a bitch no matter whose side she's on.'

'Who would do all that for Grimme?'

It had to be someone without any scruples. Someone who actually enjoyed killing. Peter thought of Felix in the hands of someone like that and a cold sweat broke out.

Cato took a deep breath. His chest emitted a loud rattle.

'I've given you enough. Got to go. The meter's running.'

'Who, Cato? It's important! Give me a name.'

Cato sighed. The seconds passed. Peter heard voices in the background.

'Some guy Grimme knows from the old days. He's done time, like us.'

'Where?'

'Djursland. That's all I know. Some sort of young offenders' institution.'

The telephone went dead.

66

Felix was frozen. She had always believed that extreme cold would numb the body, but it didn't for her. Everything hurt. Every joint, bone, muscle and organ. The cold was a worse foe than her kidnappers. She couldn't talk to it. She couldn't give it something to assuage its anger. She could only hope, endure and wait for Peter to find her. She knew he would. He would find her and save her. Or at least he would do his damnedest.

She had tried everything. She had shut her brain down and put it on standby so that her thoughts were frozen in time like the winter outside. But the winter had crept in where she was: Was it a stable, a barn or an outhouse? Or a basement perhaps? There was a smell of cats and fish, damp old newspapers and filthy mattresses.

She had also tried the opposite, feeding herself snippets from the past. She had gone over the days leading up to the helicopter crash in great detail, trying to fill every gap with memories. Episodes had emerged she had long since filed or forgotten or suppressed.

Like the time, in a fit of anger, she had slapped her brother across the face, partly to see how he would react. He was fifteen and she was sixteen and he had never forgiven her. On mature reflection, she realised it had affected their relationship to this very day, which showed how a split-second decision could have consequences for your whole life and destroy something precious. Like the time she had fallen out with her friend, Susanne. She wasn't proud of this episode, and in her foolish pride she had never patched up the breach, even though she missed Susanne terribly and realised they had been part of each other's lives ever since Year Two at school. At *gymnasium*, when they were seventeen, Susanne had stolen a boy Felix felt was hers, and Felix had frozen out her best friend. Once she came close to apologising. She sat down and wrote a letter to Susanne, but she couldn't bring herself to post it, and she tore it up and threw it in the waste-paper basket.

She had always found it easy to isolate herself, just as she had hidden herself away in the house on the cliff. Fleeing was her response to adversity. Rather than finish arguments with boyfriends, she would jump in her car and drive off, consumed with thoughts of righteousness and self-pity.

She had reviewed her relationships with her mother (not brilliant, but affectionate in a muted sort of way), her stepfather and her brother, who had long since left Denmark and settled in Spain. She had thought about colleagues and old boyfriends whose faces had a habit of appearing in her dreams and on Facebook. She had taken stock of her life and it wasn't one that filled her with pride – not if you counted success with others as the meaning of life. The only success she'd ever experienced had drowned in an orgy of water and wreckage. The only child she had borne, the only person to whom she had given life, had had her life extinguished because her mother had chosen the wrong man. Because she had been brainless. Because she hadn't seen anything, hadn't seen what he'd been up to. No, not that; no excuses. It was because she hadn't wanted to see and had closed her eyes.

The tape was still stuck to her mouth and the blindfold was so tight it felt like her skull would cave in. She mustn't cry. She must breathe calmly or else all was lost. She tried to change her position. She had tried countless times, but all she'd done was make the metal around her ankles and wrists cut even deeper into her skin. She was sitting upright with her back to an icy wall. Her arms were still stretched out, attached somewhere above her head, and her legs spread-eagled. Her muscles were strained to their limit.

She hoped Maria had felt loved by her mother in her brief life. She believed she had. Maria had been the sunshine in her life from the moment she was born. From that day on everything had been different, and all her feelings, her every thought, had been directed towards this new little being. And it had continued. The bond between them had grown stronger and stronger.

She could still see Maria in her pink leggings, a white dress on top, with white bows in her hair; flawless skin, dark hair from her Spanish genes. A little Snow White ready to steal everyone's hearts. A loving child with no inhibitions towards other people. A child with a God-given ability to wrap her thin arms around others and love them unconditionally.

She heard a sound. Footsteps were approaching, bringing a draught and waves of cold with them.

The footsteps came closer, right up to her. She sensed it was a man from the way he moved and breathed; from the way the air moved out of his way. He bent down to her and she felt the pain as he tore the gaffer tape from her mouth, taking some skin with it.

'No one can hear you. But if you start screaming, the tape goes back on.'

The voice belonged to the driver who had brought her here. It was also his body. This man filled space. He was broad and muscular, possibly not very tall, but certainly stocky. She could smell his sweat, even in the cold. He smelt as if he had just been doing some sort of exercise.

'Water . . .'

She wanted to say so many other things, but this was the first that sprang to mind.

'Here.'

He held something to her lips. A cup or a mug. She drank. The water was ice cold.

'I'm freezing.'

'What did you expect? Fur coat and champagne? This isn't a fucking five-star hotel.'

She made no reply. A large hand grabbed her hair, forcing her head back.

'You know what we want, don't you?'

'No,' she lied.

He tightened his grip on her hair and banged her head against the brick wall. It was like being run over by a tractor and for a moment she blacked out in a sea of pain.

'Bitch.'

She had bitten her tongue and tasted even more blood than before. She clung to consciousness by her fingertips, her entire body trembling in sheer terror.

'Now give me that location,' he ordered.

She moistened her lips. They had cracked from the cold. Hot blood trickled from her tongue into the cracks and she could taste her own flesh. Peter would find her. She just had to stay strong.

'I haven't got it.'

'Liar.'

He hit her head against the wall again, and once again massive waves of pain surged through her body. She longed for unconsciousness, yet resisted it.

'Well, if you won't listen, then you'll have to feel, as my mother always says. I've got a little present for you. Something that will warm you up. But first . . .'

He freed her ankles from the chains, but she knew she wasn't free. He took off her boots one by one; then she felt his hands rummaging under her jumper and in rough jerks he unbuttoned her trousers and pulled them down.

'Nooo!'

The cold bit into her bare skin as he pulled off her trousers; she didn't know whether he had also removed her panties.

It was going to happen now, she thought. Rape. In a moment something would be forced inside her. His dick, cold steel, a broken bottle.

The thought of it filled her with rage. She flung herself around trying to kick him, but she couldn't see anything and kicked out in vain. He grabbed her legs firmly and got first one, then the other, back in the shackles. She wanted to spit and scratch and claw; she wanted to plunge an ice pick straight through his megalomaniac heart. But there was nothing she could do. She was helpless.

'Oh, so that's what you think, is it?' he said. 'Do you really think I fancy a skeleton like you? You'd only enjoy it, so it would be no fun for me.'

'So what *do* you want?' she wanted to ask, but she didn't want to let him see her vulnerability, and the words remained inside her.

'I've got other plans for you,' he said, almost whispering, his mouth close to her ear. 'It's a little ritual. So we know whose property you are.'

He disappeared for a while, and she thought she would die from the cold. She tried to shout, but her voice refused to work and the pain pinned her body to the wall as if someone had nailed her spine in place. Only a tiny whimper escaped her lips. A pathetic, miserable, wretched moan, which she hated and which shamed her. She thought about Peter. She could hear his voice, his laughter and imagine him that morning after they had made love for the second time. His smile and his laughter lines; his intense eyes.

He had taken care of her. He had carried her to and from the bathroom, fed her, changed her clothes and her bed linen; he had been there for her. He didn't want to be a hero, she knew that. He just wanted to be a decent person and do what needed doing without any fuss. No fine manners, no expensive habits, no dreams of luxury. Just one man doing his best. He existed, and that was the closest she came to any kind of solace.

But evil also existed.

'Here we are.'

Her prison guard had returned. He held something close to her. It smelt of burning and radiated a fierce, shimmering heat.

'This'll warm you up.'

He sat on one of her legs and held the other in position, even though she couldn't move anyway. Fear washed through her. A scream lodged in her throat.

'You'll be part of the herd now,' he said. 'Another flower in the bouquet, if I may put it like that.'

And then it came. She registered the hiss of burning flesh and smelt the smoke from the meeting of hot and cold as he pressed the searing hot object into her thigh. A conflagration of pain exploded in her body as he held it there for long, long seconds. She screamed, but no sound materialised. She didn't have the strength.

'Now tell me,' he said afterwards. 'Or do you want another dose of the branding iron?'

She gave him the coordinates and passed out.

67

THERE WERE SEVERAL correctional institutions for minors on Djursland, but only one secure institution for young offenders. It was also the only place which had been there long enough to have housed a sixteen- or seventeen-year-old Grimme, whose real name Peter remembered as Kenneth Krøll.

Peter estimated that Grimme would now be in his mid-thirties. He had spent most of his adult life behind bars in Horsens Prison, where Peter himself had had the pleasure of being subjected to his bullying. His first adult sentence had been for the double murder of two members of a rival biker gang. He was currently doing time for drug dealing. If he had offended as a minor at the start of the 1990s, he wouldn't have been sent to an adult prison, but he might have been sent to a secure institution for rehabilitation, with social workers and psychologists. It was possible that, during his time there, he had met the person who now held Felix's life in his hands.

Peter knew it would be difficult, if not impossible, to obtain information about inmates in such institutions, current as well as former. All the staff took an oath of confidentiality. And yet he chanced it and drove there. He had no other options, and the clock was ticking.

The name of the secure institution was Svalen, near Lange Lake, set in rural surroundings outside Ebeltoft.

There were only seven such establishments in the whole of Denmark. Once they were full, teenagers ended up in remand cells or wherever there was space. At times that meant adult prisons.

The seven residents and the various staff at Svalen lived in the wing of a whitewashed manor house, which boasted an impressive avenue of pollarded poplars, now bare and frozen in the winter cold.

Peter drove his van up the avenue without any kind of strategy at his fingertips. He couldn't do anything until he knew what he was dealing with.

The snow lay thick across the yard and around the buildings. The trees and bushes looked as though they were being gradually suffocated and only their branches protruded. Three vehicles were parked outside. Two of them were 4x4s and the third was a Toyota Hiace. A man in a thick Icelandic jumper and a fur-trapper hat was clearing the main entrance. Peter parked and got out.

'It's locked,' said the man with the shovel before Peter had time to ring the bell. 'And no one will come and let you in.'

'Why not?'

'They're in a meeting.'

The man checked his watch. 'For another quarter of an hour.'

He carried on dutifully shovelling snow with long, determined sweeps. Peter guessed he was in his mid-fifties. There was a solidity about his lumbering body which seemed to fill his surroundings. He wore a pair of black biker boots of an older vintage and they were firmly planted in the snow.

'I'll hang around and wait, if that's all right.'

He started walking up and down the yard, where the snow had been cleared. The cold crept under his clothes as the snow swirled around aimlessly.

The man wiped his nose on his sleeve.

'It's not like anyone will abscond in this weather.'

'Do they usually?'

The man shook his head. Snow fell from his hat on to his shoulders.

'They try sometimes.'

He nodded towards the windows.

'They're probably playing computer games at the moment. They have to pass the time somehow.'

Peter did another round and stamped his feet to keep warm. The man sniffed again.

'The cold slows them down,' he said contentedly. 'They're like little lambs. But as soon as spring comes, they run around making trouble again.'

He nodded around him. 'It all happens out there, if they can get away with it. Down to the lake, nick a rowing boat and off they go.'

'But there's nowhere for them to go.'

'Nope. They're always found quickly.'

The man went on shovelling. 'Just as well.'

'What else do they get up to when they're down by the lake?'

The man laughed.

'Enjoy a bit of freedom. Carve their names in the big oak down there. They'd carve the staff too, given half a . . .'

'How long have you worked here?' Peter asked.

The man shook his head again, sending the earflaps of his hat into a frenzy.

'Far too long.'

'Since the early nineteen-nineties?'

The man made no reply, just carried on shovelling.

'I'm looking for a man called Kenneth Krøll. He was here around nineteen ninety-two.'

The man stared at Peter and narrowed his eyes. His mouth became a thin line. He continued shovelling.

'I wouldn't know,' he said. 'I don't remember anyone.'

* * *

At last the main door opened, and a man stepped out. He nodded to them, headed for one of the 4x4s and drove off.

Peter rang the bell. A woman in her thirties appeared at the door. She regarded him with professional courtesy bordering on hostility. He had met her type so many times before behind various public service counters: people who took pride in telling you why something *couldn't* be done. He introduced himself.

'We don't give information about residents,' she said, measuring him with her eyes. 'Why do you want to know?'

'He's an old school friend,' Peter lied. 'I've lost touch with him and I'm trying to find him.'

'Sorry.'

She puffed out her chest. It was wrapped in a synthetic fur gilet and she managed to look down on him even though he was taller than her. 'Take my advice, ask his family.'

If he had forgotten his distrust of authorities, she had just reminded him of it. His life consisted of betrayals by people like her: social workers, teachers and others who always knew best, people who had replaced their humanity with rules and regulations, busy diaries, impossible meetings and sick leave due to stress or burnout while their cases were shelved or forgotten.

One look at her said it all. He gave up and turned on his heel.

She was left like a jilted date as he reversed the van, drove down the avenue and nodded to the handyman, who was still shovelling snow. The boys used to carve their names in a tree, he had said. He drove along the main road. Lange Lake was visible now and it was covered with a thick layer of ice.

Grimme wasn't originally from Grenå, that much he did know. His family had moved there sometime in the Eighties, but where from? Krøll wasn't a common name. Perhaps the woman was right. Perhaps he should try to find his family and ask them.

On an impulse he turned off the tarmac road to the right,

where the road immediately became more challenging, not to say impossible. Finally he stopped the car in the middle of the track, got out and walked alongside the lake. There weren't many houses here, but there were a few and they looked pretty expensive. A view of your own lake, a jetty plus motorboat, or maybe just a rowing boat – a little slice of heaven. But with a detention centre just up the road. He couldn't imagine the residents were thrilled about their neighbours.

Boys. He wandered on. Where would they go? What would they do here if they managed to get outside the perimeter?

He walked into the forest. It was there that he found it: an old oak with a massive trunk and bark as thick as elephant hide. He walked around it, studying it closely, and knew he'd found what he was after. Judging from the dates in the bark, carving your name in a tree and thereby revealing a little of your history would never lose its attraction.

Back in his car, a thousand thoughts surged through his head and he barely heard the text message announce its arrival with a beep. He had put his mobile in his jacket pocket and felt the faint vibrations, enough for him to retrieve it as he drove.

The text was from Cato. He had been granted day release from prison and would meet him the following morning in a scout hut in Lisbjerg Forest. He had more info, he wrote.

Peter contemplated the message and compared the wording with what he'd just seen by the lake. At home he made a plan.

68

THE MORNING WAS still dark when Mark turned off the main road and headed for Allingåbro. It was snowing. The headlights caught the large flakes in their glare and the wipers juddered across the windscreen in a mechanical rhythm. One was broken and the rubber screeched in protest as it was dragged across the glass. While he drove around looking for a barn under construction, the light started breaking down the curtain of black, the snowfall dwindled to scattered flurries and the pale fingers of the sun clung to the horizon like a desperate prisoner scaling a fence.

He stopped at a garage in what a country singer would call a one-horse town and bought a couple of cinnamon pastries when he paid for the petrol.

'You wouldn't happen to know if anyone is building a barn around here, would you?' he asked the girl behind the counter.

She brushed an invisible speck of dust off her white blouse, whose two top buttons were open to reveal a small gold heart on a chain.

'That'll be Thorvald's farm.'

She gave him directions. He couldn't miss it, straight through the village and he would see it on his right a few kilometres after the exit sign. Mark was tempted to blow her a kiss, but controlled himself and saluted her with two fingers to the temple.

'Only the skeleton of the barn's up so far.'

'Thank you. I might be back for more pastries later.'

'You'll be more than welcome,' she said in mock dialect with a tilt of her head.

She was right. He didn't miss the red structure once out of the village. The snowy landscape spread in all directions and there it was, on a hilltop, catching the morning sun, a sparkling mixture of red and white. It was beautiful here in a rugged kind of way. In the summer the fields would be a billowing mass of green or yellow and nature would truly come into her own. He had a sudden hankering for milder weather, a longing to see the snow turn to water and be absorbed by the soil, for the first spring rain, even though the farmers would inevitably poison the air by spreading manure. Christ, how he longed for something that would germinate and grow. Something that would give him a sense of meaning.

He drove a little further, round a bend in the road, and pulled over. That morning he had put on heavy boots and a winter coat. Now he studied the field leading up to the farm thinking about Christian Røjel's grim face. The pig farmer hadn't given much away and for most of the conversation had been tight-lipped and stony-faced. But towards the end he had given him a few titbits of information.

The Poles had been crammed together in the attic because the other flats in the property were already let and bringing in rent. Officially they didn't exist; they were paid in cash and the taxman was none the wiser. It was hard to keep body and soul together as a farmer if you had to pay the union rate for every single job that needed doing. Men from the same Polish family had been coming to Røjel's farm for years to do the kind of work that would have been unprofitable with Danish labour. In the end, Røjel had reluctantly informed him that their next assignment was building a barn in Allingåbro.

Mark drove on until he could see the back of the farm in his rear-view mirror. Then he pulled off the road, got out, slammed the door and walked through ankle-deep snow across the field.

He avoided the small frozen pond, which now formed an ice rink in a dip, but kept to the edge, hoping the bare poplars around the farm would conceal his arrival.

The main building was white and blended in with the snow. Smoke was coming out of the chimney. He might have been mistaken, but he had the feeling he had been spotted. As he approached, he could see something else that was white in the whiteness behind the poplars. At first glance, it looked like a private rubbish dump, where someone had left their old, clapped-out caravan, a rusty van, a pram and a trailer. But on getting closer he could see movement behind the caravan window, the twitch of a curtain. The door opened and two men charged out, one more panic-stricken than the other, without coats but in overalls and socks. They set off, running across the field to where he had come from. He tore after them, feeling a pain in his side, but he ignored it and picked out the slower of the two, a fat little man, whose legs were going nineteen to the dozen in the snow. But not for long. The lack of footwear made it hard for him to make headway through the drifts, and his pace slowed and slowed until Mark caught his sleeve, and they rolled around in the snow.

'Police,' Mark shouted in English with all the authority he could muster, turning the man on to his stomach and forcing his hands behind his back. To emphasise the gravity of the situation, he took one of the silly cable ties he kept in his jacket pocket and tightened it around the man's wrists. Then he dragged him to his feet.

'I'm a police officer. I'm not here about work. I have some questions for you about some girls in Grenå.'

The man looked unconvinced. Further ahead, his pal had reached the frozen pond and stopped, as though he couldn't decide which way to go.

'Tell him it's not about work,' Mark said to his captive, hoping he understood English.

The man shouted something to his friend, who was still caught in two minds. Then he stuffed his hands into his overall pockets and started walking back, lifting his feet high with each step.

They spoke English. One a kind of pidgin, the other slightly better. Yes, they were from Poland, they were just visiting. Mark didn't care. He undid the cable tie and marched them to the caravan, which was clearly inhabited. There was a smell of sweat, dirty socks, garlic, cabbage and oil. Some clothes had been hung up to dry on a line and there was a pair of socks on a small electric heater. An electric cable from the farm had been fed through a window. There were rubber boots and trainers lying around, and the bed linen on the two mattresses was crumpled. It looked as if the alarm clock had just gone off.

They sat down at a folding table. There was a half a bottle of vodka in the corner with a couple of glasses. Mark nodded to the bottle and the squat Pole found an extra glass and poured vodka for all three of them, looking as if he couldn't quite believe his own eyes.

'Na zdrowie.'

Mark had learned the word on a school trip to Poland in the distant past.

'Na zdrowie.'

The little fat guy, who, Mark guessed, was around his own age, threw back his head and drained the glass in one go and wiped his mouth with his sleeve. The other man followed his example, but his eyes watered and his face went red. They put their glasses down on the laminate table with a bang. Mark earned himself cautious smiles as he tipped the vodka down his throat and felt its beneficial, burning effect all the way down, followed by the relief of dulled pain. *Highly unprofessional conduct*. He could almost hear Anna Bagger's outraged voice, but it served merely to enhance his enjoyment of the vodka. He stuck his hand in his pocket and took out the CCTV picture. The Poles looked at it and nodded. Yes, they recognised the girls.

They had been with the two prostitutes in the house. Yes, they admitted they had invited them up to the attic, but they hadn't paid for sex.

'We had fun.'

'What were their names?'

They pointed: 'Lena, Lily and Tora.'

'When did you last see Tora?'

They looked at each other and exchanged a few words. Mark guessed from their expression that they were trying to agree whether to tell the truth or not. He tried to read their body language and intonation. The fat one appeared to have more experience. The other, who was younger, early twenties perhaps, looked like a gangly teenager and was still nervous.

'Christmas,' the fat one said.

'December the twenty-fourth?'

He shook his head.

'The twenty-fifth. We drank some vodka and ate fish. Polish tradition,' he said with an airy gesture, almost reaching for the vodka bottle, but folding his hands on the table instead. 'We were with the girls from downstairs. Tora went down to the kiosk to get another bottle of vodka, but she never came back.'

Even a kiosk had to be closed on Christmas Day, surely, Mark thought.

'And the others? Didn't they start to worry?'

'They were a little drunk. But later they panicked and said she must have been *taken*.'

'Did you find out anything about the girls? Their history? Why they were in Grenå?'

The young Pole studied his lap. The fat one gazed longingly at the vodka bottle, and when Mark nodded, his hand shot out and grabbed it. He spoke while pouring out three glasses.

'When they were drunk, they talked about a treasure at the bottom of the sea – some money or something they wanted to find.'

'Were they on the run from someone?'

The fat one drained his glass as he had the first and looked at Mark as if to say everyone was running away from something.

'There were some people they didn't want to meet, but I don't know who they were. They didn't mention any names.'

Mark showed them another photo. A picture of Ramses.

'Have you seen this man before?'

They both nodded.

'Once with Lily.'

Mark looked at the first photo again: Lily, the smallest of the three, with the Mohican, pierced eyebrows, lips and nose, and a hard expression on her small, pale face. He produced the earring from his pocket and showed it to them. Yes, that was hers, they confirmed. Lily had had a couple of ear studs with a fleur-de-lis. They matched her name, she had said. A fleur-de-lis was a lily in English.

'The fleur-de-lis,' Mark said. 'Did you see if any of the girls had tattoos or brands on their thighs?'

He held his breath, but he drew a blank. Whatever the two Poles had been doing with the three girls, it hadn't been in daylight.

Before leaving, he asked to see their passports. He wrote down their names: Krystof and Marek Skopowski.

He turned in the doorway. Something didn't quite add up. The men weren't attractive, they weren't rich. They were working illegally in Denmark. They lived in a place reeking of cabbage, garlic and dirty socks. What could they possibly have to offer three young Danish women?

'What did the girls want from you? What did you have that they needed?'

Mark looked around the caravan. As a child he had gone camping with his parents. He took two swift steps, flipped aside the mattress and bedding and looked in the box beneath.

'What the hell is this?'

He counted five handguns and one automatic weapon. A veritable arsenal. He straightened up. The two Poles scrambled to their feet, ready to flee a second time. Mark launched himself at them. He was pushed to the floor, but got hold of the older man's legs and felled him. The younger man tried to get him in a headlock, but Mark found his police gun and pressed it against the man's neck.

'Let go.'

The young guy released him. The older man had struggled to his knees, but he was moving sluggishly and Mark managed to stand up before he could muster any resistance. Mark pointed his gun at the two men, who were quite clearly inexperienced fighters.

'Hands up!'

They did as they were told.

'On your knees.'

The men knelt on the floor of the camper while Mark cuffed them with cable ties again. He read defeat in their eyes and their posture.

'They bought weapons from you, didn't they?'

He pointed his gun at each in turn. 'How many?'

Finally the older man answered.

'Two automatics and two handguns. Two night-vision goggles.'

'Where did they get the money from?'

They didn't know, but he could guess: robbing shops in Grenå.

'That's why the girls went up to the attic, wasn't it? To check out the merchandise?'

It had never been about sex or friendship. It had been about business.

He frogmarched them to his car, put them in the back and locked the doors. He leaned against the car and called Anna

Bagger. He quickly explained the situation and requested assistance: two patrol cars and a search team to turn the caravan inside out.

'I can only give you one car and two officers,' she said. 'We've got too much going on here. Didn't you get my message?'

'I've been busy.'

Her voice was chilly: 'Felix Gomez's parents have reported her missing. She was on her way to see them, but she never turned up.'

'Shit!'

'We're meeting here at eleven. I'd like you to be here. I want to know what your friend Boutrup is up to and where he is.'

69

PETER COULD HEAR the chainsaw chewing its way through the wood and he knew that Manfred had been in his workshop since daybreak. Jutta had driven the children to the nursery and then gone on to her job as a carer at a centre for senior citizens. The house was empty. Only King, the dachshund, was at home. The door was open and he went straight in, bent down and chatted to the dog, who greeted him like a long-lost friend.

He went over to the window, opened the curtain a fraction and looked across the yard to the workshop. From where he was standing, the noise was muted, but it was there. Manfred was busy.

In the few seconds he stood there, scenes from their friendship flashed through his mind: their first discussions about books they had both read. Hunting trips. A shared love of carpentry. A game of chess in the evening with a whisky and Jutta and the children around. Time spent in each other's company without many words or any grand gestures.

Peter let go of the curtain. He would always treasure the thought of their friendship. When everything fell apart and he could no longer hold the fragments of his life together, he would still have that. But although it meant so much to him, he was still prepared to risk it.

Manfred kept his guns in the living room. He knew where the key was because Manfred had shown him himself.

He fished it out from a Royal Copenhagen porcelain vase on

a shelf and unlocked the gun cabinet. There were two rifles and two shotguns. He reached for the Finnish-made Sako rifle which Manfred had taken with him when they went hunting on New Year's Day. It was heavy and solid, one of the finest and most accurate rifles in the world.

He weighed the weapon, which was kept ready assembled with a magazine, and found six 30.06 calibre shells in a box. He put the bullets in his pocket, rested the butt of the rifle against his cheek and looked through the sights. For a brief moment he was back in the forest looking at the stag. The air stood still. He held his breath. His finger quivered slightly on the trigger.

'It handles well.'

Peter spun around, with the rifle still against his cheek. Manfred was standing in the doorway, calm, his arms outstretched.

'It can shoot a hole in a hole at a distance of a hundred metres.'

'I know,' Peter said. 'I hope I won't have to use it.'

'You could have asked me. All you had to do was ask.'

They looked at each other for long seconds.

'It's better this way,' Peter said, lowering the rifle.

'We're friends,' Manfred said. 'You should have trusted me.'

'Perhaps that's precisely why.'

Manfred took a step towards Peter, who raised the rifle again. Manfred stopped.

'You wouldn't do it.'

Peter shook his head.

'I wouldn't run that risk if I were you.'

He had promised himself he wouldn't explain. And yet he did.

'It's best if you say this: I broke into your house and stole a rifle and ammunition from your gun cabinet and I threatened you. Should anyone ask.'

'And why would they do that?'

Peter backed away. There was no time; the atmosphere was

too charged and he didn't want to drag Manfred into a mess that had its origins in his old world. That was how it was. His old and his new life were in a head-on collision.

'Because they'll want to talk to me,' he said. 'But I haven't got the time. There's something I have to do.'

'Perhaps I could help?' Manfred offered.

Peter retreated to the door.

'You'll get it back,' he said, and then left.

At home he changed into the white shearling jacket he had bought in a sale last winter. Kaj whined when he put on the jacket. He let him out and took him for a short walk on the cliff. The snow was now falling thick and fast, and the wind had risen so that it was blowing across the cliff. He watched the dog as he ran around and did his business. He bent down, made a snowball and threw it. Kaj raced off to catch it.

'Good dog.'

He patted his head and thought about New Year's Eve. It was only a short time ago, but the night had tightened its grip on him and his world out here, his self-chosen no man's land. Nothing had been the same since.

He let the dog back in the house and ignored its pleas to come with him. He locked the door and was steering the van down the lane when Matti called.

'You were right,' he said. 'Grimme is on day release today.'

Peter reviewed the situation as he drove. He had several reasons to believe that the text about the meeting hadn't come from Cato. There was Cato's nervousness when they spoke earlier and the abrupt way their conversation had ended. There was the background noise and the unease Peter had detected on the phone. He hadn't believed a word Cato had said and he still didn't. The scout hut as a meeting place was an odd choice. They had never met there before. He and Cato had spent their childhood in and around Ry. Wouldn't it have been more obvious to pick somewhere in the woods around Ry, a place they both knew?

The conclusion was obvious: the rendezvous had been chosen by Grimme.

Peter had been online and printed off a map of Lisbjerg Forest. The hut was situated in the northern part, approximately ten kilometres from Århus. There were several entrances to the forest. He chose the one closest to the village of Lisbjerg and the furthest from the scout hut. From the clearing where he pulled over, he could see the large incineration plant in northern Århus, whose giant chimney belched out black smoke day and night – as it was doing now, high into the air. He could see it in the middle of the white landscape to the west, even though it was still snowing. He calculated it was opposite the hut and used it to navigate his way through the forest.

The tracks had been cleared enough for him to manoeuvre his way through the forest. The road was irregular and bumpy, and the van coughed and spluttered. Roughly one and a half kilometres from the hut he parked in a dark clearing where low-hanging spruce branches would conceal the white van to some extent. He took the rifle and started walking. There was one bullet in the chamber.

Approaching the hut, he kept close to the trees and moved with quiet stealth. It had eventually stopped snowing and the sun's rays shone through, warming his neck. There wasn't a breath of wind under the trees.

It was just like hunting. With every footstep, his tension evaporated into thin air. He knew he could do this. This was his thing. The forest, the forest floor, the birds, the ponds and the small streams; the sounds and smells and feeling of nature. He breathed it all in as he walked and his confidence grew. He was doing what had to be done. Fulfilling his responsibility.

Now and then he heard a rustle in the undergrowth or the

treetops, and every time he would stop and stand very still to listen before carefully moving on. Once he saw a fox between the trees and later a panic-stricken mouse darted across the snow only to disappear quickly down its burrow. Apart from that, there was only the occasional flap of a pigeon. This forest wasn't very popular with visitors.

He heard the car long before he saw it and located the hut. He followed the noise and slunk from tree trunk to tree trunk. He hoped the white shearling jacket would act as camouflage.

Three men got out of the car. Peter crept a little closer and found a good vantage point, then lay down on his stomach in the snow, raised the rifle to his shoulder and watched. Through the telescopic sights he recognised one of them as Boxer Nose, the one he had beaten up outside the hospital. The other one could have been Anja's boyfriend, but he wasn't sure. He looked like most biker gang members: big, broad, thuggish. And slow.

The third man was in the crosshairs. He recognised Grimme, whose face had once been ripped open with a knife. It had gained him respect amongst gang members and a far from attractive appearance. That and his double murder conviction placed him at the top of the hierarchy and he had every intention of staying there. Grimme was as big as the others, but he moved with a lightness and an authority they didn't possess.

The three of them chatted amongst themselves, looking around and pointing. He could see their breath, like clouds above their heads, and hoped they couldn't see his.

A little while later they split up. Grimme opened the hut door and went inside. One of the two beefcakes disappeared around the back. The other positioned himself five metres from the front.

Peter slowly circled the hut at a safe distance. He looked at his watch. It was ten fifty-five. They were expecting him at eleven. At ten minutes past they would start to get nervous. He waited.

Ten minutes later, Grimme reappeared. He exchanged a few words with one of the guards and looked into the forest. Peter moved behind the hut, still at a safe distance. He spotted Boxer Nose. He was sitting on a tree stump, fiddling with his mobile. Every now and then he would look up and scan the area, but he was becoming increasingly distracted by his phone.

Peter sneaked up as close as he dared, pausing occasionally for several minutes behind a small hill or a tree, then taking greater risks. Finally he found a stone which he threw to one side, hitting a tree trunk. The noise made the man look up. Peter threw another. The man got up and approached the spot where the stones had landed. For a moment he stood still, holding a gun in one hand and his mobile in the other.

Peter leaped up, raised the rifle and slammed the butt into the back of the man's head. Boxer Nose fell to the ground with a grunt. Peter wondered whether to hit him again, but the man was unconscious; he had gone out like a light.

He knelt down, took Boxer Nose's gun and tucked it into his jacket pocket. Then he picked up the dropped mobile and flung it far into the forest. He was close to the hut now, at the back. It was a low wooden construction with moss and patches of snow on the roof. He swung the rifle over his shoulder, scaled the uneven timber wall and crawled on to the roof with ease, the snow muffling any sounds. He had sat on a ridge many times before to repair a rafter or a roof. Manfred was the expert, but Peter knew how to keep his balance.

He straddled the ridge, took out his mobile and texted Cato. A few seconds later, Grimme appeared with a mobile in his hand and walked over to the car. Peter aimed the rifle and fired off a 30.06 calibre bullet. The windscreen of the 4x4 shattered. The guard clutched his face as glass and metal fell in a cascade. He whimpered. Grimme fumbled for the pistol he had dropped in the snow. Peter's second shot, this time with Boxer Nose's gun, hit him in the arm. The gang leader roared like a raging bull and rolled around in the snow.

'I've got another five bullets in the magazine,' said Peter from his position on the roof. 'Plus this.'

He dangled the gun between two fingers. 'I think it's time we had a little chat.'

70

Mᴀʀᴋ ᴛᴏᴏᴋ ᴛʜᴇ winter with him into the meeting room at Grenå Police Station. He was still wearing his heavy boots and coat, and his trousers were wet up to his knees from running across the field near Allingåbro.

He sat down, took out his packet of V6 chewing gum and popped a piece into his mouth so that no one would smell the vodka. But the detectives had other things on their minds. Most were sitting back against coats and jackets thrown over chairs, quietly discussing the latest developments. Their footwear had left puddles of melted snow on the floor and there was a stale smell of wet scarves, mixed with frustration.

Anna Bagger's investigation team had been supplemented with a man from the Air Accident Investigation Board and an inspector from East Jutland Police in Århus. The two visitors sat next to each other in the front row. On the surface Anna Bagger was her usual impeccable self, but Mark could sense her tension as she got ready to chair the meeting. She was annoyed. This wasn't a textbook investigation, but nor was it a disaster. It was just a bummer of a case: unpredictable – evidence and information pointing in all directions – a bummer.

'There's been a development,' she said, to open her briefing. 'Felix Gomez from Gjerrild Cliff has been reported missing. She was last seen at thirteen-ten in the SOK building in Brabrand. In the meantime we've received two further pieces of information.'

She opened a green folder, took out a sheet and read.

'Last July Felix lost her daughter and her husband in a heli-copter crash in the Kattegat. She was in the helicopter, but survived the crash. After she was discharged from hospital, she settled down in Gjerrild to live a quiet life.'

More muttering. Anna Bagger's eyes sought, and found, Mark.

'Since the accident Felix has been suffering from amnesia. The police and the Air Accident Investigation Board have been collaborating to establish what happened that day. Evidence suggests that this crash is linked to our case, or should I say, cases?'

Her voice cracked. She reached for the water on the table.

Mark suppressed an outburst. Damn! They – he included himself – should have checked up on Felix Gomez. They had focused too much on Boutrup because of his criminal past and forgotten all about her. Felix had kept out of the spotlight, a single woman minding her own business. Small, self-effacing and quite clearly a stranger to her new neighbour on the clifftop. Who would have thought she could have had such a dramatic history?

Anna Bagger continued: 'Given the seriousness of the case, Inspector Erling Bank, who has dealt with the case . . . is dealing with the case,' she corrected herself, 'has come to see us. As has Arthur Sand from the Air Accident Investigation Board.'

She nodded to Bank, who trotted up to the whiteboard with a speed that seemed to defy nature: he was a small, thickset man. His voice sounded as if he had a peg on his nose and he was angry.

'If any of you had bothered to read back six months this might not have happened,' he said. 'It's extremely irritating, to put it mildly.'

Anna Bagger drew a deep breath.

'We'll deal with that later,' she said.

Bank continued, a little milder and in best management-speak:

'Had we been cognizant of the link between the two investigations, we could have been more proactive.'

He launched into an extended report: 'At the time of the accident, we were forced to consider the possibility that it might have been sabotage. The weather was fine and this type of helicopter has an excellent safety record, I am told.'

He glanced at Arthur Sand from the Air Accident Investigation Board before continuing: 'Gomez was an experienced, competent pilot. He appeared to be a happily married man with a good job. It was true he had some financial problems; however, that's not a criminal offence and we're in the midst of a financial crisis. Why would anyone have wanted to kill him?'

Bank displayed the palms of his hands: 'We found nothing on him. Furthermore, we couldn't prove that anyone had tampered with the helicopter.'

He held up one finger.

'The only possible witness was Felix Gomez, but she was traumatised and suffering from amnesia,' he said. 'For a while we did treat her as a suspect, but what did she stand to gain? After all, she'd lost her child and come very close to dying herself.'

Bank kept his gaze fixed on Anna Bagger, who stared stubbornly back at him.

'The case has gone cold recently, but it certainly hasn't been shelved. We kept hoping Felix Gomez would start remembering. In other words, we were hoping for some developments.'

Anna Bagger twisted a strand of her fringe tightly around a finger, but said nothing. She was angry, Mark thought. Piqued, but also angry. Primarily with herself, because her honour was at stake. But she was also irritated with Bank, who could have done more to look into Erik Gomez and possibly contacted her about the case, which she hadn't known about for very good reasons: until a few weeks ago she had been working as a detective in Esbjerg.

'But something happened yesterday,' Bank said. 'Felix Gomez had a meeting with the Air Accident Investigation Board at the SOK HQ in Brabrand.'

Bank nodded to Arthur Sand, who stood up, went over to the whiteboard and took up position in front of the gathering with his hands behind his back. He had a remarkably gentle voice which contrasted with his officer-like physique.

'For a long time Felix couldn't remember anything about the accident,' Sand said. 'I don't think she wanted to, which is understandable. I had a couple of meetings with her which left us none the wiser. Yesterday, however, was different.'

He turned to the whiteboard.

'May I?'

He found a dry wipe marker on the table and wrote up some numbers. Mark read: 56° 15° 62° N 011°34' 22E.

Sand put down the marker and turned to face the officers.

'This is a location in the Kattegat. And it's close to the spot where Erik Gomez's helicopter crashed. It's a place called Lille Lysegrund. Not deep. Roughly ten metres. On a clear day you'd be able to see a shipwreck at the bottom from a helicopter.'

Mark's pulse soared. A treasure at the bottom of the sea. Both the Poles and Gry's colleague, Helle, had spoken about it. Was that what Erik Gomez had been looking for?

Sand sat down again and Erling Bank resumed his report. It was clear that the two of them had worked closely on the investigation.

'Felix Gomez thought she recognised Ramses Bilal when she and Boutrup found his body on the cliff. A few days later her memory started coming back and she recalled that her husband had met Ramses on two occasions.'

The mobile, Mark thought. That's why she took the mobile. Everything was beginning to make sense.

Bank continued: 'Our investigation now suggests that both Ramses Bilal and Erik Gomez were part of a drugs ring led by a man called Kenneth Krøll, also known as Grimme. Their last operation failed because the police received a tip-off. Grimme was sent to prison, as was the courier who had collected the drugs in Poland. They couldn't charge him with dealing, but they could with being an accessory in connection with an earlier raid on a security depot.'

Bank's foot bobbed up and down.

'We now have reason to believe that the courier, whose name was Brian, had time to scuttle his boat containing the drugs before he was arrested. He was clearly hoping to retrieve them once he was released from prison. Only he never was. He was diagnosed with cancer and then died in hospital.'

He paused and ran his eye across the audience. Sand resumed: 'Yesterday Felix suggested that other people could be looking for the coordinates.'

From his chair he pointed to the numbers he had written on the whiteboard.

'She had found these numbers inside a briefcase her husband had handed in to a lost property office. She thinks he was given the coordinates by Ramses Bilal, who had switched sides in the conflict between the criminals.'

He made an apologetic gesture with one hand.

'She was nervous when we met,' he said. 'I regret that I didn't get her police protection immediately. But she wasn't alone. A man accompanied her to the meeting and had been expected to pick her up afterwards.'

He nodded to Anna Bagger.

'She introduced me to him when I met her at reception.'

Anna Bagger cleared her throat.

'Peter Boutrup,' she told everyone. 'Our friend from the cliff. Previously convicted of manslaughter. He was released in September two thousand and eight after serving four years in Horsens.'

'Boutrup. Peter.'

Erling Bank, still standing by the whiteboard, turned the name over in his mouth like a twist of chewing tobacco. 'We looked into him shortly after his release. He was suspected of that murder in Østergade. They found his DNA at the crime scene. It was Wagner's case.'

'But he was eliminated,' Mark interjected to clarify.

Erling Bank's nods could have been interpreted in so many ways.

Anna Bagger asked: 'Does that mean Boutrup was the last person to see Felix Gomez? Apart from Sand?'

'Plus the receptionist at SOK,' Sand added helpfully. 'She remembers that Felix, after her meeting with me, bought a cup of hot chocolate from the vending machine and waited for about an hour and that she also made some phone calls.'

Sand looked genuinely upset. Erling Bank said: 'Felix arranged with her mother to be, and I quote, "there in fifteen minutes". But she never arrived. Her parents then contacted us.'

Anna Bagger got up again.

'We're dealing with three urgent issues here. Number one: Felix Gomez.'

She looked at Erling Bank. 'You've already initiated a search in the area around SOK and at her parents' flat in Brabrand?'

He nodded. Anna continued her summary: 'Obviously we need to organise a local search. Her house has to be checked for clues. But we must *also* – and this is the second issue – locate Boutrup.'

She held up two fingers and held her index finger.

'Boutrup is the key to Felix, that's my clear understanding. The two of them have been seen together on several occasions. It would suggest they know each other better than we've been led to believe. And then there's the third issue.'

She grabbed her middle finger and held it up. 'The coordinates. We need to find out as quickly as possible what's out there. If someone has kidnapped Felix, we must assume they know the coordinates by now. They're bound to mount their own expedition shortly.'

Mark looked out of the window. The snow was falling again, thick and heavy, after a couple of hours of sunshine. He couldn't think of worse conditions for a diving operation, but at least the wind wasn't up.

'We've dismissed the divers. So who can do it?' Martin Nielsen asked.

'What about the local girl?'

Anna Bagger looked at Arthur Sand. 'You said it was only ten metres deep. Surely we don't need a whole team?'

Sand shook his head.

'One diver should do it. The coastguard has a boat moored in Grenå. If you can get a diver, I can get you a boat.'

Anna Bagger's eyes landed on Mark.

'Do you have any idea where we should look for Boutrup?'

He shook his head. 'I don't know any more than you do.'

'He has contacts in Århus, doesn't he? A mother? Wasn't he brought up in Ry?'

Erling Bank nodded. Anna Bagger selected six detectives.

'You two go to Boutrup's house. The rest of you go to Århus and Ry. Check out anywhere he might be: family, friends, ex-colleagues.

She turned to Mark.

'Do you know where the diver is?'

'I know where she lives.'

'Then I want you to find her and go with her in the boat to find that location. We need everyone available today.'

'There's one more thing,' Bank said. 'I mentioned the gang leader, Grimme.'

Everyone looked at him.

'He's on day release today. And he's gone missing.'

71

FROM HIS POSITION on top of the scout hut, Peter took aim with the gun he had taken from Boxer Nose. Grimme was lying in the snow, stained red now with the blood from his arm. The guard who had been at the front was sitting against a tree, groaning. The sky was growing darker, and ice crystals glinted around them.

'So Cato double-crossed me,' Peter said.

Grimme bared his teeth in a forced grin.

'Who says it was Cato? You've got to be careful with the company you keep, Peter.'

Peter's thoughts went into a whirl and landed somewhere he didn't care for. He pushed aside the image of Miriam.

'Where's Felix?'

'Go fuck yourself!'

The gang leader's hand crept slowly through the snow to the spot where he had dropped his gun. It was half under the car. Peter's shot whipped up the snow and the bullet ricocheted off the car. Grimme snatched back his hand.

'The first shot was for Felix,' Peter said. 'The next is for Stinger.'

Grimme snorted.

'You haven't got a clue what's going on. You fuckwit.'

Peter fired again. The bullet glanced off Grimme's boot and his leg jerked.

'I'm not used to your weapons,' Peter said. 'Wonder what I'll hit next time.'

After the adrenaline had kicked in, his body was filled with a strange heat. His mind was clear, his thoughts focused. He jumped down from the roof and walked closer with the gun muzzle pointing at Grimme's head, which recoiled further and further until it banged into the bumper. For the first time, Peter could see his bête noir at point-blank range. He had wanted to get Grimme in his sights so often. Revenge was tempting. But it led nowhere.

'You coward,' Peter snarled. 'Ramses was easy meat. Easy to get rid of. Let me see how you face up to an equal.'

He gestured with the gun. Grimme's mouth moved twice before a sound came out.

'It wasn't us,' the biker said.

'Then who was it?'

Even before he got the answer, he knew it was true. Grimme's tongue and palate struggled to meet and the name was slurred.

'Lily.'

'Lily double-crossed you? And she killed Stinger?'

Grimme grunted in the affirmative.

'And Nina Bjerre and Tora?'

Grimme ignored him.

'Tell me about Red,' Peter said.

'Who?'

'Red. Mogens Røjel. You were at a young offender's institution with him. You carved your names into the big tree by Lange Lake. Where is he?'

'How should I know?'

'He's your hired gun in Operation Lily. He's got Felix now. Where?'

Grimme muttered something.

'Louder!'

'I don't know anything about that.'

'What do you want with her?'

'She knows the coordinates.'

'What else?'

'Her husband was a greedy twat.'

'She didn't know anything,' Peter lied. 'She doesn't remember anything. Where does Red take his victims?'

'I don't know.'

'You're lying.'

'It's always best not to know too much. You know how it is.'

Peter got up and walked over to Grimme. His scarred face leered up at him.

Peter put a bullet into a tyre, causing it to explode. The air pressure shifted Grimme's hair. Something changed in the gang leader.

'You haven't got it in you,' he hissed. 'Not when it comes to the crunch.'

Peter gripped the gun. His finger tightened around the trigger, then he released it. He was back in the forest with Manfred.

'Go on, shoot me,' Grimme said. 'Be a man, press the fucking trigger and get it over with.'

Grimme was right. It would be over in a split second and the world would be a better place. Peter's neck tensed and he tried to relax his muscles. He took one step back. Grimme supported himself on his good hand and tried to struggle to his feet.

'Don't move.'

'Or what?' Grimme grinned at him, but a movement behind Peter made him shift his focus.

Peter turned as a thick piece of wood hit him in the kidney. Boxer Nose raised his arm for a second crack.

'Just so you know,' he grunted, as the blow hit Peter in the back and sent him flying. 'Your little stunt at the hospital failed. We got that bitch Anja the next day.'

Peter fell just as Grimme reached for his gun. The pain was unbearable. Peter blindly rolled on to his stomach and fired. Two shots cut through the silence of the forest. The second made a hole in Grimme's forehead. Peter fired again: into the air where

Boxer Nose was towering over him like a raging bear. The man and the weapon hit the ground at the same time, the man clutching his side. He was alive, but stayed down.

Peter's body was on fire. Grimme's bullet had hit him in the arm. He could see the hole and saw the white leather of the jacket turning red. He looked at the three men. The guard at the front of the hut was still leaning against a tree, groggy after the rifle shot that had shattered the windscreen. Grimme was dead. Boxer Nose was slumped in a foetal position, his chest heaving. Peter strode over to him and opened his jacket. The shot had hit him in the side. He went back to Grimme's body and pulled off his jacket and sweater. He tied the sweater around Boxer Nose's injury as tightly as he could, dragged him inside the scout hut and covered him with Grimme's jacket.

'Lie very still. I'll call an ambulance.'

After ringing 112, he found a rope in the scout hut which he used to tie the other guard to the tree. Then he walked back through the forest.

When he was back in his car and about to start the engine, his mobile rang. It was Matti: 'Heard about Cato?'

'What about him?'

'Grimme's men beat the shit out of him. Everything's broken that can be broken. Word is they wanted something from him.'

'Did they get it?'

'He put up one hell of a fight.'

Peter closed his eyes. Perhaps he had been wrong about Cato after all. He rewound to the conversation with Grimme and his suspicions regarding Miriam returned. But she wouldn't betray him, would she? After all, they were friends.

He shook his head in an attempt to dismiss her words, but two lingered: boy scout.

He yanked the wheel, reversed the car and drove out of the forest.

72

THE PAIN WAS keeping her alive. As long as she could feel it, she was still here.

They had chained her up again and thrown a quilt over her. Her skin felt flayed like an animal's. It was as if someone had exposed all her muscles, tendons, bones and neural paths so that they lay bleeding, accessible to anyone who felt like touching them.

They had removed the blindfold and the tape from her mouth. She knew what that meant. She wouldn't get out of here alive. Not now she had given them the coordinates. She had held out for as long as she could, but the branding had changed everything. She could no longer resist. Not that it mattered any more. She was going to die, she knew that.

Felix tried sitting up on the mattress. She was thirsty, and she was cold and shivering, while the wound on her thigh radiated a feverish heat up into her body. The temperature in the room was still at freezing point. She could see her own breath in the air.

'Water. Give me some water.'

Her voice had lost its strength. It was the voice of a little girl.

She heard a sound. An animal? It might be a cat. Or a mouse or a rat. Her eyes had grown accustomed to the darkness and she thought she was probably in an outhouse of some sort. Possibly a boathouse. She could make out ropes and netting around her. There was also the kind of tub builders used to mix cement. She couldn't see a boat, but it was difficult to get a sense of how big the room really was. She was in one corner. Behind her, the wall was cold and there were crates on both sides. She thought they might be fish crates.

'Water,' she pleaded.

She heard footsteps outside. The door was unlocked and opened. She hadn't seen their faces clearly because it was always dark inside, but she had sensed them and their outlines, and she had seen her death in their eyes.

The smaller of the two men came in. She knew that from the way he moved. He wasn't as heavy as the other one. But when he knelt down beside her there was something in his eyes that sent a shiver down her spine.

He pulled the quilt away. She was naked underneath it.

'Water.'

She was whispering now. He nodded.

'Of course. I'll get some for you.'

She wasn't fooled by his courtesy. She knew what lay behind it. And yet she was pathetically grateful and could have kissed him when he returned with a mug of water for her to drink. All the while he stroked her hair; then her skin. His hand moved across her breasts and her shoulders.

'You're so smooth,' he said. 'Nice and smooth. Your skin is so interesting.'

His hands were on her face. He forced up her chin. He felt her neck.

'I mustn't,' he muttered. 'You mustn't make me do it.'

She froze with terror as his fingers explored her body. There was no lust in his gaze, only curiosity. He pinched a nipple and tugged her breast. Squeezing it. First tentatively; then harder. He tilted his head to one side. She saw his other hand move. The gleam of metal. A small knife.

'No!'

She tried to retreat, but the wall stopped her, cold and hostile. He unlocked the shackles around her wrists.

'Shh. Be quiet. Now you can hug me.'

He spoke as though he was a teacher telling a pupil to behave. He held her breast again.

'If you promise to sit still, it won't hurt as much. You don't want to be chained up again, do you? That's not very nice at all.'

She placed a hand on his shoulder and suppressed her tears as best she could, but even so her chest started heaving. He shook his head, irritated. His fingers stroked up her thigh. Found the brand and caressed it. White pain shot through her.

'Mmm. Skin,' he mumbled. 'Soft.'

His hand moved across her stomach. Fingers pressed into her belly button. She wanted to throw up.

'Your muscles are good,' he whispered. 'They're right under the skin. They're wrapped around each other. Not like the other one.'

'The other one?'

Her teeth were chattering. The words were forced out.

'She wasn't as slim as you.'

Tora, she thought.

His hands wandered back to her chest. To her breast. He squeezed and pulled it. She whimpered.

'Shh! Quiet.'

Her stomach contracted. She was going to be sick and turned her face to the side. But nothing came out except bile, leaving a bitter taste in her mouth as it trickled down her chin.

He didn't notice.

'Put your arms around me,' he said.

She forced herself to be a statue. A plaster cast figure, a terrified woman sitting and staring her fate in the eye. Terror drained her of thought and emotion.

'Now!'

She automatically did as she was told. And then came the pain: as sharp as a needle, yet all-embracing, causing her brain to stop functioning – it registered the pain, but nothing else.

Pain upon pain. She threw both arms in the air, but then let them fall on to his shoulders again. There was no way she could resist. She didn't have the strength or, for that matter, the will.

He smiled. She saw it through her tears and the mist that had settled over her eyes. He held something up and studied it. A small, blood-stained bud. He looked at her.

'Is it true what they say that it's very sensitive?'

He stared at her other breast, fascinated. She held up a hand. Almighty God. Help me.

She nodded as best she could. Again he looked at the nipple in his hand. Then he pressed it carefully in between his lips. Sucked it. Chewed it. Spat it into his hand.

She covered both breasts with her hands. Blood was pouring from one of them. It was sticky and trickled down her stomach into her groin. He followed the flow of blood with his eyes, ran a finger through it, lovingly, tenderly.

'You're so soft.'

He mumbled something else. He was talking to himself. Discussing something she couldn't hear. His fingers felt their way down her body. Her mind whirled, trying to find ways to distract him. Perhaps he was susceptible after all – if she guided him.

'I'm so cold,' she said. 'Please can I have another blanket?'

He looked at her. He nodded.

'Blanket.'

'It's very cold in here.'

She was shivering all over now. She thought about Tora in the freezing water. Faceless Tora. She thought about his knife.

'Cold,' he said in a toneless voice.

He laid her back on the mattress and hovered over her. She was too scared to close her eyes. She had to see what he was doing, to know where the pain would come from next. He lowered his head over hers and sniffed her. He sniffed her ear and her throat and further down. He found her other breast.

She felt his tongue on her skin. He still showed no signs of lust. Only curiosity, like an inquisitive, dangerous child. He stopped at her remaining nipple. Then he closed his lips around it. Sucked it. Bit it. This time the pain was far more prolonged. She pushed him away with all the strength she had; she screamed. He sat back and looked at her in surprise.

'Shhhh.'

He got up with his eyes on her. There was blood around his mouth. He wiped it on his sleeve. His eyes were blank, without any trace of anger. He was finished with her, for now. She knew he was when he turned his back on her and walked away. She looked down at herself. Blood was pouring out. She pressed the blanket against her wounds and lay down and cried. Then she heard the noise she had heard before he came in. A rustle. Someone breathing, perhaps?

Shortly afterwards she heard the voice, a feeble whisper: 'Help me!'

73

THE PUB WAS situated on a corner. The sign above the door was shaped like a dartboard, with a dart in the middle and *Bull's Eye* inscribed in looped, red letters.

The curtains were drawn; the door was locked. There were no A-boards outside, but it was only one o'clock in the afternoon. Peter peered through the stained-glass window in the door. At first he couldn't see anything. Then he heard chairs and tables scraping and saw a man washing the floor – a slim, young man. Probably an employee. He tapped on the window, but the man didn't hear him. He went behind the building and found a rear entrance. Here the door was open and an old blue Daihatsu was parked in the yard. He gained access to the pub through a back room filled with beer crates and kegs. He cleared his throat and the young man with the mop jerked upright as if someone had held a revolver to his head.

'Sorry if I frightened you.'

'Who are you?'

The young man looked nervous, as though he was used to being shouted at for the slightest thing. Beads of sweat had gathered on his forehead.

'Where will I find Red?'

The man slapped the mop into the bucket and sloshed it back on the floor without wringing it out first. There was soapy water everywhere.

'I don't know where he is. I guess he'll be here later.'

He surveyed Peter askance. Then he froze.

'Hey! What happened to your shoulder? You're bleeding.'

'It's nothing. Where does he live?'

The man pushed the mop around under a table.

'He's bought one of the new flats down by the river.'

Peter asked him for the number.

'Who wants to know?'

The man narrowed his eyes. He spoke the line as if he'd heard it in an old spy movie and then practised it in front of a mirror. Peter backed out.

'Just an old friend. Don't worry, I'll find him.'

Peter swore softly under his breath. What was it about him that meant he couldn't frighten information out of people, but ended up shooting them?

He had been hoping that Grimme could have told him where Red lived, but it was clear he hadn't wanted to know any details. And so Peter had lost valuable time. Now he had to find the place in some other way because Felix was bound to be where Red was. He might already be too late, but he didn't dare think about that.

His shoulder was hurting and every now and then his eyes would swim. He had to concentrate to stop himself passing out. Changing gear hurt, but he managed to drive towards the centre of Grenå and park near the railway station. From there he walked over the river and across the railway to the new buildings. Black box-like structures were scattered around the area, some still under construction. 'River Promenade, Grenå. Quality homes in a unique location', said a sign which also announced the name of the construction company and the other contractors involved in the project.

Many of the flats were still unfinished. The financial crisis might have put a stop to the project. Or perhaps it was just the winter which had literally frozen the works. They'd had snow on the ground since November now. An icy winter and a financial crisis: jobs in the construction industry were in short supply.

It was still snowing and at times a gust of wind would send a flurry of sleet into his face. His kidneys also hurt and he couldn't walk upright. Sharp shafts of ice pricked his skin and the snow found paths under his clothing and down his collar to his neck.

The flats looked on to the black river flowing past, with ducks bobbing up and down on the surface. The River Grenå never froze. The current was too strong, and the ducks were quickly carried down towards the harbour.

He saw evidence of human activity here and there: a cleared garden path, a bicycle, curtains or flowers in a window, tools in a garage left open, snow blowing inside. In front of every building he noted the framework for decking, reminiscent of parquet flooring. But the work was unfinished and only the foundation of the terraces and a few floorboards could be seen under a thick layer of ice. He couldn't see any cars. If Red did live in one of the flats, he was unlikely to be at home.

After surveying the area, he decided that only three flats looked occupied. He walked up to the first and could see from the sign on the door that the owner was called A. Bartholdy. He continued to the next one. There was no door sign yet, but there was a frozen-looking double buggy outside. He knew Christian Røjel had no grandchildren because he had often heard him complain about this very issue. Red lived alone.

One flat remained. It had a wonderful location, only a stone's throw from the river. There was a garage under each flat. He circled around it trying to form an impression. Black blinds hung in the windows. He walked up the steps to the front door. No name sign. He rang the bell, but there was no reply and the door was locked. He walked down the steps and stood for a moment wondering what to do. Then he opened the garage door. It opened easily and revealed an almost empty space. But not entirely. There was a work table on two trestles and tools hanging in rows on the wall. Some boxes had been stacked on top of each other and there was an old tub filled with empty bottles. In a corner some sacks had been thrown across something he couldn't see. There was also a coil of rope. He stepped further into the darkness. He heard a sound. Something was hiding under the sacks. Whimpering sounds.

'Felix?'

Images flashed through his brain: Felix with her hands tied behind her back, savaged, just like Tora. Felix dying from exposure. Felix with blank eyes, her body defeated for ever.

'Is that you, Felix?'

Carefully he raised one of the sacks. Then he staggered back as a shadow shot past him. A cat. He looked under the sacks. In a beer crate full of old newspapers lay six tiny, freezing kittens.

74

Kɪʀ ᴡᴀꜱ ᴄʟᴇᴀɴɪɴɢ. Scrubbing floors, dusting cupboards, removing stains and scouring the sink made her feel better. It mitigated the disappointment and humiliation after the slap. The redness on her cheek had gone, but the act itself would never go away, she knew that. It wasn't the first time her father had slapped her. Far from it. But it was the first time she had felt as if the intimate world around her had disappeared beneath her feet, as if there was nothing of it left.

She missed work. She missed Allan Vraa and the others. The diving truck, the drysuit, the sensation of gliding through the water on a mission. She stood up, supporting herself on the mop, and bent over the kitchen table and read the letter again. It was from the Frogman Corps's EOD Division in Kongsøre and had arrived that morning. Allan Vraa was putting together a team to go to the Gulf of Aden to hunt pirates. Was she interested?

She returned to the mop. She had neglected housework for a long time and the kitchen floor was greasy. She could hardly be further away from the place described in the letter: the waters off the coast of Somalia, where pirates were taking Westerners as hostages. Departure in one week. Sun and camaraderie on board. HDMS *Absalon* and exciting work. Getting away from Grenå. She should have left a long time ago, but now it had suddenly become difficult. Now that she had given up on her family, something else was keeping her here. Or was that the very reason why she should say yes? Perhaps there really was nothing to stay for?

She heard the car outside and could tell from the engine whose it was. Seconds later Red filled the doorway.

'Get your gear together. You're going diving.'

She said nothing. She simply stared at him. He was dressed completely in black: black combat gear, black leather jacket and black boots. He looked like a mercenary on a secret mission. He also had that expression on his face: as if he was staring death in the face. The red birthmark was practically pulsating.

'Are you kidding?'

She blinked. But he wasn't kidding, that much was obvious. He was used to getting his way. She was his baby sister. He expected total obedience.

'And where were you thinking I would dive?'

She deliberately carried on scrubbing the floor, on her knees. She found a greasy spot under the table and worked at it with the floorcloth, her thoughts sprinting ahead. What was he up to? What had she failed to see?

'And don't walk on the floor,' she warned him, but her voice sounded uncertain. He was her brother, but he hadn't come for a chat. He was like a ticking time bomb that could go off at any moment, triggered not by acoustics, or magnetism, or movement, but by what she said or did.

'Look at you,' he said. 'Down on all fours. Just where you belong.'

She was shocked by the level of bitterness and hatred in his voice. Where did it come from?

She got up. Gradually the gravity of the situation dawned on her. She was a soldier, but her judgement almost failed her, faced with him, her brother. She gave herself a talking-to. She had to keep her wits about her. This was serious, no doubt about it. But it was a situation she could handle.

'OK,' she said carefully. 'What do you want?'

'What I just said.'

His hand moved in his jacket pocket. Any other enemy and

she wouldn't have been so shocked. He pulled out a pistol and pointed it at her.

'I didn't know you had one of those.'

'There's a lot you don't know about me. Get your gear. We're going.'

Her training took over. Patience, she thought. Do what he tells you. Wait for the right moment.

Drag the time out if you can.

She pulled off her rubber gloves, forcing herself to keep him under surveillance. For the first time she saw herself through his eyes: she had passed him in the outside lane. His baby sister had long since proved that she was stronger and more capable than him, though he was the one who, from the very start, had received all the support, all the belief from her parents. Her achievements as a mine clearance diver and as a soldier were a provocation. She was a threat. She wondered if that was really what this was about.

'I need to know how deep down you want me to go. So I know what kit to bring.'

She rolled up one glove and stuffed it in her pocket while still keeping her eyes on his. The other she left on the rim of the bucket.

'Ten to fifteen metres. Come on. Get your gear!'

She looked out of the window. It was still snowing, but not as much as it had done earlier. The wind was picking up again, though.

'How far are we going?'

'You're asking too many questions. Get a move on.'

Or else what, Red? she thought, but she knew better than to ask.

'I need to go to the garage. That's where I keep all my equipment.'

'Get your diving gear on now,' he said. 'And hurry up.'

He followed her outside. She lived at the end of the road;

her neighbours were far away and wouldn't notice a thing. The expensive EOD kit they used on assignments was at the naval base, so she used her own private equipment. She took her time checking the manometer, making sure the pressure of the tank was 280 bar. She was a kit nerd. Sports divers tended to use equipment with only 200 bar in the tank. While she was checking it, she took the opportunity to drop the rubber glove in her pocket on the floor. Then she changed and put on first the undersuit and then the drysuit. When she got to the diving knife and was about to attach it to her leg as usual, he took it from her.

'You won't be needing that.'

He kept it. She carried the gear into his car, her mind racing ahead of her. He probably intended to use Uncle Hannibal's motorboat. He had made sure he got it when it was found on Fjellerup Beach, where it had drifted ashore. It was unlikely anyone would see them setting off. He would have moored the boat in a secluded spot. But even if anyone did see them, they would think that Red Røjel and his sister were off on some entirely legitimate trip. A crazy trip, given the winter weather. But that was just like her, they would think. The crazy diver, who always had to draw attention to herself with her foolhardy behaviour. A constant source of embarrassment to her parents.

Red gave her the car keys and pushed her into the driver's seat.

'Drive.'

She started the car and reversed in jerks, almost knocking into the larch hedge. She hoped she was leaving behind conspicuous tyre tracks. Red sat on the passenger seat pressing the gun into her side. She could feel it against her diving suit.

'We're going to the harbour. No funny stuff.'

She drove down the coastal road. It wasn't far. Not much time to think or begin a conversation. Just time to do what had to be done.

The harbour was deserted. The divers had gone. No one in their right mind would sail today, except the Varberg ferry.

'Over there.'

He ordered her past the Norwegian company where rusty heaps of scrap metal were waiting to be turned into money.

'Down to the right. You can park there.'

As she had predicted, the boat had been moored in a remote location so that no one would see them, unless they had a reason to be on the breakwater today. They couldn't be seen from any of the businesses, Thorfisk, the freight company, the ferry berth or the scrapyard. All the cutters, dinghies and yachtsmen were far away, right up the other end.

He jumped out and told her to carry the equipment box.

'Over there,' he nodded.

Sure enough, moored to a post in the water, there was Uncle Hannibal's motorboat, bobbing up and down. It was a bit like a cutter with its inboard motor, small cabin and maximum speed of fifteen knots. She had many happy memories of that boat. Today wasn't going to be one of them.

'Down you go.'

She scrambled down. He handed her the box. No chance of disarming him. Not yet. He came down the ladder with his back to the rungs and the gun pointing at her. He stuck his hand into his pocket and found the keys, which he handed to her with a note. She read: 561562 N. 0113422 E.

'Shouldn't be a problem for you to find, should it?'

She checked. There was a satnav in the wheelhouse. He made her drag the boat fenders on board. Then he nodded for her to insert the key in the ignition. The engine started with a low growl. Red slipped the mooring. She put the boat in gear and reversed out. Then she programmed the satnav and steered them out of the harbour.

75

'Maria?'

Felix whispered the name into the darkness. For a long time there was no reply. Plants clung to her with their green tentacles and soft caresses, but they had no voices. Being at the bottom of the sea was wonderful. The plants undulated gently while the waves formed intricate patterns of sunlight on their leaves. It was warm and peaceful. Far away, where the water was no longer quite so clear, Maria was singing a Spanish ballad. Felix opened her arms in anticipation. In a moment Maria would come running to her.

'. . . ter.'

Someone was speaking. The sea disappeared, taking Maria with it. Felix blinked in the gloom. She must have passed out. Now she was back in her prison. She wasn't lying at the bottom of the sea, but in a freezing cold garage somewhere unknown to her. Alone, or so she had thought, but that was before the voice in the darkness. It sounded as if the walls were talking, but the voice was devoid of any strength.

'Is anyone there?'

She, too, struggled to find her voice. She listened intently for a reply, but heard nothing.

She turned her head and stared into the old fish crates and stacked coils of rope. Her eyes went up to the old bricklayer's tub and discovered for the first time that there was a hole in the wall, a rectangular opening where a door must have been.

Her neck protested and pain flashed through her breasts as

she tried to twist her body towards the doorway. The scabs split open. She placed her fingers on her breasts, but the sores hurt too much. The fever vied with the cold. Her tongue was rough, like sandpaper.

'Can you hear me?'

She didn't manage to get all the words out. She summoned all her strength and said: 'Are you there?'

The reaction was clear now. Something scraped across the floor on the other side.

'Water.'

Leaning across the mattress was agony. A nail or a spring was digging into her thigh, but the sharp tip was as nothing compared to the pain from the branding. Her ankles were still shackled, even though her hands were free. The chains cut deep into her flesh as she stretched as far as she was able. To the right, she glimpsed a naked foot.

'Who are you?'

'Water,' the voice said.

Felix closed her eyes. The sea returned with the warm sway of the water. The rim of the tub was soft. She had to rest her head against it, just for a moment.

'Who are you?' the voice asked her this time. It came from far away.

Felix sat up. She must have passed out again. Her head was pounding.

'Felix.'

She spoke her name into the darkness. Hearing her own voice helped. She reached forward again. The foot moved once more.

'I'm Anja,' the voice said. 'Are you with Lily, too?'

Felix didn't understand. She had no idea what Anja was talking about.

'Mine is called Swatch. What's yours called?' Anja asked.

'Who's Lily?' Felix asked, but there was silence and for a

moment she thought it was the last time she would hear Anja. Then the voice said: 'Water.'

Felix looked into the tub and discovered it was half full. Melted snow had dripped from a hole in the roof.

'I can't reach you,' she said.

She would never be able to push the big tub towards Anja. Or perhaps she could. If she really made a huge effort.

There was a pause, then Anja whispered: 'He's scared of water.'

76

Mark parked in front of Kir's house, which was at the end of Hasselvej, an enclosed plot in the old summer house area south of Grenå. He had tried calling her landline and her mobile, but all he got both times was a request to leave a message.

The house was old; black stained wood with white windows. There was a garage next to it. Facing the road was a tall larch hedge which effectively shielded it from nosy parkers. Kir's old Toyota was parked in the drive, close to the front door.

He rang the bell. When there was no reply, he tapped on the window, but there was no reaction there, either. He looked through the kitchen window and saw a bucket in the middle of the floor. There was a mop leaning against the wall and a cloth on the floor tiles, as if she had been in the middle of cleaning when she left the house. A yellow rubber glove hung over the rim of the bucket. He could see a letter on the table.

He pressed the handle, but the door was locked. It would take too long to pick the lock. He went back to his car, found a rug and fetched the jack from the boot. After covering the glass window in the front door with the rug as best he could, he smashed it with the jack. He looked around. Not a peep from the summer houses. He hoped no one had heard the noise to make them come rushing over, or even more ridiculous, call the police.

He removed the remaining shards from the frame, using the rug for protection, and stuck his arm through. It was a strain to reach, but his fingers finally found the lock and turned it. No problem pressing the handle then. He entered the hallway and closed the door behind him.

'Kir? Are you there?'

There was no reply, and something about the silence troubled him. She might have a perfectly valid reason to be out, of course, but who would leave their house while they were in the middle of washing the floor? Where would she go on foot in this kind of weather? As far as he knew, there were no shops nearby, but she could have gone for a walk or dropped in on a friend. Perhaps she had a boyfriend – what did he know? – who had picked her up in his car. The thought wormed its way into his brain and gnawed at him, and he had to make an effort to ignore it.

He looked around the room, which was a kitchen and living room combined. At first glance, the only alarm bell was the bucket. He didn't know a great deal about housework, but logic told him you wouldn't walk away in the middle of washing the floor. Besides, Kir had walked across the wet tiles to get out, he could see that now. There were footprints on the tiles, possibly from two different pairs of shoes or boots. One pair was a size that could have been Kir's. The other was bigger and might have belonged to a grown man. He put his hand in the bucket. The water was tepid, but not completely cold.

He did a tour of the house. He felt bad about prying in her bedroom, which was a terrible mess. Piles of clothes were scattered around two chairs and the bed – panties, bras and camouflage trousers. He thought about Helle Bjergager's tidy, feminine room in Fredensgade 27. Kir's room was neither tidy nor feminine. There was no burgundy velvet cover on this bed – it was covered with an old, faded quilt – and there was no tray of candles – just an underwater torch on the battered bedside table along with seashells and conches. There were posters of divers on the wall and large drawings of various mines and instructions on how to defuse them. He had no doubt Kir took great care of her gear and as a mine clearance diver she had to be both organised and pay attention to details, but in her own home she had no sense of order. Where was her equipment? Not inside the house. So it had to be in the garage.

On the way out he read the letter lying on the kitchen table. Kir had been invited to spend three months in the Gulf of Aden hunting pirates. During that period, the doctors had planned some experimental treatment for him. He would be getting an injection every other day and each time he would have a temperature and experience flu-like symptoms the following day. The worse the reaction, the greater the chance that the medication was having an effect on the cancerous cells. He put the letter back on the table. If he was lucky, she would be away while he was in treatment and would come back when he was well again and ready to make a fresh start. If he wasn't . . .

He shuffled the letter around the table. He didn't want to think about it. Lady Luck hadn't really smiled on him.

He went into the garage. No wonder Kir's old Toyota estate had been banished to the drive. The garage was filled with an assortment of stuff, most of it work-related. There was also a fibreglass boat on a trailer. It was fitted with a single outboard motor. Unsuitable for long trips, but big enough to take to sea, so that she could dive or fish. He guessed that her job was also her hobby. He saw a lot of fishing equipment. Personally he didn't know one end of a fishing rod from the other.

He stepped on something as he moved further into the garage, where some dumbbells were lined up neatly on a foam mat. Looking down, he saw a yellow rubber glove matching the one in the kitchen. He picked it up and sniffed it. It was dry, but smelled of fresh detergent. He thought about the tepid water and a chill started to spread down his back. He took out his mobile and called Anna Bagger.

'She's gone,' he said. 'I think someone has taken her.'

He told her about the rubber gloves and the bucket while checking the garage over again.

'And another thing,' he said. 'I'm in her garage. There's a lot of diving equipment here, but there's no diving suit.'

Anna Bagger was on his wavelength immediately.

'It seems we're not the only ones in need of a professional diver today.'

'Now what?'

'I'll sort it out with Sand. You'll have to find your way to the location without a diver.'

'Any other news?'

'We've been informed there's been a shooting incident in Lisbjerg Forest, near Århus. Grimme, the gang leader, has been found killed. A surviving gang member alleges Peter Boutrup shot him.'

'When did that happen?'

'A couple of hours ago. Boutrup is said to have been injured, so there's a good chance of finding him. I'm going there myself with the team.'

'And Felix?'

'If he's got her, he wouldn't take her to Djursland.'

'And if he hasn't?' Mark asked.

An awkward pause ensued. Then she said: 'It's all we've got to go on right now.'

She was right. She had to concentrate on a tangible incident and act. They had a shooting with a fatality and a clear identification of Boutrup. Of course they had to attend to it. It was her responsibility as a senior officer and there was no point telling her she was looking in the wrong place for the wrong man.

'We're low on manpower,' she said. 'You deal with Grenå, Mark. You hold the fort.'

77

THE FARM WAS hidden beneath fresh snow, but was given away by the new red roof on the pig barn glowing in the last rays of the setting sun.

Peter drove his van up to the main building, got out and knocked on the door. But the place seemed deserted and no one answered. He walked around the building. It had completely stopped snowing now and the sun glistened on the latest fall. He didn't like to think what would happen if he didn't find Felix before nightfall. He had no idea whether she was dead or alive. But if they hadn't killed her, what state would she be in? How would she manage when the temperature fell even further at night? He found it hard to imagine that Red would provide her with a warm bed and a hot meal.

He found Christian Røjel by the dung heap behind the barn. He was wearing his habitual rubber boots and a thick overall over an Icelandic sweater. On top of that he had an old, worn leather coat. To Peter, the furrows in his long face seemed to have grown deeper and his eyes had acquired a dull sheen. He was holding a shovel, and in a flash Peter was able to imagine the same man in a cemetery digging graves with his long, grim face and his eyes fixed on the black hole.

'Hello, Christian,' he greeted, as he approached.

Røjel's head shot up. His eyes narrowed and focused on Peter and there was no friendliness in them. For a moment the pig farmer held the shovel as if it were a weapon, but then he lowered it slowly.

'We made a good job of that roof.'

Røjel stared at him. Then he raised a hand to his cap and pulled it further down over his eyes. His gaze sought the roof and moved to the horizon where the sun was low in the sky.

'What do you want?'

There was bitterness in his voice. Peter went closer. There was a bundle at the man's feet. He saw it now. It was the family dog, a beautiful pointer.

'What happened to your dog?'

Røjel sniffed, but not from emotion. He rubbed his nose with the back of his hand.

'It's dead. Can't you see?'

It had been a young dog. Three years old, as far as Peter recalled. He had thrown sticks for her. She had bounded after them, every muscle of her hunting body under her glistening coat tensed. He stepped closer. Røjel tightened his grip on the shovel.

'Was she run over?'

The man's face turned to him in a snarl that bared a set of long, yellow teeth.

'Of course it bloody wasn't. Haven't you got any eyes in your head?'

Peter looked at the dog at the man's feet. He saw what he hadn't seen before: there was barely any skin left on the body. The back and sides were covered in large open wounds. You could see the muscles, plaited together as if someone had studied a map of a dog's anatomy from a biology lesson and then tried to make reality match the drawing. He only hoped it had happened after the dog had died.

'Who did this?'

'How should I bloody know?'

Røjel's eyes avoided his. They also avoided the dog. Peter scrutinised the man for the slightest hint of grief at the dog's death, but found only a stony face.

'It's cruelty to animals. It should be reported.'

'That's what Kir always says.'

'Always?'

Silence. Peter looked at the dog. He thought about Tora. He thought about Felix.

'Are you saying this is not the first time?'

Røjel turned to face Peter. The furrows were deep-set, the eyes sharp splinters of flint.

'So what do you want?'

They stood for a while staring at each other, the farmer's unyielding eyes boring into Peter's, uninterested in his bleeding arm.

'Red,' Peter said at length. 'Where will I find him?'

Røjel bent down and went on digging.

'How should I know?'

'He's not in his pub and he's not at his flat. What other places has he got? Where does he keep supplies for the pub?'

Røjel stopped. Peter read profound mistrust in every muscle.

'You're not one of us, Peter, and you never will be.'

'I have no ambitions in that direction.'

Røjel nodded with half a smile, well hidden in the many wrinkles by his mouth.

'That's what I like about you. You're no fool.'

Peter seized the opening: 'When he was at the young offenders' institution, Red met a man who would later become the leader of a biker gang, Grimme. He's currently in Horsens Prison, from where he still conducts his various activities. He also uses Red.'

Røjel eyed him blankly. It was hard to say if this information was news to him. He turned and carried on digging. Peter continued: 'Red kills and he's good at it. Grimme uses him to punish the gang's girlfriends when they try to break away. That girl Kir found in the harbour, Tora – she didn't have a face. Someone had skinned her. Like they skinned Zita here.'

Peter nodded towards the dog.

'But perhaps that's what you do in your family? If you haven't got any girls you can skin, you start on your dogs?'

Røjel spun round. He was furious and dispirited at the same time, a man who had suddenly grown old and lost his grip on those he used to control.

'What do you know about having sons? What do you know about bringing sons up?'

He leaned on the shovel as if it were his lifeline.

'What would you know about building a life's work over generations?'

Peter looked at the man whose life was crumbling like soil between his fingers.

'Nothing,' he admitted. 'I know nothing about that.'

Røjel spat. Peter tried to see behind the flinty look.

'Red is dangerous, Christian. He kills innocent girls.'

'Girls, pah!'

Røjel thrust the shovel deep into the dung heap. 'It's their own bloody fault. Running around, making a spectacle of themselves, thinking they can be just like men.'

'Like Kir?'

It was a deliberate provocation. Røjel reached for his shovel and for a moment Peter thought he would strike him with it. But then he seemed to run out of steam and the danger passed, leaving a man deflated by his exertions.

The pig farmer stood on the dung heap and Peter saw him against the light, a black silhouette, a tall, lean man with a bony face and hands. The silence lasted so long he began to doubt if the man would ever speak again. Then Røjel inhaled deeply, a whistling sound.

'It's called Konkylien.'

He spat out the words, laden with contempt and despair. 'It's a cottage on Nørrevangsvej between Karlby and Veggerby. On a hill overlooking Nederskov.'

He took another deep breath.

'Now go. I'm busy, as you can see.'

78

THEY HAD BEEN at sea for one hour. In another, the sun would be gone. The light was already fading and the sea was black and hostile. On the horizon they could just about make out '*Jernhatten*', Ironhat, the tall, southernmost part of Djursland, a brown hill with a white top.

'It's here.'

Kir pointed to the satnav. They were right over the location. Red stared first at her then over the railing. Was this her moment? The thought lasted for a split second, then he was back on his guard, pointing the gun at her.

'You're going down. I want you to get something for me. From a wreck.'

She looked at the screen. The sea was 9.5 metres deep.

'Swimming in a wreck isn't that straightforward. What am I looking for?'

She didn't ask the other questions: What would happen to her afterwards? Would he claim she had drowned while diving – a mine clearance diver, at a depth of ten metres?

'I want you to fetch a packet,' Red said. 'It's sealed. It's not big.'

He showed with his hands how big he thought it was. Like the sweater she had given him for Christmas and had wrapped up with sailing twine.

'Where is it? What kind of boat is it?'

'It's Brian's *Molly*.'

Brian. She hadn't heard that name for ages. He was one

of Uncle Hannibal's many friends. She had always suspected him of supplying Hannibal with Polish vodka.

'He managed to scuttle *Molly* and her cargo of heroin before he was locked up,' Red said. 'It's worth seven million kroner.'

Kir looked at him. She wasn't scared of him or the gun. Perhaps she wasn't scared of dying. She had faced death so often. She didn't want to die, but it might be a price worth paying.

'You're a real bastard, aren't you, Red?'

His face reddened. She looked across the sea and was reminded of another day on the same sea. Her, Tomas and Red in the boat. Suddenly Tomas was gone.

'You're also a liar. You pushed Tomas overboard.'

She saw the muscles tense in his neck. His face was still almost as red as his birthmark.

'I had to. It had to stop.'

She shook her head, confused.

'What had to stop?'

'You know perfectly well.'

She replayed the scene. She was back there. The water was clear and warm. They were fishing. Tomas and Red were spearing lugworms on the fishing hooks. The worms lay in a bucket at the bottom of the boat. Tomas was mesmerised. He stared at the guts of the worms as they spilled out. He touched them. He tasted them. His entire face lit up.

They started fishing and the boys caught a couple of small fish. Red threw his back in the sea after releasing them. Tomas left the hook in. He wriggled it back and forth to see how the fish would react. He took out the hook and stuck it into the eye of the fish.

The next thing she knew he was lying at the bottom of the boat with his mouth open like a fish gasping for air.

'It was Tomas,' Kir said. 'It was Tomas all along. The cockerel and the cats. I thought it was you.'

Red snorted with contempt.

'You think I get a kick out of tormenting animals? I'm guilty of a lot of things, but cruelty to animals isn't one of them. I thought you'd worked that one out.'

Tomas as a boy. Silent, cautious Tomas who always had a cold. Fragile and delicate with skin that was soft like a girl's. Always introverted. Always an enigma. You could never get a reaction out of Tomas. You could tease him or push him, or you could ignore him or give him a hug. It was all the same to Tomas. With one exception: after the accident he developed a water phobia. His greatest fear was to have his head under water.

Kir suppressed her nausea.

'But it didn't stop?'

Red gritted his teeth.

'His brain damage only made it worse. Dad has had one hell of a job keeping it quiet.'

That's the most important thing, she thought. The most important of all. No one must ever suspect there was something wrong with the Røjel family. And certainly not Hannibal, her father's brother and eternal rival, who'd never had children of his own. He always had to have Christian's family shoved down his throat so that he could see what he had missed out on. Hence her father's bitterness when she preferred Hannibal to him.

Red's head jerked up. The movement reminded her of their father, but he hadn't inherited his father's tall frame. Red had his mother's sturdy figure invigorated with masculine strength. Tomas was the tall one, but here the similarity with their father ended. Or did it? Where had his wickedness come from?

The family, Kir thought. The end of the family. That was what it was. The final destruction. The structure had been wobbling for a long time, but now the foundations were crumbling. She felt defeated, vanquished by fate, by time and by all her miscalculations and mistakes. She stared into the sea.

'It's not about animals for you, is it? It's about money,' she said.

'It's about the good life,' he said. 'It's about independence.'

'You're using Tomas now. You're using his methods. You said it had to stop. You, the person who tried to drown him.'

She stared at Red.

'You're not the same any more. You're more rotten inside than Tomas.'

Red smiled, but he was angry.

'No one can change Tomas, so I might as well exploit that side of him. At least that serves some purpose,' he said. 'You know I can make him do almost anything. So, yes, he has assisted me with his special skills. He was useful.'

Some purpose. Kir was speechless. Her anger was spent. She thought about Tora in the harbour and about Nina and Gry.

'And you think that's acceptable?'

Red shook his head. For the first time she saw something that resembled remorse.

'He went too far. I thought I could control him, but there's something in him even I can't reach. I told him to be careful and I told him to suppress his most bizarre urges.'

He looked across the sea. 'That's why all this ends here.'

'And because Nina Bjerre happened to turn up on New Year's Eve and saw you and Tomas throw Tora in the harbour? She died because Tomas had gone too far, right?'

Red nodded.

'You didn't intend for her to die?' Kir asked.

He shrugged.

'The idea was we would beat her up and dump her somewhere she would be found by the other girls so that they would know what would happen if they tried to break away. But Tomas couldn't stop himself. We decided it was best to get rid of her.'

'You sent Tomas to kill Gry at the hotel. Why, Red? Why did she have to die? A poor girl like her?'

She didn't understand any of it: 'All because of the heroin on the seabed?'

He nodded. 'That police officer got too interested in her. She started talking.'

'And what if the packet isn't there? What happens if I don't find it?'

Red looked at her. There was hatred in his eyes.

'You will. You'll find it. Or you won't leave here alive.'

79

FELIX PUSHED AND shoved. It was laborious work. With every movement her entire body ached and the iron shackles around her ankles cut deep into her flesh. She stretched until her body was as taut as wire and little by little she managed to push aside the crates and old junk. That was what separated her from Anja on the other side: junk and old sacks.

She hoped Anja had stayed conscious, but she heard only intermittent signs of life.

'Come on, Anja. Push hard. We need to make a hole through.'

There was a faint scrape on the other side. Something shifted slightly. Anja coughed. Her cough turned into a gurgle.

'You can do it. Pull yourself together.'

The words lulled her desperation as she worked. Their only chance was to work together. She stretched as far as the leg shackles and her body would allow. Her breasts were blood-stained, the wound from the brand was throbbing fiercely and her body was engulfed in a raging fever.

'I can see you.'

It was a whisper, no more than that. But Anja was right. They could see each other. A little light fell through the holes in the roof. Felix could see Anja lying on some filthy sacks with a blanket wrapped around her. Her hair was matted; her face shone, pale and tormented. She lay in a foetal position with her knees pulled up.

He had been there in the meantime, their tormentor. Felix had heard noises coming from behind the wall of junk; she had heard the whimpering and crying and his voice, which was unemotional, robotic. There had been nothing she could do, only hope that it would end soon, and think about their chances of overpowering him. Now she wasn't even sure they had a chance.

Anja was no longer chained up, but the marks on her wrists and ankles told Felix that she had been. The chains were no longer necessary. It was obvious her body was close to succumbing.

Felix stared. Beyond Anja, snow had drifted in under the boards and lightened the room. She heard dripping from the roof and now she could see a puddle of water at Anja's feet.

She looked around in the gloom and found the tub, which with considerable difficulty she managed to drag towards her. From the melted snow she removed some old bottles and they rolled across the cement floor. She grabbed a worn old broom leaning against the wall and used it to push the tub towards Anja.

'Can you hear me?'

'Yes.'

'Can you move?'

There was no reply. But her body slowly reached out. Anja grunted with the effort.

'Take the tub. Fill it with snow and push it back to me. Can you do that?'

'No.'

Anja whimpered like a child.

'You've got to.'

For a moment Anja lay still. Felix was beginning to think that all her strength had gone when she sat up halfway and pulled the tub closer to her before collapsing with a sigh.

'Keep going, Anja! Do it! You can do it!'

Slowly, very slowly, the girl struggled into a sitting position.

Felix cast around for something to serve as a shovel, but found nothing. Anja reached out. Little by little, she shuffled closer to the snow. Her hand reached into the pile. Felix heard a splash as a tiny handful fell into the water in the tub.

80

KIR SLIPPED INTO the water. The light would soon be gone. All she could see were shadows in a muddy, icy sea. As she dived towards the bottom, she could just about make out Red's boat on the surface. She had cast anchor, but the waves were pulling at the boat and rocking it from side to side.

She spent a minute floating on her back, letting the current carry her, while she tried to stabilise her thoughts. It was important to find the right moment and it had to be soon after she resurfaced. Otherwise she was lost, regardless of whether she found the heroin or not. She had to take a risk; it was her only way out. She had to remember her training and forget that Red was her brother.

Once the decision was made, she dived and quickly reached the bottom, where seaweed and sea grass waved in the current like tentacles reaching for help. At first she couldn't see the wreck and was starting to think that Brian had tricked everyone. But then she saw a dark shadow, the contours of the vessel. She flicked her flippers and soon had her hands on the hull of the boat where mussels and other creatures had already formed a crust. She swam all the way around the boat feeling her way with her hands. In the dim light she recognised the boat that had been moored in Grenå Harbour. There had been rumours that Brian smuggled cigarettes from the Baltic, but people minded their own business, and as long as he was no threat to the neighbours, they turned a blind eye.

She found the name and ran her fingers across the five letters. MOLLY.

The boat had come to rest on its side. The wheelhouse lay on the sea-bed like the shell of a snail. Kir found the hatch and pulled at the handle, but it wouldn't give. She was seized by a premonition. Someone was inside. She had worked with bodies underwater for so long that she had developed a sixth sense. It felt as if lifeless eyes were staring at her, as if someone from the beyond was trying to tell her something.

She pulled again, harder this time, and the hatch opened, creating a whirlpool. Then the water settled. She couldn't see very much, but the feeling stayed with her. Brian had died in hospital. How had he got ashore after scuttling *Molly*? Logic told her that there had to be another boat. A helper. Uncle Hannibal's boat had later drifted ashore on to Fjellerup Beach. Had Brian sailed it to Fjellerup after opening the sea valves and scuttling *Molly*?

She lay still for a moment attempting to calm her heart and pulse rate. Then she swam inside the boat. She ran her hand along the floor, examining every square centimetre of *Molly*, but there were no sealed packages, there was no heroin, and all of a sudden she felt she was no longer touching wooden planks. She recognised the sensation of touching a dead body. A body that had been there for months. Disintegrating flesh crumbled in her hands. She came across bones attached to remnants of clothing. She tried to think clearly and let her training take over, but when she found the diving knife and held it in her hand, she knew whose body it was. Panic threatened to suffocate her. Uncle Hannibal would never have gone anywhere without his diving knife strapped to his shin. He had been the ultimate old salt, the sort depicted in comics. She kept looking and also found the sheath the knife had been kept in, hanging loosely from a leg bone.

Her brain went into overdrive. The knife was in good

416

condition. This was her chance. But she had to find something she could take to the surface – something that looked like a packet. She rummaged around the wheelhouse and found the First Aid box. She ripped a flimsy curtain from the window and wrapped it around the box as best she could. With the box under her arm and the knife in her leg sheath she left *Molly* and started her ascent, promising herself and Uncle Hannibal that she would return as soon as she could to recover his body.

She took her time resurfacing, even though no pauses were necessary in such shallow waters. Now she knew what had happened: Brian had tricked Hannibal into meeting him at sea, possibly under the pretext that he had run out of fuel. Once Hannibal was there, Brian had persuaded him to board *Molly* to give him a hand and had killed him on the spot. A post-mortem would reveal how he had been killed, if she ever got away from Red and managed to contact the police.

After Brian had killed Hannibal, he had sailed Hannibal's boat to Fjellerup, from where he had found transport – probably a bus – and returned to Grenå unnoticed.

Everyone had thought that a drunken Hannibal had gone to sea and had an accident – one that was waiting to happen, what was more. He was getting on in years and could no longer handle all that vodka, and, besides, he had white spots on the brain from the numerous dangerously deep dives he had made and from resurfacing too quickly.

Hannibal, the old mine clearance diver, had met an entirely predictable end. Only Kir had known it wasn't true. She had never really believed that Hannibal would have been so drunk that he couldn't steer his own boat home.

But there was no heroin. Brian had scuttled his boat without any treasure on board. He had tricked everyone. If the treasure even existed, it was somewhere completely different.

She reached the ladder and felt the weight of her own body and the equipment once she was out of the water. Red was waiting with a gun to receive her. This was the moment, she thought. This was where her training would save her. She was an elite soldier. She knew how to overpower an enemy who was bigger, stronger and heavier than her – only she had never thought the enemy would turn out to be her brother.

'Put down the gun,' she called out to him and showed him the bundle under her arm. 'Move away from the railing, or I'll drop the box.'

She knew he wouldn't be able to dive down himself to retrieve it. Red had never been a strong swimmer, and he had only ever been able to dive a few metres, and that was only when she forced him into one of the competitions which she always used to win. She could see from his face that he was weighing up the odds. At length he did as she said. He showed her his empty hands and stood on the bows, still with his hands in full view. She didn't doubt for a second that he had stuffed the gun in his pocket and could quickly retrieve it, but it bought her some time. Perhaps it was enough.

She struggled up, water dripping off her. Red stirred.

'Stay where you are. Don't move yet.'

He hesitated, his greedy eyes focused on the box. If she wanted to, she could quickly throw it overboard. He obviously didn't want to risk that because he took a step back and held up his hands. She peeled off her diving tank, flippers and mask and felt an icy chill on her skin, but fortunately her feet were enclosed in the all-in-one. Then she took a step forward and placed the wet box on the deck between them. As she bent forward, she sensed him move towards it. She knew he had taken the gun out of his pocket. She reached for the knife in the sheath on her shin and straightened up as he bent down, threw her arms around his neck and twisted his body at the moment the shot was fired. She pressed the blade against his throat and it bit into his skin.

'Drop the gun or I'll cut your throat.'

He waved the pistol in the air. She saw his finger tighten on the trigger.

'If you shoot, you're dead. Trust me. I've done this before.'

He dropped the gun and it skidded along the deck.

'You bitch.'

She put all her strength into the blow. The butt of the knife struck the back of his head while she locked her arm around his neck. The boat swayed. She felt him go limp and collapse on to the deck, then she laid him on his stomach and quickly picked up the gun. She took two rolls of bandages from the First Aid box and tied his wrists together behind his back. He was starting to regain consciousness, but she pinioned the back of his knees and prevented any resistance by tying another roll of bandages around his ankles. He twisted in agony as she pressed her knees into him and held the gun to his head.

Half his face was squashed against the cold deck. She found some strong rope in a box under a bench and tied him up, properly this time.

It was only then that she let him go, and at that moment she heard the coastguard's siren as the vessel surfed on the black waves towards her.

She was still holding the gun with Red at her feet when Mark and two other men boarded the boat. For a moment she felt numb; there was no sorrow or joy. Then she snapped out of it.

'I was in the middle of washing the floor.'

She could hear the irritation in her own voice.

'That was lucky,' Mark said. 'I found the glove in the garage. They train you well over in Kongsøre.'

She tried to smile.

'I think I learned that trick in a Donald Duck comic.'

'If you say so.'

The policeman knelt down by Red's side and grabbed his arm. Red groaned. His eyelids kept opening and shutting.

'Where's Felix Gomez? I presume she told you the location.'
Red mumbled something.
'Where is she?' Mark repeated.
But Red simply stared at him blankly.

81

Peter drove past the property a couple of times. Then he parked the van in Nørrevangsvej near Konkylien's closest neighbour, quite a distance from the drive leading to the house. The neighbour's house was on the bend and barricaded behind a tall fence with warnings of vicious guard dogs, while Konkylien was open to all and sundry on a hilltop.

He sat in the van for a moment assessing the situation. Then he took Boxer Nose's gun, left the more cumbersome rifle behind and set out on foot, hoping that his white shearling jacket would blend in with the snow and that he would get some protection from the dark night sky.

There was a small, hand-painted wooden sign bearing the house name, Konkylien, at the bottom of the drive. The letters were in white, and a white conch had been painted rather clumsily to represent a full stop. The drive was long, about two hundred metres, he guessed, and straight. The main building was white with an old, black Eternit roof, patchily covered with snow. Several tiles were missing on the outhouse. The property must have a beautiful view of Nederskov, and it would have been easy to keep a lookout for trespassers.

He squinted to see if anything was happening, but he saw nothing. There was no movement. Perhaps there wasn't even life there any more. Or maybe the place was fortified to the hilt. It was impossible to know how many helpers Red had. A small army might have been waiting for intruders. Perhaps, at this moment, a sniper was watching him, to protect the valuable prize that Felix was for them.

He took out his mobile and walked with it in one hand while the fingers of his other hand tapped a message. Then he scrolled through his contacts. He hated the thought of it, but he could see no other way out. He found Mark Bille Hansen's number and for the second time in his life he did something he had sworn he wouldn't do. He called the police.

'Yes?'

Mark Bille sounded out of breath.

'It's Peter.'

'Where are you? We're looking for you.'

'I'm sure you are. Listen . . .'

He explained himself as quickly as he could.

'Stay where you are,' Mark said. 'We've got Red. We're on our way to the harbour and we can be with you in half an hour.'

Peter looked up at Konkylien. The house looked menacing and sombre. He couldn't keep Felix waiting. Half an hour in hell was a long time.

'I'm going in,' he said after a pause. 'Get here as quickly as you can.'

'He hung up.'

Mark stared at his mobile and then across the sea to where the coastguard was dutifully following them. Red had been transferred to their vessel and only Mark and Kir were in Hannibal's motorboat.

'Konkylien. What kind of place is that?'

Kir steered the boat towards the harbour from the wheelhouse, where they huddled from the cold.

She told him about Hannibal's property.

'Where might he have hidden Felix?'

'In the outhouse, I reckon.'

After a pause she added: 'There's also a basement.'

He nodded. They had found some warm clothing for her in the rescue vessel: overalls, a warm jacket, a woolly hat and gloves. They'd also found a pair of boots several sizes too big and a pair of socks. Her red curls sprang out from under the hat and the gap between her teeth showed when she spoke. Mark thought about what she had just done to Red and could hardly believe it was the same girl.

'He said he was going in alone,' Mark said.

'Can't you call for back-up?' she asked. 'It'll take us some time to get there.'

'They've all gone to Århus.'

He had called Anna Bagger, who said she would send back-up as quickly as she could, but she was in Lisbjerg Forest with the rest of her team. Grenå was currently unmanned.

'We'll come as soon as we can, Mark.'

He cursed her roundly.

'That's not good enough.'

'You've got Kir,' she said. 'We'll try and get there fast.'

He hung up and gritted his teeth. He looked at Kir.

'Can't we go a little faster?'

'It might capsize.'

He could feel the drag on the boat. It started jumping across the crests and swerving from side to side as Kir increased the speed to maximum.

Peter walked up the drive to Konkylien.

No lights were on. There was not a single sign of life. The house looked abandoned, like many other houses for sale in this remote area. They were the sort of places he might have bought and done up cheaply himself.

As he approached the property, he could see it more clearly. There was a main building with a low door, a cobblestone yard with a well in the middle, an old outhouse and a barn. The main house was white, but the paint was flaking badly. There was so much moss and weed growing on the roof it almost looked thatched. The roof of the outhouse sagged and looked as if it might cave in at any time. He felt for the gun in his pocket. It was good to have it. Even close up, the property seemed abandoned, but there could be all sorts hiding in the shadows. He might be walking to his death. One of Red's henchmen might be there.

He dismissed the thought and tried the main door. It was locked, so he walked around and saw what looked like a stable door. It consisted of two parts and looked home-made. With his Swiss Army knife, it didn't take him long to pick the lock.

He entered the dark house and was met by the unmistakable smell of cat pee and mildew. He didn't dare switch on the light, but groped his way around, now holding the gun in his hand and keeping the knife ready in his pocket. The ground floor was deserted. When he had established that, he found the stairs down to the basement. He turned on the light – it looked as if it was empty. Carefully, he walked down with one arm outstretched and his finger on the trigger. As he expected, there were only bare walls, crates of dusty diving equipment, coiled rope and old furniture too shabby to be used in the living room. No Felix.

82

'Your body is so supple.'

He was back. His hand moved up her leg.

'Just like the dog's.'

Felix didn't want to know what he meant.

'I can dance,' she whispered. 'I can dance for you, if you want.'

He kneaded her muscles as though wanting to expose them. She was still weak and had very little musculature left, but she had to pretend.

'I can show you a dance.'

He tilted his head. His face was long and narrow and matched his body which, at first glance, might have appeared fragile. But he was strong and could handle her like a sack of potatoes. He looked at her. His eyes were without expression.

'There's no music,' he said.

'It doesn't matter. The music's in my head. Let me show you.' She tried to stand up.

'Oh, no. The chains . . .'

For a long time he stood, appearing to consider the situation. He stared at her, his gaze still glued to her body, she sensed. Then he took out the key, crouched down and loosened the chain around one of her ankles.

'And the other one,' she begged.

He stared again. Then he shook his head.

'Now dance.'

She got up. She would just have to do her best. He sat on the mattress like a spectator at a show. She evoked the music in her head and swayed back and forth to it while singing quietly. He continued to stare. She stretched out her arms and rotated until stopped by the shackle around her ankle. She stood on her tiptoes and went down on her knees, despite the pain shooting through her, almost fainting. But it worked. He dropped his guard and his eyes were half-closed now as his head rocked from side to side to the rhythm of her movements. She danced close to the wall of junk and he shifted on the mattress to be near the dance. She knelt at his side as part of the dance and hummed in a way that seemed to hypnotise him. She caressed his hair while her other hand grabbed the rim of the tub. Gyrating rhythmically over the tub, she saw her reflection in the melted snow. He moved nearer; his breathing was close to her neck, his hand was on her naked back and she forced herself not to shake him off.

She struck when he was most under her spell.

Using all her weight, she pushed his neck and head forward. The shackle around her ankle contorted her leg and the iron cut into her bone. She reached out to pull the tub closer. He spluttered and gurgled as she sat on him using every ounce of strength to keep his head under the water.

He panicked, waving his arms around wildly and howling when he briefly came up for air. Then she pushed him back down into what for him was a hell, the sum total of all his fears. But she had reached her limit and could stretch no further because of the ankle chain, and she had to let go.

'Help me!'

But Anja had no strength left. She was lying quietly on the sacks, barely breathing. Felix tried in vain to keep her tormentor's head under the water. He struggled and flapped his arms and gurgled and spluttered, but she was losing her grip and was unable to maintain the pressure. Gasping for air, he finally got to his feet. He stood for a moment staring at her, his eyes wide, terror written all over his face. She was sure he would kill her now. Why didn't Anja help?

Then she heard a noise. Was that footsteps on the drive? Or a car?

He heard it, too. He turned his face towards the sound and stared at her again with his mouth open. Before, there had been no expression; now there was one of boundless hatred, as if she was a mistress who had humiliated and betrayed him.

Barely conscious, she sensed that he had turned on his heel and stumbled out of the darkness, sending the bottles on the cement floor clattering in all directions. Her legs gave way and she collapsed on the mattress. Again she felt the warmth of the sea close over her and heard Maria's voice.

83

Peter walked behind the house to avoid crossing the yard. He found himself at the back of the outhouse. There was a high window. He stood on tiptoes to peer inside, but the window was grimy and the light inside dim. Yet he saw a shadow move and heard a clatter. He threw caution to the wind and tapped on the window.

'Felix!'

He heard a metallic clanking, then the sound of boots. Someone was running away. Almost simultaneously he heard a car pull into the yard and stop. Car doors opened and shut. Mark Bille and Kir, he hoped, and was about to shout out when he recognised Lily Klein's voice: 'He ran across the field.'

This was followed by the sound of more people running.

He had to be quick. There was a low whimper coming from the outhouse. He drew himself up to his full height and hit the window with his elbow. It cracked at the second blow. The frame was rotten and the whole window fell in on itself with a crash. He climbed in, landing on his head and hit first his leg and then his injured shoulder as he fell. His entire body screamed in agony.

'Felix!'

There was a stench – of urine and faeces, and something else. Human decay. Bodies on the verge of succumbing. He heard the whimpering again. Light was what he needed. He couldn't see anything clearly, so he used his mobile to find his way. His hands touched something soft. A blanket, a person. He couldn't hear any breathing. Nothing. He struggled to lift the human bundle in his arms, then staggered out of the outhouse, towards the back of the main building, where he opened the stable door. He found a sofa and turned on the light. The girl was whimpering quietly now. He stared at her.

'Anja!'

She half-opened her eyes.

'Felix?'

He shook her. 'Where is she?'

Anja tried to say something, but couldn't. He limped back to the outhouse.

'Felix! Felix, can you hear me?'

He held up the mobile to see and rummaged frantically around old crates and sacks and coils of rope. He crawled around on all fours, trying to cover the entire area. Then he felt something sticky. A whole puddle. He sniffed his hand. Blood. He threw aside everything he bumped into and finally his hand touched a mattress.

'Felix?'

He fumbled for her pulse. It was hard to find, and she was freezing cold. There was a quilt over her but she was naked underneath it.

'I've got you now.'

It wasn't until then that he saw the chain. She was caught like an animal in a trap. He had to lay her down again. Then he pulled off his jacket, wrapped her in it and the blanket, and took out his Swiss Army knife. He started unscrewing the fitting on the wall. The shackles had cut right through to the bone.

He picked her up and stood with her in his arms. He staggered out with his light burden and felt the pain shooting through his whole body. Outside, he stayed close to the walls. The car was still parked in the yard, but Lily and her helper were nowhere to be seen. He managed to get Felix inside the house, went back to their silver 4x4 and took out his knife.

84

IT WAS DARK by the time they reached Konkylien.

Kir thought about the past as a weightless number of hours and days spent with a man now lying in a grave at the bottom of the sea. Everything else had been destroyed; everything she had believed and hoped for with her parents and brothers. But she still had the memory: the tiny oasis of Uncle Hannibal, precious time which had flown by as quickly as his boat had taken her and Mark ashore.

There was an oppressive silence about the place when they got out of the car. The light was on in one room. In the middle of the yard there was a battered old 4x4 with flat tyres. She touched the bonnet.

'Warm,' she said to Mark, who had his service weapon ready. She was holding Red's gun in her hand.

They had seen Peter Boutrup's white van parked around a bend in Nørrevangsvej, but they hadn't seen the man himself. Apart from the 4x4, Konkylien appeared to be deserted.

'We're going in.'

Mark made a move to go, but she stopped him.

'Let me.'

She sidled along the wall to the front door, holding Red's gun in front of her. He copied her and followed. She kicked open the door.

'Police,' Mark shouted into the house, grabbing her shoulder. She sent him a look.

'In here,' they heard from the inside.

They entered the living room. Peter Boutrup was stooped over a figure lying on a mattress on the floor. There was another person on the sofa. They needed an ambulance.

'I've already called them,' Peter said.

He straightened up. His face was racked with pain, and there were blotches of blood on his jumper.

'Tomas fled. The others went after him,' he said. 'The people in the car outside.'

'Who are they?' Kir asked.

'Women,' Peter said. 'Two of them. One's called Lily Klein. She's the ex-girlfriend of a biker called Grimme and she's in his bad books for leaking a drugs deal.'

Mark nodded as if everything made sense.

'Tora was their friend – another girl who wanted to break free from the gang.'

'And Anja here,' Peter said, looking at the girl lying on the sofa wrapped in an old duvet he must have found in the bedroom, 'her boyfriend is in a gang.'

'What about Tomas?' Mark asked.

Peter shook his head.

'I don't think there's anything else you can do.'

The same women had robbed the shops in town and been caught on the surveillance camera, Mark told them. They were the women looking for the treasure at the bottom of the Kattegat.

'They would do anything to get hold of that heroin,' Peter said. 'They want to use it to fund their own gang.'

'It's war: men against women,' Kir said.

'They're desperate,' Mark said.

Peter didn't look in the least sympathetic.

'They're killers. They killed Ramses and my friend Stinger. They attacked Felix in my house.'

Kir thought about the packet she had been looking for in the wreck of *Molly*. Everyone had believed Brian had hidden the heroin in the boat. All the rumours, all the information pointed that way, but *Molly* was empty. Hannibal and Brian were friends. Brian would never have risked hiding heroin in his own house, but he would have had no problems hiding it in the house of someone he knew.

She found an old torch in a cupboard. It still worked, even though the beam was faint. Mark followed her outside. They both had their weapons at the ready.

'What happens now, soldier?'

She smiled.

'Patience, police officer.'

Close on her heels, he followed her to the well.

'The bucket is down the bottom,' she said, almost to herself. 'Shine the torch here.'

He held it while she grabbed the rope and started hoisting up the bucket. She had done it so often as a child, hoisting up a bucket full of bottles. The pulley creaked, but this time there were no bottles. When the bucket reached the top of the well, they could both see its contents.

She reached out and took the packet wrapped in plastic.

'I think you'll find this is seven million kroners' worth of heroin.'

She had only just spoken when a salvo from an automatic pistol echoed between the walls of Konkylien and they felt the bullets whistle past. Kir dropped the bucket and its contents on the ground and they took cover behind Mark's car, but they could see nothing in the darkness. They waited. Holding their weapons, they scanned the area, but there was nothing to see.

'Drop your guns,' a woman's voice shouted. 'You don't stand a chance.'

Mark fired a shot in the direction of the voice. The response was another salvo from the automatic. Plaster was blown off the walls, sending dust everywhere. They huddled close to the ground.

'We can see you,' a woman shouted. 'You can't move a milli-metre without us hitting you.'

'They're serious,' Kir said.

Mark nodded.

'They bought night-vision goggles from the Poles. They're equipped like elite soldiers.'

'That would have been helpful to know.'

'Sorry,' he said. 'I forgot to mention it.'

She heard footsteps as they were attacked from both sides. The figures were so fast and difficult to see it was impossible to fight both of them. She fired and heard Mark do the same. Neither of them hit anything and a second later she was knocked to the ground by a big, heavy figure with a rifle butt. She heard a semi-strangled noise from Mark as the same happened to him. Then she blacked out and slumped into the snow.

85

PETER HAD HEARD the shots and the screaming outside and knew what was about to happen.

In a moment they would kick down the door. The women had automatic weapons. They would take Anja and then they would drive off, if they could. He checked his gun. He only had two bullets left.

'I'll be back. You'll be all right.'

He took a last look at Felix and Anja. Felix looked at him. Anja had slipped into a coma-like sleep.

He crept out of the back door just as the boot-clad women stomped in with a roar: 'Don't anyone move.'

He ran behind the house, across the fields covered in deep snow, and couldn't remember when he had last done anything quite as exhausting. One of his legs was barely working and his shoulder was injured, but he thought of Stinger. Old Stinger had never hurt a fly. Lily and co. had tracked him down and beaten him to a pulp to get the coordinates after failing to get them from Ramses.

Finally he reached the road and ran around the bend to his car. He felt dizzy and had to lean against it, gasping for breath like a drowning man. Somewhere in the distance he heard sirens. Ambulances, he thought. Or police. But he couldn't wait. Four flat tyres weren't enough to stop a desperate and angry Lily Klein.

He climbed into the van with difficulty, put on his seatbelt and started the engine. He pulled out and drove up the drive to Konkylien and immediately saw a set of headlights coming towards him from the yard. He revved the engine and saw at once they weren't driving the 4x4. They had taken Mark Bille's police car.

He stamped the accelerator to the floor and clung to the steering wheel. The tyres gripped the snow. The headlights from the oncoming car blinded him and he was glad he was sitting high up. The other car sounded its horn, but he clenched his teeth and held his course. Neither of them was prepared to move. So he closed his eyes and hoped for the best.

The collision shook everything. The world went under. He let go of the pain in his body and the tightrope between the past and the present. It all evaporated in the cold air to be swallowed up by darkness.

He regained consciousness with the airbag pressed into his forehead and an irritating ringing in his ears. It was coming from his car. He was slumped across the steering wheel. Blood blurred his vision. He wiped it away with his jumper, pushed the airbag aside and stared straight into Mark's patrol car, which appeared to be welded to his own in a bizarre sculpture, one bonnet entangled in the other. A door had been forced open and there was light inside. Two airbags had inflated in the faces of both the women, who stirred, groggy.

He forced himself to act, but his head was on the point of exploding and his body protested violently when he loosened the seatbelt, grabbed Manfred's rifle and jumped out. His knees buckled and he struggled to get back to his feet. The women came to with a rifle pointing at them and the sound of sirens approaching. His eyes met Lily Klein's and he could read her mind.

'Forget it,' he shouted. 'It's over.'

He could see she was evaluating the situation. Then she leaned back and closed her eyes. Seconds later the road behind them was jammed with a whole motorcade of ambulances and police cars, and the sirens fell silent.

86

I F P O S S I B L E, W I N T E R's grip had tightened still further and the frost had locked the countryside in an icy embrace. Yet it didn't feel quite as desperate as before. It was as if the weather was showing some signs of ceding, or perhaps he just wanted to believe it was.

'Have you heard they've found Nina?'

Manfred was walking alongside him with the dachshund sniffing and scenting the air. It was the 31st of January. The last day of the hunting season.

'It was on the radio,' Peter said, ducking to avoid the branches at the edge of the forest. 'She was caught in the net of a Norwegian trawler off the coast of Bergen.'

'How awful,' Manfred said. 'But a relief to her family – all things considered.'

They walked on in silence, searching for tracks. Then Peter said: 'How did you know I wasn't going to shoot you?'

Manfred turned to him with a quiet smile.

'You'd just put the cartridges in your pocket. The rifle wasn't loaded.'

'Was that the only reason?'

His friend shook his head as they trudged along. Peter was happy to walk and talk.

'Not the only one. You wouldn't have done it, Peter. You might think so, but I think differently.'

Was it at this point he should say thank you? Probably, but

it wasn't what they did. Their friendship was of another kind, and silence could also express gratitude.

'How's Felix?' Manfred asked after a pause.

'She's in Spain. Her recovery is going well, but she says she needs some time away.'

So many questions could follow. Will we see her again? What's happening with the two of you? But it wasn't Manfred's style, and Peter wouldn't be able to give him a clear answer anyway. Instead his boss said: 'This winter seems like it'll never end. But it will one day. One day it'll go and the world will become itself again.'

Peter muttered something positive.

'By the way, I've started a new book,' Manfred said.

He turned now and his face cracked in a grin.

'Victor Hugo. *Les Misérables*.'

'The one about the convict being persecuted by the police?'

Peter had read it several times.

'Why don't you read something cheerful for a change? *Tortilla Flat*, for example?'

Manfred smiled.

'And you? Any news?'

'Mark seems to think I may get off lightly. It was a set-up, after all.'

'But you killed a man.'

'He reached for his gun first.'

Self-defence. They were hoping to make the judge see it that way. Mark seemed to think it was possible in view of what had happened in the forest and at Konkylien.

They were interrupted by the dog whining. They could see it had got a scent. Its whole body trembled with excitement as it rushed off with its nose in the snow. They followed it and found tracks and droppings. The dog took them deeper into the clearing and led them over a hilltop. And there it was again, the fourteen-pointer, with its head raised and its antlers high in the air. Its nostrils were flared and its muscles quivered under the winter coat. They stood very still for a long time; everything else ceased to matter and the past and the future fused into the here and now. Then Manfred passed him the rifle. Their eyes met briefly. Peter shook his head and Manfred lowered the weapon.

'Go on, take it,' Peter whispered. 'It's your last chance. Tomorrow it'll be too late.'

Manfred half-turned towards him.

'It's also his last chance.'

They continued to watch the animal in front of them. Then it seemed as if the stag sensed that humans were nearby. It shook its head nervously, stamped the ground and trotted off across the fields.

The Lost

Claire McGowan

NOT EVERYONE WHO'S MISSING IS LOST

When two teenage girls go missing along the Irish border, forensic psychologist Paula Maguire returns to the hometown she left years before.

NOT EVERYONE WHO'S LOST WANTS TO BE FOUND

As Paula digs into the cases the truth twists further away. What's the link with two other disappearances from 1985? And why does everything lead back to the town's dark past – including the reasons her own mother went missing years before?

NOTHING IS WHAT IT SEEMS

As the shocking truth is revealed, Paula learns that sometimes, it's better not to find what you've lost.

Praise for Claire McGowan:

'A knockout new talent' Lee Child

'Ireland's answer to Ruth Rendell' Ken Bruen

'This thriller is fresh and accessible without ever compromising on grit or suspense' Erin Kelly

978 0 7553 8640 6

headline

The Unquiet Grave

Steven Dunne

The past can't stay hidden forever . . .

The Cold Case Unit of Derby Constabulary feels like a morgue to DI Damen Brook. However, in disgrace and recently back from suspension, his boss thinks it's the safest place for him.

But soon Brook uncovers a pattern in a series of murders that date back to 1963. Baffled that a killer could stay undetected for so long, Brook delves deep into the past of both suspects and colleagues unsure where the hunt will lead him. What he does know for sure is that a significant date is approaching fast and the killer may be about to strike again . . .

Praise for DEITY by Steven Dunne:

'DI Damen Brook is one of the most memorable characters in recent British crime fiction' Stephen Booth

'A well-placed, dark thriller from an author who's clearly going places' *Irish Independent*

978 0 7553 8372 6

headline

Tarnished

Julia Crouch

Sometimes the past should be left well alone . . .

Mild-mannered Peg has never asked too many questions about her unusual upbringing: her absent father; her deceased mother; her bed-ridden aunt. Peg can't remember much from before the age of ten, but she's happy to fill in the gaps with fond memories of home-cooked dinners and walks along the seaside.

But when, all grown up, Peg discovers she had an uncle who died many years ago, the holes in her childhood memory start to trouble her. Yet as the skeletons come tumbling out of the family closet and the past begins to reveal itself, Peg starts to wonder whether her youthful lack of curiosity might not have been a good thing. A very good thing indeed . . .

Praise for *Tarnished*:

'You'd be crazy not to read this book' *Daily Mail*

'[Her] best yet . . . downright terrifying. You will not want to miss this book' Elizabeth Haynes, author of *Into the Darkest Corner*

'A memorably disqueting story that twists brilliantly . . . to a chilling, destructive ending' *Daily Telegraph*

'Truly chilling . . . you won't want to read it alone in the house' *Sunday Mirror*

978 0 7553 7805 0

headline